Promise en Pointe

Beth Jancec

A catalogue record for this
book is available from the
National Library of Australia

Linellen Press
265 Boomerang Road
Oldbury, Western Australia
www.linellenpress.com.au

Contents

Prologue

Alicia Sommers stared at the cold, granite slab. As always, she had changed the wilted flowers in the ceramic vase for fresh ones, collected the dead leaves on the grave that had fallen from the surrounding trees, and brushed the headstone free of dust with a small cloth she kept in her bag.

Every week for the past three years she had stood in this same spot, doing the same thing. Today was no different, except it was. She was leaving. Leaving them. She sat on the edge of the grave, stroked the flat surface as though it lived, felt her touch, heard her voice.

"I have to go," she whispered through her tears. "It doesn't mean I don't love you anymore. You know that's not true." Her dream had morphed into reality and instead of feeling the exhilaration of success, guilt danced with her conscience. She could see their faces staring up at her. Mum, proud, smiling tears of joy. Dad, his strong arms wrapped around her shoulders, kissing the top of her head and Simon, clever Simon, teasing, laughing, loving his little sister.

She lay down on the slab, stretched her arms across its width and kissed the cold granite. Her heart, heavy with grief, beat against the stone. She hoped they could feel it, hear it. It beat for them, yearned for them, missed them. The voice of betrayal inside her head refused to be silenced. She bit into the soft flesh of her lips, tasted the blood on her tongue and begged for their forgiveness.

Questions haunted her. Had she done the right thing? Was it all worth this wrench? Training at the academy till her muscles ached so badly she could barely walk to the car at the end of the day. Working at the local supermarket in the precious hours she had free to put food on the table and pay the bills. The reason she had refused to live with Uncle Robert and his family in the country, so she could keep Sophie, her baby sister, instead of leaving her with Aunt Beryl and Uncle Stan to raise. Wasn't it all about this moment?

She closed her eyes; listened to the leaves rustling in the wind; breathed in the stillness of silence, their silence. Where were they? Why couldn't she hear them? Why weren't they speaking to her? They always spoke to her when she came to see them.

The sound of footsteps startled her and she quickly sat up, stared at the familiar face. Glad, sad tears spilled over the rims of her eyes.

Brandon sat beside her on the grave, laid his head on her shoulder. "I had a feeling I would find you here."

"Sophie?"

"With your aunt."

He took her trembling hand in his, held it against his heart. "The war is over Baby, but the battle goes on," he said quietly. "We have, and always will, fight this fight, together. You and I are more than best friends: we're family now."

"I don't want to leave them."

"Don't let their death be for nothing, Ally. Do it for them and do it with the same determination that has driven you this far. They would want you to go, to have the chance to follow your dreams. We have achieved what hundreds of other dancers failed to do. Don't think of this as leaving them behind but living the life they have been denied." He let go of her hand and pulled her into his warm embrace. "I remember one cold, wet Saturday afternoon, not long before the accident happened, we came home to find your mum in the kitchen baking hot scones for us to eat. She started dancing around the room with a rolling pin in her hand. And the two of us laughing at her clumsy attempt to do a *jete*. Do you remember what she said to us? 'Always remember, darlings … no matter where you are or what you do, I will be right there —'"

"'with you in spirit.'"

"Maybe she had a premonition."

Alicia nodded. "I miss her so much. There are times when I long for the simple things, like the way she stroked her fingers against my cheek, brushed the knots from my hair."

Alicia clung to him, listened to his breath give life to his warm body. Brandon was right, this was as much her parents' dream as hers. She brushed the dust from her hands, clasped his.

He pulled her to her feet and into his arms. "I miss them too. Every day. I miss the way they made me feel special, like I belonged. I loved them more than I did my own parents, you know that. They believed in me and I don't intend to let them down. Tomorrow, you, me and Sophie will fly across this wonderful continent to start a new life, a life we have spent years training for. It's time to let go."

She lifted her chin, fed on the sight of every flower, tree, earthy and dewy smell, cementing them to her memory.

"Don't look back. Take my hand and together we will go forward."

She gripped his hand with both of hers, focused on the path ahead. First one step then another and another until they were running, leaping and laughing as the wind whistled them along the road to hope. Out of breath, but full of tomorrow she whispered into the wind, 'Goodbye, my darlings,' hoping it carried her words back to them.

As she drove behind Brandon, up the street towards her house, she could visualize her father striding along the footpath on his way home from work, the old case he carried swinging in time with his step; mum with Sophie propped on her hip talking to Aunt Beryl outside her house under the peppermint tree; and Simon, her darling brother, running up the road with her new ballet shoes, refusing to give them back. Big beautiful memories she would file away in the closet of her mind. One day in the future she intended to write them all down and pass them on to Sophie, in the hope, when she grew older, it would give her a better understanding of who her parents really were.

Alicia, Brandon, and Sophie spent the night at her aunt Beryl's house, ready for the early flight. The morning came quickly. Frightened to look at her aunt's face for fear of falling apart, Alicia busied herself neatly repacking hers and Sophie's cases for Melbourne. Brandon had ordered an Uber to take them to the airport. When it arrived, he loaded the suitcases, ready on the porch, into the back of the station wagon.

With Sophie perched on her hip, Alicia took one last look around her aunt and uncle's home. They had lived in this house next door for all of her life. They had watched her go to school, learn to ride a bike, learn to dance, lose a family, struggle to survive and now it was time to watch her leave. Shutting the fly-wire door behind her, she wondered if she would ever come back.

Her aunt and uncle were standing on the lawn, arm in arm. Each step towards them, harder than the last. They kissed and cuddled Sophie, gave her a teddy bear to hug on the plane, then passed her to Brandon who said a quick goodbye and taking Sophie, strapped her into the Uber.

Alicia hugged her aunt first. "Thank you … for everything." Words weren't enough. Her aunt patted her back, choked back tears. Uncle Stan squeezed her so tight she thought her ribs would crack.

"Take care, love. Drop us a line once in a while. You know your aunt and I love you both." He withdrew a handkerchief from his pocket and wiped his eyes.

She couldn't bring herself to say goodbye. Goodbye was final, forever. She pulled from his embrace and ran to the car; kept her head lowered until the Uber was halfway up the street. She turned quickly then, looked out the back window, stared down the street of her youth until the car turned the corner, leaving her heart behind.

Chapter One

Alicia watched her reflection in the mirrored walls; crystal beads of sweat glistened in the light. She loved the feel of perspiration trickling down her body, the reward of her taxing effort. It drove her beyond fatigue to fresh challenges. Helen Barsby, the ballet mistress, yelled at the Company to take their positions. Dripping wet, Alicia left the *barre* and moved to *centre floor*. She closed her eyes, waited for the music to block out the world. As the first note sounded, she felt her mind and body unfold into the romantic creation of motion.

At the end of the particularly demanding day her head ached. Rehearsals had run overtime and if she and Brandon didn't hurry, they would be late for their dinner date at the Spencers'. The muscles in her neck and shoulders had knotted and she rolled her head to help relieve some of the tension. She grabbed her towel from the *barre* and wiped perspiration from her face. Her blood pumping, she pushed through the studio doors, glad to escape the thick smell of body odour, hard work, and the director, Louis' grating voice.

"Fifteen minutes and we're out of here," yelled Brandon as he peeled off his sweaty top on his way to the men's changerooms.

Alicia flopped onto the dressing room bench, needing to catch her breath before taking a shower. Dressed in jeans and knitted top, her feet feeling the freedom of a pair of Birkenstocks, she hurried downstairs to meet a toe-tapping Brandon waiting by the door. Pointing at his watch, he rolled his eyes.

Outside the Melbourne Arts Centre, she lifted her head, inhaled the salty air wafting over the edge of the city. So much about Melbourne reminded her of Perth: the city's strong, cosmopolitan flair and the warm friendly faces; the cool rush of the afternoon sea breeze that diluted the stale heat.

She missed Perth and the casual way people gathered at the foreshore of the Swan River, newspaper tented over their heads as they soaked in the midday sun. A smile played about her lips. Not often did memories of home bring a smile.

The two of them walked to the car park, glad to be in the fresh air, and jumped into their red Corolla. Brandon revved the engine, thrust the gear stick into drive and swung hard on the steering wheel as he turned onto the street. When he heard the siren, he slammed on the brake. Red and blue lights flashed past and he blew out his breath. "That was close." He glanced at Alicia, a sheepish smile on his face.

The road took them past the Docklands of outer city Melbourne and wound its way along the Esplanade of the Yarra River. Alicia eased into the seat, soaked in the sight of the sun dancing over the water. She looked across at her best friend and dance partner, his long fringe flapping in the breeze as he rudely cursed the driver of the car in front. Although the pain had dulled over time, his support was as strong as ever and for that she would forgive him almost anything, including his driving.

"Louis is determined to break my back." Brandon stretched, squirmed in his seat, before changing lanes.

A million miles away, Alicia didn't catch what he said. "Sorry, what did you say?"

"Wakey, wakey. The *pas de deux*. I think Louis is trying to kill us." He pulled up outside the after-school care centre and, scraping the tyres on the kerb, jerked the car to a halt. "I swear this car needs a wheel alignment."

Alicia bit her tongue, not trusting herself to speak. Twice last week she had been late to pick up Sophie and forgot to sign her out. If she stuffed up again, Sophie might be suspended.

"Do you want me to go get her?" asked Brandon, between sneezes.

"No, I think you should spend the time tightening the nuts on the wheels, in case they fall off on the drive home." She laughed when he poked out his tongue.

"Actually, my back is quite sore. And my throat feels a bit scratchy."

"Pulled a muscle, maybe?" She secretly hoped he wasn't coming down with the flu. Brandon was a brilliant cook. She loved to come home after a long day at work to one of his gourmet meals but tonight it was dinner at the Spencers'. The thought of a large bowl of pasta - Jenny's favourite dish - sitting in her stomach didn't really appeal but it was too late to cancel.

She ran up the path to the gate, scowled at the sign on the large building next door – INNER CITY CHAPEL – written in bold print across the front. Bitter thoughts took over. Years of believing their lies and for what? An emptiness she would never conquer. She tried to remember the last time she bent her knee and prayed. Even the echo of her mother's voice had stilled over the years but never the memories. The memories would last forever to remind her of her bitter-sweet past, and the battle she now lived with daily. If the centre wasn't so convenient, she would gladly move Sophie to another one.

A head full of ringlets turned towards Alicia when she entered. Sophie waved at her from the carpet. No longer a baby, her Sophie, but a pretty girl with a bubbly personality. Except for her slender frame so similar to her own, Sophie looked like the female version of their late brother, Simon. *The years had covered the truth well,* thought Alicia, no one doubted the child was hers, not even her good friend Jenny Spencer, a doctor, had any notion of their true relationship.

The carer dismissed the children. Grabbing her backpack, Sophie skipped over. Alicia squeezed the small hand clasped in hers and, taking the bag, raced to join Brandon in the car.

"Jump in, Button," he said. "Don't take all day. We have to be at Auntie Jenny's in less than an hour."

"How come?"

"'cause she invited us to dinner. And I need to change out of these old togs before we go." He grabbed the box of tissues from the glove box and blew his runny nose.

Home was just a few streets away, their apartment on the ground floor in a block of six was set back off the road and surrounded by Yellow-Gum trees. Brandon pulled into the driveway, jerked on the brake. After helping Sophie from the car, the two of them raced inside.

Alicia watched them push through the door, fighting over who should go through first. She didn't feel like rushing anymore and wandered over to the old wooden seat she and Brandon had found dumped on the verge, sat down in her favourite spot, content to listen to the birds chirping in the branches above. She stretched back, closed her eyes and contemplated the little problem that had been plaguing her all week.

Jenny and John Spencer were good friends, no longer just doctors she saw for purely medical reasons. Their love and support meant the world to her, making her free time in Melbourne some of her happiest memories: dinner at their place, barbecues or boating along the Yarra River on Sundays in their launch. But her last appointment with John at his rooms had sparked a fear she would rather not acknowledge. He had appeared somewhat distracted throughout their consultation, and the constant checking of his watch, as though there was somewhere else he needed to be, she found disturbing. He even cut her appointment short by five minutes.

She had explained to John how the nightmares had returned. "I listened to the tapes you gave me but they don't seem to be working. I'm just so tired all the time, struggling to keep up with everything – rehearsals, Sophie, housework. All I want to do is go to sleep but then … nightmares."

Elbows on the desk, John jotted down a few notes. He questioned her about the nightmares. Who was in them, what were they about and how she felt when she woke? When she stopped talking, he swivelled around in his chair and, scanning the shelf, pulled out a book on relaxation. He found a few paperclipped bundles in his filing cabinet, underlined the parts he thought would be most helpful.

He handed her the papers and the book, pushed back his chair, indicating the end of their session. She read the title, *Post Traumatic Stress Related Symptoms*; placed them and the book in her bag.

"When does the ballet season begin?"

"Tuesday week." She stood up, walked with him to the door, a little annoyed at his haste to be finished. "I've already given Jenny complimentary tickets for Saturday night's performance." "Perfect. How are your feet?"

She thought about the metatarsals in her left foot. They had been plaguing her all week and she promised herself to purchase the footpad Jenny had recommended last time they spoke. The thought of having cortisone injections sent a shiver down Alicia's spine. She knew dancers who had tried it and said the pain was excruciating. "A couple of nasty little blisters on my toes and another on my right heel giving me grief."

He looked at his watch, stepped in front of her to open the door. "Come for dinner one night this week, if you're free. Jenny could bind your toes while you're there. I'll remind her to bring extra tape home from the surgery. Bring Sophie and Brandon."

"Thanks. I'll ring Jenny and arrange something."

"Not just a pretty face is my wife. We won't mention her cooking, though." She felt the pressure of his hand on her back, almost forcing her out of his room. "Don't forget to read those notes I gave you. I think the exercises will help. Do them each night before bed."

And with that, he shut the door behind her.

Gwen, the new receptionist with the extremely long eyelashes, looked up from applying her red lipstick. As though her go-fast button had been pushed, she finished what she was doing, gave a thin sharp smile and quickly handed Alicia the Medicare slip to sign.

Was it Alicia's imagination or was everyone in this office in a hurry to get out of here? Not like old Shirley, John's last receptionist who recently retired, always ready for a lengthy chat.

"Sign on the dotted line," said Gwen, sounding as if she had mastered a mathematical equation. Searching her handbag, she pulled out a small round mirror, checked her hair before replacing it, then drowned herself in perfume.

The ink on the paper was barely dry when John joined them at the front desk. Gone was the serious-doctor-look, replaced with young, free and easy, trendy-shirt-over-jeans, come casual. Alicia had noticed the shirt and jeans hanging up in his office and thought maybe he was meeting Jenny for dinner or a movie. It did strike her as a bit unusual for a weeknight, the kids having school the next day.

"You still here, Alicia?"

He wasn't even looking at her when he said that. His glance fixed on his receptionist, who was looking as if a stick had been wedged between her cheeks, her smile was so wide. A horrible suspicion Gwen was the reason behind his haste skimmed through her mind. This wasn't the John she knew, the man she had come to rely on and trust for emotional support. What was he doing? "Sorry," she said, a slight edge to her voice. "I'll try to get out of here as quick as I can."

Gwen laughed. John joined her. "I didn't mean it like that."

Alicia hadn't seen John since that afternoon and wondered how dinner tonight would go. The banging of the front door startled her from her daydreams.

"Sorry to interrupt your little repose, Queen Muck, but in case you have forgotten, the Spencers are expecting us in fifteen minutes. Which brings me to my next point. Do you think John and Jenny would mind very much if I took a raincheck? My back is killing me and I think I need to rest it if I'm to be any good for rehearsals tomorrow."

Alicia thought Brandon looked a little peaky. It wasn't like him to miss a dinner date, backache or not. She wondered if she should mention her concerns about John to him but changed her mind, not wanting to start a fire she couldn't put out. "Are you okay? You're not coming down with a cold or something? You've sneezed a few times and blown your nose."

"God, I hope not. That's the last thing I need. No, my back is really sore. A good night's sleep with a hot water bottle should fix it. Either that or a scottle of botch." Laughing, he wobbled off back into the house like an old drunk. "I'll send Sophie out," he yelled over his shoulder.

***

Another fun-filled day of drama at work, thought Nick Coleman, as he trudged through Melbourne's city streets, on the way to his car. Rumours of a takeover bid were rampant at the station. Apparently, Channel Seven was being bought out by media magnate Jeremy Townsend. Nick had done a Google search on him while on a lunch break, which unfortunately proved less than encouraging. The man was known to replace the *old faithfuls* when he took over an establishment, with much younger, more hyperactive blood, causing Nick some concern. Or did it? As of late, bouts of discontentment were becoming more frequent and he wondered if he was actually relieved. Was this the push he needed to get off the bus going nowhere?

Those thoughts were quickly abandoned when he found himself confronted by a head of curly hair, squashed against his shirt front.

"Oh, dear. I'm so sorry," said the voice beneath the curly mass.

"Just make sure it doesn't happen again," he replied, a touch of irritation in his voice.

"Well, I didn't … Oh! Nick, you brute," said Jenny Spencer, slapping him affectionately on the arm. "I should have known it was you."

He smiled into the familiar face of his college mate and marvelled how quickly time had passed. Not that she looked a day older. In fact, he loved her hair, she looked … chic, sophisticated. Although he did wonder about the furrow on her brow.

"Gee, it's great to see you," said Jenny, throwing her arms around his neck. "How's things?"

"Can't complain." Nick moved from her embrace and tapping her forehead, pulled a questioning face. "What's this all about."

Jenny brushed the hair from her face, blew out her breath. "My last patient. A baby with genetic cancer of the left eye. The mother was distraught. Years of training and I still can't seem to conquer the kid thing."

"Sounds like you could do with a coffee?"

She pushed back the sleeve of her pale pink shirt, checked her watch.

"Somewhere you need to be?"

"No, not really. It's John's turn to pick the kids up from afterschool-care but it's my turn to cook dinner. Not my forte, as you well know."

Huffing out a laugh, Nick nodded. Dinner at the Spencers' generally consisted of spaghetti bolognese, probably Jenny's best effort. Throw in a roast dinner every now and then and there you had the full extent of her culinary skills. He led her to a pleasant café close by and found seats in a secluded spot; ordered coffee. "How long has it been … one, maybe two years?"

"No! Not that long, surely?"

"Shameful really, considering I only live ten minutes from you." He knew most of the blame lay at his door. Since his divorce he'd shied away from his regular haunts, the Spencers included. No excuses, just a kneejerk reaction to his single lifestyle, he suspected.

"You've kept yourself in good shape. Still single?"

His deep, infectious laugh rippled across the table. "Same old Jenny, cut right to the chase."

"You know me, never one to mince my words."

He was comfortable talking with Jenny. There wasn't much about his earlier life she didn't know, having attended university together, and later, their internship at Royal Melbourne Hospital. He lifted his gaze, shrugged his shoulders. "Seems my lot in life."

"You're not still pining, are you?"

"For Rebecca. Hell no. That flame died years ago. No, things are pretty good. Job's good, money's good. Some even say I have a certain charm about me." He winked, making her laugh. "And yet, the blissful state of holy matrimony eludes me."

"Disenchanted, perhaps?"

"You've always been good at pinpointing precisely how I feel. Your training, I suspect." He stirred his coffee. "I don't know. Foolish I suppose, but I'd like to think the real deal does still exist. Like you and John, for example."

"Like you and John," she repeated, in a somewhat forlorn voice.

If she was hoping he hadn't heard, she was mistaken. *Like you and John'*, he said to himself, as though there was a hidden meaning behind those words. The sadness in her eyes worried him and he hoped his suspicions were nothing more than wild imaginings. Jenny and John had one of the more stable relationships of his acquaintances. He thought it best to continue talking, maybe add a bit of light banter to the mix to help distract her from her melancholy. "I want it all," he said. "Sincerity, honesty, loyalty, love. My money and the media attention from the TV show I receive, are just an added bonus not the prerequisite to marrying me, if you get my drift. Don't happen to know anyone, do you?"

Jenny stopped twirling the silver spoon in her cup, stared straight through him as if he were invisible. Nick, feeling like he'd pulled the pin on a grenade, waited several seconds before continuing. "You're not saying anything. What's going on in that clever head of yours."

Jenny placed the teaspoon onto the saucer, sat back in her chair and downed the last of her coffee. He found it hard to read the look on her face. "Don't be a tease. Out with it." All he could do was wait but the longer Jenny remained silent the more concerned he became.

"As a matter of fact, I do have someone in mind," she said.

Thank God, thought Nick when she finally spoke. "Come on, out with it. Curiosity's killing this cat." He kept his voice light, playful.

"I think I need another coffee."

Nick signalled the waiter. "You're determined to keep me in suspense."

She laughed at that. But it wasn't a hearty laugh. After the waiter had placed the coffees on the table, Nick watched her skim the froth from the top with a spoon, and lick the rich taste from her lips.

"She's young, with the face of an angel and a slim fairy-like figure most women would die for, including me, and talented. She's very talented."

So, thought Nick, *there is a girl involved and a beautiful one at that. He wondered if this girl could be the real reason for Jenny's troubled mood.* "Go on."

"I'm trying to think how best to describe her personality. Gentle ... and sweet, even adorable in an innocent kind of way. She's intelligent and strong. But there's a sadness about her, something in her past she never speaks of but you know it's there. Like a ghost hovering in the background."

If all Jenny said about the girl proved correct, Nick could well imagine the steadfast John being a little distracted by this lovely creature. Provided it was a mere distraction and nothing more. "Got me in one. How do you know this girl? Where did you meet her?

"She came to see me at the surgery, complaining of sore feet." The napkin in Jenny's hand seemed to be getting its share of punishment as she twisted it round and round. "During the course of the consultation she told me she had some personal issues and wondered if I knew of a good psychologist, and of course I recommended John."

Nick raised his eyebrows, questioning her logic.

"That's the sadness about her I mentioned earlier."

"Hasn't John spoken to you about it?"

"No of course not, as you well know. He's taken the same oath as we have. Let me finish. One day, quite out of the blue, she asked John if we would like to be her guests on opening night at the ballet. She gets complimentary tickets for each new season and since she has no family here, she asked us."

"Does she work at the theatre or something?"

"I suppose she does in a way. She's one of the leading ballerinas in the Australian Ballet Company. Their home base is the Melbourne Arts Centre."

"Impressive. Now, let me get this right. This divine creature is here alone, a principal dancer of the Aussie Ballet Company with a deep and dark secret, only John is privy to? Where's she from? Where's her family?"

"And beautiful, you forgot to mention beautiful." Her voice was somewhat wistful.

"Beg pardon." Nick considered Jenny an attractive woman with her cute button nose and cheeky smile. He also loved her flawless, olive skin and her sharp intelligence. But he would never go so far as to say she was beautiful.

"Alicia's from Perth and she's not entirely alone. She has a seven-year-old daughter named Sophie, and she shares her apartment with a guy called Brandon, also from Perth, whom I suspect is gay and obviously adores her. Other than that, I don't know much."

"How old is this girl?"

"Twenty-three."

"Seriously! You know how old I am."

"Don't remind me, we're the same age."

A cynical edge touched his voice as he balanced the years in his outstretched hands. "Seven-year-old child? Twenty-three? You call having a baby at sixteen, sweet and innocent? Not where I come from, they don't."

"I can't tell you why – it's just a feeling I have – but I'm sure the child is intrinsically linked to the sadness I see in Alicia's eyes."

Nick sat forward, clasped his hands. "What … what aren't you telling me? I can see there's something else bothering you."

Jenny worried her bottom lip. It shocked him when he saw the tears forming in her eyes. Then like a burst water main, words rushed from her mouth. "If you must know it's John. He seems … distant … distracted, not his usual self and I'm worried about him."

"Like depression or something?"

"I'm not sure. I tried to talk to him about it but he clams up when I do. I thought maybe it was work but then … oh, I don't know. I'm probably reading too much into it. You know, we all go through things during our life. Maybe the two of us should go away together for a few days, leave the kids with mum. John would hate me to talk about him like this. I shouldn't have said anything. Just forget I mentioned it."

Not likely, thought Nick, his suspicion aroused. Irritation gripped him. This girl suddenly became a whole lot more interesting. She sounded to Nick like an award-winning actress, playing two of his good friends for fools. Well, not for long if he had anything to do with it. "Why don't I drop by one night this week for a drink, like old times?"

"I did intend to invite you over and I know John would love to catch up."

He took out his phone and opened the calendar app. "What can we arrange?"

"Coincidently, Alicia is coming for dinner tonight. There's a new ballet opening next week, and I usually treat her feet beforehand. It's almost a standing arrangement. Why don't you join us for coffee?"

For one moment he thought he might have to do dinner. He'd moved past spaghetti bolognese. Steak and salad were more his thing these days. "Perfect. What time?" He snapped his phone case shut, shoved it in his shirt pocket.

"Around eight?" She hesitated. "Are you sure you want to do this? You might not like her."

"Too late. I'm hooked, line and sinkered. Besides, what have I got to lose."

"You won't mention …?"

"Jenny, we're friends. Of course not. Besides, I might be meeting the love of my life." He very much doubted it but it sounded like a reasonable excuse for a visit.

They finished their coffee, Nick paid the bill and led her into the street. "I'll see you tonight. Bye for now." He leant in and dropped a kiss on her cheek.

As he walked towards his car, Nick's mind drifted down a path he knew only too well – betrayal and the degrading fear it provoked. The same fear he recognised in Jenny's eyes when she'd mentioned John. There was more to this story than she was saying. Jenny described this girl as angelic, sweet and innocent. Enough to tempt most men, including John. Which he had to admit did surprise him. Nick never thought of John as a player. Steady as a rock, good old Spencer, loyal to the backbone. Hence his nickname, Gibraltar, given to him when he was at university.

At home, he made himself a light meal and showered. Staring in the mirror as he brushed his teeth, his mind flashed back to the sight of his former wife, Rebecca, in bed with Alex Braun, his supposed good friend. A bitter taste burned a path along his throat. He tried not to completely blame the girl, or let his own painful past be the benchmark for judgment. But, of one thing he was certain, his need to save his good friends from the hurt that he still struggled with. If this girl was the problem between the Spencers: age and experience had taught him over the years how to charm his way into her life, and get her out of John's.

***

Nick rang the doorbell and wasn't surprised to find Jenny answering it. Her smile was tight. He leant forward, lowered his face to hers. "Stop worrying."

She smiled then. "Come through."

He followed her into the dining room. His first sight was of a slender young woman sitting on a chair with her back to him, both feet propped on the table. Her auburn hair was twisted into a bun atop a long elegant neck. A young boy sat across her lap, winding a loose strand of hair around her ear and John, peering over her foot, his fingers pressed against the tape on her toe.

"Ouch!" she said, when John accidently pressed too hard.

"Sorry Alicia." He ripped his hand away, pulled an apologetic face.

"I think your mum and dad are trying to kill me, Oliver. Do you know what I need?" came the lilting voice from the chair. The boy in her lap shook his head and the woman continued. "I need a big, strong, handsome man to give me a cuddle and a kiss."

"Only too happy to be of service," said Nick. A cocky smile on his face, he waited for the coming reaction and was rewarded when she swung around, her colour rising to a delightful shade of pink. She stared at him until her rudeness became obvious then swung back to Oliver. *Jenny was right, the girl was exquisite, no surprise there.*

John stepped forward to greet his old friend. "Jenny said she'd bumped into you today. Glad you could make it." They hugged affectionately, patted each other on the back. "We shouldn't be much longer. Jenny's almost finished taping Alicia's toes."

Nick joined John at the table. Being a doctor himself, he couldn't resist the urge to examine the blistered feet and leant forward to get a better look. "Alicia is it?"

"Oh, beg pardon," said Jenny. "Nick Coleman, Alicia Sommers. Alicia, Nick."

A quick nod was the sum total of the dancer's greeting. He tried smiling, only to receive a slight acknowledgement of the lips before she turned her attention back to the boy.

Nick had never met a ballerina before and the bone structure of her foot fascinated him. When she stretched her foot into a pointed position, he itched to prod the unusually high-developed arches. "What have you been doing with your feet to get so many blisters?"

"Alicia is one of the principal dancers in the Aussie Ballet Company. Hence the sore feet." Jenny explained. "It's opening night in less than a week. Unless we tape her toes to keep them firm during rehearsals, the blisters could bleed. I'm just a bit worried about the tape sticking to the broken skin."

Nick sensed Alicia's reserve, which he found surprising in someone who held such a prominent position in a ballet company. *If this was an act it was a good one*, he thought as he stared into her hazel eyes, marking some shadowed mystery. *Innocent, shy or dangerous, which was it*, he asked himself.

"Sorry, Alicia, won't be much longer," said Jenny looking for the scissors. "Time for bed, Oliver. Hop off Alicia's lap and off you go."

Alicia lifted Oliver off her lap, tapped his bottom, sending him on his way. "I do feel a little silly sitting here with my legs stuck out like this in front of your visitor."

Nick gave a dismissive wave. He watched her fidget, shift position and couldn't help thinking how gracefully she moved. "Please don't give it a second thought. I'm amazed anyone can walk with feet in that condition, let alone dance."

When she stretched back on the chair, he felt a quiver of pleasure shoot into his belly as the round-eyed face of innocence smiled at him. He checked himself. He was beginning to understand the kind of dilemma in which John might be finding himself.

"There, finished." Jenny snipped the tape, placed the scissors on the table. "Coffee anyone?"

Alicia lowered her legs, pulled down her rolled-up jeans and slipped her feet into a pair of pumps.

"All done," said John, placing his hand on her shoulder. She squirmed, like she was uncomfortable with John touching her, which surprised Nick. It also eliminated from the list, his suspicion of her being a threat to Jenny. Definitely not dangerous which left only shy or innocent.

"I think I'll pass. I'm quite tired and it's time I took Sophie home to bed." She kept her head bowed as she spoke.

"Just stay for a quick coffee. It's still early."

"No, I won't. You have company and I'm sure the three of you have a lot to talk about, but thank you, Jenny."

Nick was tempted to laugh at the pleading look Jenny flung his way. "Don't go on my account. I refuse to accept the responsibility of driving the Spencers' delightful guests from their home."

"Besides, Alicia, it's your turn to make the coffee, right John?"

"So, it is. You can't get out of it that easily, young lady. Now off to the kitchen you go."

"But …"

"Go!" said Jenny. "John and I will clean up. Nick, you can help Alicia with the coffee."

As Alicia headed for the kitchen Nick caught the frown on her face. Another surprise, it seems she really did want to go home. Eyeing the full length of her delicate and graceful frame, finely tuned from the extensive training she must have been exposed to, he followed her without any objection. And long slender limbs, he observed.

She busied herself placing the cups, sugar, and spoons on a tray. She kept her eyes lowered, as she filled the coffee machine and the milk container.

He found her reserve refreshing, attractive, not something he experienced with most women he knew. He rested against the bench, his arms folded and his ankles crossed, bothered by the knowledge she seemed more interested in setting the cups on the tray than conversation. He found himself watching her every move. Even in her nervousness, she was controlled and graceful, just as he imagined a ballerina on stage, and he wondered what it would be like to see her dance. "Should I ask if you want some help?"

She stole a look from under her lashes, flicked her glance to heaven. That's when he noticed the dimple in her right cheek and let out a chuckle, lightening the mood. She poured coffee into the cups, then lifted the tray from the bench.

"Now that, I can help you with," he said, accidentally stepping on her foot as he took hold of the tray. The muffled gasp came first, followed by a pool of tears, filling her eyes. Momentarily stunned, he stood staring as she pushed her clenched fist against her mouth. Ripped from his daze, "I'm so sorry," he said placing the tray back on the bench. Instinctively reverting to his medico experience, he dropped to his knee. "Take off your shoe."

As she slipped off her pump, he stared at the blood soaking through the newly applied dressing. In one swift movement he swooped her into his arms and sat her on the bench. "If I take the plaster off, I think I'll make it worse."

She grimaced several times. "Just give me a few minutes. I'm sure the pain will subside." She gripped the edge of the bench with both hands, bit hard on her bottom lip, and closed her eyes.

"I can't believe what a clumsy oaf I am," Nick said apologetically. He placed his hand under the sole of her foot for support and began to massage her ankle. Her pained look distressed him.

"Don't worry. It's beginning to feel better already. A good cup of coffee is exactly what the doctor ordered."

She gave him a tiny smile and he quickly responded. Before he could say another word, John and Jenny entered the kitchen. At the sight of Alicia's bloodied foot in Nick's hand, Jenny rushed over to see what was wrong, John close on her heels.

"Clumsy fool that I am," said Nick, feeling more than a little embarrassed, "I trod on her foot. I thought it best not to remove the tape, it might make the bleeding worse." To his relief, Jenny agreed.

Nick lifted Alicia from the bench and, ignoring her protests, carried her into the dining room and gently lowered her onto a chair. Jenny placed the tray in the centre of the table, poured cream into the coffee. The golden aroma filled the room. It smelt good, soothing. An unusual quiet came over him. He glanced across at Alicia, watched her swirl the coffee in her cup. Her sweet, unassuming nature appealed to him, something he hadn't anticipated. A thought occurred to him. "Opening in a week, did you say?"

"Yes," she answered, twisting her fingers.

Nick suspected her toe still throbbed and wished there was something more he could do to ease her pain.

"Actually, this ballet has been created especially for Alicia," John explained, smiling across at her.

"It's a tragedy," Jenny chipped in, the back of her hand on her forehead and an exaggerated tilt to her head. "Blighted in love!"

"That's a little dramatic, my love," said John, tapping at the corner of his lips with a napkin.

The smile left Jenny's face.

Nick watched her closely after that and decided Jenny's attitude towards Alicia was one of genuine affection. He detected no signs of jealousy or suspicion. And as far as he could tell John's interest certainly wasn't directed at the ballerina. But there was definitely something wrong, a friction between the couple he hadn't witnessed before.

"Isn't that a rather large workload for those somewhat mangled feet?" he asked.

"No, not really. Comes with the job. Besides, I have a few days to let them heal and I won't be doing every rehearsal e*n pointe.*"

"*En pointe?* Tippy toes?" Nick placed two fingertips on the table to imitate dancing feet. She released a breathless laugh, sending a spark of joy through his body. "Interesting. Are you two going?"

"Wouldn't miss it," said Jenny. "We have tickets for the following Saturday night, courtesy of Miss Sommers."

"How would a clumsy oaf like myself go about acquiring one of these tickets?"

Alicia opened her mouth to speak, words forming hung mid-air, she suddenly snapped it shut. He had the distinct feeling she was going to ask him why he wanted a ticket and realising how rude that would sound, changed her mind. It was something of a shock, catching him off guard. Years of working on live television had taught him how to recover quickly. "I thought, that is … I have a midday TV show and … and … I'm always on the lookout for new material … wondered what it would be like to interview a ballet dancer." He hoped he didn't sound too much like a babbling idiot but blundered on. "It might help to see a ballet before I do. Besides, I can appreciate ballet with the best of them."

"I am sorry. Of course, I'd be happy to get you a ticket. I'll organise with the theatre staff to hold it for you at the box office."

Although he didn't like to admit it, he was glad she was sorry, justifying his wounded pride. "Excellent and forgiven." He pulled a sulky face. Everyone laughed including Nick, but deep down he was a little miffed. Definitely not the reaction from her he had expected. "I'll ask for it under the name of oaf, will I?"

She returned his smile. To counteract his awkwardness, he skilfully diverted the conversation to the weekend's football game. Her constant attempts at stifling a yawn convinced him her interests didn't lie on the footy-field.

Alicia placed her cup on the tray. "I really must go. It's getting late and Sophie has school tomorrow. She's been a little grumpy lately, not wanting to go to school. I'll have the headmistress ringing me if I'm not careful. And poor Brandon will be waiting for me. I promised to make him a hot cup of tea before I went to bed. Not often he opts out of dinner at his favourite friends. Thank you both again for a scrumptious meal, I'm full as a goog."

"You hardly ate enough to fill a bird," said John.

"John, get Sophie, and Nick and I will see Alicia to the door."

"I can see Alicia to the door," said John.

"Would you prefer me to carry Sophie down the stairs?" replied Jenny, scowling at her husband.

"I'll get her." Alicia rushed from the room before anyone had a chance to object.

Nick raised his hands at the two of them to stem further argument and hurried after the girl. Unsure of which room she had entered he waited at the top of the stairs until she appeared with the Sophie in her arms. "Here, let me." It had been forever since Nick had carried a child. He glanced down at the sleeping face against his chest. Blonde curls bounced in time to his steps. The porcelain skin, the cherry lips, all identical to her mother's. The urge to kiss the top of the little head surprised him.

"Thank you so much. She's quite heavy."

"You're welcome." He carried the child to the car and bundled her into the back seat. Jenny pushed him aside and strapped a sleepy Sophie into the seat. When she finished, she turned and kissed Alicia goodnight, who said her goodbyes and slid in behind the wheel.

Nick stood with his hands in his pockets and watched the little red car drive away with his mind full of possibilities.

Chapter Two

Saturday night, Nick took one last look in the mirror. Adjusting his grey tie, he rehearsed in his mind how to capture Alicia's attention. "Fairly casual," he said to the mirror, "with an element of caution added. Maybe throw in a pinch of flirty but not straight away – too obvious." A rogue curl refused to behave and he pressed it into place for the tenth time before heading out the door.

As he drove his black Range Rover along the highway, his mind drifted back to the night he visited the Spencers. Two hours after Alicia left, he was still sitting at their dining table, drinking coffee. The Jenny and John of old emerged as they laughed together about the many pranks, they'd committed in their university days. He reminded himself what good friends they had been to him: loyal and supportive, and never more so than when Rebecca had betrayed him.

Some painful memories had resurrected themselves that night, assailing him with a series of regrets. He loved being a doctor and deeply missed the intellectual challenge the medical profession demanded. And, the compassion he discovered within himself when dealing with the sick, had given him enormous satisfaction, something he now lacked and greatly missed.

He clenched hard on his jaw as he pondered the existence he felt he had been forced to adopt. Disappointment, bitterness, and a need for self-preservation had robbed him of his sense of worth. He had found a home at Channel Seven, a place to lick his wounds. But the wounds from his failed marriage had healed and it was time to let go of the past and become the doctor he believed he was meant to be.

Running his fingers through his hair, he wondered what was wrong with him. Most of the men he worked with claimed to envy his bachelor lifestyle. No mortgage, no wife or brood of kids tying him to the front door of the picket-fenced house. Instead, he owned a house in Toorak, a unit in the city and delightful beach house down the coast in Dromana. Yet, after a day at work, he wanted to come home to something more welcoming than the latest computerised stainless-steel fridge.

It annoyed him that he couldn't shake the damned age-old belief in marriage and children, the happy-ever-after, something he blamed his mother and her Christian values for. The vision of Alicia Sommers with her high cheekbones, popped into his mind. Those hazel flecked eyes that rarely blinked, seeing but revealing little, fascinated him. He hadn't detected anything frivolous or superficial about her, and her quiet, mysterious nature intrigued him. As he pulled onto the Spencers' lawn, he realised how much he was looking forward to seeing Alicia dance.

When Jenny answered the front door, Nick thought she looked a trifle flustered, even angry. He also noticed her shapely figure in the hip-hugging dress; the skin on her shoulders pale against the midnight blue fabric; and her hair, piled in big curls on her head, reminded him of the young Jenny he went through medical school with.

"Love the dress!"

"Glad someone noticed." Turning abruptly, she headed up the stairs; called back over her shoulder. "I'll check on the kids, and as soon as John has finished dressing, we'll go."

He waited by the door, his mind occupied with visions of the night ahead when he turned to see John and Jenny descending the stairs. The body language between the couple led Nick to believe they had been arguing, and by the dour look on John's face, none too pleasantly. The lame handshake, the sharp smile, the silent drive to the theatre, confirmed his beliefs. He tried making conversation but with little success and gave up to enjoy the glorious array of city lights beaming through the window.

The auditorium was filling fast. He collected his ticket at the box office then followed John and Jenny up the carpeted staircase. Dropped pearl earrings, diamonds, white collars, and ties, reflected brightly in the seats of the dress circle.

The lights faded and the draped velvet curtains opened, revealing a hazy blue-lit stage and multiple white chiffon curtains falling in moon shapes across the backdrop, setting a romantic mood. Alicia's entrance onto the stage drew immediate applause in which Nick enthusiastically contributed. Mesmerised, he watched her leap and spin with a strength that belied her slim legs and petite body. Her graceful movements reminded him of African gazelles, leaping with the same timid and gentle quality. And yet, the skill she displayed when e*n pointe*, astounded him. But it was her tender portrayal of the role that enchanted him the most.

Heart-rending music ebbed and flowed through the theatre. It swayed the audience into a world of emotion as they clung to the last few minutes of the ballet. A hush greeted the finale before applause exploded across the theatre. Her partner escorted Alicia back for a final *encore*. Cries of *"Bravo"* echoed around the auditorium. She placed a hand on her heart, sank into a deep curtsy. And as the crowd settled, the curtain slowly closed, shutting out the audience and their mutterings.

Nick, transfixed, stared at the stage. John's voice reminding Jenny not to forget her shawl, brought him back to reality. Outside in the foyer, the crowd dispersed, and the three of them moved to the sofa by the door. Jenny explained to Nick they always waited here to see Alicia after a performance. Twenty minutes passed before she appeared. She waved, hurried down the steps, a flustered expression on her face. John sprang to his feet. Nick noticed her features soften as she walked towards them.

"I'm sorry to have kept you waiting. I dressed as fast as I could."

She'd changed into a pencil-skirted black dress with her hair pulled into a high ponytail. He tried not to stare, but *nobody*, he thought, *who danced with such sensitivity could be so calculating as to steal another woman's husband.* He felt a surge of envy when she affectionately embraced Jenny, wishing it was him.

"I see you picked up your ticket okay?"

Nick gazed into her eyes, trying to focus on what she had said. "Yes. Yes, thank you."

"I'm happy you made it."

A sharp thrill shot through his body. He wanted to say he too was glad but she was already addressing Jenny.

"I have a small favour to ask," she said measuring the amount with her thumb and finger. "There's an after-performance party I'm expected to attend. Several sponsors and the famous - or infamous according to Brandon - Roland de Beau, will be there. You're all welcome to come, of course. I promise not to be too long. Hope you don't mind?"

"No," Jenny said, her back facing her husband. "Of course not. I love being part of the hype after a performance. You okay with that, Nick?"

"That's the closest you'll ever get to being a ballerina, my love" cut in John as he sized up his wife's figure.

Unable to control himself, Nick looked sharply at John, spread open his hands as if to question the man's logic. "I didn't realise your *wife* was trying to enter the ballet world. I would have thought being a doctor was a reasonable enough achievement in itself." He deliberately stressed the word wife to remind John of whom he was speaking about, and was glad to see the man felt some discomfort, as he tried to laugh it off. "And yes, I would love to come to the party."

Not knowing what to expect at a ballet-after-performance-party, he braced himself for an interesting evening.

The conference room was filled with dancers, families, and

dignitaries. A young man, whom Nick was certain had partnered Alicia in the ballet, bustled towards them, a heavy frown across his brow. "Where the heck have you been?"

"I told you I was going to collect John and Jenny. Brandon, this is Nick Coleman, a friend of theirs. Nick, Brandon Hastie."

Brandon turned to face Nick; the scowl still visible. "John, Jenny and, Nick, did you say?" He gave Nick the once-over, then continued, "Did she tell you what she's done? No, I thought not."

"Please, don't do this here, Brandy. You know I don't have any choice." Alicia patted his arm but he pulled it away.

"That temperamental creep, who dares to call himself a dancer: wait until you see him Jenny, he's so old he needs glasses to see where the stage is, thinks he can just waltz in here from Tasmania and demand the lead."

Nick grinned at the sight of Brandon mimicking an old man on a walking stick, peering short-sightedly over the rim of a make-believe pair of glasses.

"And, you might as well know, he's notorious for bedding his leading ladies … has insisted she dance with him when we tour Tasmania. And get this – I just can't believe it – she agreed! No objections what so ever. Just, okay, lets kick Brandon out and give Roland the role."

There it was: the raised eyebrows, the twisting of the fingers, and the barely hidden anxiety. Alicia looked as if World War Three had broken out and the crowd was pointing the finger at her. Nick had an urge to tell Brandon to shove a sock in it, but it wasn't his call.

"I'm so angry with you for giving in to his demands. It's not my fault Louis owes him a favour. Nobody, especially fat old Roland, dances with you better than I do. You know that."

Her expression warmed. Like a big sister soothing a naughty boy, she tucked her arm through Brandon's. "Excuse us, we won't be long."

Nick watched her move off with the brooding Brandon. A passing waiter offered him a pink champagne. It felt good to quench the fire burning in his chest. He watched her shake hands with a pout-lipped man. *Obviously the old creep who dared to call himself a dancer,* thought Nick, *by the way he stood, poised, his feet pointing outwards.* And not quite the ancient, Brandon had led them to believe. The other man, with gossamer hair and a black and white striped scarf draped across his shoulder, seemed to be doing most of the talking between the pair.

Nick felt a stirring inside him. He couldn't put a name to it. All he wanted was for her to look at him, to see and understand why he had come but she was too engrossed listening.

"It's like entering another world," said John, trailing Nick's gaze.

Breaking his stare, Nick huffed out a grunt. Reluctantly he accepted what John had said to be true. Every way he looked, talent surrounded him. Poised, long, thin bodies gliding like swans that fed on success, lived in this alien world of passion and determination. Even those who weren't dancers seemed to endorse the energy.

He wondered if there was a place for a man like him in such a world. He looked back at Alicia and, much to his surprise, found her watching him. He was determined to hold her gaze long enough for her to acknowledge the force that flowed between them. She looked confused, blinked several times before drawing her attention back to the conversation. He was satisfied, a thin sliver of recognition, she understood he hadn't come just for the ballet.

"All done," said Jenny when Alicia returned. "You look a bit flushed."

"She's full of her own importance, if you ask me." Brandon lifted his nose to the air, flicked it with his forefinger.

"Thank you, Brandy."

Nick, amazed she accepted the harsh assessment of her so-called flawed character without comment, was impressed.

"Brandon, would you like to join us for a drink back at our place?"

"No thanks, Jen. I think I'll turn in." He reached out to tilt Alicia's chin and dropped a quick kiss on her lips.

Nick observed the gentle way she brushed her cheek against Brandon's fingers before rushing off to collect her gear from the change room. He was glad Brandon had declined Jenny's offer. Selfishly, he wanted as much of her to himself as he could get.

When they arrived back at the Spencers', Alicia headed up the stairs while Jenny paid the babysitter and watched her run down the street to her house. John and Nick made their way through to the lounge.

"Drink, Nick?

Conscious of the fact he had to drive home, Nick settled for a diet Coke, whilst John mixed Jenny and himself a whiskey and soda, adding a scoop of ice and a slice of lime to each glass.

"Alicia won't be long. She's checking on Sophie." She smiled at Alicia when she entered the room.

"Jenny hires a babysitter, for her children –"

"– a young neighbour, two doors up, needs the pocket money," chipped in Jenny.

"I can leave Sophie here instead of at the theatre. It's such a relief not to have to worry about her for a change, although she did fire up when I told her." She tiptoed across the room, sat on the couch with her legs and feet tucked up tight. "Excuse my bare feet, but they are still a bit tender. They've had a big night."

Nick had noticed every toe was wrapped in tape, the dried blood still visible on the one he had trod on. How she had managed to jump, repeatedly, on those blistered feet, astounded him. "I'm not surprised. That was some performance. How is your toe by the way?"

The raised eyebrows, the surprised expression but this time her eyes revealed her pleasure. "Oh, it's fine. Did you really like my … the show?"

He enjoyed seeing her obvious excitement. How he would like to take her face in his hands and taste her zeal. Another time and place he might have. "Yes, you were enchanting. I can't remember when I enjoyed a ballet more."

Seconds passed. A dimple appeared. "And how long is it since you last went to a ballet?"

"Let me think, maybe ten, twenty years ago." He kept a straight face but he hoped she could see the mischievous spark in his eyes.

Everyone laughed.

"I should throw my ballet shoes at you for that."

"I hope you're a good shot. Nick played a mean rover in his footy days, dodging players," said John.

Nick tried to focus on what John was saying, but his gaze kept drifting towards Alicia. There was something tantalising about hair being freed from an elastic band, fingers shaking loose the tension. Several times she stifled a yawn. Then, to his astonishment, she stretched along the sofa, eased her head onto the decorative cushions and fell asleep. Had she not looked so adorable he would have been seriously offended. "It's not often my company sends a woman to sleep." He sat forward, his hands clasped between his knees and studied the peaceful face.

"She's not being rude, Nick, just extremely tired."

He checked his watch. "Mm, in any case, it's late. Time I left." He walked over to Alicia sleeping soundly on the sofa. "How are you going to get her to bed? I gather she is staying here tonight?"

"Yes, she is," said John stretching his spine.

And this is the consolation prize, thought Nick, as he picked her up, before John succumbed to the task. She wriggled, sighed, then nestled her face into his chest. He followed Jenny to the guest room down the passage and lowered his beautiful bundle into the queen size bed beside a sleeping Sophie; basked in the whispered touch of the ballerina's breath against his skin. But for the Spencers, he would have kissed those full pink lips.

"Shouldn't we take her dress off or something," said John.

Nick choked back a laugh. Pretending to cough, he wondered what John was thinking.

"Oh God, give me strength," said Jenny, storming from the room, her husband following behind.

"I didn't mean it like that," echoed in their wake.

Left alone, Nick pulled the doona up under her chin and, kissing the tip of his finger, placed it on the beauty's forehead before turning out the light.

***

Nick lay in bed, staring out of the window with his hands behind his head, and pondering what was going on with the Spencers. John's behaviour reflected his disgruntled, frustrated and outright rude, state of mind. There was definitely something bothering the man, and he was taking it out on Jenny. Nick wondered if perhaps it was his work, or money worries or God forbid, another woman. From the little he'd been able to observe thus far, he was fairly positive it had nothing to do with the ballerina. It was so out of character of the person Nick knew and respected, he was tempted to ask Jenny what, if anything, was happening behind the bedroom door. More convinced than ever John was the real reason causing Jenny's anxiety, Nick considered approaching him. Conscious of the fact his relationship with John lacked the strength it needed for him to interfere at that level, he decided against it and turned his mind to a more personal level.

After his divorce, he had made it a point to learn all he could about the women he dated, determined not to be bitten again by an ambitious gold digger. What was it about this shy slip of a girl that had him so bamboozled? He saw no evidence of John's

35

attentions being reciprocated, aside friendship, and to think of her as a temptress, almost made him laugh. Her slight, sylph figure and fine-boned features, reminded him of a young Audrey Hepburn – no Marilyn Munroe there. And yet, her grace and poise fired every nerve in his body when she entered the room.

It amused him how effortlessly she drifted off to sleep in his presence, as though it was the most natural thing in the world. His biceps tensed at the memory of her in his arms. He thought about the daughter. Nick's involvement with children was non-existent and he questioned himself; how would he cope if he had to take on someone else's child. He pulled the reins on his galloping thoughts. *It might be an idea to go on a date first*, he reminded himself. He had no idea when he would see Alicia again but see her, he must. He decided to give Jenny a call in the morning.

He walked into his office the next day to find Clarissa, his PA, placing a pile of paperwork on his desk, alongside a steaming hot coffee. "Thanks for that. Any news?"

"If you mean, do we still have a job now that the takeover is finalised and Townsend is officially our boss?" She pulled a *I've-got-no-idea* face before shutting the door on her way out.

Nick nodded, picked up the phone and called Jenny's number.

"Well-timed," said Jenny. "I'm just about to usher the first patient through the door. What's up?"

"Let's say … a slight dilemma."

"Does this slight dilemma go by the name of Alicia Sommers perchance?"

"Yes. Surprised?"

"You kidding? I'd have been surprised if it wasn't. I saw the way you looked at her. I did warn you, Nick."

Yes, she did. "I might have known – can't hide much from a woman, and a doctor at that." He leant back into his chair and, crossing his legs, mulled over how best to articulate what was on his mind without sounding chauvinistic. "It seems I have developed a need to satisfy my caveman instincts. The thrill of the hunt, as they say."

"Ah! A new experience for you, Nick."

Not particularly pleased with the confession, and about to make another one, he drummed his fingers on the table. "Trouble is … once bitten …you know the rest." *Rebecca, his cheating ex-wife's parting gift,* he thought, suppressing a curse. "Our dancing swan strikes me as being quite naïve, even a little immature."

"Alicia may be naïve but she's definitely not immature. So, if you're asking my advice, I would strongly suggest you take it slow. In the three years I've known her, the only male I have ever seen or heard of in her life, is Brandon."

"Interesting. Where's the child's father?"

"As I told you the other day, I know very little about her past. She deliberately avoids personal questions. I've learnt not to ask."

"Right." Nick found that rather strange. In general, his experience of women led him to believe their friendships went much deeper than the superficial. That was more a man's domain. Unless of course, Jenny was sworn to secrecy. "Suggestions?"

"Um, let me see. How about lunch at my place next Sunday? Barbecue; bring your bathers and all that jazz," she said singing the tune. "Oh gosh, hang on a minute. I forgot the ballet season has two weeks to go and she won't do anything before that's over."

"Well, you did say, keep it slow." He sighed heavily. "Guess I'll have to amuse myself for a couple of weeks."

"I'll organise something in the meantime and give you a call."

"Much appreciated. Not expecting too much, am I Jen?"

"No. Not at all; pleased to oblige. Umm …"

Nick waited apprehensively; hoped she wasn't about to spill the beans on her and John's relationship over the phone. Through the silence, he could almost feel the cogs of her mind ticking over. He didn't want to get involved in their marriage. And considering his history, he was the last person to give advice, friend or not.

He blew out his breath when she said goodbye.

***

Nick walked across the manicured lawn swinging his Adidas bag. The Spencers' house appeared different during the day: bigger, brighter, full of lush green foliage and age-old oak trees that watched over the house like a wise old gypsy. He was glad the Spencers had convinced him to purchase a house in the same suburb. He loved Toorak and the Federation style homes that dominated the streets. He took the paved steps with a spring in his spirit he hadn't felt in years. Nobody answered when he knocked and, finding it unlocked, he let himself in.

Jenny had a knack for design, thought Nick, as he stepped onto the wooden decking outdoor area, with its high-pitched cedar roof and built-in kitchen. John and Jenny were seated on the lounge chair facing the pool with another couple he hadn't met before and a young blonde, enjoying a drink and nibbles. John sprang to his feet when he saw Nick approach and pulled out a chair for him to join them while Jenny did the introductions: a married couple who rented rooms in the same building Jenny worked at, and John's new receptionist who had recently moved from Albury after a broken relationship. He hoped this wasn't a setup. Her eyelashes were a trifle too long for his taste.

"Drink?" John asked, pointing to his glass of amber fluid.

The high-pitched squeals emanating from the pool diverted Nick's attention. Alicia was sitting on the steps, waist-deep in water with Oliver on her lap, watching Brandon tease two little girls. Glad he'd had the foresight to wear his bathers underneath his clothes, he ripped off his shorts and shirt and chucked them on the outdoor lounge. "Wouldn't mind a dip before I do. Sun's a scorcher."

The child with the long blonde hair, he recognised as Alicia's daughter. The other little girl, he realised, was Chloe, John and

Jenny's child. She had grown taller and rounder since he'd last seen her. The fluorescent pink bathers highlighted her olive skin, so similar to her mother's. It amazed him how children were simply purer versions of their parents. Her toothless smile made him laugh.

He lowered himself beside Alicia on the step, loving the feel of the cool water on his legs and feet. She looked tired, empty of energy. The black swimsuit clung to her thin body. He wanted to take her in his arms and smooth away the tension, the way she was doing with Oliver.

"The mysterious Nick," said Brandon, a child clinging to each leg.

"No mystery here, just a friend of the family." Nick decided now was as good a time as any to test his plan. "I'm glad I caught you both on your own."

Brandon disengaged the girls from his legs, sent them off to play on the blown-up floaties and squatted on the bottom rung of the steps. "Oh yeah. Why is that?"

Thinking back over his conversation at the café with Jenny, Nick recalled her saying something along the lines of Brandon adoring Alicia, which would explain the big brother act. "Because I have a favour to ask. I assume you know I host a midday show at Channel Seven. I'm always on the lookout for new material; thought perhaps you two might do a short dance routine, followed by an interview about a dancer's life and the medical challenges it presents."

"Are you serious?"

"Eh … yes, actually, I am." Nick, smiled to himself at the change in Brandon's tone.

"Television. Interview. Wow, we'd love to. We'll need to confirm it with Louis, our director, of course, but I'm sure he'll agree. We leave for Tasmania in a few days, but I'll mention it to Louis before we go. We have a short break when we return before rehearsals start for our next production.”

“Excellent,” said Nick. When he looked at Alicia, he wasn’t too sure Brandon’s enthusiastic response was shared. In fact, she looked slightly rattled.

“Do I have to speak?”

What an odd question. “As far as I know grunting is still considered unacceptable on TV.” He was immediately sorry he’d said it when she blushed scarlet.

“Of course, you have to speak,” Brandon piped up. “What do you think, sign language? Sorry, Nick, if she wasn’t the best dancer in the country, I’d disown her.”

“I really am very bad at that kind of thing,” said Alicia, apologetically. “It’s so different from being on stage; more confronting; personal.”

Nick found this difficult to fathom, coming from a girl who spent her life being scrutinized by some of the harshest critics in the business. “I’ll direct most of my questions to Mr Excitement over there if it will make you feel better. Then, of course, you could always go to sleep if it becomes too much.”

The horrified look on her face wiped the smile from his. She was way too sensitive. It was meant as a joke, which she obviously didn’t find funny. Either she needed to relax or he needed to brush up on his idea of humour.

Her words tumbled out like leaves in the wind. “Oh … I’m so sorry … I … I didn’t mean to be rude. Please, don’t take offence … I get so tired from the stress …”

Was he offended? A little bruised in the ego department perhaps but offended, no. “Joke, Joyce. Forget it.” He grabbed the beach ball floating past and hurled it at Brandon. “Fancy a little volleyball, matey?”

Stunned by the slap to the chest, Brandon retaliated, throwing the ball back as hard as he could. “Not one to knock back a challenge, old man. Sophie, Chloe, come on, out you both hop.

Brandon is going for a swim in the deep end and I can't watch you two at the same time."

Somewhat miffed with the term 'old man', Nick spun the ball on his index finger, plotted his revenge.

When the girls had finally left the pool, like a shark discovering his dinner, Brandon flung himself at Nick and, knocking the ball out of his hand, bolted to the deep end.

"Coming?" said Nick, his open hand ready to help her up. "I can tell by your muscular arms what a great advantage you will be."

"Don't be mean. And yes, I'm a lousy swimmer, even worse at treading water for too long."

"I thought all us Aussies could swim." He was pleased to see a smile replace the frown.

"I didn't say I couldn't swim, I'm just not very good. Not my *forte*."

Looking at her slight body he had no trouble believing that. "I promise to save you if I see you drowning."

"And if you don't?"

"Not a chance." With Oliver propped on her hip, he helped her up the steps.

She set the child on his feet and pointed him in the direction of the house. "Go tell Mummy you need to change out of your bathers, Beautiful. Alicia's going for a quick swim and will be there soon. Will you remember all that, Oliver?" She ruffled his hair when he gave three exaggerated nods, making her smile. She unlatched the pool gate and watched him run up the path.

Nick, who had been waiting by the side of the pool, took hold of her hand when she approached. With his fingers curled around hers, he led her to the deeper end. He held his breath when she slipped into the water smoother than a mermaid. The cool liquid eased his rising temperature.

Brandon kept popping up out of the water, dodging about like a duck. Nick was amazed at his agility and speed when they raced each other for the ball. They tussled and fought like school kids, sending water spraying into the air. With Brandon fighting like a terrier for the ball, Nick quickly threw it to Alicia, blissfully floating on her back. To his horror, the ball smacked her on her forehead.

Brandon started laughing when he saw her spluttering as the ball bounce off her head. Nick quickly ducked him under the water to shut him up.

"That's not funny, Brandon," she said, wiping hair and water from her eyes.

"Crikey Moses! Nick did that, not me," he said, after he'd come up for air.

She was right about one thing, thought Nick, *swimming wasn't her forte.* She seemed to be struggling to stay afloat while she caught her breath. He swam over to her and slipped his arm around her slim waist.

"Oh thanks," she gasped.

"Said I'd save you." He trailed his thumb down the side of her face to her chin, lifted her head. "Here, let me examine the damage. Hmm … a nasty red mark. Diagnosis … you'll live."

"Very cute. But it's my temper you should be worried about."

There was a hint of victory in the moment and he tightened his hold. The feel of her small body in his arms sent his heart rate soaring. The smile left her face. Large curious eyes stared into his. He almost forgot where he was until John's booming voice, calling them to lunch, reminded him. Nick did a double-take at the blonde at John's side, wearing an extremely brief bikini. She was standing way to close to his mate, for Nicks liking and her high-pitched laugh made him want to send her packing. He hadn't paid her much attention, apart from her eyelashes, when the introductions were being made but she now seemed a whole lot more interesting. When his glance returned to the beauty in his arms, judging by the worried look in Alicia's eyes, he realised she too understood the Spencers' problem.

"I'd better go," said Alicia, moving out from his embrace.

"Yes, we mustn't keep the good doctor waiting." Sorry he had allowed his annoyance to show, he quickly smiled when she flashed him a frown.

"Beauty, I'm starving," said Brandon, spinning the ball.

"Thanks for the game, Nick. Bad luck you couldn't keep up."

"Nice try, Brandy, 'old boy'."

Nick, burdened by his thoughts, decided to do a few quick laps of the pool before joining the others. He sliced through the water like a torpedo, hoping to ease his concern about John and his voluptuous secretary. Several laps later he stopped, out of breath but in control. He swam to the edge of the pool, rested his arms on the paving and let his gaze traverse the lush green property. John had it all, the wife, the kids, the house and the picket fence. Nick could never understand how a person could throw away everything they had spent years building, on a moment of chance. He was young and foolish when he fell in love with Rebecca and missed the signs of her ambitious nature, but John was neither young nor foolish and Jenny was a far cry from a party girl with a pretty face looking for excitement. If the man wasn't careful, he stood to lose a whole lot more than his dignity, which at the moment was in serious trouble.

He dried himself off, wrapped the towel around his midriff and followed the hearty smell of barbecued steak and sausages, to join the others at the table. Swimming had given him an appetite and he hoped his stomach wouldn't betray him by rumbling.

"How many snaggers?" called John.

He was tempted to say ten but kept it to a polite three. Oh, to be a kid, he thought as he watched the three littlies drown their hot dog, along with everything else around them, in tomato sauce. Oliver looked as though he'd dunked his face in the sauce bottle.

Alicia stepped out of the house dressed in a pair of linen shorts and matching top. Her wet hair fell in curly tangles over her shoulders, and dark sunglasses covered her eyes. Like a slow soft wind came the smile. His hunger for food was quickly replaced with desire. She sat beside Brandon on the opposite side of the table, pulled the scrunchy from her wrist and tied her hair back. His attraction to her was growing with every precious moment.

John placed a plate with a small serve of steak in front of her. "Eat," he ordered. He lifted her chin, baulked at the red mark on her forehead, then shot Nick an accusatory scowl. Nick returned his glare. *If you know what's good for you, you would be wise to turn your attention to your own affairs, and less on Alicia.* His thoughts were interrupted by a well-cooked piece of steak on the end of a fork being waved in his face.

"So, Nick, question time. What brought you to the ballet?" said Brandon.

"Curiosity."

"About what?"

"About whether or not I would like to interview a dancer." Wanting to avoid further interrogation, he tried to concentrate on lunch, helping himself to a large spoonful of creamy potato salad.

Brandon popped the last morsel of steak into his mouth and, cheeks bulging, continued. "So, how do you know the Spencers?"

He wondered where Brandon's questions might be leading. "We all went to university together, and later, Jenny and I completed our internship at the same hospital."

"And now you're a TV personality?" Brandon spread open his hands, signifying an explanation.

"Opportunity too good to refuse came a-knocking." *Just in time to save my sorry self from a breakdown, thanks to my cheating wife.* He pulled at his shirt to let in some air, hoping to stop the sweat running down his back. He hated rehashing his past in public.

"Your accent. A touch of Yankee or Canadian?"

"Right the first time. My parents emigrated from the US when I was twelve. Some things are hard to shake. Correct me if I'm wrong but I think Jenny mentioned the two of you are originally from Perth?"

The clang of Alicia's fork hitting the floor, stopped conversation and she quickly bent down to pick it up. Nick couldn't help noticing when she surfaced, her normally pink complexion had paled. She placed the fork on the table, and excusing herself, rose to join the children.

What! What had he done! Or said? Perth! Something she doesn't want to talk about that happened in Perth. Perhaps the child's father lives there. Perhaps he wants custody, perhaps, perhaps, perhaps. His curiosity talons dug into his psyche and his need to discover the truth increased.

A high-pitched giggle coming from the other end of the table diverted his attention. The blonde had her hand on John's arm and the two of them seemed to be enjoying a joke. He glanced over at Jenny. Her face a mass of pain. His heart went out to the girl – she looked broken. He thought about inviting John out for a drink, perhaps try to approach the subject during the course of their conversation but he feared his interference might spark John's anger, making matters worse. The man was obviously besotted with the young blonde.

After lunch, everyone ended up in the pool. All but Alicia, who opted to watch Oliver and the girls on the swings. She sat on the bench, her head resting back on the wooden slats with her eyes shut. Nick eased down beside her and pretended to study the ground, all the time planning how to win her confidence.

"Mind if I join you?"

She took a moment to respond. Twisting her fingers, she smiled unconvincingly. The tender moment they'd shared in the pool was gone, and in its place was a tension he intended to remedy. As he sat back to ponder the complexities of this woman, his arm brushed against hers. She flinched as if a match had fired on her skin. Was she frightened of men, or just sick to death of husbands behaving badly, who should know better? Simple questions, hard answers. How to talk to her so that she opened up, released some of that anxiety she kept cocooned inside and hopefully, gain her trust. He decided to try some reverse psychology, revealing tiny snippets about himself. He settled back, stared at the children in the playground.

"I loved being a doctor. It gave me a sense of worth, if that makes sense. It challenges me in a way nothing else can. Don't get me wrong, I've really enjoyed my time at the station. But it doesn't stimulate my intellect like medicine does." He lowered his head, twisted the ring on his right hand. "I hope that doesn't sound too arrogant, but it's the truth."

"No, not at all."

Slowly at first, Nick let words draw a picture of his life until he felt he'd captured her attention. The intensity with which she listened spurred him on, and he found himself telling her about his work and life at the station. She began to relax, even laugh at some of his funny stories.

"Ballet can sometimes have its funny moments," she said, "especially when dancers become emotional or fight with their partners. Once I saw a dancer take off her ballet shoe and smack her partner on the head because he said she wasn't sharp enough *en pointe*. When he cringed from the slap, she asked him if that was sharp enough for him. Nobody dared laugh, except Brandon of course, who let out a whopping hoot."

"I have no trouble imagining Brandon doing that." They smiled at each other and he felt a small but real connection. He wanted to ask her so many questions: did she have siblings, why

Melbourne, where … who was Sophie's father? But he had to content himself with the minuscule victory of her sharing anything with him at all. God, it was agony exercising so much restraint, but, in another sense, he found it challenging, stimulating, working to uncover the personality of this fascinating girl. "All jokes aside, I did enjoy your performance the other night."

"Thank you. I'm so glad. Why don't you still practice medicine?"

Nick didn't expect that. Wanting to give the answer its full merit, he hesitated.

"I'm so sorry, I shouldn't have asked. It's none of my business."

Nick felt pleased she had. It meant the door had swung open enough for him to take the same liberty. "Hey, it's fine. I don't mind. Age-old story, really. My ex left me for another doctor, a psychiatrist who worked at the hospital. A pretty ugly scene there for a while." He huffed out a laugh. *Hindsight is a wonderful thing,* thought Nick. "A talent scout from Channel Seven Studios came to the hospital looking for a doctor to host a medical show. Seemed the perfect solution. Self-survival. I resigned a month later. Not particularly stoic of me but to say I was in a bad place at the time was an understatement. I couldn't bear the whispers, the sympathetic smiles. Everyone down to the cleaning lady knew what had happened."

"That's awful, Nick. I'm so sorry. I can't imagine having to quit ballet. I love it so much. It has been my dream since I was a child."

"I caught something of that the other night. The emotion you portrayed couldn't have been merely acting. Do you have a favourite role?"

"Juliet, I think. You know, Romeo and Juliet? By Prokofiev?" She didn't wait for an answer. "But there are other strong character roles in which I can lose myself. I'm never happier than when I'm performing. Ballet is my lifeline; it has sustained me through … some … … difficult times."

He wondered what she was really going to say. Jenny's words reminding him to go slow, kicked in and he decided not to ask. "You certainly have achieved remarkable success for someone so young."

"Twenty-three's not that young in the ballet world."

"Seems pretty young to me." She was staring ahead, or was it into the past. He wished he knew what she was thinking, could interpret that facial expression, understand the meaning of the raised eyebrow. One day, he promised himself, he would.

"I've been lucky to have been blessed with three main ingredients for success."

"And they are?"

"Please don't think I'm bragging when I say I have a perfect body for a dancer."

He had no problem with her bragging about her body: it looked perfect to him too.

"It's pretty much imperative if one wants to succeed. Then there's my passion to dance, to push through the pain and dwell in a world of make-believe."

"Interesting," said Nick, imagining what it would be like on stage, acting out fantasy. "I've never lived in a world of make-believe. Instant and urgent, fit my profile. And the third?"

He followed her gaze across to the children on the swings.

"Sophie."

Silence fell between them. Nick reached over to take her hand, but she snatched it away. So, he thought, Jenny was right, slow, very slow. Puzzled, he tried to think how to ask if he could see her again. Before he could say another word, he looked up to see Brandon striding across the lawn.

When he reached the bench, Brandon knelt in front of Alicia and claimed both her hands. "Jenny's mobile rang just now. It was your Aunt Beryl. She's been trying to contact you and finally called Jenny."

Alicia stood up, panic written across her face. "Stupid me, I left my phone in my tote bag in the kitchen. Did she say why?"

"I think you had better call her back," said Brandon, attempting to wrap her in his arms, but she pulled away. "Something's wrong, isn't it?"

When he nodded, she stepped past Nick and ran inside.

Brandon slumped down on the bench, buried his head in his hands.

"What! What the hell is wrong?" asked Nick.

"Her Uncle Stan died of a heart attack earlier this morning." Brandon lifted his head, stared at Sophie on the swing. "She gave Aunt Beryl Jenny's number in case of an emergency, but I never thought…"

Nick sprang to his feet. "Why the hell don't you go after her."

"Because I know her better than you do and Alicia wouldn't want that. She does grief in private."

Nick rushed towards the house with Brandon yelling at him to stop. He hesitated, but only for a moment. Inside he found Jenny staring down the sink, John propped against the pantry door, watching his wife. There was no mistaking they had argued: the anger on Jenny's face said it all. Without stopping he headed down passage to the same room he had put Alicia to bed after the ballet. He was about to open the door when he heard the sobbing. Not sure if she would receive him under such emotional circumstances, he hovered, argued the point with himself then decided against it, knowing the connection between them lacked the strength it needed for him to intrude. What was it Brandon had said? *She does grief in private!* A prominent piece to the puzzle. Alicia had tasted grief.

Chapter Three

Alicia spent that evening packing for Tasmania. Folding her clothes neatly into the suitcase, she contemplated if she should be packing for Perth instead. The thought of going home, staying with her aunt, being next door to the house her family had lived in, brought back the pain. Tears pricked her eyes. Could she face all that again?

The memory of Pastor Matthews standing in her parents' kitchen, telling her it wasn't God's fault that her parents and brother were killed, resurrected her anger. "All things work together for God's glory," he had said. How that man thought their death could be glorious is something she would never understand. It would be a Christian funeral for her uncle. She hadn't been to church since her family's funeral.

She shut the suitcase and went in search of Brandon. She found him in the kitchen, clearing away the breakfast dishes, and propped herself against the doorframe. "I thought perhaps I should go home for Uncle Stan's funeral."

Brandon finished wiping the bench before he answered. "I don't think that's such a good idea, Ally. You'd be exhausted, flying from Melbourne to Perth, then over to Hobart. And you know how much this tour means to Louis. He mentioned Lauren Mason will be flying across from New Zealand to see us perform. Apparently, he is looking for a dancer to perform his next ballet. I'm sure Aunt Beryl wouldn't expect such a sacrifice."

"I know all that but I feel … oh, I don't know what I feel. Aunt Beryl is my mother's sister. She and Uncle Stan were very good to Sophie and me after the accident. Don't I have some sort of obligation to my Aunt?"

"Of course, you do. Send flowers, phone her tonight and explain it all. She'll understand."

"I guess," she murmured. "I know Louis is relying on me to dance at least three performances with Roland. And I can't bear the thought of Yvette taking my place. You know how much she wanted this role. She nearly scratched my eyes out when Louis gave it to me."

Brandon frowned, flicking the tea towel into the air several times, a sure sign something was on his mind. "I need to talk to you about Roland."

She raised her eyebrows. "Now there's a match, Yvette and Roland."

"I know Roland can be a frivolous bore at times but he can also be an animal when it comes to women. I wasn't joking when I told you he likes to bed his leading ladies."

Her mouth fell open in shock. "I can't believe you just said that to me." She thought about the promise she'd made to her mother before she died. A promise given loosely as a teenager, now meant the world to her. She would never break it. "In all the years you have known me have I ever given you cause for concern?" And, the idea of losing her virginity with someone as shallow as Roland made her shiver.

"You don't know Roland. Men like him know all the right moves to entice naive girls like you."

"Great! Now I'm naive."

"Well, not naive exactly, but inexperienced."

"Brandy, I might be inexperienced but I'm not stupid."

"I know that. What I'm trying to say ..." Running his fingers through his hair he blew out his breath, sending his fringe fluttering.

"What are you trying to say?"

"What I'm trying to say is ... some men, worldly men, men who are used to getting their own way – you know the type – well, they can often get bored. They long for a taste of the unexpected. Then one day a woman or young girl, sweeter or a bit naïve, unlike his usual type, comes along and he thinks to himself, this could be exciting. He acts, you know, sincere at first, makes promises he rarely keeps, then after a while the novelty … excitement – call it what you like - wears off and he very soon becomes bored again and moves on. Commitment isn't his thing. Do you get what I'm trying to say?"

Yes, she got it all right. This speech had little to do with the flirtatious Roland, and everything to do with a dark-haired TV host. "Yes, I think I do. You think I could get hurt if the wrong man, whom I thought might be the right man, were to take an interest in me?"

"Spot on." He dried his hands on the towel and hung it on the cupboard rail. Pleased as a peacock, he dropped a kiss on her cheek. "Gotta pack," he said, and left the room.

"Love you," she called. That was her Brandon: duty done, no time to hang about.

"Dittoooo …"

Memory of the dark-haired TV host with the wild wet curls and smiling eyes, holding her in the pool, popped into her thoughts. She rubbed a hand over her waist where he'd held her. His arms weren't like Brandon's. Nick's were stronger, safer, more like her father's. And the way he looked at her ... No one had ever looked at her like that before. And worst of all was, she liked it, wanted it, yearned for it. If not for John interrupting them, she might have let him kiss her. Although she had often wondered what it would feel like to be kissed, it had never occurred to her she might actually want to.

She had promised herself, after her family's death, never to love anyone but Sophie and Brandon. So, the possibility of not seeing Nick again, she convinced herself, consoled her. There was no place in her heart for love, only a desperate, Godless need to survive the harsh reality life had dealt her. Sophie, ballet, and Brandon had to be her focus, her reason to keep going. She wasn't about to let a handsome face distract her from her purpose. New York City, Royal Ballet, even the Bolshoi, if the opportunity presented itself. But love. She huffed out a laugh. Love was a dangerous and powerful emotion she had no intention of meddling with.

***

The plane for Hobart departed at 7 a.m. Waking a seven- year-old in the wee hours of the morning was like drawing blood from a stone, as her dear mother had been known to say.

"Come on, Baby, wake up." Alicia lifted Sophie from the bed, pulled her to her feet. "I've put your clothes on the end of the bed. The Uber will be here in twenty minutes, so hurry up and get dressed."

"I don't want to go to Tasmania and I hate flying," said Sophie, rubbing her eyes.

"You're just tired. Go wash your face, you'll feel better."

"I hate you," said Sophie, echoing Alicia out the door. The everyday stress of raising Sophie seemed to be increasing, the older Sophie grew. Time was her enemy. Soon she would be forced to place Sophie in a private boarding school. She tried not to think of the reaction Sophie would have when she found out. Lately, the child seemed reluctant to go to school at all. She had asked Sophie several times if anything was wrong but always received the same answer. No, and to stop asking.

Alicia, Sophie, and Brandon hurried from the house and piled into the Uber waiting to take them to the airport. Hustling a tired and grumpy child through the sliding doors, they weaved through the crowds. One look at Yvette's face and Alicia was glad she had decided not to go home for the funeral.

"Watch it!" called a man striding past."

"I know you're tired, darling, but try not to knock the other passengers with your bag. We'll be on the plane soon and you can go back to sleep."

"I'm hungry too and I don't want to catch a plane."

"As soon as mummy finishes checking us in, I'll buy you some raisin toast. Look, there's Louis and Linda."

"Alicia, darling, thank goodness." True to his French heritage, he kissed her on both cheeks and, cupping Sophie's chin, tapped her nose.

"Sorry to keep you waiting, Louis. Hello, Linda. Sophie say hello to Linda."

"Hello."

"You be good girl for Linda … Oui," said Louis.

A stony-faced Sophie stared at Louis. "Why do you make my mummy go away. I want to stay home."

"Sophie!" Alicia sent Louis an apologetic smile. Laughing, he dismissed her concerns with the flick of his wrist.

"Come on," said Linda, taking Sophie's hand. "Let's go line up behind the others and wait for mummy to join us."

Alicia breathed a sigh of relief, glad to know she had Linda to help her, with Sophie, on this tour.

"I want to say 'be nice to Roland," said Louis. "I know he can be hopelessly theatrical sometimes but, poor man, he finds it hard to grow old."

Aware of Roland's intense dislike of Brandon and his extraordinary talent, having witnessed firsthand the jealousy displayed by Roland whenever he saw Brandon dance, she reluctantly nodded. The difficult task of soothing Brandon's battered ego, should Roland choose to be obnoxious, would fall to her. She boarded the plane with a less than happy heart.

Stepping onto the tarmac at Hobart Airport, she inhaled the wonderful scent of Huon pine drifting through the air. As they taxied to the hotel, the afternoon sun, pitched high in the heavens, winked between the clouds at the picturesque countryside below. The Tasmanian Blue Gum, the State's floral emblem, blossomed in bright coloured patches along the highway approaching the city, proudly announcing the coming of spring.

Alicia instantly fell in love with Hobart and its fresh sweet smell, and its quiet personality, so different from the fast pace of Melbourne. The Grand Chancellor Hotel, where the Company was staying, was within walking distance of the theatre in Campbell Street.

Before checking into her room, Alicia arranged with Linda to meet her and Sophie at the theatre the following day. With a small back pack slung over her shoulders, Alicia set out with Sophie the next morning, ready to embrace the interesting personalities to be discovered in a city infused with its own unique culture. Although the sun shone, there was a nip in the air, making her glad she had insisted Sophie wear a light jacket. She stopped at a local café on the main street to buy a coffee for herself and a cup of hot milk with a doughnut for Sophie, and stayed longer than she intended.

This was the first time she had danced in Hobart and, as she walked up the steps of the Theatre Royal, the oldest continually operating theatre in Australia, she experienced a tremor of excitement. She noticed the time on the reception clock was eight forty-five and checked her watch. "Oh, my stars! Sophie, hurry up, we're late."

With a moustache of milk, and clutching a half-eaten doughnut, Sophie stumbled through the doors.

"Come on, come on! You can finish that when we get inside."

"But I'm hungry."

Several members of the Tasmanian Ballet Company, Roland de Beau amongst them, were warming up. Keeping her eyes lowered she scooted backstage, through a side door leading off the auditorium to the dressing rooms.

Linda jumped from her seat as Alicia entered. "Thank heavens. I was beginning to worry."

"Sorry, Linda, I lost track of the time." She threw her bag on the chair and yanked out her gear.

"Come here, Miss. Look at that face."

"Milk and doughnuts," said Alicia, pulling up her leotard. Her hair was a jumble of knots from the wind and brushing it was like untangling fishing line. She wound it into a roll, pinning it with several clips and grabbed her pumps.

"Be good for Linda and I don't want to hear any whining about doing your schoolwork."

"I'm still hungry."

"There are some cookies in my bag." At a minute to nine, she ran onto the stage, to be confronted by two waiting Companies.

"Nice of you to join us, Miss Sommers," said Helen Barsby, the ballet mistress. She hurried to the *barre*, taking her place in front of Brandon, who was glaring at her as if she had played truant.

From the beginning, it was clear to everyone, that Roland's jealously of Brandon's unique talent was an uncontrollable obsession and he goaded Brandon at every opportunity he could in an attempt to upset him. He even pleaded innocence, when standing to closely behind Brandon at the *barre*, swinging his front leg into *grand-battement-en-cloche*, smacked Brandon in the back of the head.

Alicia had heard rumours over the years, concerning Louis' obligation to Roland. She knew Louis had struggled in earlier days as director of such a large Company and needed a name to draw an audience. He had begged a young inspiring Roland to join as principal dancer, which he did, giving up a chance of becoming an international soloist on the European ballet circuit. Roland, much older now, and in the twilight years of his dancing career, was determined to take full advantage of the present situation. He insisted on having his own personal dressing room, constantly disparaged Louis' choreography as lacking imagination, and the dancers' ability to perform at a standard to which, in his opinion, he was accustomed.

Each day his demands grew more difficult to endure. Although Alicia respected Roland for his experience and dancing ability, she reached a point where there was very little she liked about him, including his partnering.

So, when he asked her out on a date, she had no hesitation in refusing him. After a week of rigorous rehearsals, Roland sought his revenge by insisting she partner him, instead of Brandon on opening night, as well as the following Friday and Saturday nights, the three most important nights in the season. She was almost tempted, for a brief moment, to let Yvette her understudy, take the lead.

"Why should I play second fiddle to him?" said Brandon kicking a stone along the footpath as they walked back to the hotel. "I'm the principal dancer of this Company and this is my role. Besides that, I'm ten times better than him. I always do opening night, it's my earned privilege. I worked hard for that right, Ally."

"I don't like that nasty man Roland," said Sophie, pretending to ride a bike. "He's a big bully."

"Sophie!" said Alicia, eyeballing Brandon. "I know, Brandy, but once this week is over so is Louis' obligation to Roland and none of us will have to endure him or his behaviour a minute longer."

"I don't know how you tolerate him, honestly I don't."

Alicia wondered herself, thinking about their last rehearsal together and the way he yanked her off *pointe* into his arms at the end of the *pas de deux*.

Opening night was a surprising success even though Roland managed to complain about almost everything from the timing of *corps de ballet* to Alicia's lack of control in the *deadlift*. When Sunday came the entire Company breathed a sigh of relief, ready for their two-day break.

Alicia liked to take Sophie away from the theatre during these breaks, giving Linda a chance to do some sight-seeing. She enjoyed her own company, relishing the space to clear her mind of the stress that came with performing and the fractured relationships touring could sometimes provoke. And Sophie often became difficult to manage when she had been cooped up for too long; dancing up and down the corridors of the hotel, talking to strangers in the foyer and befriending the kitchen staff, for food. Once, Alicia found her by the pool, talking to a group of young teenage boys on holiday with their parents.

She found a pamphlet, on a stand in the hotel foyer, advertising a day trip to Bruny Island. There were bikes for hire if you chose to ride around the island viewing the wildlife such as dolphins and seals swimming in the bay or dozing on the rocks beneath the cliffs; and exploring caves along the coastline. Morning tea and lunch were provided, plus a tour of the Bruny lighthouse. She booked ferry tickets through the concierge for her and Sophie, for the following day.

From the top deck of the ferry, Alicia listened to the wind whistle over the sea. Soothed by the swaying motion of the boat, she felt the tension of the past week drift away. Watching a young couple cuddled together on the seats, more interested in each other's lips than sightseeing, conjured thoughts of Nick's kissable lips. She shook her head. It was no use dreaming of what might never be. Her life was different, she was different. There was no place in her heart for love.

Sophie, on tip toes, watched over the side of the boat, her long blonde hair floating in the breeze. She was a bright child, vivacious and comfortable around strangers, but lately Alicia had noticed an anger in her behaviour, which was beginning to worry her. And her dislike of school seemed to be increasing. Sophie, my Sophie, mused Alicia as a pair of sun-warmed arms wrapped around her neck.

Sophie sprang to her feet at the shriek of the ferry whistle and grabbed Alicia's hand. "Come on, Mummy, the ferry is almost stopped."

On Sophie's insistence, Alicia hired a bike each for the two of them to explore the island.

"I love riding bikes. All the kids at school have a bike, and a daddy. I want a bike first then a daddy. You will buy me a bike when we get home, won't you, Mummy?"

"We'll see." With nowhere in the unit to keep it Alicia doubted that request would ever be fulfilled. As for a daddy, that thought didn't bear thinking.

After a long and tiring day exploring the island, observing the unusual wildlife, and taking a quick dip in the ocean, they boarded the ferry back to the mainland and strolled back to the hotel, picking up Chinese Takeaway on the way.

"I loved riding …" said Sophie, stretching like a Siamese cat on the floor of their hotel room.

Alicia put her to bed, cleared away the leftovers, wondering how to fulfil Sophie's wish for a pink bike. Glad to rest her sore bottom, she slumped on the settee to watch a movie, when her mobile rang. "Hi," she said, stifling a yawn as she picked up her phone.

"Alicia. It's Nick. Nick Coleman."

"Nick!" She hadn't bothered to check her phone; certain it would be Brandon ringing. She sat up, pushed at the strands of hair that had escaped her ponytail and took a slow deep breath.

"Haven't got you at a bad time, have I? You sound tired." "No, of course not," she said, stifling another yawn.

"I called to let you know I've arranged for you and Brandon to appear on the show I mentioned a while back. I've spoken to Louis. He seemed quite enthused with the idea, good publicity and all. He said Brandon had choreographed a short piece that would adapt nicely on the set. He also mentioned you have some free time after the tour. Provided the two of you agree, it might be a good time to do a shoot. What do you think?"

"Sounds fine. Have you spoken to Brandon at all?"

"No, not yet. I rang Jenny first; she gave me your number. Don't mind me calling, do you?"

"No, don't be silly. It's just that I can't really confirm anything until I speak to him tomorrow."

"Not a problem. So, how's Tasmania? I've never been there, it's on my bucket list."

"It's quite stunning, lots of touristy things to see. I took Sophie for a ferry ride to one of the islands and we rode bikes all the way around. Sophie's favourite thing to do. She loves riding. And the weather has been perfect."

"How is Sophie?"

"Also, perfect. She's asleep."

Nick laughed. "So, you're sitting up alone, in a strange place and I'm guessing, in need of some company."

"I am in a strange place but I'm not exactly alone," she said, glancing at Sophie.

"Shame. How's the ballet going and what about that Prima Donna you have to dance with?"

"Very successful so far, packed house every performance. Roland finished up last night." She wanted to say 'thank goodness' but held her tongue.

"And did he get to bed his leading lady?"

For a moment, Alicia wondered if she had heard correctly. Did he think she was the kind of woman who slept with a man so easily? Maybe he was joking. With so little experience she felt at a loss to know how to respond. She cursed Brandon and his wayward tongue, under her breath, for saying something so stupid. "I have a big day tomorrow." She cleared her throat, hoping to stop the awkwardness in her voice. "I think perhaps I'd better go."

"You don't take all that kindly to my jokes, do you. My sense of humour can be a little dry at times but I promise to be more careful in the future. No offense intended. I can be a bit of a clumsy oaf at times."

It was her turn to laugh. "None taken." He had promised to try harder in the future. She wasn't sure if there was to be a future, and filed that thought in the too-hard basket.

"What day are you due home?"

Now why would he ask that question, she wondered apprehensively? But she answered all the same. "Sunday, the fifth."

"The last time I saw you, you were very upset about your uncle. Are you okay?"

Was she okay? Her brain said yes, her heart said no. Her brain also told her 'don't start something you can't finish.' She chose to ignore her brain and pressed the receiver hard against her ear, glad he had asked. "Yes, I'm fine. I did consider going home for the funeral."

"I'm glad you didn't."

Glad. He said he was glad. Those words both thrilled and terrified her. Did he mean what she thought he meant? She had to ask. Should she ask? "Why?"

He laughed at that, loud and hearty. "You might decide you like Western Australia and never come back, breaking my pathetic heart."

Alicia wished that was all it did take to break a heart. "Now I know you're joking."

"Maybe just a little."

Alicia could hear Daniel Johns singing in the background, one of the few modern artists she actually liked listening to, and wondered if he enjoyed listening to classical music. She laid down with the phone at her ear and listened, laughed and lived as time ticked on. His easy conversation flowed with a confidence she envied. Nothing too personal or intrusive, yet it was enough to know there was someone who thought about her, when she worked away from home.

"Nick, we have been talking for hours. The battery will run out on your phone."

"Charged it up before I rang. Besides, I enjoy talking to you."

"You do?"

"Yes, Alicia Sommers, I do."

She enjoyed talking to him too but kept that information to herself. Sophie stirred. It was eleven-thirty and she had promised to take her on a tour of the city in the morning. The bus would pick them up at eight o'clock sharp. "Sorry," she said, yawning.

"Time to say goodnight."

"Do you mind?" She didn't want to hang up but she felt troubled by the warm tender feeling, stirring in the pit of her stomach.

"Yes and no. Goodnight Alicia. Sleep tight and I'll call you when you get back."

She slipped under the covers and cuddled up beside a sleeping Sophie.

He rang! He even said he enjoyed talking to her. Did he mean it? He certainly sounded as though he did. She rolled onto her back, switched off the light and stared into the night.

"I liked talking to him too," she confided to the dark. Nobody ever rang her when she was away. No family to say they missed her, no father or brother to tease her and no mother to share her thoughts with. Loneliness was like a pair of hands, twisting and pulling at her wretched heart.

She remembered her mother once said that no one was alone when they walk with God. Was her mother right? Could God fill her empty void?

"I have lost so much, Father. Please don't let me lose anything else. I know nothing about the love between a man and a woman. Nick Coleman could be playing games with me, games I don't know how to play. Loneliness I can deal with, heaven knows I've learned the hard way, but a man … love … another loss?'

The following morning, Alicia and Sophie, rising early, had a quick shower and hurried downstairs to catch the bus, which took them on an extensive tour of Hobart, and its beautiful historic attractions. The crisp morning air against her skin had lifted her spirits and by the time they arrived back at the hotel for lunch she felt revived. She tried to push thoughts of Nick from her mind but his deep voice kept interrupting her peace. It bothered her to know a simple phone call from him could affect her in such a profound way.

Glad to be back in her room, she dumped the few souvenirs she had bought during the tour, on the bed, and went in search of Brandon to discuss Nick's arrangements for them to perform at his studio, on their return. Clutching Sophie's hand she wandered down the passage to his room, knocked on the door.

"Just a minute."

Sophie, bouncing like a bean threw herself into Brandon's arms when he opened the door, wrapping her legs around his waist. The last two days had been happy ones on the island with Sophie and she was glad to see her back to her sunny self.

"And you want to be a ballerina. Point those toes, straighten your back and give me a smacking kiss," he said, tapping his finger to his cheek.

Alicia watched the two of them as Sophie squeezed Brandon in a bear-like grip around the neck and, pulling a face, he pretended to choke to death, his tongue hanging out the side of his mouth. He fell backward onto the bed with Sophie on top of him, giggling. "Mummy hired bikes for us to ride around the island. We went to the animal park and fed the kangaroos, didn't we mummy?"

"Yep, we did." Gazing around the room, she smiled. Neat to a pin was her Brandon. The new clothes he had bought were stacked in an orderly fashion on the settee. Several pairs of shoes were lined up in plastic bags on the floor, and his pyjamas were neatly folded and placed on the pillow.

He hopped off the bed with Sophie still in his arms and greeted Alicia with an affectionate kiss on her cheek.

"Nick rang me when we were on Bruny Island about appearing on his show. Apparently, he arranged with Louis do the piece you choreographed for the opera. Any objections?"

"Are you kidding? It's a great piece. Australia will be getting a taste of my superb choreography. Brandon Hastie, the world's leading dancer slash choreographer." Lowering Sophie, he twirled her in a circle before taking a bow.

Alicia agreed, Brandon's talent extends beyond performing. And when his dancing no longer sustained him, he was certain to find a future in choreography and artistic direction.

During the last two weeks of the season in Tasmania, the theatre was packed every night, right up to the last performance. Alicia wished Louis had been there, to see how many dignitaries attended the reception. But with his wretched hip joint steadily deteriorating, he had scheduled the operation for a hip replacement to take place while the Company was on tour.

It was a grand affair with the men looking immaculate, in dinner suits, crisp white shirts, and bow ties, escorting wives and partners dressed in bright coloured, laced or satin ball dresses. The ovation she and Brandon received when they entered the reception room, in the theatre complex, brought a heartfelt glow to her face. Congratulations flowed like champagne. And Roland de Beau, centre floor, lapped up the effervescent spray of praise.

Alicia arrived back at her hotel room to find Linda asleep on the couch with the television on. It was well after midnight when she finally crawled into bed. The blare of the phone alarm jerked her awake. She checked the time, and groaned, seven o'clock.

"Come on, darling, time to get up," said Alicia, tapping the small bottom beside her.

She threw back the covers, grabbed a pair of jeans and denim shirt from the closet on her way through to the bathroom for a much-needed shower.

Alicia was about to set the locks on the cases, when a violent knocking on the door, interrupted her.

"Have you read this?" Brandon said, waving a newspaper in her face as he entered.

No, but I think I'm about to, she thought, shaking her head.

"Well, listen to this." He ran his gaze over the paper. "Ah, here it is. *'And of course, de Beau's performance was indicative of the great man himself.'* Oh, God that makes me sick. Great man. Great man ... ... can you believe it, that obnoxious, spoilt, useless piece of ... ..."

"Brandon!"

"Sorry, Soph, but Uncle Brandon is very upset." He flopped on the bed and like a magnet Sophie climbed onto his chest.

"I hate that Roland," she said.

"Me too," he whispered in her ear, his fingers curled around her pigtails.

"Did you bother to read the rest of the article, Mr Dramatic? No, I thought not. *Brandon Hastie and Alicia Sommers' world class talent brought to life Louis Batiste's brilliant interpretation of Gershwin's Lullaby for Strings. Their faultless performance wooed the audience, assuring the Company's return.'"*

"But that's the truth!"

"Whoa. Modest too. Have you packed yet?"

"Bag's downstairs in the foyer."

"Come on then, let's go."

After the late night, the long day of travelling, and Sophie's incessant whining from the hotel in Hobart to their apartment, Alicia's head pounded louder than a drum by the time they reached their apartment. The place smelt from being shut up for so long. Dropping her bags, she flung open the windows and took a deep breath of Melbourne air.

"It's so good to be home," she said as she soaked up the familiar surroundings. The thought of a whole week off her busy schedule, eased her headache.

Two days later, Louis called to confirm their appearance on Nick's show. "I'm very excited about this, Alicia. The publicity will be good for the Company. I would like you or Brandon to mention the coming season of Manon, if possible."

"Louis, you know how much I hate talking in public, especially on television. Just the thought of it makes me feel sick. If you don't mind, I think I'll leave that to Brandon. He's so much better at that sort of thing than I am. How's your hip by the way?"

"Oui, much better. Merci. I think it good idea you both come tomorrow for quick rehearsal. Maybe, nine o'clock. Fantastic report from Hobart press, Ma Cherie."

"Especially the bit about Roland de Beau. Brandon loved it." His laughter faded down the line as he hung up.

Chapter Four

Channel 7 Studios, situated on Harbour Esplanade, Docklands, reminded Alicia of an overly large, grey Meccano set. She entered the building, into a hub of activity.

"Nervous?"

"Terrified," she replied, clutching Brandon's hand with her sweaty one. She'd only ever performed on stage, where lights, darkness and the music hid faces and cocooned her in another world. This world seemed all too confronting.

"You're kidding! How can a silly TV shoot scare you that much?" Brandon gently nudged her in the ribs. "Just think of it as your first performance at Covent Gardens, partnering Nureyev, that ought-a do it."

She was tempted to return the gesture but they had reached the main foyer.

The receptionist glanced up at their approach, smiled politely, her bright, red fingernails tapping the computer mat beside her. "Can I help you?"

Sounding like he was related to Prince Charles, Brandon told her they were here to appear on the *Medicine for Melbourne* show. Alicia would have laughed if she hadn't been so nervous.

"Could I have your names please, and I'll let Mr Coleman know you have arrived."

"Brandon Hastie and Alicia Sommers. Principal dancers from the Australian Ballet Company." If he expected a reaction to his elegant introduction, he was extremely disappointed, judging by the expression on the woman's face. The smile remained but her eyes had already switched to business as usual.

They waited quietly taking in the plush surroundings: big name personalities smiled on them from the walls above; a huge vase of artificial flowers, symmetrically placed in front of the window, highlighted the mocha-coloured carpet; coffee machine steaming away at the ready. A few minutes later Nick came bounding down the stairs. His easy, pleasant smile made her glad she had come. He looked exactly how she imagined, in his light grey suit and navy tie, sophisticated and confident. He shook hands with Brandon, clasped hers with his own. "Alicia, Brandon. It's so good to see you both."

He introduced her and Brandon to his colleagues, who measured her head to toe, curiosity alive in their eyes.

A young woman approached, introduced herself as Carissa, Nick's PA, and on Nick's orders, led them to their dressing rooms.

Pleased to see the room was lit with bright lights above the mirrors, Alicia removed her red tutu from her bag and hung it on the rack provided. Unlike other dancers, she was not superstitious and placed her red ballet shoes on the bench.

A loud knock caused her to swing around. "Hi. I'm Bree, the makeup artist," came the booming voice from a large girl who burst into the room, another hard on her heels. "And this is Jodi … she'll be doing your hair."

"It's nice to meet you both. I'm …." Alicia held out her hand but drew it back when Bree slapped her on the back.

"Alicia Sommers. We know. We've been dying to meet you," said Bree, taking the ballet shoes off the bench and smoothing them against her cheek. "Oh, they're so small and cute. I love the feel of satin against my skin. I've always wanted to wear a pair of these." She replaced the pumps on the bench, giving them one last touch. "Have you seen the size of my clod hopper?"

Alicia was pleased to see no smudges marked the red satin. But she couldn't help gawking at the large foot waving the air.

With a hand on Alicia's shoulder, Bree eased her into the swivel chair as Jodi flipped a plastic cape around her shoulders. The wide leather belt around Bree's waist was loaded with an assortment of makeup paraphernalia: brushes, blushes, grease sticks, lipsticks.

"You remind me of a porcelain doll my mother gave me when I was a small child." Bree cupped Alicia's chin in her hand as she studied her face. "Perfect structure, high cheekbones, full lips and almond-shaped eyes. This will be a breeze."

Half an hour later when Alicia stood for inspection, both girls let out appreciative sighs. Touched, she asked if they would be watching from the sidelines.

"Are you kidding? A truck couldn't hold us back."

Alicia and Brandon warmed up on a makeshift bar comprised of two chairs pushed together. Bree and Jody chattered exclusively to Brandon who was busy charming them with his artistic guile.

"Ready," called the producer.

As she walked out in her bright-coloured costume, a parade of onlookers, including cameramen who were focusing on her from different angles, did little to improve her nerves.

Brandon stood *centre floor,* mentally adjusting the *pas de deux* to the proportions of the room while Alicia pushed resin into her dampened toe shoe to prevent herself slipping on the wooden floor. They waited for the producer's nod and counted time to the introductory music filling the studio.

Brandon's unique choreography captured the sensual feel of Debussy's Clair de Lune. Alicia flirted and teased her lover until his frantic heart could stand it no more, submitting to her power and giving the viewers a glimpse of the scarlet character inside the red tutu. Everyone, including the crew, ummed and uhhed each time she leapt into Brandon's receptive arms, stretching and sliding over his taunt body in sensual demonstration of awakening love.

When the performance finished, all Alicia could hear was a deafening silence. Then, to her relief, applause and cheers erupted.

Holding Brandon's hand, she executed a low and grateful curtsey. The camera swung across to Nick who was still clapping enthusiastically, a delighted smile spreading across his face. Introductions complete, he invited them to join him on the settee. Folding her hands on her lap, she sat on the couch provided, the tips of her toes resting *on pointe.*

Nick, as promised directed most of the questions to Brandon, regarding the life of a dancer and the challenges they faced. He also asked about the future of the Company and coming productions. Alicia marvelled at Brandon's cool, confident manner, as though he was quite familiar with making TV appearances.

"Alicia," said Nick, leaning forward to look at her. "I have heard a ballerina's feet can give them a bit of trouble from time to time. All that jumping on your toes. Is that true?"

Nick's unexpected question caught her off guard causing her left foot to fall off *pointe,* sending her nerves to jelly and her mind into a blank panic. "Um, yes that's true. But mine are fine, thank you." Deeply embarrassed by her jumbled response, she lowered her eyes but not before she caught sight of Nick's tightly pressed lips fighting back a grin. He politely thanked her for her comment.

On their way back to the dressing room, Alicia wiped perspiration from her face with the hand towel she had left on a chair. "Oh, thank goodness," she sighed.

"Um, that's true, but mine are fine," mimicked Brandon. "Pathetic."

She slapped him across the back with the towel. "Ok for you, Mister Cool, in front of the camera." Back in the change room she collapsed into the swivel chair. As she removed her shoes, she thought about Nick and the easy way he flirted with the audience, mostly full of adoring women. She never flirted with the audience unless the director demanded it in his choreography. Every step, every head or hand movement was meticulously studied and calculated. Only after hours and hours of practising difficult and strenuous movements did she begin to develop the personality of the character.

She sat forward, rested her chin on her hand, and glared at the girl in the mirror. Doubt crawled through her like a spider. She wasn't like Bree or Jodi or Nick, secure and confident. She might look normal on the outside but inside her, lurked many demons from her past.

A knock brought her back to earth. She turned to see a couple of cheeky faces peeking around the door.

"You were absolutely gorgeous," they cried out, bursting into the room.

"Go on Bree, ask her."

"We were wondering ... that is, if you have no objection and you don't mind ... of course if you do mind please say ... um ... could we ask a small favour, well a large one really?"

"Yes, of course."

"We thought you might give us your ballet shoes, one each as a souvenir from a great dancer."

Laughing, she bent down to retrieve them from the floor. Dancers often gave away their shoes to fans as a souvenir. It was almost a custom in the ballet world. She, herself had a collection of shoes from various dancers who had left them behind at His Majesty's Theatre, in Perth, after a season – Marilyn Russell, her favourite ballerina, amongst them. She handed each girl a shoe, happy they thought of her as a great dancer.

The girls shrieked with joy.

Nick poked his head in through the open door. "What's all the noise about?"

"Nick, look. Alicia has given us a ballet shoe each as a souvenir," cried Bree as she proudly waved the red shoe in front of his nose.

"Lucky, you. Such fortune seems to have escaped me."

"Oh Nick! Don't be silly, you can have anything you like. You only have to ask." Although what she had to give him, left her thinking.

"Anything I'd like, eh!"

He stood with his hands in his pocket, a cool, calculating look on his face. Something about his manner, started warning bells ringing in her head. "Well, yes, I …"

"Is that a promise?"

"Ooooh … be careful, Alicia," said Bree, clapping her hands. Alicia looked from Nick to the girls. Her heartbeat quickened. He raised his eyebrows waiting for a reply. She could feel heat rising though her body and only hoped the costume would absorb the colour. "I … I promise. I mean, I don't know. It depends … what exactly do you want?" She stared at him unblinking.

"What I want, Miss Sommers, is something a lot more tangible than a worn-out pair of ballet shoes."

"Whoa," said Bree, nudging Jodi, whose eyes were popping out of her head.

Alicia felt a sliver of panic. What did he want?

"A promise is a promise."

"Yes but … …"

"Sorry, no buts … dinner, the two of us. I'll call you." They stared at each other until, accepting the challenge, Alicia nodded.

"You did promise," Bree reminded her.

"So I did."

"Good. Come on you two. I think the lady might like to change."

After Nick and the two girls left, Alicia stayed rigid in her seat. Twice she stood to change and sat down again. She tried to figure out what had just happened and how skilfully he managed to manipulate a simple situation. "I can't go out with him. I can't. Me on a date with a man …" She had seen first-hand the type of women he associated with: sophisticated, confident women who were accustomed to handling men like Nick.

When she finally plucked up the courage to emerged from the

dressing room to join an impatient Brandon and his toe tapping foot, she felt a little more composed.

"You've been ages. What have you been doing?"

"I've been chatting with the young girls in the dressing room. They asked me if they could have my ballet shoes." The minute the words left her lips, she realised her mistake.

"Why would they want your dirty ballet shoes?"

"You know very well why, Brandon."

"Well, that's lovely. They didn't ask me for anything."

He was miffed. She would never hear the end of this little *faux pas*.

"Okay, well, let's go." He gave a slow sigh, turned to Nick, who was striding towards them. "Thanks for inviting us. I loved it. If you ever get stuck for someone to interview, you know where to find me."

"Top of the list. Bye, Brandon," he said, shaking hands. "Alicia."

"Bye, Nick."

All the way home in the car, Brandon whined like a turbo engine. "To think I answered every one of their dumb questions and they never even said goodbye."

The slight headache she woke with that morning had now escalated to a throbbing migraine. She had taken a couple of Nurofen before the show but they were proving ineffective. By the time they arrived home, she was ready for bed.

Brandon, accustomed to these attacks made her a sugary tea, drew the blinds and put a cold compress on her head.

"Pick up Sophie for me, will you?"

"Yep." He dropped a kiss on her forehead and tucked her in. "Bring her home, make her dinner, put her to bed, and everything else, 'miss-who-gets-to-give-her-ballet-shoes-as-a-souvenir," he mumbled before closing the door.

After collecting Sophie from school, Brandon stopped at the local markets. Aside from dancing, he loved to cook, having grown up on the good old staple diet of steak and three vegetables six nights a week, and scrambled eggs on toast, the seventh. Cooking helped calm his inner psyche and gave him a chance to create, away from the theatre. Tonight, he decided on traditional Chinese: beef in black bean sauce, accompanied by fried rice. Michael Gillespie's favourite. He ought to know: he'd cooked it for him often enough. It still hurt to think of him and how happy they had been together. Unlike Alicia, he had never known what it was like to be truly loved, until Michael came along. Brandon would always wonder why … why Michael betrayed him so cruelly.

He thought about his childhood and the father he hated. There were so many things about home he missed, but his family wasn't one of them. Mr Hastie, a bigoted, small-minded man, had rejected Brandon most of his life for his gentle and artistic disposition. 'A pansy boy,' his father labelled him. It was Jason, his younger brother – the star footballer – whom his father adored. By the time he was seventeen, his father's contempt for Brandon was so obvious, he knew he had to leave before the man destroyed his confidence completely.

A few days before he left Australia, he dropped a letter in his parents' letter box. He'd addressed it to his mother, telling her of his plans to leave Perth for Melbourne, and that he could be reached at the Australian Ballet Company. That was six years ago, and he hadn't heard a word from any of them since. Not a phone call, text, nothing. He shook his head, hoping to rid himself of the hurt.

"Ah, Mr Brandon, how you are? Not seen you for long time."

"Afternoon, Mr Chong. I've been busy touring but tonight I'm cooking Chinese in my own kitchen."

"Very good, very good. Fresh bok choy jus' arrive. Very cheap for best customer and maybe Chinese cookie for Sophie."

"You're a crafty old codger, Mr Chong."

Mr Chong nodded, a wide smile on his face. Brandon smiled too but for quite a different reason. He was certain the Chinese man had no idea what a crafty old codger was.

Loaded up with two hessian bags of Asian vegetables, they headed for the car.

"Try not to get cookie smeared all over your uniform."

As they walked from the car to the apartment, the straps of the hessian bags cut into his palms and he was glad to dump them on the kitchen bench.

"Go wash your face and hands and then you can help me cut up the beans." He emptied the vegetables into the sink.

Sophie returned with water dripping from her chin and climbed onto the stool. Brandon handed her a tea towel, a blunt knife and a handful of stringless beans. "Here, wipe your face then cut the tops off these babies and don't eat any or I'll chop your tongue up for mincemeat."

Giggling, she poked her tongue at him. He pretended to grab it, and she slipped it back inside.

Whenever Brandon cooked, he like to sing. It helped him release some of the anxiety he harboured. Slicing the raw veggies, he broke into singing, "By the Light … of the Silvery Moon," with Sophie attempting to harmonise when instructed. He was almost done when Alicia's mobile rang. "Answer that, will you, Soph. I'm elbow deep in food. And speak nicely."

"Hello, Sophie Sommers speaking." She looked at her uncle for approval. Brandon nodded. "Yes, but she's in bed with a headache."

"Soph, who is it?"

"It's Nick."

"Okay, give it to me." He threw the last of the veggies into the wok, gave them a quick stir and wiped his hands. "Nick! What can I do you for?"

"Actually, Brandon, I was hoping to speak to Alicia."

"Sorry, matey, she's in bed with a migraine."

"I see. Has she had it for long?"

"Full-blown by the time we arrived home from the studio. She gets them sometimes when she's worked up about something, which is every second week for Miss Stress Attack. Oops, dinner calls. Won't be a sec." Brandon dropped the phone, grabbed the tea towel and raced to rescue his meal before it burnt to a crisp. He gave it a good stir; added some soy sauce. "Okay, back again."

"What are you having?" asked Nick.

"Beef in black bean sauce and fried rice. Why, hungry?"

"Is that an invitation?"

"Yeah, sure, why not? Plenty to spare and we could do with some company, couldn't we, Soph?"

Sophie nodded vigorously.

"Done! See you soon."

***

Nick rang the doorbell, hoping Alicia might have recovered. The look of pleasure on Sophie's face made him smile. Too bad it didn't run in the family, he thought. "Well hello, little lady."

The big adoring eyes, looking up at him as if he were her saviour, made him smile. He touched her cheek. She reached for his hand and led him through to the kitchen. He found Brandon with an apron tied around his waist ladling food onto plates.

"Ah, just in the Nick of time. Sorry, couldn't resist."

"Been hearing it all my life."

"Good. Then you'll be used to it. Here, carry this to the table. You too, Soph. Here's your dinner. Right, that just leaves me." He filled his plate and carried it through to the dining room. "Mmm

… smells good, even if I do say so myself."

"You're right, does smell good. Tastes even better." Gulping down a mouthful, Nick waved his fork at Brandon. "You know what you can do if you should break a leg."

"Hush your mouth." Brandon shuddered at the thought. "Curses, Nick, curses. Cooking's a hobby, ballet's my life."

Envy surged through Nick as he ate his meal. Just like Ballet was Brandon's life, medicine had once been his. He could still feel the exhilaration, the adrenalin surging through his blood stream as he stood over an open chest, watching a human heart pump life.

Shaking free of regret, he surveyed the room. He liked what he saw. Modern, light-coloured furniture clothed in a type of linen fabric with wooden frames, filled the room. Pictures of yesterdays' ballet dancers hung on the walls; magazines lay scattered across the coffee table; and white ceramic figurines of dancers were displayed in a glass cabinet. Yet, it lacked something and he couldn't work out what that something was.

After the meal, Brandon took Sophie off to have a bath while Nick cleared the table. He had just finished the dishes and made himself comfortable on the couch when Brandon returned with Sophie in a pair of princess pyjamas. "Say goodnight to Nick and then off to bed with you."

She stood in front of him, chewing on her bottom lip. "Will you come back again when Mummy is awake?"

"Sure, if she'll let me."

"Goodnight," she said, with a broad smile.

"Goodnight, sweetie." He leant forward to receive a kiss on the cheek and watched as she skipped off with Brandon.

The TV was showing a re-run of the latest Aussie League Football game. Nick, a keen and reasonably good player all through his university days, soon became engrossed in the game. He barely looked up when Brandon entered.

"Don't tell me you like this horrendous game."

"Guilty as charged," replied Nick.

"It's so … oh, I don't know, brutal." Brandon shivered in mock fear.

"It's actually very skilful. I bet you've never been to a football game in your life."

"Truthfully, no," admitted Brandon with a thoughtful sigh.

"If I can go to a ballet, one horrendous football game shouldn't be too much to ask of you."

"Never one to knock back a challenge. Name your poison."

"Next Sunday, Geelong versus West Coast Eagles, your home team. I've got season tickets. More than happy to take the three of you."

"Dinkum?"

"Dinkum," said Nick, putting on his broadest Aussie accent.

"Works for me. Company has the day off, so it fits perfectly. By the way, could you make it four tickets, might bring a friend?"

"Sure."

"Brandon, why are you watching foot …?" Alicia had wandered into the room, barefoot and wearing a long tee over baggy pj bottoms.

She stopped, rigid, frowning at Nick. He rose from the couch, feeling awkward and for some ridiculous reason, guilty. Her ghastly white pallor worried him.

"Oh, blame Nick, he loves football."

No response, Brandon looked from one to the other. "Crikey Moses, you two. Sit down, make a coffee, do something, you're making me nervous glaring at each other like you're ready to commit murder."

Alicia and Nick both started to speak at once, words rambling together like a couple of turkeys.

"That's it! I'm off to bed with a good book. Don't forget about Sunday, Nick. Give me a bell."

"Will do." His lips moved but his brain was focused on a pair of anxious eyes. He tried reading her expression. *Annoyed?*

"What are you doing here?"

That stung. What was he doing here? The way she put the question made him feel less than welcome. "Brandon invited me to dinner." She looked exhausted, standing there with her arms folded across her chest. "Are you alright? You look very pale."

"I need to change. I won't be long."

He stayed standing, conscious of her disapproval. Those eyes, fixed on his as though he had committed a mortal sin, made him uneasy. Maybe he should have given it more time before coming over. But when she reappeared, wearing a close-fitting pair of jeans, her hair clipped loosely at the nape of her neck, he realised why he couldn't stay away.

"You look tired. How's your head?"

"Better. Thanks."

"Do you get them often?"

"I suppose so."

"Any reason for them?"

"Stress, I guess."

"Are you on any medication?"

"No."

"I'd like to take you out to dinner."

"Nick, I …"

"Alicia." He stepped forward but stopped at the palm flexed in his face.

"No, don't. Stay where you are. I can't concentrate when … and I'm desperate for a cup of tea. Would you like one?"

"Okay, but I'll make it. Ah! Ah! Ah! No arguing, you're sick. Now sit down and do as the doctor ordered."

He returned to find her resting back against the couch, eyes closed and breathing deeply. If not for her clenched fists he would have assumed she was asleep. Hearing the cup clatter on the coffee table, she opened them.

"Are you sure you're alright?"

"Yes, I'm fine. The tea will help."

"Alicia, I'm a doctor. Tell me what I can do for you."

"Honestly, nothing. The worst is over and it will be completely gone by morning."

That brought a smile to his face. She would be better by morning, which meant she was free to go out with him. "With the rest of the week off, it's the perfect opportunity for you to keep your promise."

There was no mistaking the worried lift of her brow or the dark rings beneath her eyes. She placed the cup on the saucer and gently rolled her head, he assumed to ease the pain attacking the muscles at the back of her neck. He knew he shouldn't push her when she was ill but if he missed this opportunity, he might never get another one.

"Even though you tricked me," she said, "I suppose I did promise. But there are certain conditions that come with that promise."

He sipped at his tea. Intrigued, he tried to imagine what the conditions might be. Perhaps he would have to bring her home at a certain time, or be expected to take her somewhere special. Maybe he had to ask Brandon for permission. "I see. And they are?"

"There is to be absolutely no physical contact between us at all. I mean nothing."

He almost choked on the hot tea. He put his cup down with a clang. It took a moment before he could speak, annoyed at being treated like a teenager. "Are you serious? Would you not expect me to hold your arm or hand if we should cross a road or … or enter the restaurant together?"

"That's right. And, if you do, I will immediately go home."

"That's ridiculous. Why would you do this? I don't molest

women on first dates or any date for that matter."

She flushed to the roots of her hair. He was glad. He wanted her to realise how much she had insulted him.

"And that's the second condition – no explanations."

Nick ran his fingers through his hair. He couldn't remember a time he'd taken a woman out and not at least held her hand. He felt at a loss. "So, if I don't agree to your conditions then there is no date, correct?"

She nodded, a determined set to her jaw.

Nick sat back, irritation swirling. Baffled and more than a bit curious he begrudgingly agreed. "Right then, conditions set, I'll pick you up tomorrow night at seven-thirty. There's a nice restaurant within walking distance from here. Wear stable shoes: you're on your own if you trip." He stood up, not pleased he had allowed anger to seep into his voice. "It's getting late and you look exhausted. I'd better go."

She rose, walked with him to the door. He felt an irresistible urge to slip his arm around her waist, pull her hard against him and hear the sharp intake of her breath. Instead, with his hands in his pockets he stepped into her comfort zone. She immediately took a step back. As he continued to move closer so she continued to step away until she was pressed against the wall. He stared into her eyes, conscious of her parted lips and the rising of her chest. Satisfied he didn't need to touch her to get the reaction he wanted, he opened the door and walked out.

In the car, Nick sat motionless, staring up at her apartment, his arms resting on the steering wheel. The last time he suffered a knock-back for a date was in high school, by the gorgeous Simone who had the pick of the bunch. He started the engine, backed up the driveway, his car and mind in reverse. He didn't regard himself as a conceited man but merely accepted his characteristics as part of the package that normally guaranteed his success. He reflected on his courtship with his ex-wife. In the initial stages of their relationship, he couldn't remember her ever rejecting his advances and was certain she never found him repulsive. In fact, quite the opposite. Rebecca's problem wasn't a lack of affection, merely a lack of what he couldn't supply. She wanted, demanded, more fun, more excitement, more money. Enter, Alex Braun. The hospital's resident psychiatrist, with his Porsche and mansion on the coast. Goodbye boring Nick.

This was the second time Alicia had vetoed his touch: once at the Spencers' barbecue and now this date. So far, every move had been initiated by him. The thought niggled, almost to the point of questioning himself. But she fascinated him, more than any other woman had in a long time. And the mystery of her past whetted his appetite to learn the truth about who she really was.

It suddenly occurred to him what was missing in the apartment. *Photos. Not one photo of family, hers or Brandon's.* He knew of an Aunt Beryl and her husband, Stan, who died recently. But what of parents or siblings or husband? She'd never mentioned them. But then, she never mentioned anything about her past. Perhaps Jenny had it wrong – could Brandon be the father? So why the secrecy? And why would Sophie call him uncle? No, that made no sense. He drove home in a reflective mood, trying to put together the fragmented pieces to the Alicia puzzle. John Spencer knew the answers and for some inexplicable reason that bothered him. A lot.

Chapter Five

After Nick left, Alicia leant against the door and shut her eyes. How could she go out with a man like Nick? She had nothing to offer him. Hugging herself, she slid to the floor, rested her head on her knees. Even the conditions she had stipulated hadn't deterred him, as she was so sure, even hoped, they would. And how dare he be upset with her. She hadn't asked him to take her out. She pulled the elastic from her hair, pushed back the fallen strands and re-tied it. She scrambled to her feet, gathered up the teacups and took them to the kitchen, careful not to spill Nick's half-empty one.

She pressed her palms against her temples to ease the pain still throbbing in her head. Damn him! Did he think her some kind of intriguing play-thing? Was it the ballet that had him so interested? Oh sure, she can dance. Ballet is easy; she'd been perfecting it for years. But if he thinks she can love or feel the way he will expect her to and can't, because of the promise she made to her mother … *then let's see if you still find me worth pursuing.*

Everything about dating was foreign. She had never been alone with a man other than Brandon; never kissed a man. The thought of being ridiculed aroused a flood of new emotions. "And how many women must he have slept with?" she asked the cup before placing it in the warm soapy water. *I'm going to bore him to death.*

She placed her wet hands against her hot cheeks, wondering what he would do if he knew her darkest secret. Guilt, haunting relentless guilt, one pair of ballet shoes and the part they played in her family's death. How would he react if he knew the truth about Sophie? *Inside this wretched body, is nothing but misery. Are you ready for that, Mr … Cool Man? Are you ready to hear how my heart continues to beat because I'm too gutless to stop it? Would you still want to go out with me if you knew all that? Or would you brush the dirt from your polished hands and run as fast as you can in the other direction?*

It was a risk she couldn't afford to take. Her heart was in no condition to be rejected or broken. *You've picked the wrong girl to trifle with. Choose someone else to be fodder for your social scrapbook. One date and we're done!*

She searched through the medicine box for some pain killers, washed them down with a glass of water, and tottered off to bed.

The next morning, with the dreaded date foremost in her mind, she dropped Sophie off at school. After parking the car in the main street of Hawthorne, she strolled into J J's Barista and ordered a weak cappuccino. A mannequin, clothed in a sleeveless, teal blue dress in Rosie's Boutique across the road, caught her eye. The temptation to go inside and have a look, got the better of her. Not to buy anything, of course, what with Sophie's education fees due in a month, the rent on the apartment, not forgetting the electricity bill, her phone, and the car rego, there would be little left for a dress. Especially as it was only for one night.

"It looks absolutely gorgeous on you," fussed the sales assistant, zipping up the dress. "It shows off your figure to full advantage."

"Thank you, I'll take it," she said, handing over her card and asking herself if she had rocks in her head. After paying for the dress, Alicia walked up the road to a shoe shop. *You can't have a nice dress without shoes to match,* she repeated all the way home. She knew she'd spent an exorbitant amount of money but the roller coaster of emotions churning her insides, over one silly date, was more nerve-wracking than opening night. There were other dresses in her closet she could have worn but, the simple truth was, she wanted to impress him.

At seven o'clock that evening when the doorbell rang, Alicia felt anything but impressive. She could hear Nick talking to Brandon.

Calm down, take a deep breath and relax, she said to herself in the mirror. It took four attempts to pluck up enough courage to leave her room. This was a first for her.

The sight of him looking like a Vogue model, dressed in pale grey pants and a sports jacket, did little to help her confidence.

"Ready?"

She wanted to say no, I'll never be ready for this but turned to Sophie instead. "Be a good girl for Uncle Brandon and don't forget to read a few pages of your book before you go to sleep." She lingered, unsure of what came next.

"You've told her that seven times already, now go," said Brandon.

"Where are you going with my mummy?" asked Sophie.

"I'm taking her to dinner." Nick pinched the small chin pointed up at him.

"Why?"

"Because I think she's very hungry."

Sophie giggled. "Can I come next time?"

"No! No, you can't." Alicia didn't miss the shocked reaction to her words on Nick's face but she meant every syllable. This was never happening again. She kissed Sophie goodnight, checked her bag for keys and headed out the door. With eyes downcast, she waited for the lift to open, not daring to look at the man by her side. His silent, self-controlled manner rattled her.

"I feel like a naughty boy who mustn't move until the teacher says he can."

The light-hearted tone in his voice brought her head up and she smiled.

"That's better," he said, returning her smile. "I promise to behave."

She nodded, asking herself if he had any idea how terrified she was of seeming ignorant or foolish, in front of him.

"You look beautiful, by the way. Love the dress, matches your eyes."

God, she wished he hadn't said that. The last person to tell her she was beautiful, when not on the stage, was her mother. How she wished her mother were here – she would have told her how to handle a man like Nick. "Thank you," she said in a quiet voice.

He had booked a table by the window. A waiter showed them to their seats, pulled the chair out for Alicia, and placed a napkin on her lap. She tried to study the menu but a sense of him watching her, made comprehension impossible.

He worked hard to amuse her with funny anecdotes about the show. His deep, lyrical voice lulled her into relaxing, giving her a chance to see beyond the handsome face. She began to admire his ability to acknowledge the superficial crust the media attention provoked, recognising it as a security blanket to cover the difficulties he faced at the time of his traumatic separation. And she loved that he loved medicine. She detected from his brief mention of his past life as a surgeon, it gave him immeasurable satisfaction. It fascinated her how anyone could find the courage to cut into the chest of a live human being and touch the very pulse of mankind as it pumped life, love, and spirit, into a body. If only her heart could be mended so easily, she would gladly hand him the scalpel.

"One day, in the not too distant future, I intend to return to medicine."

"I truly hope you do."

"Really?"

"Yes of course. It's what you love doing." An argument in the street between a young couple made her glance out the window. It saddened her to see them angry with each other. Didn't they know, tomorrow might deal a hand they hadn't expected and as quick as a blink, tear their lives apart.

When she glanced at him, his eyes were so full of understanding and warmth, it frightened her and she looked swiftly away, too swiftly. Striving for calm she sipped her coke, hoping the cold liquid would cool the tumult of emotions assaulting her.

"I do admire you; you know. Managing a career and raising a child at the same time. It can't be easy. Not sure I could do it."

Him a doctor and he admired her. She tried to remember the last time anyone said something so encouraging to her. Those earlier days when Sophie was a baby, alone and grieving, with only Brandon for support, were the hardest days of her life.

"Thank you for saying that, it means a lot."

"I mean every word. It must have taken great courage and strength."

He was beginning to chip away at her heart, not with a scalpel but with kindness. His hand lay on the edge of the table. She wanted to reach out and touch it, a small gesture of gratitude, but that would be breaking her own rules.

"Why Melbourne?"

The question caught her off guard and this was the sort of question she worried he might ask. She ate a mouthful of salad, playing for time. Why Melbourne? Because she wanted to escape her memories. Could she trust him with her story? God, she wanted to, but there was always that terrible fear, should he decide she wasn't worth the trouble and leave her guttered, fighting despair, again.

He had the potential to break her completely, and she couldn't … *wouldn't* … take that risk. She had to hold on to what little strength she had left. The less she gave of herself, the less he could take away and so she gave him the simple answer. "Louis offered Brandon and myself contract."

"Louis has excellent taste."

She smiled. Waited. Wondered what he would ask next.

"Your dinner is getting cold."

Not the words she expected but at least the questions had stopped. For now. She ate slowly, acutely aware of the frown forming on his face. She guessed her answer had left him dissatisfied. The waiter collected their plates. Nick ordered coffee.

When the coffee arrived, she wrapped her hands around the cup, glad the caffeine would soon put a zing back into her mood.

He suddenly looked at his watch. She was boring him. Anxiety tightened its grip, striking at her confidence. She tried not to think about it, not let it bother her. Hadn't she argued this point with herself last night, deciding she wanted to discourage him?

"Shall we go?" he asked, indicating to the waiter to bring the bill.

Outside she turned to face him. His profile silhouetted in the moonlight caused a flutter in her stomach. He slipped his card back into his wallet, which reminded her; dutch, that's what the girls in the Company called it. "Nick."

"Yes, Alicia."

"Should I ... would you like ... have I perhaps offended you by not offering to pay half?"

He snapped his wallet shut, shoved it into the back pocket of his pants. "Your opinion of me isn't particularly high, is it? You think after I'd persuaded you to come out with me, I'd expect you to pay for yourself? Gee, thanks!"

Embarrassed, she bit on her bottom lip, took several steps backward. Louis had often growled at her in rehearsals but Nick's censure seemed more compelling. "I ... I'm sorry ..." she stammered. He lifted his gaze. His expression had changed from annoyed to anxious. He stepped closer, his jaw tight. She raised her trembling hands, turned and headed off down the street towards her home.

"Alicia, stop!"

She hesitated. He stepped across her path and she crashed into his chest, bumping her forehead against his collar bone. He cupped her chin, gently tilted her head up, until her gaze met his. The muscles of his legs, chest, and arms against hers sent messages through her body she had never known before. The words *let go, walk away,* sounded in her head, but not her heart: her heart begged him to hold her tighter. Conscious of the fact he was breaking the rules, she clung to him. "I'm sorry," he said. "I shouldn't have snapped at you like that."

She wanted to move away but his hand, firm on her back, his strong physique, protective and warm, made her feel as if she belonged there. "I didn't mean to offend you either; I thought that's what people did when they went out together."

"Not this cookie."

His lips, close to hers, parted. The temptation to touch them with her own sent shock waves to her brain and she tried to break free, but he held her captive.

"I'd kiss you if I hadn't given you my word I wouldn't. As it is, I've overstepped the mark."

Unable to read those penetrating eyes, she dropped her gaze. It seemed like hours before he released her – not sure she wanted him to when he did. As if by an unspoken mutual agreement, they began to walk back to her apartment, tension ripe between them. She was sure she had bored him during dinner and insulted him over the bill: failure ripped at her psyche until she could barely speak. The arm of depression had its hand around her throat and she struggled to focus on what he was saying. She wanted to tell him how sorry she was and how much she loved listening to him share stories about his life, but instead, all she could offer was a quick nod or an occasional smile.

They stood in awkward silence at her apartment door, listening to the laughter coming from inside. "Brandon must have a visitor." She was glad to hear Brandon happy again after his bitter break-up with Michael Gillespie. It had left him gutted for months afterwards.

"I'd say so. Sounds to me like they're having fun." He pushed his fingers through his hair. Then, from the inside pocket of his jacket, he pulled out an envelope. "I almost forgot; would you mind giving these to him. Tell him I'll ring later in the week to confirm the arrangements."

She could feel him watching her as she took the envelope. When he lifted his hand to her cheek, she flinched and he dropped it immediately.

The short, sharp smile didn't touch his eyes. With his hands shoved deep into his pockets, he walked to the lift without even a backward glance. She waited to hear the doors slide shut before she took a breath, only to inhale the faint smell of his cologne that hung in the air. She wanted to twirl in the fragrance until the feelings she had experienced when he confided in her about his life and his desire to be a doctor, returned. But the scent disappeared as fast as her confidence.

She had been tempted to ask him what was in the envelope when he handed it to her but decided to ask Brandon instead. Reluctant to go into the apartment, she paced the corridor.

The fingers of loneliness crept up her spine and she rested against the wall. She loved being in his arms, more than she believed possible. If only he hadn't touched her, like he'd promised, stirring up emotions she had no control over. He didn't understand how fear and grief had set the pattern of her life. She looked alive, danced like she was, but deep in the empty chamber of her heart was a grave, and buried in that grave lay her broken soul, he didn't have the power to heal.

***

Monday classes, after her week off, proved difficult. The date with Nick had affected her more than she cared to admit. The vision of him checking his watch kept returning. At twenty-three she could dance an audience to its feet, bring *Balanchine's Jewel* to life, but enter into a normal relationship with a man and she failed on every level. She wanted to believe that Nick's opinion of her meant nothing, and not let it bother her; stay focused on what Helen Barsby, the ballet mistress, was saying about the *plumb line* of one's body. But the truth was, it added to her feelings of inadequacy, feeding her belief she wasn't capable of functioning in the real world. She wanted to enjoy the natural flow of a relationship without the fear of having her love ripped away.

"You have all become fat and lazy after your week off." Helen walked the length of the *barre*, poking at dancers' *derrières*. "Flatten your stomachs and tuck in those butts. Don't look down in *Plie`*, Alicia, look up. Fonteyn would never look down."

Alicia loved the ballet, *L'Histoire de Manon*, and was thrilled Louis had chosen it as their next production. It conveyed a message of passion and love, and ultimate hopelessness: emotions she understood all too well. An enormous amount of mental and physical endurance would be required for such a sensitive role and she would need all her energy to concentrate on capturing the exact sentiment Louis would expect. The season commenced in less than six weeks and Louis had made it clear to the Company the long hours of practice this ballet would demand.

In the middle of rehearsal, the Company secretary popped her head in through the studio door, bringing the Company to a standstill. "Excuse me, Louis, but there is a phone call for Alicia."

The room went quiet. Nobody rang her during the day. It had to be Sophie's school. She looked over at Louis for his approval.

"Go! Go!" Louis gestured with his hands.

Alicia whipped her towel from the *barre*, wiped the sweat from her face and neck as she hurried after the secretary. What now? thought Alicia as she hurried down the steps. Had Sophie fallen ill or been naughty? She licked her dry lips before picking up the phone. "Alicia Sommers speaking."

"Hello, Alicia. It's June Heywood here, Sophie's headmistress."

"Hello, Mrs Heywood. Is Sophie okay?"

"Yes, she's fine. However, we have experienced a little incident in the school grounds today that I think needs some discussion. I wonder if you would mind coming by the school this afternoon."

"Yes, of course. I'll come as soon as I can."

Puzzled, she replaced the receiver. Returning to class she tried to imagine what kind of trouble Sophie could be in for Mrs Heywood to call her at work. As she entered the studio she smiled reassuringly at Brandon, hoping to dispel the worried look on his face.

"Excuse me, Louis, but that was Sophie's headmistress. They would like me to come to the school for an interview."

As soon as Louis was able to release her from rehearsal, she drove to Camberwell Grammar School, her mind in turmoil.

On seeing Alicia enter, Mrs Heywood put down her pen and rested her elbows on the desk. "Hello, Alicia, it's lovely to see you again. Won't you please sit down?"

"It's nice to see you too, Mrs Heywood." She hoped she still felt the same way after the meeting.

"The reason I wished to see you so soon is because Sophie became involved in a scuffle today. The second one this week." She picked the pen back up and began tapping it on a pad. "Now, I don't want to alarm you. It's nothing serious in itself and no one was hurt."

Alicia held Mrs Heywood's steady gaze. The woman had made it abundantly clear in the past, although she sympathised with Alicia's situation as a single parent and her career commitments, it was against the Education Department's policy to continue taking Sophie out of school, every time the Company went on tour.

"I realise this is a delicate subject and I will try to be as diplomatic as possible. It has come to the attention of several staff members, myself included, that Sophie is displaying disturbing behaviour concerning her father, or more precisely, her lack of one. I have just re-read your file and although I do understand your desire for privacy, I can't help but wonder if you may have been too guarded about the truth of your situation, to Sophie."

Mrs Heywood cleared her throat, waited for the anticipated reply. When Alicia said nothing, she continued. "Perhaps I should tell you, Sophie punched a child in the face who was apparently teasing her because she doesn't have a father."

Alicia sat rigid as she listened to Mrs Heywood explain to her that children are more resilient than we sometimes give them credit and have a right to be fully informed of their situation, in order to deal effectively with the trials that may occur, concerning them. Shame and guilt fought for first position to add another cross on her page of mistakes. This was the reason for Sophie's reluctance to go to school – the underlying cause of her bad moods and grumpy behaviour. She should have realised it sooner but being so busy with travelling, performing and everything else she had to fit into her life, it had skipped her attention.

"Where did it happen?"

Peering over the golden rim of her glasses, Mrs Heywood continued: "In the playground by the swings. As I said, the second time this week. Some of the children from her class formed a circle around Sophie calling her 'Orphan Annie'. Under the circumstances, her reaction was predictable. Many parents in this school are either divorced or separated, there is no shame in that, but children still have contact with both parents. Sophie appears to have no knowledge of who, or where, her father is. It's seems unusual."

Alicia bit on her lower lip as the beast of anxiety attacked her for the second time in a week. "Have you spoken to Sophie or the other children?"

"Of course, and the parents of the children involved have been notified. We have a very strict rule in this school regarding physical aggression. Our policy provides a number of sanctions, with serious consequences attached, including expulsion if the behaviour continues. Alternatively, Sophie must change her behaviour. She cannot continue to hit children."

"No, of course not," Alicia began, searching for the right words. "I know it appears like I'm being difficult but I do find it hard to address the issues concerning Sophie's father."

Alicia thought she had explained her reasons to the school, for not telling Sophie about her parents, when she first enrolled her and wished with all her heart, she didn't have to repeat herself a second time. But she owed Mrs Heywood a worthy explanation. "I have always avoided telling Sophie about our parents' death, mainly because I lack the courage to do so. She was only a baby when the accident occurred and has never known any other parent but myself. It seems so cruel. I just keep thinking perhaps I should wait until she gets older."

"I can only imagine how hard it has been for you losing your family and raising Sophie single-handed. Most young women would have buckled under the pressure. You are a brave girl, Alicia, and believe me when I say you have my absolute admiration. I have had many years of experience dealing with children. Would you mind if I made a small suggestion?"

Praise for her efforts came so rarely that when it did, Alicia struggled to keep the tears from her voice. "Please do."

"Sophie is dealing with something she knows nothing about, which is not her fault and makes her extremely vulnerable. Children pick up on weaknesses in their peers and can make their lives miserable. She has the right to know, as well as having the means to handle it. You ought to tell her and soon."

"Honestly, I don't quite know how."

"There is never a right or wrong way to go about these things. Children are more resilient than we give them credit for." Mrs Heywood looked over at her family photo on the desk. "In a way, my dear, it's just as cruel not telling her."

"As I'm beginning to realise." The school siren sounded and

Alicia stood to leave. "I will take your advice, Mrs Heywood, and tell Sophie in the next few days."

Mrs Heywood walked to the door and held it open. "Don't be too hard on yourself, my dear, life and parenting, especially in your case, doesn't come with a book of rules. We are only human after all. By the way, I see your next production is Manon."

"Yes. Do you like ballet?"

"I do and Manon is one of my favourites. I've already booked seats for myself and my long-suffering husband."

Alicia smiled at her witticism, thanked her again, before leaving her office. It was pick up time. Propped against the brick pillars at the entrance gate of the school, she welcomed the fresh air. As she waited for the final siren, Alicia watched parents, mostly mothers with prams, some pregnant, others with little ones clutching their legs while they chatted and laughed together. This is what normal people did who had children. She remembered her mother doing the same when she was little. A flash of sadness tugged on her heart. If things were different it would be her mother standing here but her mother was dead and she was just a sad young girl, caught in a role she never intended.

In the distance, she caught sight of Sophie and waved. Pigtails flying, with a smile the size of a watermelon, Sophie came rushing towards her. She bent to greet her little girl. "Oh Sophie Darling, I love you so much … you know that, don't you?"

"Yes, Mummy, I love you, too." Sophie squeezed Alicia around the neck, hitting her on the head with the backpack as she did.

"Here, give that to me before you knock me out."

The street was busy with traffic, and she held Sophie's hand when they crossed the road to the car. She decided to go straight home, knowing Brandon would hitch a lift with one of the dancers who lived nearby.

Later that night, with Sophie in bed, she kicked off her slippers and settled on the sofa next to Brandon who was twiddling his thumbs, a terse look on his face. She knew that look. "What?"

"Are you going to tell me what Mrs Heywood wanted to see you about or am I expected to guess?"

"Brandon, you baby. I haven't had a chance up until now. It's not great. Sophie hit a child in the playground who was teasing her about not having a father. Mrs Heywood asked me why I haven't told Sophie who or where her father is. She thinks I should tell her and soon."

"Mrs Heywood's right and I'm glad it came from her and not me."

"Why?"

"Would you have listened to me if I had told you the same thing?" She didn't answer. "No, I thought not."

"I just don't know how to tell her. What do I say … your father is dead?"

"Why don't you ask John: he is, after all, the expert?"

"I suppose so," she said, thinking over her last visit to his practice. She hadn't seen the Spencers since the day of the barbecue. The look on Nick's face in the pool when John called them to lunch was one of pure shock, then recognition as his thoughts fell into place. His suspicions heightened her own and her disappointment of John was growing. She wondered if she should mention the incident to Brandon but he hated gossip. "Brandon …"

"Here we go." He flicked his fingers across her shoulder. "All still there those demons, alive and well."

She glanced at him from under her lashes. "Do you remember our agreement when we left Perth?"

"Here it comes …"

Alicia knew Brandon understood, more than anyone, why she fiercely guarded against forming more intimate relationships. But even Brandon didn't know about the promise she made to her mother. A simple promise born of love, now glued the fractured pieces of her heart together. No one would take that from her. "Brandy, as long as nobody knows the truth … I feel safe, protected in a weird kind of way. You understand what I mean?"

"Yes, I do. But one day you will have to tell the truth, all the truth, even to Sophie. You can't hide behind a lie forever. Things change, people change," he whispered.

"I know, but I'm not ready for that day just yet. Promise me, Brandon."

She watched him search her face.

"I'd never betray you, Ally. It will go to the grave with me unless you tell me otherwise. You saved my life, I owe you everything." He laid his head on her lap and she stroked her fingers through the blonde hair, wondering how he could keep up such a brave face, day after day. Alicia was certain he never heard from his parents. How he coped with their rejection of him she would never understand. She had only met his father once, but it was enough to convince her of the man's arrogant and bigoted nature.

She would never forget the day poor Brandon rocked up on her doorstep after her parents funeral. He begged her not to leave him to go and live with her uncle and his family in the country. Brandon persuaded her to stay in Perth, live with him in her parents' home and continue studying ballet at the Academy. They both had part-time jobs to keep them going in food and petrol, and she had enough funds from her father's savings to afford to put Sophie into day-care. He promised to support her in every way he could, including the raising of Sophie. With her Aunt Beryl living next door it seemed the perfect solution. They had been together ever since. He was family now, and she loved him as much as she did Sophie.

***

When John opened the door, the smell of spaghetti bolognese

wafted up Alicia's nostrils.

"Come in, come in … dinner's almost ready," said John, rubbing his hands together.

Walking into the kitchen behind John, Brandon held out his hand, palm up and waited for Alicia to smack it with her own.

"Ten bucks, thanks," he whispered in her ear. Grinning, she nudged him in the ribs. The two of them had bet on which meal Jenny would serve up, there being only two choices: Spaghetti bolognese or roast lamb. Jenny's culinary skills, ended at the medical centre.

Alicia was pleased to see Jenny happy, humming like a bee as she served dinner, while John placed a Greek salad and crusty loaf of bread on the dining table. Alicia also noticed his steady gaze linger on his wife's hips every time she attended to the children or left the room for something. They had been on a short break over the weekend without the kids and she hoped their time together had something to do with repairing the tension between the couple. Glad to see them back to their old selves, she helped herself to a small scoop of spaghetti and a large portion of salad.

"Chloe, Sophie, take Oliver upstairs and get him and yourselves ready for bed," said Jenny, gathering up the plates. "Come on, Brandon, you and I will clean up while these two talk business."

"Gee, thanks," he said, pulling a face.

"You want a coffee now or later?" called Jenny over her shoulder.

John turned to Alicia. "How about we join them for coffee later."

Alicia nodded, happy to have the John of old back on track. He pushed his chair closer. "Now! What's up?"

She explained the incident with Sophie at school and Mrs Heywood's opinion and asked him if he agreed.

"The headmistress is right. Sophie isn't a baby anymore and has a right to know about her father. She needs to develop skills to defend herself in these potentially explosive situations. Kids can be nasty, particularly if they discover a weakness."

"Mrs Heywood said much the same thing."

He talked briefly about her need to move forward. "Guarding your secrets so fiercely is robbing you of true happiness. But we've discussed this, many times. If you want to develop into a stable and balanced woman you need to trust people and let them know who you are."

At the sound of his wife's infectious laughter, he patted her on the hand as though she was a confused child, indicating their consultation was over. "Now how about we join the others."

Jenny poked her head through the door. "Ready for that coffee?" she called. On seeing John waving for her to enter, she pushed through the door with her bottom, bearing a tray of mugs and a coffee pot. Brandon trailed behind, flicking a packet of biscuits into the air.

John took the coffee tray from his wife, dropped a quick kiss on her lips. The smile on Jenny's face was bright enough to light a fire. "Brandon and I have been busy arranging our social calendar," she said, excitement escalating in her voice.

"So that's what all the carry-on I kept hearing was about," remarked John as he placed the tray on the table.

"No, that was Brandon trying to sing *Figaro*. I warned him not to give up dancing."

"Hurt my feelings too. I love singing … thought I might audition for the next opera."

"Whoa, poor delusional boy." Jenny threw up her hands in protest.

"So, what have you two arranged that has caused such excitement?"

"Party," said Jenny, doing a jig. "Then sailing on the high seas to iron out all those aches and pains."

Alicia's mind had drifted a million miles away, mulling over how she would break the shattering truth to a seven-year-old, when she became aware all eyes were on her. "I'm sorry, what did you say?'

"Wakey! Wakey! Party at our place in two weeks, then sailing on the high seas the day after," said Brandon.

"Oh, okay." It wasn't really okay. She could never get used to her home being opened to others. It was her refuge, her safe haven. Unlike Brandon, she cherished her privacy.

She was relieved when they left the Spencers' early. With her mind in turmoil, she found it hard to concentrate on conversation, although she did catch the part where John mentioned he had employed a new receptionist. The old one, he said, seemed more interested in her make-up than his clients. It crossed Alicia's mind Jenny might have had something to do with John's decision to change receptionist.

Sophie was still awake when they arrived home. Alicia followed her into the bedroom to help her into bed. She picked up the small hand, and turning it over, tried to think of words that would explain to Sophie how her father, had been killed in a car accident, in which she, a one-year-old baby, miraculously survived. God knows that dreadful experience was too horrid for a seventeen-year-old to comprehend. It had changed her life forever. How could she expect a child of seven to understand?

After tucking her in, Alicia sat on the edge of the bed and watched the long lashes slowly close, reminding her of her brother, Simon's.

"What difference could one more night make," she whispered, her courage in tatters.

The next night came quickly enough. Sorting through the washing spread across the dining table, Brandon began to sing in his Rod Stewart voice. "Tonight's the night. It's gonna be alright."

Alicia hushed him with her finger against her lips as she led Sophie into her bedroom and shut the door. "Hop into bed, there's a good girl." Images of a fluffy-haired baby curled up in her cot in their home in Perth, flashed into her mind. They were dark days. If it hadn't been for Brandon, she would never have survived alone, with a child to raise.

"Darling, Mrs Heywood ..."

Eyes wide as saucers, Sophie flinched at the mention of the headmistress's name. Alicia's heart went out to this darling girl, who was soon to find out some awful truths about her life. "Mrs Heywood phoned me yesterday at work and asked me to come and see her. I was shocked when she told me that you had hit a little girl in the face."

Two large tears rolled down Sophie's cheeks and she pulled her hand away.

"Come here and give me a cuddle."

Sophie climbed onto her lap, wiped away the tears with the back of her hand.

"Do you want to tell me why you did such an unkind thing?"

"Cause she said mean stuff."

"But you mustn't hit someone just because they say mean things. Can you tell me what it was she said?"

Sophie shook her head, lips pressed tightly together.

"You know, darling, mummies often know what mean things people can say. I won't be angry or upset."

"Do you promise?"

"I promise."

"She said you were a bad girl and that's why I don't have a daddy. She said daddies don't love bad girls. Is that true?"

Alicia breathed deeply before replying. "No, darling, that's not true." She pushed the loose hair back from the tear-stained face. She knew only too well the stories people invented if they weren't in possession of all the facts. "I wasn't a bad girl. The truth is ..." Could she do this, should she do this, it seemed so cruel. She hesitated for what seemed like an eternity. "The truth is your daddy died in a car accident when you were a baby." There she'd said it.

Alicia stayed still, waited.

"Why?"

Not quite the response she expected and wished she too knew the answer to that question. "I don't know why. Accidents just happen. That's why they're called accidents."

"Well, I don't want him to be dead. All the kids at school have a daddy; even ugly Lilly Parker has one. That's why I hit her."

"Sophie!"

"I don't care because she is ugly and I hate her. Why can't you get me another one?"

Alicia was momentarily lost for words. "Well … be … cause … I don't want another one. I have you and Brandon and that's enough for me."

Sophie slipped off Alicia's lap, a fierce glare on her face. "I want one!" she yelled, stamping her foot. "I want a daddy and I want a pink bike!"

"Darling, you don't understand …"

"Yes, I do. You don't want me to have one because you'd have to cook and look after him like other mothers do. All you want to do is dance."

"That's enough. I dance because I love it and it's my job … I haven't … I don't want to …"

"See! I told you. You're mean and I hate you more than I do Lily Parker."

She stared at the child, disturbed at the extent of the anger Sophie had kept tucked inside. A father and a bike would make her normal, like all the other kids, and it didn't matter who the man was as long as she had a daddy. Bewildered, she tried to smile away the problem; reached out to Sophie.

"Go away," she screamed, slapping Alicia's out-stretched hands. She scrambled back to bed and, grabbing her teddy, cried into the pillow.

Ten seconds passed before Alicia could move. Thoughts of how she had struggled to raise Sophie, all the time fighting dreadful grief; how she had worried herself sick trying to compensate for the lack of a father for Sophie, as she pushed her body beyond pain, day after day, to make a life for the two of them. Every step, every blistered toe, add to it all the uncountable hours of rehearsals, always with Sophie's welfare at heart … for what? To be hated because she hadn't the courage to love again or to rent a home with enough space for Sophie to be able to store a bike.

She stumbled out of the room, grief wrenching at her heart, all her careful plans, swirling in her head until it ached, gone in a shock of disappointment.

Alicia flopped on the couch beside Brandon who was balancing an orange on his forehead. "That went well," he remarked, rolling the orange off his face and into his hands.

"I can't believe it! When I think of the hours I've spent worrying how she would cope once the truth was revealed … when really, any old Joe would do as her father. And our dear, dear … … father."

"She's a kid, Alicia. She never knew her father. She just wants to be like the other kids."

"I know, I know, but it's hard to hear that someone you have spent the last six years sacrificing your life for hates you."

"She doesn't hate you, she just thinks she does. Trust me, I know the difference. Go to bed, you're tired and being melodramatic."

"Thank you, Confucius. I feel so much better, now."

Alicia checked in on Sophie on the way to her room. She looked like an angel, curled up with Taffy, her teddy, in her arms. The urge to pick her up and hold her close was strong, but one rejection in a day was enough. Sophie was only a baby when they'd died but Alicia sensed she missed their mother. She was a poor substitute, struggling to know how to cope with a baby.

Six years later and still the tragedy was having a profound effect on her life. She thought about God and how long it had been since she bent her knee and prayed. She wondered if she did, would God hear her, see her pain, help her conquer her grief, her struggle to survive, and raise a child?

***

It was Sunday morning, the first day off in a week of ten-hour-a-day rehearsals. Alicia checked the time on her watch. Nine o'clock. She had slept in. She could hear the TV going and figured Sophie must be up and wondered how she was feeling after last night. Dragging her tired body out of bed she ambled into the lounge. One glance at the pouted lips and crossed arms was enough indication she wasn't forgiven.

"Have you had breakfast, Sophie?"

No communication, just lips pressed tight and a frantic shake of the head. Alicia flicked on the kettle. She needed a caffeine fix to kick start her muddy brain. Sipping the rich liquid, she decided a peace offering might help calm the waters.

"Would you like to go to McDonalds for breakfast? I hear they make fabulous pancakes with ice cream and maple syrup on top."

"Do they have strawberry ice cream?"

"I'm sure they do, Sweetheart."

Sunday was family day at McDonalds and the place was full of sugar-induced, children. Every table seemed to be covered in spilled coke or left-over waffles with maple syrup dripping off the plate. The revolting mess made Alicia glad she had eaten a small tub of yoghurt before leaving home.

She ordered Sophie a pancake with strawberry ice cream, lathered in maple syrup, and asked for a cloth to wipe the table. The assistant handed her one immediately, adding an apology.

Sophie ate every morsel and was about to lick the plate clean if Alicia's hadn't stopped her. She played on the swings and the climbing apparatus in the playground outside until it was time to go. With Sophie skipping cheerfully alongside her on the way home, Alicia felt satisfied her crafty plan for peace had worked its magic.

It was almost lunchtime when they arrived home. She noticed a familiar car parked outside her apartment. It was Kieran's, a male soloist from the Company. The whispers she had heard in the dressing room rang true. Both men rose from the couch when she and Sophie entered.

"No, not the Queen of Sheba. Just us." The joke went down like a deluge of rain. There was no mistaking the anger on Brandon's face.

"Where have you been?" he asked abruptly.

"I took Sophie to breakfast at MacDonald's. Why what's the matter?"

"The matter is, Nick will be here soon to take the lot of us to the football, which you well know."

At the mention of Nick's name, Sophie shot to her room like a bullet from a gun. Now that Brandon mentioned it, Alicia did recall him saying something about a football game, when she handed him the envelope, Nick had given her the night of their date. But had dismissed the idea in the same instant. "I'm not going to watch some stupid football game."

Pink patches on his cheeks exposed his anger. Rarely did she witness this side of him, and she gritted her teeth.

"I asked Nick if he could get us tickets so we could all go together and one of them is for you. So, go and get ready."

The anger in Brandon's voice distressed her but she resented him ordering her around like a child, especially in front of Kieran. Who did Brandon think he was, her father? "That's all very well, but you didn't ask me if I wanted to go, did you?"

In one, fast swoop, he latched onto her forearm and ushered her into the kitchen. He slammed the door with his foot and spun her round to face him. "If you think I don't know what this is all about then you're wrong. Now that Sophie is partly aware of the truth, you're scared witless someone else might discover a few more home truths." His eyes flashed anger sending a sliver of apprehension down her spine.

"I refuse to watch you become some bitter, twisted old maid who can't do anything but dance and by that time not very well. I won't! Your life is worth more than that. I'll walk out on you before that happens. It's time to let go of some of this baggage you carry around day after miserable day and live a bit. I mean it, Alicia! Don't think for one minute I don't and it's no use dropping that lip, it doesn't work for me anymore." He stepped closer, gentled her in his arms. "I know it feels like we have been fighting this fight forever, Ally, but one day, I promise you, it won't be this hard."

As he pushed through the door, she heard muffled voices, and then silence. Brandon had never spoken to her like that before and it felt like he'd punched her in the stomach. But worse than anything, it reeked of reality. Fear gripped. Ballet would only last as long as her body stood the pressure. Sophie would most likely marry or move away, maybe return to Perth; and Brandon … his life was bound to change, probably taking the path into choreography. She rubbed her arm, still tingling from the pressure of his grip. Perhaps he wanted to leave, to move in with Kieran and get away from her and her misery. Deeply caught in the whirlwind of her thoughts she didn't hear the footsteps.

"Even if you hate football, you'll love the hot dogs."

Startled, she swung around. "Nick!"

"Right the first time."

She became aware of her dishevelled appearance, in contrast to Nick's, who looked immaculate as ever in a light blue pair of jeans and long-sleeved shirt. She pushed the fallen strands of hair from her face. "What are you doing here?"

"Waiting for you to get ready, so we can go to the game."

She wished he wouldn't look at her like he understood how she felt. "I'm not going."

"I don't know what you and Brandon were fighting about, but the little I overheard sounded pretty spot on to me. There's also the chance you might actually enjoy yourself. Besides, I'll make it my mission to see that you do."

She looked up to see him smiling and some of the built-up tension inside her slipped away. She had often gone to the football with her parents to watch her brother, Simon, play when she was little. She remembered how excited they all were whenever he kicked a goal. One game of football couldn't hurt. For the first time in her life she let herself wonder what it would be like to walk into a man's arms and be loved until the ache disappeared. He looked so strong and dependable with his shirt sleeves rolled up to his elbows. And those penetrating eyes. She inhaled a shaky breath, nodded, just as Sophie crashed through the door wanting to know when they were leaving.

Alone in her room, she sat on her bed and stared at the floor. What was happening to her? Feelings she thought were suppressed were slowly taking control. Longing and desire were just two that immediately came to mind. Did he feel the same? How could he? When he looked in the mirror, he had to be aware of the reaction he had on women, beautiful sexy women. So why did he persist with her. What possible reason would he want with one skinny, messed up ballerina? Time ticked on and she needed to get changed.

Clothes went flying on the floor as she rummaged through the drawers trying to decide what to wear. Jeans, where were her jeans? Make-up, hair. Dear God, how to look her best in such a short time. Fifteen minutes later, she joined Nick and the others in the lounge, the question *why, what did he see in her*, perched on her shoulder.

The Melbourne Cricket Ground, famous for Australian Rules Football and more affectionately called the MCG was packed with thousands of excited fans. The five of them climbed the cement staircase to the grandstand just in time to see the players run onto the field. The crowd went wild, shouting and stamping their feet. Nick settled them in their seats before going off to buy them each a hot dog loaded with the trimmings and drinks.

The day might not have started out as smoothly as he had hoped, he thought as he stood in line waiting to be served, but he was determined to make it end on a happier note. There was no mistaking her troubled look in those almond shaped eyes, after Brandon had given her a dressing down earlier, in the kitchen. If he wasn't so unsure of her reaction, he would have wrapped her in his arms and kept her there for as long as she let him.

Loaded with hot dogs and a cardboard container of drinks, he headed for the steps but stopped at the top, captured by the delicate features of her profile, framed by a shock of long hair. She was an enigma, his ballerina. Gentle yet determined, timid and unconfident around him, but courageous enough to leave her home in Perth with a child and start a new life in Melbourne. And he loved and respected her passion and ability to dance. She had him by the teeth, only she didn't have a clue – another aspect of her unusual nature he found appealing. He tried to recall ever meeting a woman, other than Alicia, who wasn't acutely aware of her beauty or the hold she had over him. "No game would be complete without one," he said, handing Brandon and Kieran their hot dogs. He seated himself between the two girls. He loved football and was determined to impart some of his enthusiasm while trying to adjudicate the game. He felt a nudge in his thigh and apologetically handed Sophie her dog.

"Nick, I can't eat a whole hot dog in the middle of the day,"

Alicia protested when he handed her one.

"Why not?"

"They're fattening."

He rolled his eyes. "I've trudged through layers of screaming people hurling abuse at me, just to get these dogs. The man charged me double as thousands of others were denied the pleasure of the only hot dog known to man to make you scream louder, and you say you don't want one!"

She laughed. God, she laughed. The girlish sound set his juices flowing. "You should laugh more often, it suits you."

"One bite!" She leant across him, steadied his hand with hers and took a bite. She touched him! One point for Nick, she voluntarily touched him. First a laugh, now a touch. There was hope yet!

He couldn't be sure, but her interest in the game appeared genuine. She clapped when he did, cheered along with the crowd, even jumped to her feet when the Eagles scored a goal. He did notice her enthusiasm wane during the last quarter, certain he heard a sigh of relief when the final whistle blew.

"Well Nick, not bad, not bad at all. Might give it a while though, before I come again," said Brandon.

"Point taken."

"Not me! I loved it, right up to the final whistle," said Kieran. Brandon flicked an upwards glance.

Nick, wary of anti-social behaviour, after a game, issued a few instructions concerning alcohol-infused spectators' intent on causing havoc in their haste to get out of the stadium. "Brandon, if we get separated, met us out the front by the Bill Ponsford Memorial. I'll take the girls with me. Sophie, come here and hold my hand. You two," indicating with his head at Brandon and Kieran, "go first and we'll follow."

"Roger, Roger," Brandon responded with a wink as he trotted off with Kieran in tow.

Sophie grabbed Nick's outstretched hand, a big cheesy smile on her face. He guessed the sticky substance all over her fingers might be tomato sauce.

"Now your turn, Miss Sommers, so pay attention." He smiled back at the grin she threw his way. "Stay behind me and hold the belt of my pants, and don't let go. Do you hear me?"

"Yes, Sergeant." Alicia saluted, making Sophie laugh.

Geelong's victory had given the fans an edgy boost, provoking a noisy bunch of drunken youths, to remind the crowd that their home team had won. Nick reached back to check Alicia's fingers were securely tucked into his belt before merging into the swarm of bodies. The crowd pushed forward and she wrapped both arms around his waist. Happy to feel her body pressed against his, he worried how to protect her.

Without warning, one of the youths behind them tripped over his own stupidity and crashed into Alicia's back, knocking her off balance. She grabbed hold of Nicks shirt as she slid to the ground, ripping apart the buttons, as she went. The violent impact had jerked him forward, forcing him to latch onto the shoulders of the man in front.

"Mummy, Mummy." Sophie tried to pull away but Nick tightened his hold. The last thing he needed was to lose Sophie. The sound of Alicia's cry sent shock waves through his body. He tried to see where she'd fallen but the flow of the crowd made it impossible. He could imagine her being trampled, and panicked. Sophie started to scream as he pushed against the pulsing crowd.

"Sophie, stop it. I have to get Mummy."

"It's okay, Sir, I've got your little girl," cried the lady next to him, taking Sophie's hand. Out of the corner of his eye, he saw the lady pull Sophie to the side wall.

He elbowed back through the crowd until he saw Alicia trapped beneath a youth. Concerned spectators held the intoxicated youth by the legs, trying to pull him off her. She couldn't move, pinned by his dead weight. Another youth, also drunk, jumped on top of his friend singing; stacks on the mill. Alicia screamed.

Nick's eyes connected with hers. Recognising the signs of her terror, he launched himself at the two drunks like a demon possessed. He drove his shoulder into the side of the singing youth and didn't stop pushing until the boy rolled off, taking his buddy by the collar with him. Nick, also losing his balance, landed on Alicia's legs but thankfully they were quickly helped to their feet.

"Are you okay?" he asked, pulling her tightly into his arms. He kissed her forehead, troubled by the fear he saw lurking in her eyes.

"I think so … bit shaken," she said, panting and twisting her clothing back into shape. "My hip hurts a bit from the fall, probably bruised. Luckily, he landed on my legs and not my back."

"You have a nasty graze on your arm," he said, examining the damage.

She went to open her bag slung across her shoulders but stopped. "Where's Sophie?"

He'd forgotten about Sophie amidst the confusion. With Alicia still in his arms, he spun around and frantically searched the crowd. Relief flooded him when he spotted the lady crammed alongside the wall, waving at him.

Catching up to the woman, Nick grabbed her hand. "Thank you so much for your help." She brushed him off with a quick tap on his arm and disappeared into the crowd.

Sophie flung her arms around Alicia. "Are you all right Mummy?"

"Yes, thanks to Nick."

Taking Sophie's hand, he slipped the other around Alicia's waist, determined on keeping it there. "Are you sure you're okay, you look very pale."

Alicia nodded.

"Come on you two, let's get out of here." No objections this time, she stayed tight within his hold. Every cloud … he mused.

"That's the first time I've had three men throwing themselves at me, literally," Alicia whispered into his ear.

He threw back his head and laughed, impressed at her attempt to see the funny side of her ordeal.

"Thanks for saving me from being trampled to death."

"Nothing any decent man wouldn't do. And not quite to death but maybe a broken bone or two." Seeing her trapped beneath a couple of idiots, and the fear that emanated from her eyes, he would have torn the place apart to save her.

They made their way slowly through the stadium to the turnstile where Kieran and Brandon were waiting on the other side.

"Wow Nick, what did you do to your shirt, have a boxing match with the crowd on your way out?"

"Something like that." On the verge of thanking Brandon for bringing his appearance to everyone's attention, Nick shut his mouth and pushed his buttonless shirt into his jeans.

"Mummy was pushed over by a silly man."

Brandon spread wide his hands, shrugged his shoulders. "Care to elaborate?"

"Nick is being modest. It's true what Sophie says. Some guy who had had a few too many, tripped over and landed against my back, knocking me to the ground. Thanks to Nick and his quick thinking, rescued me from what might have been a very nasty accident."

Brandon said nothing, offered a slight nod. "Well folks. This is where our football journey together ends. We're off. See you anon, you lot. Take care of them, Nick, they obviously need it."

On the way home, Nick picked up a pizza to take back to the apartment.

"Hot dog and pizza in one day. Lettuce for breakfast, lunch, and dinner for me tomorrow."

"By the look of you, you could do with a few more pizzas.'"

"I'll remember to tell Brandon next time he pulls a muscle trying to lift my pizza-filled body off the ground."

After dinner, Sophie insisted Nick put her to bed. First, she wanted a glass of milk, which he fished from the almost empty fridge and placed on the bedside table. He rescued Taffy the teddy from the floor, and sat on the bed to read Dr Suess' Cat in the Hat.

"The lady at the football stadium called me your little girl. Is that true?"

That hit him from left field. He needed to tread carefully with this, understanding Sophie's vulnerability. "I definitely don't have any other little girl in my life so I guess for the moment, you are."

The large beaming smile made him somewhat nervous. He pinched the soft cheek before planting a kiss. The wild mop of blonde curls tickled his face.

"I love you," she whispered.

Head locked by a pair of skinny arms around his neck he whispered back. "Me too."

She rolled onto her side, teddy in her arms and closed her eyes. He was beginning to see the unfinished picture. Standing by the door, his mind in yesterday, he studied the little girl wrapped up in innocence. He understood how it felt to be an only child, whose father paid him and his mother minimal attention. Every year he'd pray his father would make it to parent nights at the school, and every year there was another excuse. Business deals, emergency meetings, overseas trips, anything to spare him spending time with his family. Even when he graduated as a doctor his father had declined the invitation to attend the ceremony. The real excuse this time was an oversized bosom with dollar signs flashing in her eyes. By that time, Nick, immune to disappointment, had lost all respect for his father. But at least he had one, for better or worse, he knew who his father was.

He turned off the light and shut the door. When he walked into the lounge, a pair of dainty feet, hanging off the end of the sofa confronted him. Nick guessed, hours of practice must be needed to develop such extraordinary arches, and the deformed bone structure had to be exceptionally strong to endure a two-hour performance, as she repeatedly jumped on them.

He rested his arms along the top of the couch and watched her as she slept. Controlled, even in sleep, her body lay perfectly straight, her arms tucked by her side and her head poised on the cushion. Every minute in her company made him want her more. She had ignited a fire in his belly and it was burning a path to his heart. He walked around, sat beside her and lifted her hand to his lips. She stirred, tried to turn, and her eyelids flew open.

"Oh, Nick. I've done it again." The hand he held was wrenched away as she pushed herself up. "You must think I'm awfully rude."

"I think you work too hard."

"Brandon works just as hard, so do many other dancers for that matter, but they don't seem to struggle with the same degree of tiredness I do."

"They don't have a young child to worry about." He watched her straighten her clothes and hair. "When will Brandon be home?"

She shrugged, unable to meet his gaze, plucked make-believe fluff from her sleeve. "It isn't as though I'm not used to it. In fact, …"

"In fact, what?" he said, tilting his head towards her.

"In fact, I'm often on my own with Sophie. I don't mind it, honestly."

Sliding his fingers through her hair he gently gripped the back of her head and pulled her closer until their foreheads touched.

"Did anyone ever tell you how frustrating you are?"

"Nope, you're the first," she said, suppressing a grin.

He wanted to stay, to touch the pale skin, to love her. But instinct told him it was still too soon. He dropped a quick kiss on the crease between her brows; gently pulled her to her feet.

"Make sure you lock up and promise to call if you need me."

"I won't, but thanks."

"Promise?"

"Huh! The last time I made a promise, some conniving creature tricked me."

"I had to do something to get you to go out with me." He laughed at the outrage on her face and put his finger across her lips to silence any rebuttal. Her impish look almost undid him; she looked so agonizingly beautiful. "I'm not going to wait weeks before I see you again. Performances, rehearsals, Brandon, Sophie and anything else on your list, I don't care what, you'd be wise to make time for me."

"Or else?"

"Or else, young lady, I'll be forced to come looking for you at the Arts Centre. Then politely tell whoever is interested, you have a pre-arranged date with a very persistent and eager man, who will pick you up and carry you out over my shoulder."

"I'll tell Louis to expect you."

He ran his fingers down the side of her face, and cupped her chin. This time she didn't pull away but tilted her head into the palm of his hand and closed her eyes. He rubbed his thumb over her lips. There was a limit to his control and it was fast withering with his burning desire. Before it was too late, he said, "Goodnight, Alicia, and don't forget to lock the door."

Chapter Six

Alicia walked into the studio a few minutes early to an atmosphere charged with excitement. Lauren Mason, Artistic Director of the Sydney Dance Company, had phoned Louis to say he was in Melbourne for a short visit. After seeing the Company perform in Hobart, and Alicia and Brandon's guest appearance on Nick's show, he asked Louis if he would mind if he dropped in to watch rehearsal of *Manon*. He was on the lookout for someone to dance the lead in his new ballet, *Reticence*. No-one said 'no' to Mason. His reputation as the best choreographer in Australia was well known. He could snap his fingers and any dancer in the country would eat their ballet shoes to perform one of his ballets.

Alicia looked at Louis, who was seated in front of the mirrors. His bloodshot eyes glared at her over the rim of his coffee cup and she guessed he'd had a restless night. Helen Barsby stood at his side strumming her fingers against her leg, waiting for the dancers to take their places at the *barre*.

"Come, come, everyone," she said clapping her hands with an edge of impatience. "Time marches on and we have a lot to cover today. You all know Mr Mason is due to arrive any minute. You need to be warmed up and ready."

With *Manon* opening in a week, Mason's timing was dreadfully inconvenient. Louis' stress levels were high enough. Twice last week, a dancer had run from the room in tears when he called her a flatfooted baboon, while another was labelled a sausage-fingered ape. He had put his reputation on the line directing *Manon*, first performed and made famous by Antoinette Sibley and Anthony

Dowell from The Royal Ballet Company. Every day counted.

By the time Alicia had finished tying the ribbons of her shoes, most people were at the *barre*. Was it her imagination or were the girls wearing new shoes? No tacky leotards or ladders in their tights and definitely no leg or foot warmers. Yvette looked as if she had been to the beauticians for a makeover. Even the boys looked sharp in white tees and black tights. Securing a few strands of hair, she wondered if she too should have worn new shoes but decided comfort out-weighed aesthetics.

They had just finished class when Lauren Mason appeared at the door. Louis beckoned him in and gestured towards a chair. Alicia could almost hear the Company suck in their stomachs, and tighten their butts. She was tempted to laugh at Brandon and his swan-like neck: all he needed was a red beak to perfect the pose. Louis had said nothing about Mason needing a male lead. Brandon wanted to help make him change his mind.

Lauren put his briefcase on the floor beside his chair and handed a sheet of music to Helen who placed it on the piano. He kissed Louis, cheek to cheek, and took a seat. When he crossed his legs, Alicia watched the pointy, tan coloured shoe swing back and forth. She had often seen his photo in Dance Magazine but the real man seemed vastly different in the flesh. She found him more imposing as he fingered the heavy gold chain around his neck. Not a man easily pleased, judging by his cold expression. No smile or frown, no nodding or movement of his head in time to the music, like Louis. Just a hard, empty stare, revealing nothing. If she was going to impress him, she needed to focus on her abilities and not on the man himself.

Louis started rehearsal immediately. Half an hour passed before Mason moved off his seat, took a pair of ballet pumps from his bag and put them on. With arms folded, he prowled the room like a panther ready to pounce. Several young dancers stumbled under his piercing gaze.

As if lightning had struck the building, he clapped his hands, bringing rehearsal to a standstill. He pointed at Alicia, Yvette and another principal dancer with the Company; motioned for them to join him. *Don't look around, stay focused,* she told herself as she moved centre floor with the others. This was her chance to shine. He flicked his wrist at the Company to clear the floor. "Watch, listen and do."

Feeling like she was on trial for her life she repeated his every instruction over and over until the *adagio* was firmly planted in her brain. It was a difficult routine, full of *high-held extensions,* a controlled *penché,* and double *pirouettes,* triples if possible, in *attitude and arabesque.* She knew Yvette would opt for triples to impress him. She asked to hear the music before she cemented the two together. Mason spun around, pointed to Helen who, waiting by the piano, handed the sheet of music to the pianist.

Listening carefully, Alicia thought she recognised a similar tune to Adolph Adams' Giselle, helping to evoke an emotion to complement the music. She drafted the steps with her hands and feet, counting time.

Standing *croiseé, deg ageè derriere* with the left foot, arms *demi – second,* she waited for the him to give the go-ahead. Concentrating on her *pirouettes,* she pulled hard on her supporting leg, *plumb line* tight as she successfully completed each turn. Her confidence grew with each beat, allowing her to capture the spirit of the *adagio.* After executing a perfect *triple pirouette,* she finished on one knee, held her position and waited.

Sharp eyes focused on her face, yet he remained motionless. She slowly rose from the floor, breaking his stare. He flung around, talked briefly to Louis. They shook hands. He slipped on his shoes, picked up his bag and sheet of music, gave a quick nod to the room and left. No one moved.

"Come, come, back to work," said Louis, waving his arms at the class.

Alicia grabbed her towel off the *barre;* dried her face, trying to analyse the last hour.

"Ten bucks you get the role," said Brandon as he passed her.

She threw her towel over the rail and followed Brandon across the floor to work on their *pas de deux,* wondering if he had seen the blank stare on Mason's face at the end of the routine.

After her ballet class, Sophie *polkaed* into the studio, backpack over her shoulders. "Mummy!" Sophie's voice echoed across the room.

Louis threw his hands in the air in a show of frustration at being interrupted, and a smattering of giggles followed.

"Pippa said I could come to her place for a play and stay for dinner. She asked her mummy and she said I could. She even said she would bring me home. Please say I can, Mummy. I hate waiting in the studio."

Alicia had met Pippa's mother and father and felt comfortable with Sophie going there. She looked at Brandon for approval, who, shrugging his shoulders, nodded. "Okay, darling. Be a good girl, won't you."

"I will. Bye, Louis. Bye, everyone." Sophie waved and made for the door, bumping dancers with her backpack on her way out. Alicia was relieved to see Louis grinning as he returned Sophie's wave.

At six o'clock Louis suddenly called a halt to the day's rehearsals. Although unexpected, it had been a stressful day and the feeling of relief was like a cold wind gushing through the room on a hot day. She sat on the floor, took off her shoes and rested her head on her knees.

"Alicia. Could you come over here please?" Louis motioned with his head for her to join him near the chairs. She noticed the heavy droop of his eyelids. She sat beside him, his arm resting on her chair. His tight, thin smile put a knot in her stomach. She hoped the pressure wasn't getting to him. Maybe it was something Mason had said, or not.

"Lauren asked if he could talk with you after rehearsal. We're to meet him for coffee at Food for Thought. I hope you don't mind such short notice but he's leaving Melbourne early tomorrow morning."

At least that explained the reason for the abrupt end of rehearsals. "Of course. Give me five minutes to change."

Food for Thought was a popular meeting place for aspiring dancers. A few older students from the ballet school were there drinking coffee. Conversation stopped when they saw her and Louis enter. Lauren Mason was already seated, mug in his hand, reading the paper. He stood when they reached his table. His friendly smile helped smooth some of the surliness from his face and she felt the muscles in her shoulders relax a little.

He hailed the waitress and ordered them both a flat white, no sugar. "Louis may have explained: I'm looking for a ballerina to perform my ballet this coming season in Sydney. I would like that someone to be you." This time the smile reached his eyes.

The chance to perform one of his ballets was every dancer's dream. With effort, she remained calm, but she had much to consider. She looked at Louis. Mason was a hard man to say no to, even for Louis, but she needed his approval. She laid her hand on his arm. "I beg your pardon, Mr Mason, I don't mean to appear ungrateful or rude … if Louis has no objection, then I would love to."

Louis patted her hand. "None, *moi petite*. It's a great opportunity. Besides, Yvette will leap at the chance to perform *Manon* in Singapore, which should be about the same time you will open in Sydney."

Alicia thought his words didn't quite match his demeanour.

"Are you sure, Louis? I don't want to let you down."

"Of course. You have worked hard; you deserve this chance."

She still wasn't convinced Louis was all that happy about her going for so long but accepted his approval without argument.

"Louis mentioned your next tour after Melbourne is Queensland. When the season finishes, I was hoping you could fly to Sydney for orientation week and help you familiarise yourself with the Company. You could also organise for a place to stay; the Shangri-La Hotel is probably the most suitable. It's close by, pleasant rooms, and so on. All expenses paid, of course, courtesy of Sydney Dance Company."

Alicia nodded, overjoyed at the prospect of performing one of his ballets but for one slight hiccup. "You do know I have a child to consider?" At the mention of Sophie, she hoped Brandon hadn't forgotten she was due home from Pippa's around six-thirty and to put her to bed by seven if Alicia was late home.

"Yes. Louis told me earlier." The smile was gone and a thoughtful expression took its place. "I have spent a long time looking for a dancer to portray the story of my mother's sad life. It's a courageous story and one close to my heart. I want someone who knows pain beyond the surface, who can bring that pain to life through my choreography. I will work something out to suit your … little girl is it?"

After finalising most of the arrangements, she left the café with Louis who hailed a cab and waited until she was safely inside. Alicia's mind buzzed with possibilities. He said he wanted someone who understood grief beyond the surface. How did he know? She had never told Louis her story. Did her pain sit so blatantly on her shoulders that anyone and everyone could see it? She slumped against the seat, too tired to think another thought.

The cab pulled up outside her apartment block. Cars were parked on each side of the road. Not until she stood outside her apartment did the noise coming from inside jolt her memory. *A party.* The last thing in the world she wanted after a long day was a truckload of people traipsing around her home. With her forehead resting against the door she closed her eyes and stayed there until she found the strength to go inside.

Jenny and John sat at the dining table nibbling chips and peanuts, along with a couple from the third floor and a married couple from the Company. Brandon had pushed back the furniture to make a dance floor and was doing an energetic cha-cha with Kieran and several other dancers who he had invited.

"Ah, at long last, the lady of the house." Jenny raised her glass as Alicia joined the group.

"Take a seat. Eat, drink and be merry," chipped in John.

"I'm a bit sweaty," said Alicia. "I might take a shower first."

"Well, don't take long. There's a party going on out here."

Laughing, the group raised their glasses in another toast. She managed a lukewarm smile and promised to be quick. With her bedroom on the other side of the living room, dodging Brandon was another matter. A mischievous sparkle shone in his eye as he cha-cha-ed up to her. He grabbed her hand, pulled her into his arms and swung her in a circle.

"You haven't said much to me since our little tiff the other day over the football. Truce? Or do I keep you swinging until you agree?"

"Truce," she said, resting her head on his shoulder. Still dressed in tights and leotard with a slip-on skirt over the top, she stepped onto his feet for support as he rocked her from side to side.

"You know I love you, Ally. I only want the best for you, not the worst."

Those words meant more to her than Mason's offer. Her life would be unbearable without Brandon and she regretted that they'd argued. She wrapped her arms around his neck, kissed his bony cheek and slipped from his embrace before the threatening tears fell.

"Sophie's in your room, by the way. Less noise in there, if that's possible."

Taking off her dirty, ballet-sodden clothes, she flopped onto the bed beside Sophie and examined her feet. Pleased with their condition – no broken skin – she slipped into the bathroom, flicked on the taps in the shower. With her hair clipped to the top of her head, she eased under the warm liquid flow.

Why a party, she grumbled, *and why tonight?* Not that any other night would make a difference. The soap slid from her fingers and she banged her head on the tiled wall as she bent to pick it up. Her hair tumbled loose into the cascade of water, and she counted backwards from ten.

By the time she'd finished in the bathroom, her mood matched her drenched hair. She eased down onto the spongy mattress, careful not to wake Sophie and fought the urge to keep her eyes open. But the regular rhythming of Sophie's breath, slowly wore her down and she slipped under the doona, hoped no one would notice she was missing, and gave into the dreamy sensation of sleep.

***

"Get up you two, it's late and we're supposed to be meeting the Spencers at the Yacht Club at nine o'clock," said Brandon, yanking apart the curtains.

The morning sun flooding the room felt like a trumpeter blowing reveille and she pulled the doona over her face. "It's our day off," Alicia groaned.

"No better way to spend it than sailing up the Yarra on a beautiful sunny day." Brandon, full of mischief and fun, proceeded to play-act his way through the choppy waters of an imaginary rapid river, making Sophie giggle.

"I love being on Uncle John's big boat. Will Chloe and Oliver be there?"

"Of course. Don't forget your hat … and a change of clothes; oh, and those new yellow bathers I bought you last week. The old ones your mother lets you wear look like you pooped your pants they're so perished."

Sophie scrambled to her feet and clapped her hands, set to launch herself from the bed into his arms.

"Aim at my chest. Ready, one, two, three, jump." He caught her mid-air, twirled her several times, and kissed her just as many. "Okay, Button, let's go rustle up some breakfast. And you, lazybones, get up."

With her arm slung across her eyes to shield them from the sunlight breaking through the morning, Alicia stretched. Her stomach growled, reminding her she had missed dinner. Eggs on toast sounded good.

She found the two of them, their faces swimming in bowls of cereal, Sophie's mouth covered with milk. Brandon's usual enthusiasm made her smile. He loved a day out on the boat, cruising through the harbour into Port Phillip Bay, mooring outside one of the restaurants along the coastline. He once told her it was like being in a moment of normality, a chance to escape into another world completely disconnected from ballet.

"I'm making eggs on toast, if anyone cares to join me."

"Nope, we're good, aren't we, Button?"

Alicia took the eggs from the fridge, cracked them into a pan. Breaking two slices of bread from the loaf in the freezer she popped them into the toaster. As she waited for the eggs to cook, she thought about Mason's offer. She would have to live in Sydney for at least six weeks while rehearsing and performing. In the six years she and Brandon had lived together, she couldn't remember being parted for so long, if at all. She looked over at the two fair heads bent over their breakfast bowls. "I accepted Mason's offer."

"That'll be ten bucks, thanks."

"Fat chance, smarty pants."

Sophie giggled. "Uncle Brandon is a smarty pants."

"Watch it, Missy, or your bum will ache from the smart I put on your pants." Brandon took his plate to the sink. "So, when do you leave? And Sophie?"

"Will come with me of course. Mrs Heywood won't be too happy but it's not for long. Lauren's ballet opens almost the same time as you will open in Singapore with *Manon*, Yvette as the lead. He wants me to fly to Sydney after Queensland for a week's orientation with Sydney Dance, to see how I go. I think I'll be partnering Sergei Vassilkovski from the States."

"Wow! Lucky, you."

"It's a bit daunting, actually."

"Um … I'm hearing ya."

"Will I be going to Sydney with you, Mummy?"

"Yes, darling. Mr Mason very kindly invited you to come too. I promise to make time to take you to some fun places."

"Can't I stay with Uncle Brandon?"

"No, Button. Uncle Brandon has to go to Singapore with the Company but I promise to ring you every day." He blew her a kiss which she caught mid-stream and placed on her cheek. "But," he continued, "I could take her home with me after

Queensland when you shoot off to Sydney for the week."

"Please, Mummy, say he can."

"We'll see. You know I can't bear to be without you."

"Okay, I'm done." Brandon stood up. "Hurry up and finish, you two. We can discuss this later. Time is marching on." He washed and dried his plate and waddled off like Charlie Chaplin.

Not quite up to his standards, Sophie dropped her plate in the sink and, mimicking her uncle, waddled off to change. Alicia had just finished eating her eggs when Sophie returned, dressed in a pink floral dress and sandals. Which seemed odd, she usually wore shorts on the boat.

"Do I look pretty, Mummy?"

Turning in her seat, Alicia straightened the crooked tip of Sophie's collar. "Yes, darling, you look gorgeous."

"Do you think Nick will think I look pretty?"

Alicia hesitated. No-one had mentioned that Nick was joining them. "Who said Nick was coming today."

"Uncle Brandon. I'm going to ask Nick if he would like to be my daddy."

Alicia's entire body froze, all but her heart, which felt like it was somersaulting faster than an acrobat. "Sophie, darling, listen to me very carefully. I understand how much you want a daddy but you can't ask such a thing of Nick."

"I knew you would say that. You don't want me to have a daddy, do you?"

Alicia held her by the shoulders, her mind struggling to find the right words. "Yes, I do. I wish with all my heart you had a daddy but you can't just pick someone out of the blue."

"But I know Nick and I love him," cried Sophie, hands on hips and her chest thrust forward.

"Oh Sophie, try to understand. For Nick to be your daddy, I would have to marry him."

"Don't you like Nick?" Her hands slipped from her hips.

Thoughts banged together. Did she like Nick? "Nick is a nice man and I like him very much but not enough to marry him." Pushing back her chair she lifted Sophie onto her lap. "Darling, you can't ask someone to be your daddy. Couples fall in love, get married and have children. Nick isn't in love with me: he's a friend. And what if he doesn't want to be a father? How will you feel if you ask him and he says no?"

The bottom lip began to quiver and then came the tears. Alicia's heart nearly broke in half. She too wanted a father, mother and brother but one thing she knew from hard-learned experience, all the wishing in the world didn't change a thing.

***

It was Sunday morning and Nick had been invited by Jenny to come boating up the Yarra River with her, John and the kids, on their luxury cruiser. Jenny also mentioned she had invited Alicia, Sophie and Brandon. He stood staring out the bay windows of his lounge-room, his mind locked on Alicia and how to win her trust. Shaking the cobwebs from his brain, he looked around the room.

The familiar surroundings, his books, the solid wooden furniture and earthy tones of the paint and carpet, seemed to bring a calmness to his dishevelled thoughts. He knew he was falling deeply in love with her, a state he hadn't been in for years. She'd awakened emotions in him he thought were past reviving and he had begun to re-discover the man he once was, the man he liked before his wife had ripped his heart to shreds and left a cynical, empty carcass in her wake.

The sweet nectar of tomorrow was gradually replacing the bitter taste of the past. But the very qualities he found so irresistible – her youth and naïveté – also stood at the core of his concern. Was he too old, too sceptical, for this gentle young woman with the sad eyes and inviting lips? He thought about the women he had been with, sophisticated, gregarious women who had certainly filled a need but invariably left him empty. Alicia only had to smile at him to make his knees go weak. How ironic, he mused. Not so long ago it took more than a smile to stir his blood. But he wanted more than weak knees. He wanted her to trust him and let him discover the real Alicia, the Alicia who Brandon knew, the Alicia that came to life on stage. He rubbed over his chin. "Alicia, Alicia, Alicia. What are you hiding from me and why?"

He wanted to take the relationship to another level and perhaps today on the boat might give him that opportunity. He clamped on a pair of sunglasses, snatched up his bag from the floor, and headed for his car.

The Yacht Club car park was almost full. He spent several minutes driving up and down lanes until he eventually found an empty space. As he walked towards the marina, he spotted Brandon head-deep in the boot of his car. "Brandon, good to see you."

"Not as good as it is to see you," replied Brandon, thrusting towels under his arm. "I wish you'd take this pair of sad sacks and sort them out."

It didn't take a rocket scientist to see something was wrong. Both girls wore miserable expressions. Sophie came over and stood in front of him, arms extended, and he picked her up. "Well, Sweetie, what's this sad face all about?"

"My mummy won't let me have a daddy and I hate her." She laid her head on his shoulder, sniffed into his neck. From the corner of his eye he noticed Alicia's arms folded, head high and a scowl on her face. "That's not a nice way to speak about your mummy. I think you better say sorry."

She pushed her face into his neck and mumbled against his skin. "Sorry, Mummy."

Amused, he patted her back. "Well, I suppose that will do for now."

"Don't worry about me, I'll carry all the gear. You just stand there and look miserable," said Brandon, the towels slipping from under his arm as he hoisted a large bag from the boot.

Suppressing a grin, Nick put Sophie down and took the towels. "Thank you, Nick."

Brandon strutted off with his bag hooked over his shoulder but stopped abruptly, and swung around. "Come on then, Button. Come with me … and don't talk or I'll throw you to the sharks." Sophie, quick to do what she was told, skipped off beside him.

Nick strolled over to stand in front of Alicia. He wanted to touch her, stroke her cheek, hold her in his arms and kiss away the crease in her brow but his arm-full of towels made that impossible.

"Want to talk about it?"

She dropped her head, pushed a stone with her foot. "Thanks, but no thanks."

"That's it! Thanks, but no thanks." He shook his head. "One of these days, Alicia Sommers, you will learn to trust me!" And with that, following in Brandon's footsteps, he marched off.

Determined not to be distracted by a pair of long shapely legs in front of him, disappearing into denim shorts, climbing onto the boat, Nick helped John with the ropes whilst the others put on life jackets and settled themselves on the cushioned seats. He watched John manoeuvred the boat into the still waters of Port Phillip Bay, impressed by the man's skill. The day was crystal clear, and the tranquillity of motion seeped down into his bones, helping him to relax.

He gazed up to see Alicia loosen her hair and let it swing in the breeze. Nick had decided to keep his distance, annoyed by her off-hand behaviour but was finding it harder than he anticipated. If only he didn't have this damn need to win the battle.

It was lunchtime by the time they arrived at St. Kilda Pier, a popular beachside for locals and tourists alike. John anchored the boat as close as possible to the shore, giving easy access to the jetty. It took two trips in the inflatable dinghy to transport everyone, plus the luggage. Nick and Brandon carried most of the gear to the park and placed it on the first available setting, while John secured the dinghy to the jetty bollard.

Nick, catching sight of the windsurfers racing across the bay, often lifting into the air on a rush of wind, thought he might try it if time permitted. The sound of palm fronds rustling in the breeze took his thoughts in a different direction. He blinked away a distasteful memory of himself and ex-wife making out under the trees; turned towards the complex girl with the distant eyes. She was helping Jenny feed the kids. *He'd never before met a woman who had him so bemused,* he thought as he joined them all at the table. One minute he was riding on the crest of a wave, only to crash the next. Her refusal to share even the smallest part of herself with him was driving him crazy.

Brandon's voice cut through his thoughts. "Fancy a game of volleyball after lunch, old boy?"

"Are you sure you want to risk losing a second time, matey?" said Nick half concentrating. He was aware of the people at the next table, who kept turning around to look at them as if they knew someone from his group.

"That's it! You're on," said Brandon, shoving the remainder of his sandwich into his mouth.

"Can we go for a swim now, Mummy?" begged Sophie.

Alicia looked to Jenny for approval.

As Chloe and Oliver scurried to retrieve their swimsuits from their beach bag, Jenny said, "I don't see why not. As long as you stay close to the shore. There are buckets and spades at the bottom, Chloe. But you're not to go in the water until I've finished my lunch."

Nick, about to take Brandon up on his offer, saw the young girl from the nearby table walking towards him. Alicia had bent down to get Sophie's swimsuit from her bag and surfaced just as the girl approached.

"Excuse me, I apologise for interrupting but, well … aren't you Alicia Sommers?"

Alicia, ashen-faced, shot Brandon a sharp glance before nodding.

"My name is Meg Thomas and I'm studying at the Australian Ballet School. I've watched you dance so many times. I think you are the best dancer in the world."

The pale complexion changed to a delicate shade of pink. "Thank you, that's very nice of you to say so."

"Hello, Brandon Hastie here! Best male dancer in the world." He raised his arms in the air above his head, lifted his chin high and poised.

Everyone laughed, including the girl.

"That's my parents sitting over there. They don't understand. They think I'm wasting my time dancing. They want me to go to college to study business and give up what they call, my ridiculous fantasy. I thought maybe … if you don't mind … you could talk to them, explain that dancing isn't just a hobby, and what a great opportunity it would be for me if I were to be accepted into the Company."

Alicia looked at the girl's parents then back at the desperate face. She switched her gaze, first to Sophie and then to Jenny.

Jenny held out her hand. "Here, give me her bathers. You go. I'll look after Sophie."

"I won't be long. Watch her, won't you, Jen. She thinks she's Dawn Frazer when she hits the water. And don't let her go out too far, will you."

"I won't take my eyes off her, Grandma," laughed Jenny.

Alicia followed the girl across the grass. How could she refuse, when she too had followed her dream? Alicia soon realised the parents were good honest folk who loved their daughter very much and only wanted the best for her. A precious feeling, she once cherished.

They listened attentively as she tried to explain her passion to dance: how it made her feel when she performed, releasing the talent God had blessed her with; how she tried to impart a piece of herself to the audience, leaving them with a feeling of joy as they journeyed home. She wanted to tell them how much she wished her own beloved parents were alive to offer the same love and support but was afraid she would break apart. And she fed them hope for their daughter's future.

As she rose to leave, she saw Jenny running towards her, panic on her face. Something was dreadfully wrong. Heart thumping, Alicia gripped the table for support.

"It's Sophie, I can't find her. Everyone is looking …"

Without waiting for Jenny to finish, Alicia jumped the seat, kicked off her thongs and pelted towards the beach yelling Sophie's name. When she reached the foreshore, she looked both ways but there was no sign of Sophie. *Which way to run!* Brushing sweat from her eyes she charged towards the bend in the foreshore, stumbling in the hot sand beneath her feet. When she reached the turn, still no Sophie; she bit hard on her shaking fist, desperate to work out what to do next, too terrified to believe Sophie had drowned. She could feel the sea at her side, daring her to look at it and see if it had Sophie in its clutches. Bile rushed into her mouth and she gagged. 'No, no, no. Oh God no, not again. Please don't do this to me again," she screamed as she sank to her knees in the hot sand. With a million frantic thoughts crashing into each other, she repeatedly punched her forehead in an attempt to clear her mind. "I have to keep going," she mumbled, when a thought flashed into her mind. *The boat!* Adrenaline returning, she ran along the coast, faltering at the pain in her scorched feet; turned onto the jetty.

"Ex …cuse… me." Alicia tried to push past a group of young people who were meandering along the jetty.

"Got me a live one here," joked one young man, blocking her way.

"Please! Let me through." She swung her arm to push him out of the way but he caught it mid-air and held it in a firm grip.

"Let her go, Jarred," shouted a young girl. But Jarred, happy in his taunting, continued to laugh. Alicia fought like a tiger, yelling at him to let her go until her voice cracked. Exhausted and with her energy almost spent, she wrenched her arm out of his grip at the very moment he let her go.

Stumbling backward, Alicia's heels caught on the ledge of the jetty and, with no railing for protection, she went flying over the side, her head hitting the aluminium dinghy tied next to John's inflatable.

Chapter Seven

"Nick! Nick! Over here."

Spinning, around he hurried towards Jenny. "What's up?" he said, panting.

"Chloe has something to tell you." Jenny pushed her daughter forward. "Go on tell him."

"Sophie's hiding behind the toilets, over there." Chloe's head drooped as she pointed to the ablution block. Oliver, emulating his sister, did the same.

"The little monkey …" Jenny broke in, "… hiding, to get at her mother. My two were appointed watchdogs. Could you go and talk to Sophie?"

"Right." He found Sophie huddled in a corner, her knees tucked under her chin, crying, and he crouched beside her. "Do you want to tell me what all this crying is about?" Sophie shook her head.

"Okay, but we had better go find mummy. She's very worried." He took her hand and pulled her to her feet. "Come on."

Jenny and her children were waiting by the table when they emerged.

"Look after her, will you? I'd better go find her mother before she has a heart attack."

"The last time I saw John, he was halfway up the beach to Melbourne. Let him know if you see him, will you." They exchanged smiles and Nick jogged off to the beach, wondering how he could mend Alicia's broken heart.

His leisurely jog quickly turned into a bolt when he saw her tussling with some young guy on the jetty. He had just about reached her when, to his horror, she toppled backward over the edge of the jetty. He heard the thump before she hit the water. With his heart in his mouth, he hurled himself off the side between the two dinghies. He hit the water like a bullet, felt the full force of impact engulf him.

He blinked to clear his vision, caught sight of her floating, submerged face down, some distance away. Chest tightening, he swam to the surface, gulped in a lungful of air and duck-dived back underwater. He swam hard to reach her, grabbed her ankle. Stunned by his touch, Alicia awoke from her shocked state. She went crazy, kicking and punching at him as though he was trying to attack her, making it impossible for him to get a firm grip. With his lungs ready to burst, he dived deeper and came up behind her, pinning both her arms at her side. With only his legs free, he frog-kicked to the surface, trying hard to ignore the kicks he was receiving to his shins. It took most of his strength to tow her underneath the jetty. She hung limp in his grip and he feared she wasn't breathing. He paddled to the inside ladder, placed his foot on the bottom rung and turned her to face him. Through the tendrils of her wet hair, two bulging eyes stared back at him, while blood trickled down her face, giving her a death-mask appearance.

"Sophie."

"Safe," he said, his relief overwhelming. He swam to the outside of the ladder and using his free arm, clutched her to him with all his might, her head banging against his chest as he climbed the steps. Eager helpers lifted Alicia from his grasp, onto the wooden boards of the jetty.

"Let me through, I'm a doctor," yelled Jenny as she pushed past the group of teenagers gathered around Alicia's limp body. Crouching, she pressed her fingers against Alicia's carotid artery feeling for a pulse before tilting her head back to clear her airway. Jenny then took a large breath, exhaled evenly into Alicia's mouth, counted time and repeated the action until finally, Alicia coughed up a mouthful of seawater. Jenny turned her head sideways as she spluttered the last mouthful of water from her lungs, Alicia collapsed, exhausted. Blood oozing from the gash on her head dripped onto the slats of the jetty, matching the stains on Jenny's pink top.

"Mummy, Mummy," shouted a distraught Sophie as she ran up the jetty, her hair flying in the wind. She threw herself on top of Alicia, grasped the bloodied face in both hands and began shaking her head. Brandon tried to lift Sophie off, knocking Jenny aside as he did.

Nick crouched down beside the frightened child, clasped both her wrists. "Sophie! Listen to me! Mummy's had a nasty fall but she's okay. I want you to be a big girl, stop crying and stay with Uncle Brandon while I carry Mummy to the boat. Can you do that?" She looked at him, fear radiating from her eyes, and nodded. His calm control seemed to have a ripple effect, causing others to take a few steps back.

"Bring her to the boat. I don't think we need to call an ambulance. I always carry an emergency bag with us, for this very reason. Even have a stethoscope," said Jenny.

He picked up Alicia and, as he stood with her in his arms, he caught sight of John running towards them, panting heavily. The young ballerina and her parents, seeing Nick, waved from the shore, and with their arms around their daughter, the three of them walked off.

While John and Jenny climbed into the rubber dinghy, Brandon led Sophie, Chloe, and Oliver back to the picnic site to retrieve the gear. Only the young man who had caused the accident remained, his head bowed. "I'm sorry," he said, "I didn't mean ..."

"No one ever does," said Nick scowling. He guessed the boy meant no harm, probably showing off in front of his girlfriend.

"It's a nasty cut. Needs stitching."

"I'm really sorry. I was only having a bit of fun."

"You might consider the consequences next time you decide to have a bit of fun at someone else's expense."

There was no reply; just a quick nod before the teenager left the scene.

Alicia had drifted to sleep in his arms. Although John and Jenny helped guide Nick's steps, carrying Alicia into the dinghy was no easy task. He scanned her face. It looked so pale against his damp shirt.

By the time they reached the boat and man-handled Alicia aboard, exhaustion and shock had set in and he was barely able to carry her to the main cabin. His arms shook with her weight; even his legs felt unsteady. Jenny spread several old towels over the bed, and Nick lowered Alicia's wet body onto them. He choked back a sob when he looked at the beautiful, blood drenched face.

Jenny went to talk with John before he rowed back to the jetty, leaving Nick alone in the cabin. Stroking the wet hair from Alicia's face, he leant over and gently feathered kisses on her lips. Guilt ripped through him. He wished with all his heart he hadn't been so aloof with her. He also wished he'd been more responsible and helped Jenny with the kids. He put another pillow behind her head to prop her up, in order to attend to the cut. She stirred.

"Ssh, ssh, it's okay, Baby. Lie still, there's a good girl."

Jenny returned carrying a medical kit. "I have every ointment under the sun in this stupid bag but no sutures or anaesthetic to administer a local. I can't believe I left them off the list. But I've been thinking. I picked up a little trick from Miles Buckhannon when I worked at the hospital, which I think should work." She parted Alicia's hair so they could see the cut more clearly.

"Nasty." She mopped up the blood while Nick tenderly stroked the lifeless white hand that hung over the side of the bed.

"I think we should remove her wet clothes before I dress that gash. The last thing we need is for her to go into hypothermic shock," said Jenny, re-examining the wound. "You'll need to make a visit to the hospital, after we dock. She'll need a tetanus shot. It's a bit out of the way but I think it'd be quicker than going home to get the keys to the surgery."

"You're the doctor."

She gave him a sharp look. "Are you up to this? You're a bit pale. I can call John if you like. You've suffered an awful shock too, you know."

"Just don't tell her I helped you to take off her clothes. That, I'll never live down."

"My lips are sealed." She rummaged through the overhead locker for some spare clothes for Alicia. Together they removed the wet and bloodstained clothes. Every muscle in his body tightened at the sight of her delicate porcelain skin, covering a taut, trim body, decked out in white lacy underwear. She was pure as the lace itself. He held his breath as they carefully dressed her into a pair of shorts and t-shirt of Jenny's — too big but they would have to do.

The cut had started to weep again, blood dribbling down Alicia's face. Jenny pressed it dry with a wad of gauze, and then, using Alicia's hair, drew strands of equal strength from opposite sides of the gash and tied them in knots. They worked together, with Nick holding each knot in place until Jenny had sealed the length of the cut. "Don't let go. I need to fetch the Betadine." After applying the antiseptic, she placed a strip of gauze over the wound and secured it with plaster, then doubly securing it with lengths of cloth she had cut out of an old shirt belonging to John, around her head. "There, that should do it for now. Not a bad effort, even if I do say so myself." Finally, Jenny checked Alicia's vital signs, pulse and breathing.

"Thank you, Miles Buckhannon," said Nick stretching his back. "Would you mind if I took a shower? I feel disgusting."

"Of course not. Towels are in the cupboard. Help yourself. I think there might be some of John's old clothes in the top drawer.

Yes, here you go. Sorry, not your usual standard but better than the wet ones you have on."

"Thanks, Jen. I feel better already." He left Jenny to finish tidying; went to the bathroom and locked the door. Years of dealing with medical emergencies had taught Nick how to control his emotions, but this episode had stretched him. He leant against the door, dropped his head into his hands. The image of Alicia's bloodied face flashed before him and he couldn't control the shudder that attacked his body. Lifting his head, he shook himself free of the frightening thought of what might have been. His anxiety was relieved a little as the pain up his shins reminded him of the kicks they received, and brought a lazy smile.

Showered and changed, he emerged from the bathroom feeling better. Alicia was still asleep and he checked her pulse, made sure her breathing was even. He needed to clear his mind and decided to go on deck for a touch of normality.

Sitting on the side of the boat, he looked out over the ocean and inhaled deeply. The swish of the sea, the cry of seagulls, even the dull purr of the motor helped reshape his thoughts. A tap on the shoulder brought him back. A tear-stained face stared at him. He lifted Sophie onto his knee, held her head against his chest.

Much of Nick's childhood resembled Sophie's. He knew what it felt like to be seven, alone and insecure with only a mother for support. All this made him think about his dear mother and how hard her life must have been as a single parent. Although she loved Nick dearly, he knew he alone wasn't enough to fill the empty space in her life. He saw that same emptiness in a certain ballerina.

"Mummy will be okay, Sweetie. Jenny stitched her up and you and I will take her to the hospital on the way home to make sure she's okay."

"It's all my fault," she snivelled.

"Well, it wasn't *all* your fault. The boy on the jetty wouldn't let go of her arm. He thought it was funny to tease Mummy, and then of course when he did let go, she flipped off the edge and I think she hit her head on the boy's dinghy." If the boy hadn't interfered, thought Nick, Alicia would have realised that Sophie couldn't have reached the boat without rowing over in John's inflatable dinghy. In which case, the dinghy wouldn't have been tied up at the jetty. Besides, Sophie was too little and too weak to row a dinghy of that size. "We'll give Mummy a bit more time to wake up and then you can see her."

Nick was glad John decided on the more direct route home. When the Yacht Club came into sight, he led Sophie down the steps to the main cabin, and felt relieved to find Alicia awake.

"Darling," she whispered, her gaze resting on Sophie who had started to cry. "Come here, it's okay."

Sophie looked at Nick for approval. She crawled onto the bed, wrapped herself around her mother and blubbered an apology. Alicia stroked her fingers through the mass of curls.

Nick leant against the door frame, arms folded. How he wished it was him lying in her arms while she stroked his head. His heart quickened when she glanced at him, a warm look in her eyes. Taking a chance, he went and sat on the other side of the bed, and clasped her hand in his.

She swallowed hard, her lips trembling. "Sorry …"

He shook his head, placed his fingers over her lips. No, he was the sorry one. Sorry he wasn't fast enough to save her from falling, sorry he hadn't watched the children instead of playing volleyball and sorry he let her down. He leant across Sophie, wrapped his arms around the two of them. "My poor girl, how do you feel?"

"Sore. Is it bad?'

"Nasty, but not too bad. Unfortunately, there weren't any dissolvable sutures on board, so Jenny used your hair to close the cut. A little trick she picked up back at the Royal Melbourne." He grinned when she frowned. "You're also going to need a tetanus shot. We'll head straight for the hospital on the way home."

"I'm not going to hospital," came the cold reply.

The panicked look shocked him, as if he had hit her in the face, and he drew back confused. Sophie moved off the bed, biting at her fingernails. What had he said to cause such a fearful reaction? "Why on earth not?"

"Because I can't."

He sat up, touched her cheek. "Just tell me, darling, tell me why you can't." Fear and anger looked back at him, and instinctively, he seized both her hands. "Don't do this. Don't shut me out. Tell me why you can't go to hospital. I can't help you if you don't trust me."

As if someone had released a valve, the tears fell, but the fear remained, locked behind compressed lips. He slipped his hands around her back and lifted her into his arms. "Alicia, listen to me. You need medical attention and the only way you're going to get it is at the hospital."

"I won't go."

"You will because I am going to take you there."

"He will, Mummy – he said he would."

She punched her fist into his shoulder, letting it fall down his side. Sobbing against his neck, her tears slipped inside his shirt, pooling in the hollow of his collar bone. *At last*, thought Nick, stroking her hair. He rocked her gently until she calmed then laid her against the pillows. He considered the terrified expression. What was this demon on her shoulders? More in the dark than ever, he dragged in his tattered breath. Something terrible had happened involving a hospital: that much he'd figured but now was not the time to press the point.

When the boat jarred against the jetty, Nick knew they'd arrived. "Don't move until I get back. Understood?" He waited until she agreed. "Good. Come on, Sophie; let's go see what's happening upstairs. We'll pack the car first before we come back and get Mummy."

He was thankful to see Brandon helping John secure the boat.

Jenny had packed up the gear, including the Esky, and was stowing the life jackets under the seats.

"Is she awake?" she asked.

"Yes. Thought I'd check out the situation before I collect the patient."

Jenny nodded. "Good idea. The sun still has a sting to it and sitting in the car for too long won't do her any good."

"Anything I can do?"

"No, all done. This lot here," she pointed, "belongs to Alicia, which I think Brandon is going to take home with him, and I've put your bag on the seat over there."

"Great. Thanks, Jen. We might get going if you don't mind. Could be a long wait at Emergency." He looked at his watch – three-thirty – and tipped his chin to heaven.

"No, you go. We've nearly finished here anyway. Let me know how she is, won't you? That cut will need suturing and might be an idea to have a chest x-ray just make sure there are no problems with her lungs."

"Yep. Give you a ring at work tomorrow. Now, Me-lady, hold my bag and wait here while I get your mother."

When he walked into the cabin, Alicia was hunched over the edge of the bed.

"Easy does it," said Nick, scooping her into his arms before she had time to protest. She rested her head on his shoulder, her arm tight around his neck. It took a bit of careful manoeuvring to get her up the narrow stairwell without knocking her head.

On deck, everyone said goodbye and wished Alicia a speedy recovery. Brandon lifted her foot and kissed each toe, over and over, until she managed a sliver of a smile.

"Better go," said Nick. John helped Sophie onto the jetty and Jenny, adjusting the strap of Nick's bag, slipped it over her small shoulders.

After settling the two girls into the car, he drove to the hospital.

Parking was always difficult, bays filling by mid-morning and he drove around the parking block several times before finding he found one.

He sensed from the stormy look on Alicia's face a battle was brewing. When he opened the car door, she pushed at his chest.

"I can't," she cried.

"You can and you will." He held up his hand when she opened her mouth to protest and lifted her from the car to her feet. "Come on, Sophie, out you jump." He locked the car, pocketed the keys and, taking hold of Alicia's arm, draped it over his shoulder.

The closer they came to the entrance the more she tried to pull away. When the doors slid open, she grabbed the front of his shirt and started gasping for breath, forcing him to stop. Sophie began to whimper. Several people passing, stared. He pulled Alicia against his chest, held her close while she continued dry-retching on his shoulder. With his other arm, he cradled Sophie to his side, patted her back and wondered whose grave he had stepped on.

"It's okay, Baby. It's okay," he whispered, trying to calm Alicia down.

"I'm going to be sick."

"Alicia, look at me! Breathe when I do. In and out … look at me! That's a girl, slowly … in and out, and again, in and out." It took several attempts until finally her breathing regulated. Where was the courageous woman, he wondered, who had fought like a virago for her daughter's life? And now, in his arms was a panic-stricken girl out of control at the idea of entering a hospital?

With no choice but to carry her, he pushed through the doors, a frightened Sophie close by his side; he placed Alicia on one of the seats inside the emergency waiting room. He started to move away but she had twisted the front of his shirt into a tight knot, preventing him standing.

"Alicia, let go of me. I need to see the reception clerk."

"Don't go!" she cried, tugging on his shirt, squeezed tight.

Swallowing down his frustration he began to free each clenched finger from his shirt, releasing the hairs on his chest which had been caught up in her grip.

"Are you going to leave us?" cried Sophie, a tremor in her voice.

"No, Sweetie. I need to talk to the nurse behind the counter to register Mummy, so the doctor can see her."

"Alicia, open your eyes. Good girl. Now, Sophie, sit with Mummy and hold her hand. I'll be right there." He pointed to the reception counter less than a dozen steps away. "Don't shut your eyes, just keep looking at me. I won't be long."

He prised the remaining fingers from his shirt, and her eyes filled. He cupped her face in his hands, dropped a kiss on her forehead, the tip of her nose and lips. Straightening, he rearranged his crumpled shirt and walked over to the counter. The triage nurse looked up and smiled.

It seemed strange to be on the other side of the counter. The sight and antiseptic smell of the hospital notched another cog in the wheel of his desire to return to medicine. After completing the relevant forms, with as much of Alicia's details as he knew, he turned around to see two pairs of eyes staring into his. A glimpse of what his future might bring filled him with an unexpected joy and made him want to burst into laughter.

Judging by the number of patients in the waiting room he prepared himself for a long wait. The nurse eventually called Alicia's name, and Nick helped her through the swinging doors and into a half-curtained cubicle, with Sophie clutching at the stained fishing shorts Jenny had given him. He helped Alicia onto the bed, sat on the only chair in the room with Sophie on his lap and studied the distressed girl, wringing her hands.

"Nicky, is that you? What brings you here?"

Recognising the voice, Nick turned. "Mattie!" *Matthew Mason, just my luck,* thought Nick, smiling. Judging by the sly grin on Matthew's face, a nervous feeling erupted and he braced himself.

Lifting Sophie from his lap, he sprang to his feet, grabbed Matthew's hand and pulled him into a warm embrace. "Well, well, well, look what the cat dragged in."

"Excuse me, but I'm not the one that looks like I've been dragged anywhere," said Matt, his voice as loud as ever.

"No, I guess not," said Nick running his fingers through his uncombed hair. "Met with a slight accident."

Matt looked at the two girls, a smirk on his face. "Seems to me you've met with more than one accident."

Nick cleared his throat. "Matthew Mason, this is Alicia Sommers and her daughter, Sophie."

"Hello," replied Alicia, studying the floor.

"And hello," said Matt, a whistle in his voice, eyeing Nick.

"Not like you to work on a Sunday." Nick spoke quickly, hoping to re-channel Matthew's thoughts.

"ICU called me in to view an interesting case brought in earlier, Prinzmetal Angina. I came down to speak to Liam Ford, the Attending in ER. You remember Ford, the guy with the squinty eye. Apparently, he treated the same chap once before. Hence, my dear man, my presence."

It had always fascinated Nick how quickly Matthew could change hats, playboy one minute, cardiologist the next.

"Do us a favour, Mattie, should only take a minute. Alicia fell backward off the jetty and whacked her head on an aluminium dinghy. Jenny Spencer did a quick patch up but she needs a few sutures and a tetanus shot."

With his gloved hand Matthew removed the plaster from Alicia's head, pulling out a few stands of hairs as he did. She flinched. "Sorry. Quite a decent gash by the look. You're going to need a local."

While he waited for the anaesthetic to take effect, he found a disposable razor and shaved the surrounding hair.

Nick watched the competent fingers stitch the wound, envy

swirling in his gut. He looked at Alicia, still as a mouse, back straight, jaw jammed tight, staring at the ground and breathed a sigh of relief.

"A bit of plaster, a quick jab in the arm, and we're done." He prepared the syringe and injected the vaccine. He placed a plaster over the small puncture, stood up, ripped off his gloves then handed Nick a card of six pain killers. "How about lunch one day, Nicholas?"

"As it happens, I'm coming into the hospital this week. I'll call you."

"Look forward to it. Must go. Pleasure to have met you, Alicia and So – Sophie, is it?" he said winking at Nick.

"Goodbye, Mattie, and thanks – you're a lifesaver," said Nick.

***

In the car on the way home, Alicia sat quietly. But to Nick's surprise she appeared not so anxious. He wondered if some of her demons seemed less threatening face to face. He reached over and squeezed her hand. The smile she gave him toyed with his heart. He sensed a shift in their relationship. Trust. Maybe she trusted him a little bit more after today's ordeal.

Brandon was half off the couch when they opened the apartment door. He threw aside the magazine he'd been reading, rushed over and pulled her into a firm embrace. "That wasn't nice what you did today. You frightened me."

"What was I thinking? Pure stupidity. I'm so sorry."

"It's not funny," he said pouting. "Now go have a shower, you're in desperate need of one."

After kissing him on both cheeks, she turned to Nick. "Can I wash my hair?"

"Best not. You need to keep it dry until the skin knits."

"I can't go to ballet class tomorrow smelling like this."

"Class! Get that right out of your head. You won't be in any state to do class, tomorrow or the next day."

"Nick, it's opening night on Wednesday. I have to go."

He couldn't believe she was serious. The gash on her head was at least three inches long. "Well, you, for one, won't be performing, opening night or otherwise. I mean it."

When she looked across at Brandon, Nick felt affronted. Why would Brandon be more qualified to answer than he?

"I think he's right, Alicia," said Brandon, pulling a nervous face at Nick.

"You can't mean that. You of all people know how much this means to me. Yvette will take the lead. I've worked too hard to give it up."

"For heaven's sake, you've cut your head half open."

She stormed out, taking Sophie with her. Nick, still slightly annoyed, followed Brandon to the kitchen to help prepare dinner. It had been a confusing day and he wanted answers to a couple of niggling questions. He gave Brandon a sideways glance. "Pretty exciting for a quiet Sunday cruise, wouldn't you say?"

"We, my good man, obviously have very different ideas of what constitutes exciting." Brandon rinsed his hands under the tap. He rested his elbows on the bench, a thoughtful look on his face. "Will she be able to dance tomorrow?"

"I'd put money on it she'll have a mighty big headache. I doubt very much if she'll be able to get out of bed, let alone dance."

"She can be determined when she wants."

And that was the opening Nick needed, to probe Brandon, about Alicia's problem with hospitals. "Determined and terrified?"

Brandon lowered his eyes, worried his bottom lip. *So*, thought Nick, *there is a story in the mix*. He waited for a reply but none was offered so he prompted again. "Of hospitals?"

Again, nothing. A quick lift of his brow, a transfer of weight to the other foot, a roll of his shoulder blades, but still no eye contact.

"Care to elaborate?"

Brandon blew out his breath, ran his hand over his hair. "Nick, Nick, Nick, where do I start?" He paused; looked out the kitchen window into the night; inhaled the breath he had just released.

"The beginning might be a good place."

"I wish it were that simple but it's not."

"Never is."

He shifted his gaze, looked Nick straight in the eye. "Years ago, when I was young and desperate, with nobody in the world to turn to, I turned to Alicia. Darling Alicia." He stopped; stared into the past. "At the cruellest time in her life she helped this very unhappy and unloved, pathetic boy. I owe her everything, absolutely everything. I don't know where I'd be today if she hadn't helped me. I gave her my word that when we left Perth, we would leave the past behind us and never mention it to anyone. Unless," Brandon waved his finger at Nick, "unless, she tells me otherwise, I'll keep that pact. I promised myself that one day I would pay her back. Keeping her trust is one small part of the payment. I like you a lot Nick, and I would really like to tell you the truth, but she would never forgive me and that I couldn't bear."

Nick clasped Brandon's shoulder, held it in a firm grip. "You're a good friend, Brandon. Alicia's lucky to have you. I'm sorry I asked."

How Brandon managed to turn dinner into a gourmet meal baffled Nick. All he could see when he looked in the fridge was a carton of eggs, a few tomatoes, and a tired-looking lettuce.

But the atmosphere around the table was far from festive. Alicia spoke little, ate less. Although she had attempted to tie back her hair, matted strips of bloodied curls framed her pale face. She cut the meagre salad she had scooped from the bowl into smaller pieces but ate nothing.

"I can't eat this. I'm sorry but I need to lie down."

"Are you in pain? The tablets Matthew gave me are in my

pocket."

"No, not too bad. I need sleep." She rose to go, but stopped, her hand gripping the chair for support. "Don't let Sophie stay up late: she has school tomorrow."

"Can you believe her? I've been looking after Sophie for years. Now stop annoying us and go to bed before you collapse."

Nick cleared the table while Brandon put Sophie to bed, and together they did the dishes. Finished, he sat down to enjoy the remainder of the evening in Brandon's company.

"I have a strong feeling Alicia is in for a rough night. Might sleep on the couch if you have no objections. What do you think? Will she go crazy if I do?"

"God Nick, who cares. But I warn you the couch can be a killer for a big bloke like you."

They talked for a while, but both men were tired and said their goodnights quite early.

Making sure he had the painkillers in his pocket, Nick opened the door to her room, so he could hear if she stirred. A brief look brought a smile. She looked like a wounded princess wrapped up in a pink doona, strips of rag and plaster taped to her dark curls, spread over the crisp white pillow slip. He tip-toed into the lounge, eased down on the couch and settled himself into an almost comfortable position, bar his feet, which dangled off the end. Brandon was right, he was in for a rough night. More tired than he realised, he soon flew off the planet.

The moaning woke him with a start. It took a few seconds to orientate himself and he jumped off the couch and into her room. "Alicia, it's Nick. What's wrong?"

"I'm…going…to be…"

Hand cupped to her mouth she pushed past him and rushed into the bathroom. He crouched beside her on the cold white tiles as she heaved into the toilet bowl. He held her hair off her face with one hand and steadied her forehead with the other. When he was sure she had finished, he carried her back to bed. Her temperature was higher than he liked. He found a washcloth in the bathroom cabinet, rinsed it under the cold tap, and laid it over her forehead. She would need something in her stomach before swallowing the tablets, so he went to the kitchen and made a cup of sweet tea. When he returned, she was moaning in pain.

He placed the tea on the side table, slipped his arm behind her back. "I'm going to lift you up so you can swallow the painkillers."

She flicked open her eyes, and nodded slightly.

He eased her forward, placed the tablets onto her tongue. Reaching for the tea, he tilted the cup against her lips, held her steady until he was sure she'd swallowed the pills.

He stayed with her until her breathing evened. Thinking back to the first time he'd seen her at the Spencers', he remembered Jenny said she would surprise him. Her beauty didn't surprise him. It was when he looked into those troubled eyes and saw her pain, he was hooked. Everything inside him wanted to take that pain away, protect her, love her, make her his. Brandon used the word 'cruel'. He wished she would talk to him. Tell him what troubled her so deeply. He stroked her arm, determined one day to get to the bottom of the mystery.

He woke the next morning feeling as if someone had smashed him about with a baseball bat and made a mental note to pump iron at the gym before the next catastrophe. His knees ached, having been bent up under his chin most of the night, to avoid his feet from getting a cramp. Even his brain seemed fogged. He rubbed his face, conscious of the stubble, and sat up to stretch his legs. He shook his head free of cobwebs and moseyed on down the hallway to Alicia's room, knocked gently on the door. To his delight, she was awake.

"How are we this morning?"

"Awful."

"Surprise, surprise." His eyebrows lifted, and he gave her a knowing nod. "Hungry?"

"Everything, including my teeth, aches. I don't think I have the strength to eat."

"That bad!" He laughed. "You haven't eaten for hours and you need something in your stomach. I'll see what's in the fridge." From what he could remember, not much, but he did recall a carton of eggs. She was about to protest, but he silenced her with a raised index finger. "Doctor's orders."

Silence and darkness greeted him in the kitchen. He groped for the light by the door, flicked the switch and waited until his eyes adjusted to the glare. Taking the eggs from the fridge, he cracked two into a bowl, added some butter and beat them until they were light and fluffy. Searching the cupboard for a frying pan, he turned at the sound of a yawn. "Fancy scrambled eggs on … do you have bread?"

"Thanks, but I'm a cornflakes man myself," said Brandon. "And yes, somewhere in this pantry is a … ah yep, here it is.

Burgen with Pumpkin seed, Alicia's favourite."

"And Sophie?" Nick's mother had cooked his breakfast most of his young life, a habit he still enjoyed. He couldn't imagine getting up each day to nothing more than a bowl of cornflakes.

"Same. Don't worry about Soph, I'll fix her."

With Alicia's breakfast, of scrambled eggs and toast, laid out on a tray, Nick carried it to her room, only to find her sleeping like a baby. Unable to resist the temptation, he stood over the bed, basked in the pleasure of watching her unheeded, before placing the tray on the bedside table. She stirred.

Easing down, he gentled her face with his fingers, stroked back her bloodied hair. "I have to go home and get ready for work but I want you to promise me you'll eat the breakfast I made for you."

She rolled her eyes at him, winced when she nodded. He leant forward to check the dressing; pulled the card of painkillers from his pocket and placed them on the tray. "Take two of these with your tea. It'll dull the pain and help you sleep." Taking hold of both her hands he kissed the tip of her nose and lips several times before finally leaving.

He drove home in a reflective mood. After a long and exhausting twenty-four hours, Nick needed a shave and a shower. At the same time, he recognised his longing for something more in his life. The show, the media lifestyle, the false sense of importance no longer satisfied him. Not that they ever did, only now, he could no longer justify the reasons. His wounded pride had healed long ago, and being in the hospital with Alicia had helped him realise what he'd always wanted: a challenge, a purpose and a chance to fulfil himself in the healing of others.

How strange, he thought, that a young woman whom he barely knew had inspired in him so much. He might feel physically tired but mentally he felt revived and ready for a fresh start. He looked forward to his appointment with the Head of Service, Cardiology, at the Royal Melbourne, a chance to consider his options.

***

Alicia woke in the afternoon to the buzz of the doorbell. It couldn't be Brandon: he had a key. Besides, there was a full-dress rehearsal at the theatre, and he wouldn't be home until later in the evening. When she sat up, the dizziness started. She held her breath, hoping it would pass. It took a while to get to the door, her head throbbing with every step.

"Oh! Alicia, I'm sorry Baby, I don't have a key."

Nick had called her *Baby*. Although the endearment implied an intimacy, she wasn't familiar with, she rather warmed to the idea of being his Baby. "What are you doing here?"

"I told Brandon if I finished work early, I would pick up Sophie, as you see."

Sophie pushed past the two of them and flung her backpack on the floor. "Miss Myers asked him if he would like to come in and see my work. You think I'm very clever, don't you Nick?" She turned on the television and flopped onto the couch.

"Insanely clever," said Nick, tongue in cheek. He eyed Alicia. "You look white as a ghost. You shouldn't be out of bed."

"Someone knocked on the door. I usually try to answer it when that happens." She swayed slightly, and was scooped into his arms as if it was the most natural thing in the world for him to do and carried her back to bed. Considering the last twenty-four hours, and how many times he had picked her up, it had certainly become a natural thing to do. Apart from her accident, she had thought of little else but Nick when she lay awake. He was slowly worming his way into her life, becoming important, necessary to her every day, and peeling back the layers of doubt. Dazed as she was when she had fallen off the jetty, she had subconsciously known it was Nick who had taken control of the chaos that followed.

His firm but gentle manner at the hospital, the way he had cared for her overnight, had been a pleasant surprise. Also surprising were the deep feelings of trust she had experienced, feelings she hadn't known since the death of her parents, feelings she thought she would never know again. Perhaps it was time to release the padlock holding her heart locked and allow these new emotions to run free.

He had taken off his coat and tie, released the top button of his shirt, and was watching her with those smiling eyes as if she was the most beautiful woman in the world. His pale blue shirt, which stretched across his chest and outlined his muscular physique, ignited a warm glow within her. "Nick, Louis rang today and asked me when I thought I'd be well enough to dance. I said I'd ask the doctor. That's you."

"I'd give it a good week," he said, taking her hand.

"A week! Oh, Nick, no. Please don't make me wait that long. It will kill me." Although she pleaded with him to let her go back in a few days, he remained adamant, infuriating her with an offhand shrug. He didn't understand how important this was to her, how hard she had worked over the last few months perfecting the role of *Manon*. Yvette would never let her forget that it was she who had performed on opening night. She knew her resentment of Yvette was unreasonable but her competitive streak was one of the reasons she had survived in the ruthless world of ballet.

"I'm fairly positive nothing so far has been written up in the medical journals concerning patients dying from rest."

"Very funny." Although he looked weary from yesterday's ordeal, there was something different about him, an energy, or was it confidence, she'd not noticed in him before. "Nick, there is something I need to say to you." The warm smile faded, replaced by an anxious frown. But the glow in his eyes remained.

"Yes, Baby."

Oh, my stars, that word again. "Yesterday and last night, everything you did for me —"

His eyes fixed on hers. He took hold of her hands, shifted closer.

"I don't know how I would have coped if you hadn't been there for me."

When he went to kiss her, she planted her fingers on his lips.

She needed to finish what she wanted to say. "You must …" She stopped, her voice unsteady. She had never shared her emotions with a man before and found it difficult.

"What must I do, darling?"

Hold off with the Baby and Darling endearments for starters, at least until I've finished what I have to say. "Be patient with me." There, she'd said it. Her heart raced. She had shifted the gear stick from neutral into drive.

Framing her face with his hands, he placed his forehead on hers. "I'll try, but if I go much slower, I'll trip over my own feet." He nipped at her lips with his own. "I want you to know I would never hurt you, Alicia. I wish you would trust me a little."

Oh yes, more than all the stars above she wanted to believe him. She wanted to trust him, confide in him, tell him about her family, the accident and the years of fighting to survive the tragedy, but it would take time. This was all new – a big step. With her heart moving off first base, she nodded through the blur in her eyes and he gently wrapped her in his arms, encouraging her to believe he meant every word.

Chapter Eight

Nick brushed a speck from his suit as he approached the desk, licked his dry lips. The receptionist peered at him over her glasses. "Mr Coleman, nice to see you again. Take a seat. Mr Manning-Brooke will be with you in a minute."

Surprised she remembered him, he grabbed a medical journal from the counter and took a seat. He flicked through the pages, put it down, went to get a glass of water. Too restless to concentrate, twiddling his thumbs, he read the title above the door, Nelson Manning-Brooke, Head of Department, over and over until he could spell it backwards. He took another sip of water and thought back to the last time he'd sat in Manning Brooke's office, the day he'd tendered his resignation.

"Mr Coleman, Mr Manning-Brooke will see you now." Nick stood, straightened his coat and walked to the door.

"Go straight in, sir. He's expecting you."

Manning-Brooke rose when he entered. "Mr Coleman! Good to see you again."

Nick was relieved the man seemed pleased to see him. After shaking hands, he took the offered chair as he scanned the office. Same leather embossed desk and chesterfield chair. A library of medical books in wooden and glass cabinets lined the walls. His nerves calmed in the familiar setting.

Manning-Brooke hadn't changed much over the years. A little greyer at the temples perhaps, but the same cut he had ten years ago with his hair brushed back off his face. He was a large man who carried himself with dignity, always polite, but suffered no fools. He had held the position as Head of Cardiology with the hospital ever since Nick could remember and had been officially recognised for his excellence in administration, both financially and medically. Nick noticed his file was open on the desk.

"What's on your mind, young man?"

Straight to the point, thought Nick, and he followed suit. "I would like to return to medicine."

"Ah! I can't say I'm not pleased. I was sorry to see you throw away a very promising career."

They talked for a long time. Nick explained his reasons for wanting to return to medicine, hoping to convey his sincerity.

"Reading through your file, I believe you are more than capable of specialising in Cardiology, but I do question your choice of hospital."

"I beg your pardon, sir?" asked Nick, puzzled.

"I'm assuming you know Alex Braun is now Head of Psychiatry at this hospital. Will this be a problem?"

So, he remembered that too. "I can truthfully say, no. I have grown stronger and wiser since then. Shouldn't be a problem."

Manning-Brooke stood. "Your application has to be put before the Board, of course; however, you will have my full support." They shook hands, firm and warm.

Pleased with how the interview had gone, Nick left on a high. He shot the receptionist a confident smile and almost skipped out the door. He wondered why he hadn't recognised earlier how much he needed to take control of his future.

Glancing at his watch, he saw that the interview had taken longer than expected. He picked up a ham and salad roll and coffee from the staff servery on his way through to join Matthew in the doctors' lounge. "Sorry, Mattie, the interview ran a bit longer than I thought." He sat down at the laminated table, amused the furniture hadn't changed in the seven years since he'd left.

"I've only been here a short time myself. How did it go?"

"Good. Manning-Brooke seemed keen enough to reinstate me. Ultimate decision is up to the Board, as you know. I made sure I kept up to date, and registered so no problems there. Might be a bit rusty at first but shouldn't take me long to get back into the swing of things. I'm pretty excited, if you hadn't noticed."

"I'm glad – it's about time. I'm guessing Cardiology is still your preferred choice."

Nick flicked the lid off his flat white, took a sip then nodded.

"It will be good to have you back, Nicky, old son. I have missed your lovable face. No doubt a few nurses might say the same."

Smiling, Nick knew only too well where that comment was leading.

"Tell me, is the long-haired beauty with the angel face the latest?"

Shrugging his shoulders, Nick faked ignorance.

"Oh, come on! I saw the way you looked at her. I want to know who she is and how you met."

"Whoa! Down boy." Nick laughed. Matthew never changed, forthright as ever. He felt somewhat embarrassed admitting Jenny had set the whole thing up and decided to tone it down a little. "We met at the Spencers'. I hadn't seen them for a while and decided to pay them a visit. Just so happens she was dining with them that night."

"How very convenient. You just happened to drop in at the Spencers' one random night and, low and behold, there's this ravishing beauty in their living room, waiting to be met. Sounds like a set-up to me."

Nick huffed out a laugh. Knowing Matthew's unique sense of perception, he knew he'd have to stay close to the truth. "Call it fate. She's one of the leading ballerinas in the Australian Ballet Company. Her feet often blister from overuse. Jenny used to treat them at the surgery but over the course of time they developed a friendship, with invitations to the ballet and so forth; hence her presence at dinner and the treating of her feet in their house."

"A leading ballerina with The Australian Ballet. Impressive."

"I think so." An uneasy feeling snaked up his spine. Matthew and his overactive imagination piecing random bits of information together could prove dangerous. He gulped at his coffee, and to his annoyance, burnt his tongue.

"A ballerina, a mother as well if my memory serves me, and beautiful. Full package."

"Correct again." Nick could almost feel the man's mind ticking over.

"I've heard it said ballerinas make for versatile lovers. True or false?"

Bang! Typical Matthew, direct and predictable. "That's a bit personal, even for you."

Matthew gave a low whistle. "You never used to be so coy. What are you not telling me? Or should I say … what don't you have to tell me?"

"My teenage days of kiss and tell are over. I would have hoped yours were too."

"Nice try but I'm not so easily fooled. You haven't slept with her yet, have you?"

Damn Matthew and his uncanny knack of hitting the mark. He changed the subject. "How's Sally?"

"Okay, I get it – mind my own business – but I'm not stupid, I can read between the lines. One last question and I'll drop it. Are you in love, Nick?"

Matthew was too astute for Nick not to confess the obvious. But in truth, he hadn't fully processed that he was deeply in love with Alicia. It had been a long time since he'd felt anything more than a mere attraction and was somewhat shaken from his comfort zone. "Yes, Matthew, I think I am."

"I knew it." He swung back on his chair, folded his hands behind his head, grinning from ear to ear he looked like he had just solved the million-dollar puzzle. "I never thought I'd see the day. It's been a long time coming. Wait till I tell Sally."

Matthew's expression changed when he mentioned his wife's name. His brow tightened and the cheerful grin slowly turned into a thin smile. He sat forward, picked up his coffee, swirled the contents.

Matthew was never good at hiding his emotions. Nick thought he looked like he needed to get something off his chest. "You didn't answer my question. Fair's fair."

"Sally ... well, you know... she's fine, I guess."

"You don't sound too convincing."

"She's gone all maternal on me. Says her biological clock is ticking and she wants a baby."

"Is that bad?"

"No. Yes … I don't know. It's me, I suppose. Kids just don't do it for me. I enjoy my freedom too much. Selfish I know, but truthful."

"Got to grow up sometime, Mattie, my man. You can't play Peter Pan forever. Sally deserves better. She's a good woman and a good wife."

"For God's sake, don't you start. I get enough lecturing at home."

Nick studied the face opposite. He'd often heard others label Matthew as a Jekyll-and-Hyde. Brilliant on one hand, a party animal on the other. He drank to excess when he went out, growing louder and more obnoxious as the night wore on. And yet, his ability to analyse, calculate and react under pressure at the operating table left other doctors in awe of his brilliance. "I hear he is Head of Psychiatry?" said Nick.

"By 'he', I'm assuming you mean Alex Braun."

"I do."

"Unfortunately, yes he is and don't he know it. Never could take to that man. I swear he majored in arrogance. He parades around the hospital like he owns the place, barely acknowledging us lesser mortals when he passes. Makes me want to puke. In any case, I would have thought you'd be over that by now, Nicholas."

"Just curious, Matthew. Just curious."

"Changing channels … I'd like to become more acquainted with this ballerina who has the most sought-after bachelor in Melbourne by the short and curlies. In fact, I'd rather like to see her dance."

"You at a ballet! Since when?" Although he was joking, the thought of introducing Alicia to his friends, giving them a glimpse of her extraordinary talent, suddenly appealed.

"Oh, ye of little faith! I've been to several ballets over the years. Swan Lake for one. How about we get the crew together

– a night at the ballet then dinner to finish – like old times?" "Like old times." That took him back.

***

On his way to the TV station, Nick rehashed his meeting with Manning-Clarke: full of positives and possibilities. But his mind soon switched to Matthew and his comments about the so-called crew and old times. Rebecca had been part of the crew, for a short while.

Those early days, dating her and working at The Royal, were some of the happiest times of Nick's life. He thought he was the luckiest dog alive when she agreed to marry him. But he had buried the pain of her betrayal long ago. It was his puppy-like adoration that still caused him misery. She had played him for a fool, carrying on behind his back, humiliating him in front of his friends. Just thinking about the smug look on Alex Braun's face when he walked in on his cheating wife, locked naked in Braun's embrace, made his blood boil.

He remembered well the day he was working in the Emergency Unit. It had been uncommonly quiet that day, and like all dedicated interns who worked around the clock, Nick looked and felt exhausted. The Senior Registrar, finding him in the bathroom splashing water on his face to keep from falling asleep, said he looked as though he could do with the afternoon off, and sent him home.

He called Rebecca at work, hoping they could do something crazy together. The receptionist told him his wife had signed off early that afternoon, complaining she felt unwell. Worried, he stopped at the local florist and bought her a small bouquet of pink roses. He spent a lot of time choosing them – nothing but the best for Rebecca – and raced home to surprise her. Oh, he surprised her all right. Except, not quite the surprise either of them expected.

He could still recall how shocked he was, standing like a stuffed dummy, staring at the two of them lying on the dishevelled sheets on his bed, Braun's hand resting on Rebecca's naked butt. Braun had made a sarcastic remark – he couldn't remember what it was – and then, laughing, they pulled the sheet over their faces.

He stumbled from the house, stunned and into his car. He drove aimlessly for hours. Finally, he pulled into a parking bay along the coast, fell out the car door, and spewed until his stomach ached. And there he stayed, slumped face-deep in dirt until he woke several hours later.

When a talent scout from Channel Seven Studio turned up at the hospital looking for a young innovative doctor to host a medical program that would be telecast state-wide, Nick saw it as the perfect escape. With only two weeks left, he finished his internship. About to start a postgraduate degree specialising in Cardiology, he resigned from the hospital.

Several people, including Matthew and Sally, tried to talk him into reconsidering, but he remained adamant. Rebecca told him, being married to a boring doctor drove her insane, said she wanted more fun out of life than waiting for Nick to return home stinking of blood and guts each day. Braun became the preliminary stepping-stone to financial freedom. She later left him too, bestowing her favours on a richer, worthier beneficiary.

Sweet revenge came a few years later when she turned up on his doorstep, whimpering like a wounded dog. She swore she'd changed; promised to make amends, if only he would give her a second chance. He had no trouble refusing: everything down to her shoes repulsed him. Nick later heard the last sucker had dumped her for a twenty-year-old model.

As they say, love is blind. How he could have misjudged her character so completely, he would never understand. In hindsight, he realised the relationship was destined for failure from the start. Eventually, he would have needed more than a party girl with a pretty face to share his life.

Without the setback, and given the same circumstances, he would be a qualified cardiologist by now. But he knew he would do it again if he had too. Thanks to the TV show, he could afford to live comfortably through the next five years while he specialised.

What was it Matthew had said? Like old times. Old times, he thought, were way overrated.

***

Alicia was determined to get back into shape. Knowing she would be performing in front of Nick's friends, she decided to attempt a training session, even though Nick had warned her to wait until she'd completely recovered. She thought she might try doing a class with the senior ballet school, which tied in perfectly with Sophie's ballet lessons after school.

The first person they ran into was Meg Thomas, the young dancer she met at St. Kilda the day of her accident.

After giving her a hug, Meg stood back, eyeing her head. "Alicia, how are you? My parents and I were so upset at what happened. We feel responsible for taking you away from your little girl."

"I'm fine, really. Don't blame yourselves, whatever you do." Alicia looked down at Sophie wriggling beside her. "Off you go then." Sophie ran up the corridor to the junior studios, swinging her shoes by the ribbons. "And be good." She looked back at Meg, "… if that's possible."

"Poor little thing … is she okay?"

"Poor little thing, my pink ballet shoe! She frightened me half to death." Meg returned her smile. She really was a sweet unassuming girl, and Alicia hoped Meg's ability matched her desire to dance.

"I know you missed opening night and several other performances. How long before you can go back?"

"Actually, I thought I might do class with you today, to see if I have my ballet legs yet. Do you think anyone would mind?"

"Mind! Are you kidding?"

Meg hooked her arm through Alicia's and walked with her to the change room. When they entered, the other students went quiet, their jaws dropping at the sight of Meg, her arm linked with one of the principal dancers of the Company. If she hadn't been so worried about how her body would cope under the pressure, Alicia might have enjoyed the moment a lot more.

"Alicia, come in, put your bag in my locker. Move over, Laura, so Alicia can sit there. She wants to take class with us."

After seeking approval from Miss Hathaway, the school ballet mistress, Alicia went to the end of the *barre* to avoid distracting the students from their lesson. Her hamstrings were tight from spending too much time in bed and she was glad when the music started. Feet in *first position*, she bent into a *demi plié*; then, holding her breath, her heels to the floor, she continued into *full plié*, happy to be doing what she did best. She worked hard at the *barre*, ignoring the faint dizziness that appeared at the end of *grand battement en cloche*.

Meg, moving past her to take her place in the centre, asked how she was going. Alicia nodded but with little conviction as she wiped the sweat from her brow. By the time she had finished the *allegro* section her head pounded, but it was the *pirouettes* that finished her off. With the room whirling like a kaleidoscope, she excused herself, grabbed her towel and rushed to the bathroom to splash water on her face. Gasping for breath, she held the towel to her mouth as she fought the nausea swirling in her stomach.

Meg was first through the door of the dressing room, full of concern. "You don't look at all well. You've gone really white. Perhaps I could call someone for you?"

"No, but thanks." She knew Brandon would probably be having an afternoon sleep. It had been well after midnight when she heard him in the shower and he had to be up early for a morning class. Besides, she had the car. Each time she leant forward to take off her shoes the dizziness increased, and she was forced to sit up.

"Here, let me do that." Crouching in front of Alicia, Meg untied the ribbons of her flats, slipped them from her feet and put them into a plastic drawstring bag.

By this time several other students had wandered in and were keen to help. She felt like an invalid, and even more of a fool when she tried to stand and had to sit down again.

"Alicia, you can't go home in this condition."

"I'll be okay once I'm in the fresh air. If you wouldn't mind helping me outside, I need to find Sophie."

"Of course not." Meg hooked her arm through Alicia's and assisted her off the seat. She was thankful to see Sophie skipping up the passage, munching an apple and holding the hand of one of the dancers from Meg's class.

"Thank goodness." One less problem she had to face out of the many more to come.

"Don't you feel well, Mummy?"

"No, not too good, darling."

"Are you sure I can't call someone for you?" asked Meg,

lowering her onto the garden wall outside the building.

Sophie sat beside her. "Why don't we call Nick?"

"No!" He was the last person on earth she wanted to find her in this condition. Several times over the last few days, she had asked him, even begged if she could do class. Every time, he had said no. She knew he would be annoyed if he found out she'd deliberately ignored his advice.

"Thanks so much Meg, for all your help, but honestly I'll be okay once I take a few deep breaths."

"Are you sure? Because my mum will be here soon and I know she wouldn't mind giving you a lift."

"No, my car is parked just around the corner. I'll be fine."

"If you're sure, then I'd better go. I always meet Mum on the other side of the road near the ice-cream shop. Although I don't have one very often, Turkish delight is my favourite," she said, pulling a cheeky face. "Bye Alicia. Bye Sophie."

Alicia watched Meg spring across the road, wishing she felt as spritely. "Okay, let's give this a go." No more than two minutes passed before the dizziness returned and the throbbing in her head escalated to a crescendo. Desperate to lie down, she sat on the wall of a built-in garden outside an accounting firm, and rested her head against a small tree.

Sophie grabbed her bag and pulled out her mobile. "I'm going to call Nick," she said, skipping out of reach.

Too weak to argue, Alicia watched Sophie fiddle with the buttons. She felt so sick she thought she was going to throw up on top of the petunias.

"Hello, Nick, it's Sophie."

"I'm good but mummy is sick and we can't get home." That stung. Alicia could almost feel his heated words from where she sat.

"Yes, she has, and now she's sick. She didn't want me to ring you, but Uncle Brandon is asleep and I want you to come and get us."

Sophie started looking around. "Mummy's sitting on a wall, of a very big building. A … C … C … it has plants growing in it."

"Yep, it's just there," she said, pointing to the Arts Centre.

***

The traffic was fairly intense on a Saturday morning and driving through Melbourne was almost bumper-to-bumper. Not until he drove up Collins Street did he get a free run. Nick was glad he had chosen to live close to the city and not the outer suburbs. Although it was a lot more expensive, it was also a lot more convenient to where he worked as well as to the coast; and soon to be the hospital; and now, of course, the ballet centre. Turning into Kavanagh Street, he spotted a group of young women all with the same bun hairstyle, their feet pointing in an abnormally outwards direction, walking along the footpath and knew he must be close.

He spotted Alicia sitting on a brick wall slumped against the trunk of a small tree with Sophie fussing around her, stroking her arm. He pulled up on the opposite side of the road. If he wasn't so vexed because she had ignored his advice, he might have felt more sympathetic. Sophie was first to see him and jumping off the wall, waved.

"Sophie, don't go near the road," he heard Alicia say. She lowered her eyes when she saw him crossing the street. He was glad to see she at least felt some remorse for dancing when he told he not to.

"Mummy's been sick in the garden."

"Funny that. I'm sure the doctor advised her not to dance for this very reason." She peaked at him from under her lashes, guilt written on her pale face. Far from letting her off the hook, he raised his eyebrows, before scooping her into his arms. "This is becoming a habit. I feel like a human ambulance, transporting you in my arms all over Melbourne.”

“I can w …”

“Be quiet!” He was in no mood for a stance on independence. As far as he was concerned, she deserved to be chastised. Next time she might listen to the professional.

“Sophie, hold on to my pocket while we cross the road and don’t let go.”

“Nick, listen … I …”

“No! I won’t! I told you not to dance and you should have taken my advice.” He dumped her in the back seat of the car, and having fastened Sophie securely in her seat belt, drove to Camberwell.

Brandon was sipping coffee at the kitchen table, the paper opened in front of him when Nick entered. “Crikey Moses, what now!”

“Exactly!” Nick kept hold of Alicia in his arms. “Sophie tells me your car is still at the Centre. Do you need a lift to the theatre or somewhere?”

“Eh! Should be okay.”

“Sophie can come with me for the day until this one gets better.” He felt like a brute. Alicia’s complexion had sallowed even more – if that were possible. She needed bed and he carried her through to her room. He removed her shoes before tucking her under the covers. She looked so miserable he didn’t have the heart to just walk away. “I don’t have anything to give you but I think a good sleep should do the trick.”

She twisted the button on her shirt, thanked him. He had grown to love her habit of twisting things when she was nervous or upset and he hated seeing her weak and vulnerable. If she hadn’t needed sleep so badly, he would have taken her in his arms and kissed the life out of her. “Next time, do what you’re told.” Her lids were fluttering to stay awake and, taking one last look at her sweet face, he quietly left the room.

“Ready Sophie?” he asked, walking into the kitchen. Like a

magnet, she slid her hand into his. "I might need a key to get back in."

"Roger." Brandon slipped a key from the hook inside the pantry and threw it to Nick, who having promised to return it, left taking Sophie with him.

***

Alicia listened to the footsteps receding down the passage, then the door closing, followed by silence. She lifted the doona up under her chin, turned away from the light coming through the window, to see Brandon leaning against the door frame of her room, a cup in his hand. He raised his eyebrows, a crooked smile on his face. "Phew … trouble in paradise?"

"He's a bit miffed with me and I feel so sick." She hated Nick being angry with her and loved that he had come to her rescue. She could have accepted a lift with Meg's mother but it would have been an inconvenience. With Nick it was different. She wanted to be his inconvenience, his problem.

"Why, what happened?" Entering her room, he placed the tea on the bedside table and lowered himself to her bed.

"I took class with the senior school. Afterward, I couldn't even walk, I felt so dizzy. I threw up in the garden."

"Ouch! I hate to say it, but he did warn you."

"I know, but the thought of Nick and all his clever doctor friends coming to the show to see me dance scared me witless. I figured if I didn't get out of bed soon and back to class, it'd be Yvette they saw, not me."

"You stoopid goose! It'll be Yvette they see if you don't take it easy. Besides, you're outstanding even at your worst. As though Nick's dumb friends would be able to tell the difference. They might be doctor-smart but they're certainly not world critics in ballet. In any case, he wouldn't be bringing them if he didn't think you were unbelievably great." He felt her head with the back of his hand. "You're as white as a sheet. I'll bring you a couple of Panadols; save some of that tea to drink them with. Think of it as lunch, guaranteed cure."

Alicia woke hours later, pain-free and hungry, which she considered a healthy sign. Careful not to tempt fate, she slowly hung her legs over the side of the bed, waited to see if the dizziness had completely gone. To her relief, it had. Her room was in darkness, and instinct told her the apartment was empty. Wandering into the lounge she turned on the light. Brandon would be at the theatre of course but he had left her a note telling her Nick had a key to let himself in. It was already seven o'clock, close to Sophie's bedtime and she wondered where they were.

She hadn't eaten for hours and decided to make herself an omelette. She was searching for a bowl when she heard the front door open. For a split second her heart skipped a beat until she remembered the note.

"Mummy, Mummy," called Sophie, running into the kitchen, followed by Nick.

Alicia bent down with her arms outstretched for Sophie to run straight into them. "Have you had a good day, darling?"

Sophie looked from Nick back to Alicia, a smile on her face as bright as the sun. "I went to Nick's place," she said, taking Alicia's face between her hands.

Alicia peeked at Nick over the top of Sophie's head. He was leaning against the doorframe, an unreadable look on his face. "Are you hungry, darling?" she asked Sophie.

"No, that's what else. Nick bought me a burger, with the works. That's what the man said, didn't he, Nick?"

"Yes."

The deadpan face convinced her he was still annoyed. Once she settled Sophie, she would explain to him why she had gone against his advice. "Come on then, let's get you showered and ready for bed."

After tucking Sophie in her bed, she decided to take a shower while Nick said goodnight to Sophie. She'd been too sick to change her clothes after he'd brought her home in the morning. When she walked back into the kitchen, it was empty, he'd gone.

The stillness was suffocating. Determined not to let his leaving affect her, humming Chopin's Sylphide, she cracked eggs into a bowl. "What does one more miserable night alone matter," she mumbled as she whisked away, splashing some of the yoke onto her fingers.

"I refuse to let myself fall apart." No sooner had the words left her lips when the tears fell. She brushed them away with the back of her hand smearing sticky egg over her face. As she tried wiping it off, fallen strands of hair stuck to her gluggy fingers and she stamped her foot.

Brandon was right! – she was a stupid, stupid goose! Why would anyone want to hang around a miserable, incompetent, sad sack like her?

Using the back of her wrist, she pushed the lengths of hair behind her ears. But when she poured the mixture into the frying pan, her hair fell forward, blocking her view and she spilled some of it on the bench. Counting backward from ten, she placed the pan on the stove, turned on the gas. Heaven help her if Brandon came home to this mess. Bowl, whisk, spatula all went in the sink and, turning on the water, she started to wash dishes.

There were times, like now, when she craved the loving arms of her mother. Precious words of wisdom she knew would wash away the dreadful longing, threatening to break her spirit. So, caught up in a whirlpool of misery she forgot about the omelette until the pungent smell of burnt eggs wafted up her nostrils. "Oh no!" With water dripping from her hands she ran to turn off the gas; stared at the charred piece of rubber still sizzling in the pan.

"What are you doing?" asked Nick, from the doorway.

She swung around knocking the handle of the frying pan with her arm and flipping the burnt offering into the air. It splattered on the floor, landing next to the spinning pan.

Nick burst out laughing.

Two bags of groceries filled his arms. He must have gone out to buy food for dinner but he should have told her … or left a note … something. His laughing was the final straw. As he moved to put the groceries on the bench, she stepped aside but he too moved sideways blocking her path.

He walked her backward, pinned her against the bench and placed the bags on either side, keeping her trapped within the circle of his arms. Hurt, confused, embarrassed, heat flooded her face. And that stupid smile of his made her cross. "How dare you laugh at me!"

"Callous I know but you did look funny – still do." He grabbed the tea towel from the bench, wiped egg from her face and hair, and taking both her hands in his, lifted them to his lips. She hoped her face wasn't as red as the flames dancing in her heart. He released her hands and wrapped his arms around her waist until their bodies and lips touched. *This is all happening too fast …* voices in her head – her mother's – the promise – God – Church … yelling at her to stop. She placed her hand on his chest to ease him away.

Nick threaded his fingers through her hair, soothed away her qualms with sweet, tender words full of kindness. Happy to rest in his strength, she lay her head on his shoulder. Nobody told her about desire … desire that swept through her body like fire. She wanted him, needed him. One kiss, just one kiss. With his lips pressed against her ear, he whispered her name. Desperate to see what was written on his face, in his eyes, she lifted her head abruptly and smacked him on the chin with her wounded head. Startled, he jerked back, stepping into the greasy omelette. Unable to counter-balance with Alicia still in his arms, he lost his balance, toppled over, and crashed to the floor with Alicia on top of him.

Fearing the impact from his chin might have reopened her wound, she pressed at her stitches. Finding no blood on her hands, she hunched to her knees.

Nick lay as stiff as a board staring at the ceiling with the omelette stuck to the sole of his shoe. She wondered if he could be concussed with his eyes open. "Nick, it's me … Alicia. Are you alright?"

When he didn't speak, she dropped her head onto his chest. "Oh God, Nick, talk to me?"

She felt his stomach shake and looked up to see him chuckling. Before she could react, he rolled her on her back, and settled himself on top of her. Her heart beat so loud she wondered if he could hear it. She closed her eyes and settled into the warmth of his affection. The touch of his lips nuzzling the skin on her neck, the feel of his legs entwined with hers and his muscular chest and shoulders pressing against her flesh, left her craving.

"I've been so terribly stupid."

"True," he said, kissing first one cheek then the other.

"I did the class because I didn't want you to be disappointed in me in front of your friends."

"Oh," he said, nipping at her lips with his own.

"And when I came into the kitchen, you were gone ... Are you still upset with me?"

He lowered his head until his lips joined hers. Nervous and unsure, she lay quite still, hoping he wouldn't guess she'd never been kissed before. His soft teasing lips slowly prised hers apart.

He tasted of coffee, strong and delicious, filling her head with the aroma of desire. She couldn't fight the urges begging to explore, to feel, to be with a man like Nick, and to let her body enjoy the sensation his kiss had ignited. But, like the chords of a violin floating through an opus, came her mother's voice reminding her of a promise she'd made at sixteen. It was only a kiss but a kiss awakened a yearning to know more, more than she could give a man as experienced as Nick would expect. Guilt tore through her like a hurricane and, scrambling out from under him she sprang to her feet, the weight of her past a heavy burden on her shoulders.

Nick also stood and grabbing the sponge from the sink, wiped remnants of egg from his shirt and pants. "Not the normal reaction I get when I kiss a woman," he muttered, the muscles in his jaw tightening as he spoke.

Alicia noticed he hadn't made eye contact with her since he had moved off the floor. She had embarrassed him. "I'm not your normal woman."

"I won't argue with that."

No, she supposed he wouldn't but did he understand why?

"If you want this relationship to continue you had better find a way to tell me what it is that's troubling you." He threw the sponge in the sink, spread his hands, prompting a response.

She had to agree, standing in his shoes she must appear very abnormal. She wanted to explain to him why she couldn't love him like he wanted her too. But how could she tell him now when he struggled to even look at her.

"I'll see myself out," he said. Reaching into his pocket, he threw the keys to her apartment onto the coffee table. Without so much as a goodbye, he left her standing alone wondering if he would ever return.

Chapter Nine

Alicia walked into the kitchen, noticed the Herald Sun on the table, opened at the page with Yvette in Brandon's arms. She read the review with an aching heart. It mentioned Louis' choreography; how his unique imagination strengthened what was often described as a morbid and unsavoury ballet. It also praised Brandon's ability to adapt to whichever dancer he partnered, and complimented Yvette on her dramatic and sensitive interpretation of the depraved prostitute, *Manon*.

She had to get out of this house and back to dancing before Yvette became too comfortable in the role. A week of inactivity since the accident was enough. Nick might be the doctor but she was the dancer and this was her life. The cut on her head no longer throbbed or hurt to touch, and the dizziness had stopped, even after multiple sequences of *pirouettes*. Her muscles craved to be stretched, and she craved to escape the prison cell of boredom that waged war in her mind the longer she stayed home.

Driving with Brandon to the theatre in the early afternoon, Alicia inhaled the breeze blowing through the window of the car. Its gentle warmth on her skin helped ease the tension in her neck and shoulders. Although she hated being out of action, the break had revitalised her enthusiasm. She looked forward to feeling the *barre* beneath her hand and tasting the salt from hard-earned sweat on her lips.

Backstage, several dancers said how pleased they were to see her. It was customary for *the prima ballerina* to have the main dressing room in the theatre but she was unprepared for the depth of her resentment when she found Yvette seated in front of the mirror, tying her ribbons.

"Great write-up in The Herald, Yvette." She hoped she sounded genuine.

Yvette accepted the compliment, somewhat begrudgingly judging by the stiff nod of thanks she received as Yvette shifted her gear closer to the wall, to make room.

After class, Louis beckoned Alicia to join him in the auditorium. When she sat beside him, he lowered his feet, propped on the seat in front "How are you feeling, Ma Petite?"

"Much better, thanks, Louis."

"Bon, bon. I think Yvette should finish the week. She's done an excellent job of *Manon*. Good reviews too. You can take over on Monday night. I'll be at the studio on Sunday if you need to slip in some extra practice."

She was glad to take Louis up on his offer and spent most of the weekend rehearsing for Monday night's performance. Yvette had become far too comfortable with the role and Alicia needed to remind Louis why he had chosen her for his leading lady.

***

Back on stage! She soaked up the atmosphere and the excitement a performance generated. She loved it all: it was part of who she was, where she belonged. Her body thrived on the physical commitment this ballet demanded. At the end of the final act, Brandon led her to the front of the stage for the fourth and final call. She sank into a deep curtsey and waited for the curtain to close.

"It's so good to have you back. You were exquisite tonight. Absolutely sensational! Not even Antoinette Sibley could have done it better."

"Thank you, Brandy. I missed it all so much, and you, of

course."

"Oh, don't overdo it. You might kill me with praise."

Laughing, she threw her arms around his neck; squeezed him tight.

"Coming?" he asked, holding out his hand for her to go with him to the change rooms.

"No, you go ahead. I won't be long."

Alicia stood in the middle of the stage; her right foot poised *on pointe*. She loved to dance for Louis. He never failed to praise her for giving the audience the exact verve he wanted portrayed in his ballets. He likened her dancing to that of the willow tree whose long supple limbs captured the graceful flow of simplicity.

But tonight's performance felt different, disturbing. *Manon* was a sensual woman, whose passion and mystery finds her embroiled in a web of love, deception, and death. Alicia understood passion, death – particularly death – but she knew little about sensual love. She was nothing like *Manon*, the prostitute, and everything like *Manon* the broken-hearted. She looked up at the rich drapes. *You are like the windows of my heart. I come to life when you open and shut down when you close.*

Nick was chipping away at the protective shield she had spent the last six years building. Emotions she thought were safely locked away were escaping. Alicia gathered the curtains in her arms, pressed the silky velvet against her skin and inhaled their rich smell. She had thought performing on stage was the most exhilarating feeling she could hope to experience. But she was wrong. One long, loving kiss and her world had turned upside down. She walked into the front wing of the stage, sat on a stool, and untied the ribbons of her pointe shoes.

Brandon pulled back the side drape, worry lines about his eyes. "What are you doing?"

Shrugging her shoulders, she asked herself the same question.

He crouched in front of her, rested his arms on her knees. "Are you okay?"

She twirled the ribbons around her shoes and, staring at the floor with her bottom lip between her teeth, she shook her head. She wanted to tell him how lonely she was; how much she wanted to be like everyone else; to be able to love and be loved, like him and Kieran. But the knife lodged in her chest twisted and she couldn't bring herself to release it.

"I love you, Ally. I always will, you know that. Nobody understands you like I do, but I can't help you unless you tell me what's wrong."

Taking his hand, she cradled it in her own. "Something about dancing *Manon* tonight – her life, her death, maybe her pain – I'm not sure exactly, but it opened old wounds. I don't think I will ever get over their death. I miss them more than ever. Nothing new and nothing you can do." She smiled softly, knowing their kind of love wasn't enough anymore. Not for her, not for him, and not forever.

He nodded; dropped a kiss on her forehead. "I'm going out. Take the car. I'll bum a lift home."

Alicia was pleased Sophie had stayed at Jenny's for the night instead of at the theatre. It meant regular meals, early nights and no sleeping on a makeshift bed on the dressing room floor, then being carried by one of the stagehands to the car after the show. But it also meant Alicia arrived home to an empty apartment. She had learned to deal with her grief and loneliness over the years, but there was something unbearable about the stillness of an empty house with no presence or body keeping it alive.

The tributes had been outstanding after her performance. Praise and congratulations flowed like champagne through to the last member of the *corps,* and the flowers from Louis filled her dressing room with a rich, rose fragrance. But the accolades brought little comfort as she sat in the dark with her hands wrapped around a mug of warm milk, staring at the flowers on the kitchen bench.

She remembered those earlier years after a performance with

the Academy, going home with Sophie to her house in Milton Street, aching for her mother and pleading with God for answers, in the dark, cold kitchen. Why? Why her? What had she done to incur such punishment? Six years later she had adjusted to her situation. No more unanswerable questions. But she would always wonder how different her life might have been had the accident never occurred. Perhaps she would have stayed in Perth, married, had children, lived as a Christian, believing in God and his promises. Instead, she was alone in Melbourne, staring down the tunnel of a precarious future. In ten years' time she would be thirty-three, nearing the end of her ballet life. Many dancers in the past, consumed with their careers, ended up single and living on the pittance of a ballet mistress' wage, with only their memories for company. Would this be her fate too?

She touched her lips, the memory of his kiss still there. She hadn't heard from Nick since that awful night in the kitchen and wondered if he had changed his mind about bringing his friends to see her dance. Next time. *There will never be a next time.*

***

The final night of the season arrived and Louis reported a full house. Nick had rung earlier confirming he and his friends would be sitting in the dress circle. He sounded excited and the relief she felt was enormous. The lights faded out, quieting the crowd. Alicia stood in the wings with Brandon beside her, both his hands on her shoulders as they waited for the orchestra to finish playing the introduction.

"I can't believe you're this nervous," he said, massaging her neck.

"They'll all be watching me."

"No!" he remarked dryly. "Is that what they do at the ballet?"

"You know what I mean."

"No, I don't. Together we will dance till their eyeballs fall out. Now stop this craziness and let's show them what they paid to see."

He dropped a good luck kiss on her shoulder and, taking her hand, led her on to the stage and into instant applause. So many different emotions tapped into the heart of the character, *Manon*. Surrendering Alicia, she became the sister who adored her cheating brother, the conniving prostitute who would do anything to obtain wealth, and the damaged woman who died in her lover's arms of a broken heart.

Each act was an emotional challenge, but the last one most of all. She gave it everything she had, throwing herself into the role and into Brandon's steady arms with complete confidence. They were daring lifts which took skill and strength. Hesitate for a second and she could find herself dangling upside down or worse, sprawled out on the stage floor. Sweat poured from her till the very end, with Brandon slumped over her dead body, sobbing at the loss of his true love.

One of the ushers presented her with a large bouquet of ruby red roses. With the conductor on her left, Brandon on her right, Alicia took her final curtain call. When she curtsied low, with the flowers cradled in her arms, the audience rose from their seats, cheering loudly. Random cries of *Bravo* could be heard around the auditorium. One young man, clutched at his heart, raced to the foot of the stage and threw a small bunch of flowers to her. Picking them up she blew him a kiss. Laughter rippled across the theatre until the curtains drew together for the last time, bringing the production to an end.

In the dressing room, Alicia placed the flowers on the bench and sat to catch her breath. Smiling at the thought of the young man who had given them to her, she gently fingered the velvet petals of the roses in the larger bouquet, when she noticed a card and a maroon pouch with gold drawstrings attached to the cellophane paper. Louis always gave her flowers on opening night but not normally at the end of a season and never with a present attached. She turned the card over in her hand, opened it up. *Wear them with love, From Nick.* She lifted out a pair of diamond stud earrings; stared at them until her eyes stung.

How many times over the years had she watched dancers receive presents from their loved ones? It hurt knowing her family would never come to the theatre, never see her dance or bring her flowers. She had schooled herself not to look at the gifts for too long, had pretended it didn't matter, and to act happy for the person who had received them. When she opened her hand to look at the diamonds twinkling under the lights she wondered if he had any idea how much his gift meant to her. They were more than mere earrings sparkling against her skin. They were priceless shards of joy, a joy she had almost forgotten existed, dancing in her heart.

***

Spellbound by her performance, Nick remained glued to his seat. The audience started to shuffle toward the exits. Matthew's wife, Sally, reached over and patted Nick's arm.

"That was amazing. She's beautiful Nick, absolutely beautiful. Made me cry."

"I knew you would enjoy it." Nick took her hand, slipped it through his arm as they moved out of their seats into the aisle. He walked with her behind Matthew who was talking to Jack and Lynette Bronson. He tried to concentrate on what Sally was saying but his thoughts kept drifting. The last time he had waited in the foyer of this theatre, his interest in Alicia was barely a spark. Now, it was a wild fire burning out of control along with his doubts about a possible future with this talented woman and her career.

Matthew joined them. Nick thought he looked annoyed, irritated. Something was eating at him and Nick was reminded of their conversation over lunch, at the hospital.

"How is a two-left-footed klutz like you going to live up to that?"

"Matthew! Nick is nervous enough."

Nick wondered if he had made a mistake inviting everyone tonight. Nothing ever stayed the same and, looking at his friends he realised they had all changed: they were no longer students with exams to worry about, but adults and parents with work responsibilities. Nick realised he'd let his ego dictate over logic inviting his friends to the ballet. Did it really matter to him what Lynette or Jack or any of the others thought of her?

"I think she's coming," said Sally

He looked up to see Alicia walking down the steps, wearing the same dress she had worn on their first date. Her delicate skin pearled against the dark fabric, her hair swept back off her face, revealing a pair of diamond earrings, and carrying the bouquets, one in each arm. She stopped at the bottom step and handed the flowers to Brandon who waved at Nick before heading out the doors with Kieran.

He couldn't take his eyes off her. His heart beat so hard he thought his chest might explode. He kept his pace steady as he went to join her. The smell of roses lingered. He caught hold of her hands, mouthed her name.

With her hand in his, he led her over to the group. He made the introductions, ignoring the fact she was twisting his fingers out of shape, as everyone congratulated her on a wonderful performance.

"You certainly look different from the last time we met," said Matthew. "How's your head?"

She looked up at Nick. "Better, thanks."

Jack looked at his watch. "Shall we go? It's late and I'm hungry!" He guided his wife towards the exit.

The restaurant was close to the theatre and Nick enjoyed the evening breeze on his face, the moonlight guiding their steps as he moseyed along behind the others with her arm linked in his. "You were stunning tonight." He couldn't see her face in the night-light but could visualise the faint blush he'd become accustomed to as she thanked him.

As the others entered the restaurant, she pressed her hand against his chest. "I want to tell you something before we go inside."

Apprehension flooded him and he braced himself. Searching her face, he tried to smile away his fears. "I'm all ears."

She stared at the button she was twisting on his shirt. "Being in Melbourne … alone … I mean … well, not completely alone … but on my …"

"Alicia!"

"No one has ever given me a present or flowers before." She peered up at him then. "Apart from Louis, of course, who always arranges for a bouquet to be presented on stage. They're beautiful. I love them. Thank you so much."

With her head turned into the light, he fingered the diamond earring. He remembered giving Rebecca everything she had wanted when they were dating. As a young medical student, it had cost him heavily and he always felt it was never enough. And here was this darling girl looking at him like he had given her the world. He placed his hand over her fingers to stop her twisting the button off his shirt. "Should I be jealous of Louis?"

"Louis! No, it's his job. He gives all his leading ladies flowers on opening night." She smiled at him. "Even Yvette."

He smoothed the back of his fingers along the side of her face. "Better go inside before Matthew sends out a search party." He could think of other things he would rather be doing, and polite conversation wasn't one of them.

Nick didn't need to ask where his friends were sitting. He led Alicia toward the roar of laughter coming from the back of the room. Matthew's hand tightly wrapped around a half empty bottle of wine caused him a momentary pause. Past experienced warned him to tread carefully. Matthew and alcohol didn't mix well. "Something funny?" he asked, addressing the group.

"Matthew's been telling tales out of school," said Sally, causing another outburst of giggles amongst the group.

A strong suspicion he was the butt of their entertainment, crossed Nick's mind. In the warmth of the restaurant, he removed his coat and hung it on the back of the chair.

"Am I supposed to pay half this time?" asked Alicia.

He took her hand, cocooned it between his own. "My treat," he whispered against her ear, drinking in the delicate fragrance of Coco Chanel.

The bulldog frown hanging on Matthew's face, worried Nick. Sally, too, looked upset. She placed her hand on her husband's arm, preventing him from taking another drink. He shrugged off her hand and gulped down the remainder of wine in his glass. To Nick's surprise he poured himself another, emptying the bottle, and gulped that down too. Then he slammed his glass on the table, called to the waitress to bring him another bottle. Sally grabbed her handbag; shot to her feet.

"Need to pee – won't be long."

If Nick wasn't mistaken this was the third time Sally had been to the bathroom in the space of two hours – twice at the theatre and again now. It started him thinking. If what he thought was true and Sally was pregnant, it would go a long way to explain Matthew's mood. He felt for Alicia's hand and lifted it to his lips. "Would you like a drink?"

"No, thanks, water's fine. I have a plane to catch in the morning."

"A plane! Where are you going?" Nick felt as though he had been socked in the stomach.

"Queensland."

"Queensland," he repeated under his breath. Now she mentioned it he did remember her telling him she was flying to

Brisbane, then to Sydney for a trial dance or some such thing, but he hadn't realised it was so soon.

"Are you some kind of parrot? "Plane! Queensland!" said Matthew, mimicking a parrot as he poured himself another drink.

If that was supposed to be Matthew's attempt at humour, Nick wasn't laughing. He reminded Nick of a spoilt child, chucking a tantrum because his life wasn't going his way.

He was glad when dinner arrived: it would shut Matthew up for a while and give him a quiet moment with the beauty by his side. "When do you open?"

"Tuesday week."

"That's ten days away. How long is the tour?"

"Two weeks. Then I fly to Sydney for a trial week with the Sydney Dance Company. I did tell you Nick, when I was sick, in bed, remember."

"I know, I know. I didn't realise you were leaving so soon and for so long. I'll miss you."

She rubbed her cheek against his arm, smiled at him and he kissed the button nose. The thought of a whole month without seeing her, killed his appetite.

"For God sake, you two! Get a room," said Matthew, between drinks.

"From what Matthew tells us you're not very interested in rooms," Lynette quipped.

They all laughed, except Matthew. A pair of tight eyes stared at Nick from across the table. Matthew's flushed cheeks matched the crimson table cloth, and his glass, held aloft towards Alicia, swung like a pendulum, splashing wine over his dinner.

Close to shoving his fist down Matthew's throat, Nick too, faked a laugh. He placed his arm around Alicia's shoulder and gave her a quick squeeze.

"Sounds like you're jealous, Mattie." Jack grinned, pointing his knife at Matthew.

Nick kept a steady eye on Matthew, watched him gulp down another mouthful and waited for Jack's provocative comment to work its poison. *And Bingo.*

"Jealous!" Matthew spat the word across the table on a splutter of red wine. "Told me himself, he's still pushing to find out if ballerinas make for versatile lovers. That's why you're trying so hard, hey, Nicky boy!"

A paralysed hush spread over the group. Nick tensed, his fury itching for retaliation. He felt Alicia flinch when a smothered giggle came from the far end of the table. He seized her hand. She tried pulling it away but he tightened his grip.

"I think you've had enough to drink," Sally said, pale-faced, then mouthed the word 'Sorry'. Matthew snatched up his glass, splashing the remainder of his wine over Lynette's white pants. She and Jack scraped back their chairs and jumped to their feet. Grabbing a handful of napkins, they dabbed at the stain. "I think it's time we made tracks." Jack's annoyance was unmistakable.

"Besides it late and I have an early start tomorrow," said Lynette.

Nick could almost feel Alicia's anger sizzling like an overheated radiator. He knew that once he moved, he would have to let go of her hand. But she pushed back her chair, stood, and he was forced to release his grip. Their eyes met for a brief second. He wanted to yell so loud it would blow Matthew's eardrums apart. Months of building her trust, destroyed in one insane drunken moment.

He pulled out his wallet as the group divvied the bill, gave the cash to Jack. Clutching her bag, Alicia followed the others outside. She stepped away when he joined her on the sidewalk. He wanted to explain, but one glance at the clenched jaw, the dark flashing eyes and he changed his mind. As they walked silently behind the others to the carpark, he prayed for an answer, something he hadn't done for a long time.

Everyone muttered their goodbyes as they stepped from the

carpark lift, and hurried off to find their vehicles. Sally gave a quick wave, battling to support a dishevelled Matthew, leaving Alicia and Nick standing like cracked pillars.

Alicia started walking towards the lift. Nick caught hold of her hand. "Wait."

"Let go of my hand!" The venom in her voice startled him and he dropped her hand, instantly.

"Can we talk about this?"

"I think Matthew said it all," she said continuing to walk.

Not willing to give up without a fight he recaptured her hand. "Get this straight … if you think I'm going to let you walk the streets of Melbourne at midnight, you are very mistaken. I'll drag you to the car kicking and screaming if I have to."

He watched the rise and fall of her chest, the clenched fist at her side, as she weighed her options. At last she relented, indicated with a quick nod. He slowly released her hand until he was sure she wasn't going to bolt and followed her to his car.

The silence, tense and explosive, filled the space between their seats. His thoughts knocked together, arguing his own defence. When he pulled up at the apartment block, Alicia scrambled out of the car, slamming the door.

He chased her up the driveway, planted himself in front of her and she stopped. "Alicia, can we please talk about this?"

"From what I heard you've said enough."

He wanted to take her in his arms, hold her until her anger died, and give him a chance to explain. "What Matthew said derived from a very drunk and disgruntled man, whose perspective was extremely tarnished. And I might point out, if I was in this purely for the sex, I doubt I'd still be standing here. It wasn't what you think."

"And you're an expert now on what I think."

"You've made it pretty clear."

She blushed scarlet, bit down on her trembling lips. She held out her hand, bounced it against the air, searching for words. "Did you and Matthew have a good laugh at the dumb dancer's expense?"

"I had hoped you knew me better than that"

"Honestly! And yet your friends seemed to find Matthew's jokes extremely funny. 'telling tales out of school,' I think is what Sally said. I can't help but wonder what that tale was. Trust me, darling. Remember that, Nick? Now there's a good joke."

"That's a bit harsh. We …"

"Forget it! Matthew said you have been trying so hard."

"Alicia, don't do this. Give me a chance …"

"To what? … explain why you told Matthew personal …" She swallowed and he could see she was fighting back tears. "… and then he repeats it to a table of strangers, as a joke. Not even with Brandon, do I discuss … … you have no idea about me. I have guarded my privacy for good reason, which, I am glad to say, you don't understand. I'm sorry to hear you've been bored all this time but believe me, you won't have to try quite so hard anymore."

"I'm not bored and I haven't been trying so hard, as you put it! And the reason I don't understand, Alicia, is because you tell me nothing about your life."

"Rather a good decision under the circumstances, wouldn't you agree, Nicky Boy. Now if you don't mind, I'd like to go inside."

The words hovering on his lips slipped into the darkness. He felt defeated. She refused to hear the truth, leaving him little space to plead his case, he stepped aside. The sweet smell of Coco Chanel whipped past him. He listened to her high heels tapping on the path, until they faded into the night. He wanted to punch something, yell until his lungs ran out of air, and curse Matthew to Hades after he had ripped him apart, limb-by-limb.

Staring into the night, he clasped his hands behind his head, desperately trying to work out what to do. Tomorrow she would disappear for a month. A month. He knew he couldn't stay here all night, but he couldn't bear the thought of leaving. He opened the car door. Slammed it shut.

How could he fight the obvious? No matter how he tried to explain what Matthew had blurted out, she would still accuse him of betraying her.

He drove home in a daze, his mother's words ringing in his ear. 'I pray son, one day God will find you a woman who won't give in so easily, and you just might discover the thrill of the chase.'

He stood at the window of his apartment, watching the morning sun tint the night. It was true: had Alicia given in to him, he most likely would have become bored. It surprised him how much the thrill of the chase, the fight to earn her trust and prove his worth, stimulated his need to win her over. Every minute in her company had been a challenge. *Bored! What a joke.* Not once in the last few months had he been remotely bored.

Tired and dispirited, he made himself a strong coffee. She said she was leaving that morning and he wondered what time. He checked his watch. He needed to talk to her, try to explain, and downed the remains of his drink, thinking perhaps he should have had something stronger for a confidence booster. He picked up his mobile. What could he say? What would she do? If he did nothing, he lost anyway.

"Hi Nick, it's Brandon. Was kinda wishing you hadn't called."

"How is she?"

"On a scale of one to ten – zero."

"I'd like to speak to her if I can."

"Sorry Nick, no can do. Strict instructions. She won't come to the phone, hence why I'm answering it."

"When are you leaving?"

"Soon. Plane leaves at ten-forty-five." Brandon clicked his tongue. "Want some advice?"

"Try me."

"She needs you, Nick. Don't give up."

His grip tightened. He didn't intend to give up but what could he do if she refused to speak to him? He threw the phone on the couch, slumped down next to it. The vision of her walking down the steps of the theatre in that clingy dress put a lump in his throat. He was so proud of her – proud of her ability and courage to enthral an audience with her talent like it was the most natural thing in the world. He loved her shy, unassuming nature, and her quirky habits; the way she twisted the skin on his finger, the button on his shirt when she was nervous. It kindled in him a need to protect her. Instead, he had hurt her.

The knock at the door broke through his thoughts. Wiping a hand over his prickly face, he dragged himself off the couch, wondering who the hell was calling this early on a Sunday morning.

"Hello, Nick, can we come in?" said Sally.

Matthew stepped out from behind his wife, his blood-shot eyes little more than slits above the bulging bags beneath them.

"I'm fresh out of booze." Nick couldn't control the tremor in his voice. He saw Matthew wince but he was too annoyed to give a damn about the man's feelings.

"Matthew has something he would like to say."

"What! You didn't quite finish ripping off my ..." Mindful of Sally, Nick finished that sentence under his breath as he walked into the kitchen, leaving the door ajar. He felt he needed another coffee and grabbed two more cups.

"I drank a bit too much Sal tells me; said things I shouldn't have. It's not much of an excuse but I did have an intense week at work. I apologise for being a jerk."

Nick squeezed his eyes closed, pinched the bridge of his nose. His anger slipped away when he looked up to see Matthew's head hung like a naughty boy. Would the man ever grow up?

"Forget it. Doesn't matter now. It's too late."

"What do you mean, it's too late?"

"She flies out today for Queensland, remember."

Sally crossed the room and rested both hands on the bench. "Nick, look at me. Are you going to give up so easily because of some silly thing Matthew said?"

He wondered why everyone presumed he was going to give up. "You don't know her, Sal. She thinks I betrayed her. She trusted me." He punched the bench, rattling the cups. He didn't want to talk about it and he wished they'd go away; give him some breathing space so he could work out what to do.

"You forget I'm a woman and we gals know when another woman is in love."

His attention caught, he glared at her.

"My mother used to say 'if it's hard to get, it's generally worth fighting for.'"

"Interesting. So did mine." A fissure of hope opened in his chest. He checked the time. "The plane leaves at ten-forty-five."

"I'll drive, so you don't have to park. Just run straight in."

Thoughts jumbled in his mind. Could he go to the airport?

He wasn't even sure which airline she was on: Qantas or Virgin. Would Alicia talk to him? Could Sally be right? Did she love him?

The drive to the airport was a good thirty minutes and even then, that would depend on the traffic. Boarding time was generally half an hour before the plane was scheduled for take-off. It was already nine-thirty. He had fifteen minutes up his sleeve if everything went according to plan.

Sally drove like a woman possessed through the heavy traffic, yelling abuse at the cars in her way. Nick breathed a sigh of relief when they finally exited the causeway to Tullamarine Airport. Taking a left, they screeched to a stop outside the departure terminal.

Nick sprang from the car, tucked in his t-shirt as he rushed to the entrance. Barefoot, hair uncombed, he swung around to salute his co-conspirators who were laughing like a couple of kids.

Taking the stairs two at a time, he sprinted past surprised

onlookers to get to the upper floor. In his bedraggled state, with no luggage, he was allowed through security screens and into the Departure Lounge only after he'd explained his situation and agreed to a full-body search. He managed to convince them he posed no threat, scooted up the escalator and stopped at the first overhead screen. He scanned the flights until he found Qantas Airlines, the only plane leaving at ten-forty-five for Brisbane. With five minutes to go, he was still in with a chance. Emulating Usain Bolt, he pelted along the thoroughfare, dodging hordes of disembarked passengers, past the shops and cafés, until he came to Gate 54. Disappointment surged through him at the sight of an empty departure lounge.

A flight attendant closed the gate doors to the jet bridge, whilst her co-worker packed up their gear.

"Excuse me, has the plane left yet?"

"It's just about to taxi up to the runway." "Any chance I could send a message?"

"If it is an emergency sir, we can request to have a passenger brought off the plane. Otherwise, I'm very sorry," said the attendant. Nick leant over the counter. The nervous attendant took one look at his fisted hand and threatened to press the alarm button if he didn't move away.

"Okay! Okay! I promise not to do anything stupid." Hands spread open, he backed up, politely thanking them for their help, and went in search of Matthew and Sally who'd arranged to wait for him in the car park.

Nick arrived home feeling worse than he did when he left. If only he'd been thirty minutes earlier, things might have been different. Instead, she was in the air on her way north.

Catching sight of himself in the hall mirror, he realised why the airline attendant seemed so nervous. He needed a shower, a shave, and several hours sleep. When he walked into his bedroom, the brilliant rays of midday sun blazing through the window made him squint. In his haste he'd forgotten to close the wooden shutters before he left.

He walked blindly over, snapped them shut, and pulled close the taupe silk curtains his mother had insisted on him buying when he'd bought the apartment. She'd eventually convinced him they would be more effective in the summer months and, of course, she'd been right. They cut the glare considerably but still allowed a clear view of the Yarra River, which he often spent time enjoying. He wondered what his mother would think of Alicia.

His mother! His mother! Of course, why hadn't he thought about his mother sooner? So caught in his misery he'd totally forgotten his mother lived in Queensland. Oh, what a fool he was. A stupid, confused, fool. Jubilantly he kissed the curtain, play punched the wall. It had been years since he'd asked his mother for help. Now, he was considering asking her to do the outrageous, but first he needed sleep to clear his mind.

He called her early evening. At fifty-six, his mother still enjoyed an active social life, especially living in a lifestyle complex where organised events such as ballroom dancing were held several times a week. To the best of his knowledge, she stayed home on a Sunday night to recuperate over a movie.

"Hello, son."

"Mum."

He listened to his mother's silence seeping through the phone, and hesitated. "Hate to ask but I need a favour. I've stuffed up."

Seconds passed before she answered. "Will I like this one, darling?"

"Yes, Mum, this time I think you will.

Chapter Ten

The short flight to Brisbane left little room for Alicia to dwell on the failed date with Nick and an eternity of time dealing with a disgruntled little girl who hated her mother for making her go away again and confused why Nick hadn't come to the airport to see them off. Trudging through the doors of the Marriot Hotel, Sophie whinging in her wake, Alicia felt the full weight of her responsibilities. Sophie needed stability, and travelling all over the country, pulling her from school and her friends every few months no longer seemed an option. She would inquire about boarding school when they returned to Melbourne.

"When we're settled in our room, how about we go and buy you an ice cream? We could take a ferry up the Brisbane River. Would you like that?" said Alicia as she ushered a nodding, if somewhat sulky Sophie, into the lift.

Not particularly keen on spending her free afternoon cruising in the heat, inside her room she flopped down on the bed, wishing she could curl up and sob into her misery. Angry, frustrated tears threatened. *Why did he do it? Why did he confide in that drunken fool of a man? I thought doctors were more circumspect than that and infinitely less drunk.*

She touched her ears, fingered the diamond earrings she couldn't bring herself to remove and breathed in the memory of his hand on her cheek.

"Come on, Mummy, get up. You said you would buy me an ice cream."

"So, I did." Alicia dragged herself off the bed. Unzipping her case, she searched through the contents for hats, when the hotel phone rang.

She lifted her head, stared at the phone, hoping it was Nick. The desk clerk said a lady by the name of Mrs Dorothy Johnson was asking to see her. Alicia repeated the name several times but failed to make a connection. Positive she had never heard of a Dorothy Johnson, Alicia asked the clerk to check the lady had the right person. He assured Alicia she did and waited for directions. "Okay, tell her I'll be down in a tic."

Alicia tried to imagine who the woman was and why she would want to see her. Perhaps she sold *pointe shoes* or some type of new ballet product. *Pointe shoes* were generally custom-made to suit the shape of individual dancer's feet, and most people connected with the ballet world would know this. And how would she know the Company was booked into the Marriot Hotel? Louis never divulged such information. It all seemed very strange, even presumptuous of the woman to assume Alicia would be interested in speaking to her. "Sophie. I have to go downstairs for a minute. I want you to stay here and watch television. You're not to answer the door unless it's Uncle Brandon, and don't leave this room until I get back. Do you hear me!"

"How long will you be gone?" Sophie groaned and collapsed on the bed.

"I promise not to be too long, darling, and then we can go get an ice cream."

A quick touch up to her hair and Alicia headed out the door to the lift. Stepping into the open area of the lobby, she glared at the lady sitting in the high-backed chintz chair, reading New Idea. On seeing Alicia, she placed the magazine on the pile and stood. It quickly became clear this tall elegant woman with the long graceful limbs and beautiful thick grey hair swept back off her face was no sales representative. She reminded Alicia of someone but she couldn't quite work out who. "Mrs Johnson?"

"Yes, my dear, I am."

"The desk clerk said you wanted to see me."

"True." The woman looked around. "Please, won't you join me on the sofa – much more comfortable than standing."

Alicia hesitated, not sure she wanted to be more comfortable. But she sat, determined to be firm with the woman if she didn't soon explain herself.

"My name is Dorothy Johnson as you already know … slash Coleman, if that helps. Most people call me Dee Dee for short."

For a fleeting moment, Alicia didn't think it did help until she realised Coleman was Nick's surname and that, much to her dismay, he was who the woman reminded her of. Her face must have shown her realisation.

"Yes, my dear. I'm Nick's mother."

"Oh! Mrs Johnson, I beg your pardon. I didn't know … Nick never said … …" Alicia supposed he must have rung his mother and told her where she was staying, but why?

"I hope you don't mind my showing up unannounced. Nick mentioned you were in Brisbane so I took the liberty of calling on you. I had a few errands to run in the city and thought it might be a good opportunity for us to become acquainted. I was hoping, if you aren't too busy, perhaps you could join me for coffee."

"Yes, well … no … I mean, I do have the afternoon free." She felt awkward, embarrassed and wondered exactly what Nick had told his mother about her, or their relationship and how it ended. To leave her sitting in the foyer seemed rude but she didn't particularly want his mother to come to her room. What would they talk about? "My little girl, Sophie, is upstairs. I hope you don't mind waiting while I fetch her. I know she will be thrilled to meet you. Perfect timing really, I promised to buy her an ice cream. I won't be long."

"No, not at all. Take your time. I'm happy to wait."

Controlled as Mrs Coleman appeared to be, Alicia didn't miss the faint lift of the lady's brow when she mentioned Sophie. Nick had obviously failed to mention she had a daughter. As she waited for the lift to reach her floor, a dozen questions filled her thoughts, the most prominent being, what was his mother really doing here? The story about her having a few errands didn't ring completely true.

Alicia rushed through the door into the bedroom. "Come on Sophie, turn off the TV. There's a big surprise waiting for you downstairs."

"An ice-cream?"

"No silly. It's a lady, Nick's mummy. Mrs Johnson."

The bright smile on Sophie's face reeked of mischief and Alicia worried she might ask some uncomfortable questions.

"Did she tell you why Nick didn't say goodbye to me?"

And there was the first one. "No, she didn't and don't you dare ask." Brushing Sophie's hair into a neat ponytail, Alicia had a nervous feeling this meeting had the potential to go horribly wrong.

"Ouch, you're hurting me."

"Sorry, but I'm in a hurry. Done. Come on, let's go. Behave yourself and don't ask too many questions or I won't buy you an ice cream."

When the lift doors opened, Sophie charged straight up to Nick's mother and plonked down beside her. "Are you really Nick's mummy?"

The striking similarity between mother and son was uncanny — the same casual smile Alicia had become familiar with, the steady, almost arrogant, way they held their heads, the way they looked at her with that cool, confident grace.

"I certainly am," she said, gently pinching Sophie's pink cheek.

"Mummy says I mustn't ask why he didn't say goodbye to me."

Alicia wished Sophie was closer so she too could pinch the pink cheek. Although it was only fleeting, Dee Dee's glance conveyed a poignant message: she knew enough to make Alicia uncomfortable.

"Dearie me, that is disappointing." Dee Dee drew her eyebrows together. "How about I promise next time I talk to my son, I ask him why he didn't say goodbye. I'm sure he has a very good reason."

He has a very good reason, all right, thought Alicia as she followed Dee Dee out of the hotel. *Because he's a rat, a loose-lipped rat who I hope I never see again.*

Sophie slipped her hand into Dee Dee's as they strolled along the South Bank to the café. Dee Dee insisted on paying, and ordered coffee for herself and Alicia and a chocolate-coated ice cream for Sophie.

"Thank you for joining me, Alicia. I know my dropping in this way must have come as a surprise, but I do appreciate it."

"Oh, Mrs Johnson, don't be silly. It's nice to have company. I know Sophie is pleased, aren't you, darling." They both looked at Sophie licking chocolate from her fingers, and laughed.

"Do call me Dee Dee. Mrs Johnson makes me feel very old." She patted Alicia's arm. "I was wondering ... being alone, I rarely venture into the city at night. *Manon* is one of my favourite ballets and, knowing you will be the lead, I thought I might treat myself and book a ticket for this Saturday night."

"Mrs ... Dee Dee, please don't feel that you have –"

Dee Dee shook her head; cut her short. "I certainly don't. I really do enjoy the theatre. Phillip, my dearly departed husband, not Nick's father in case you hadn't guessed, often came home with tickets for the two of us." Pressing her hand on her chest, she attempted a smile. "Going on my own isn't quite the same. This will give me something special to look forward to." She paused; took a breath. "I was also wondering - that is, if you are free on Sunday - whether you might like to come and stay with me for a short break. I live close to the sea, on the Gold Coast and Sophie could go swimming."

Sophie's ears pricked up at the mention of swimming and

clutched Alicia's arm. "Please say I can. I love swimming."

Alicia dropped her gaze, traced circles on the table cloth. "I do have Sunday and Monday off but there is something I need to tell you."

Dee Dee wrapped her hand around Alicia's arm. "Please, don't say no. You see, I lost Phillip several years ago and since his death I'm often lonely. It would be such a pleasure to have you both stay. You could come home with me after the show and I'll drive you back whenever you wish."

Sophie turned to Alicia. "Can we mummy? Please say yes." And turning back to Dee Dee. "Do you have a bike?"

"I'm afraid not," said Dee Dee half laughing.

Touched by the gracious offer from the older woman, Alicia struggled with her emotions. She recognised and understood the loneliness and grief that lurked behind the calm exterior. But what of Nick? He must know his mother was with her and if he didn't, what would he think of her after the disparaging way she had spoken to him, only to find out she had spent the weekend with his mother? But how to refuse such a simple plea for company? "Of course, we'd love to, wouldn't we, Soph?"

Nodding vigorously, Sophie licked the last drop of ice cream from her lips, wiped her face clean on a Wet-One Alicia handed her, and the three of them left the cafe. They stopped to check out the jewellery stalls and artwork displayed along the bank of the Brisbane River, watched a man on stilts dressed as Pinocchio, perform a funny skit.

It both pleased and perplexed Alicia to see Sophie skipping along with her hand tucked safely inside Dee Dee's, talking faster than a jet plane on the runway, as they strolled to the hotel. She seemed so comfortable with Nick's mother. The grandmother she subconsciously craved, perhaps.

They arrived at the hotel late in the afternoon. Dee Dee said her goodbyes but not before pinkie-promising Sophie she would return and take her to the beach.

***

Alicia woke Saturday morning to Thomas the Tank Engine, on the television, tooting his whistle. "Sophie, turn that racket down, it's so loud." Leaning over to check the time, she groaned. She had gone for a coffee after the show, egged on by Brandon and a few members from the Queensland Ballet Company who had attended the performance. It was past midnight when she finally said goodnight to Linda, Sophie's sitter and fell into bed.

"I can't wait to go swimming. How long till Nick's mummy comes."

"It's only eight o'clock in the morning. You know she's not coming until later on tonight." Alicia pulled the covers over her head, hoping to catch up on sleep, but gave up when Thomas tooted into the station.

Lying on her back, she stared blindly at the television and thought about the repercussions, should Nick's mother fail to turn up. Alicia knew somehow Sophie would blame her and she dreaded the tantrum that would inevitably follow. The whole situation was beginning to play out like a nightmare. Nick had obviously spoken to his mother about her, but how long ago and had he mentioned their last date was anything but amicable. Dee Dee's invitation seemed genuine enough, and Alicia couldn't imagine she had some kind of ulterior motive brewing.

Sick of thinking, she rolled out of bed. "I have to go to the theatre a bit earlier today. When we get back from breakfast, I'll help you pack an overnight bag, which you can bring with you tonight. I've arranged for Linda to take you out for the afternoon, buy you some dinner and then bring you straight to the theatre."

"Where's Linda taking me?"

"She mentioned something about the opening of a fair in a park by the foreshore, not far from the hotel."

"Why couldn't Nick's mummy take me. I don't want to go with Linda."

Alicia sighed and spoke slowly. "Because Nick's mummy won't be here until much later, which you already know. Now go and change for breakfast."

Returning from breakfast, Alicia started packing for herself and Sophie, when she heard the knock.

"That will be Linda. Let her in, will you, while I finish here."

"I'd still rather go with Nick's mummy."

"Of course, you would," mumbled Alicia under her breath.

"Don't forget to pack my bathers."

Alicia let out a sigh of relief when she finally closed the door on a harassed Linda trying to manoeuvre two overnight bags and a grumpy child into the passage.

Alicia knew Brandon would be waiting downstairs and quickly finished dressing. He had organised with the principals of the Queensland Ballet Company, for the two of them to watch rehearsals of *La Fille Mal Gardee* at their studio. and then join them afterward for a late lunch. This suited her fine as she wouldn't need to worry about snacking before the show. A cup of warm milk should see her through.

She was impressed with the standard of the Queensland dancers as she watched them capture the playful charm of Frederick Ashton's ballet. And she thoroughly enjoyed the ballet-banter being bandied across the table over lunch. But strolling across the bridge to the theatre, her arm linked in Brandon's, she felt anxious about her stay with Nick's mum on the coast.

They arrived in plenty of time to change, ready for the warmup class. Knowing Nick's mother would be in the audience, she took extra care over her hair and makeup, checked that her costumes were lined up in the correct order of appearance. She placed her shoes on the bench, along with a couple of spares. Often during a demanding performance, the soles of her *pointe* shoes would give way, sometimes even snap clean through, which meant a quick change.

Standing in the wing on one side, Brandon, in the role of *des Grieux, Manon's* lover, and Julian Parry as *Lescaut,* her brother, on the other, with her nerves on fire, Alicia waited. Taking a deep breath, she stepped onto the stage, moving into the music as it took her on the journey of *Manon's* life. By the end of the first act, her costume was soaked in sweat. Linda had only just arrived with Sophie when Alicia pushed through the dressing room door.

"Great, you're here! Would you mind undoing me, Linda? I'm sopping wet, sorry about that. See if you can get Sophie to have a little nap before we go, otherwise she'll be exhausted tomorrow."

"Will do," said Linda, pulling at the skin-tight costume. "But you know what she's like. Stubborn little thing. Bit like her mother."

Alicia smiled at Linda through the mirror. Time was precious during intervals and, slipping out of her costume, she threw it on the bench; whipped off her shoes, before checking her hair and makeup.

"What did I do with my extra pair of shoes?" Panicked, she circled herself looking everywhere and nowhere.

"Alicia! They are under the costume you just took off. What's gotten into you tonight? You're a bundle of nerves."

Linda was right. She needed to calm down, and took several deep breaths. She hung up her costume, put on a clean but used pair of *pointes* and slipped into the long *tutu* for Act Two.

"Do you want me to do you up?"

"Thanks. I need to get out of here and put some resin on my shoes." Alicia loved this costume: the feel of the full skirt swirling around her legs, the sound of the net swishing in the air as she moved. It helped her adapt to the strong tempo of the music as *Manon* transformed into a scheming seductress, disregarding the love she had for *des Grieux,* to enchant the wealthy *Monsieur* and steal his money.

By the end of the second Act, the emotional strain of the role had begun to kick in and Brandon gave her a quick massage when they came off stage, kneading the top of her shoulders and neck, working out the knots in her muscles.

"Thanks, Brandy, I needed that."

Giving her the thumbs up, he shot off to change. Sophie was still awake when she entered the dressing room, her lids fluttering to say open. Alicia said little to Linda, turning her mind to the last but most difficult of the three Acts. The long *tutu* with its layers of tulle was replaced with dirty, stained, flesh coloured tights, making her legs look unclean and bruised. The filthy ripped tunic barely covered her buttocks, and the shorthaired wig looked as if someone had taken to it with gardening clippers.

After the final curtain call, she hurried backstage, relieved it was over. She hadn't been able to see if Dee Dee was in the audience because the overhead lights blacked out everything past the end of the stage.

"As I said, stubborn like her mother." Linda mouthed a quick 'Sorry' at Alicia who was frantically pulling hairpins from her wig.

"Two minutes in the car and she'll be asleep."

"Alicia, would you mind if I took off now? I've arranged to hook up with some of the others and make a night of it."

"Of course not. You go, and thanks for tonight."

"Pleasure. Have fun on the coast. See you Tuesday."

Alicia threw her tights into the washing basket for the wardrobe mistresses to launder and removed her makeup. Slipping into a black sweat-suit she brushed her tangled hair into a low ponytail. She turned to see Sophie sitting on the chair with her backpack on and yawning. There it was again, the guilty feeling tapping on her conscience. What effect was her hectic lifestyle having on Sophie? "Okay, sleepy-head, let's go."

Dee Dee was sitting by the theatre entrance and rose when she saw them enter by the theatre door. Alicia tried not to stare at the woman walking towards her: the way she held her head, regal and assured, her smile, warm and welcoming, even the black layered chiffon skirt and lace blouse, everything about her reminded Alicia of her own mother. She wrapped her hand around her throat hoping to ease the tension inside but her eyes refused to blink as they fed on the uncanny similarities.

Sophie ran straight into Dee Dee's outstretched arms and laughing, Dee Dee dropped a kiss on the top of her head.

"You came!" The words fell from Alicia's lips before she could stop them.

"Yes, of course. Did you think I wouldn't?"

"Yes. I mean, no." Whatever was wrong with her? She didn't normally sound so silly.

"I loved the ballet, Alicia. *Manon* is such a powerful story. It reminds me a bit of *Les Miserables*. It's right up there on my list of favourites. And you, my dear … what can I say? You were absolutely amazing. I really am in awe of your extraordinary talent. You should be very proud of yourself."

"Thank you so much. I'm glad you enjoyed it."

"That, I surely did." She picked up Sophie's bag from the floor and taking her hand, smiled at the two of them. "Shall we go, it's getting late. I managed to get a spot in the car park directly opposite. Not far to walk, thank goodness."

It was close to midnight by the time they arrived back at Dee Dee's home. Alicia carried Sophie inside, following Dee Dee who guided her through to the spare room at the end of the passage.

"I hope you don't mind sharing a bed. I thought Sophie might be a bit nervous in a strange room on her own."

"No, not at all. We often share a bed on tour."

Dee Dee placed the bags on the floor and turned down the covers. "Is there anything I can get you? A drink, something to eat?”

"No thanks. I ate earlier and I have a bottle of water in my bag."

"In that case, I think I might say goodnight. Sleep tight and I'll see you in the morning." Dee Dee stepped forward, rested her hand on Alicia's shoulder and, brushing a kiss on her cheek, left the room.

And I liked having someone I know in the audience watching me, she whispered to the closed door as she sank down on the bed and stared at the wall. A wave of exhaustion washed over her as she pulled her nightdress from her bag. Too exhausted to think past the comfortable bed she sat on, she curled up next to Sophie and drifted off to sleep.

***

The sound of the sea echoed through the open window above her head. Rolling over, she stretched across the bed like a Siamese cat, her foot feeling for Sophie. When she discovered it empty, she lifted herself onto her elbows and glanced around the sun-crisp room with its lime green accessories, and inhaled the fresh smell of lemon-scented pot-pourie. The china timepiece on the dresser showed nine o'clock and she flopped back on the pillow, unable to believe she had slept so long. Her body and mind felt rested, relaxed as if she was at home in her own bed. She was tempted to stay where she was but knowing Dee Dee would be busy entertaining a yappy Sophie, she threw off the covers and headed straight for the adjoining bathroom.

Seated in front of the mirror, wrapped in a damp towel, she gathered her hair at the nape of her neck and worked it into a braid over her shoulder. Deciding not to wear makeup for a few days to give her skin a chance to breath, she slipped on her faithful old jeans and sleeveless top. She gave a quick pinch to her colourless cheeks and followed the dull drone of voices coming from the other end of the house.

She thought she detected a baritone amongst the laughter but shrugged off the thought as the sweet smell of maple syrup teased her nostrils. It had been hours since she'd eaten, and the idea of pancakes smothered in maple syrup, with cream on top, made her mouth water. She rarely indulged in such decadence and, pushing through the door, she decided today was the day.

"Um! I smell … Nick!"

"Not a good start." Perched on a stool with Sophie balanced on his knee, he pretended to sniff his shirt.

But for the pounding of her heart, Alicia stood paralysed, her eyes darting from Dee Dee to Nick. A small voice whispered something about love, but she shut it down.

He lowered Sophie to the floor and rose from the stool.

"Mummy, Nick came as a surprise," said Sophie, clutching his hand.

"So, I see." Oh, she saw alright. She saw the sultry pout of his lips, a small pulse beating in his neck and longing in his eyes that was making her legs go weak.

"Alicia, would you mind if I took Sophie with me to church? It starts at ten o'clock and, if we leave immediately, we should make it just in time." Dee Dee's expression betrayed nothing as she waited for an answer.

"Where are we going, Dee Dee?"

"Well, if your mummy says yes, I would like to take you to meet a very special man called Jesus."

Her mother had said much the same to her when she was a child. She wanted to smile but a pair of eager eyes held her captive.

"Can I go? Please say yes. I would really like to meet Jesus." Unable to stop the smile forming, Alicia nodded.

"Okay then, we're off." Dee Dee took Sophie's hand and, already answering questions about Jesus, led her out the door.

Nick stepped closer. "One word from you is all I need and

I'll leave."

She frowned, wondering what word he wanted her to say. Did he expect her to order him from his mother's house? And did she want him to go? What then? Was she supposed to ask him to stay? Maybe he wanted her to leave. The thought sent her colour rising. "No! Stay! I'll go."

"That's not what I meant."

Unsure what he meant, she backed out of the room, trying not to look as awkward as she felt. She wanted to put some distance between them, to give herself time to think without a pair of intense eyes sending her thoughts into cyberspace. Nothing made sense. Why had he come? Had Dee Dee asked him and if so why hadn't she mentioned he was here? The passage went both ways and, in her confusion, she couldn't remember where she had come from. She heard his steps and fled.

"Alicia, wait! Alicia!"

He was right behind her. She grabbed at the first available handle and found herself in the laundry. The washing machine and dryer stared at her. She flung around to face him, her breath coming in short sharp bursts. "Don't you dare come any closer, Nick Coleman. I can't concentrate when you … are … I just can't concentrate."

"Why not?" Pushing his hands in his pockets, he took a provocative step.

"I … get… I don't know, I just can't, that's all."

"I won't come any closer, but I won't let you pass either. At least, not until you talk to me."

"I'm not quite as loose-lipped as you, Nick."

"That's not fair, Alicia,"

"Fair! You know nothing of what's not fair. I'll tell you what's not fair, Nick. It's…" She stopped suddenly, the words dying on her lips. How could she tell him how unfair her life had been - death, grief and endless loneliness - without revealing part of herself he didn't deserve to know? At least not after the way he had treated her and not until he declared himself. "It doesn't matter."

"It matters to me. For once in your life, talk to me, tell me what's not fair." His steady gaze burned through to her spine.

"You didn't …" she whispered through the lump in her throat.

"I didn't what?"

"I waited."

"You waited for what? Tell me!"

"For you! But you didn't come."

"I didn't come …?"

"To see me before I left."

"Oh, Sweetheart, to the airport?"

He called her 'Sweetheart'. First 'Baby', then 'Darling', now 'Sweetheart'. Painfully aware of the odd feeling shifting inside, she forced herself to stay in control and turned her back to him.

"Go away, Nick."

"You're wrong, you know."

The tender tone of his voice creeping closer, cut into her resolve.

"I did come to the airport. Barefooted and unshaven, I raced like a frantic dog up escalators, past groggy-eyed passengers until I reached Gate 54. Missed you by minutes. Even caused a couple of hosties a few nervous moments."

He stood so close Alicia could feel the warmth of his body. His heart pressed against her shoulder, he smoothed his hands up and down her arms. The touch of his breath blowing against her cheek brought goosebumps. She fought hard, arguing with herself not to give in. He had betrayed her.

"Forgive me," he whispered as he turned her to face him.

That was all she needed to hear to break the last remnant of her will. She rested her head on his chest, succumbing to the comfort of his firm embrace. Dear God, how she cherished having this man hold her. The last time she remembered being held with such comforting tenderness was by her father after she told him she'd been accepted into the Dance Academy in Perth.

Nick lifted her chin and covered her lips with his. She closed her eyes and let the feelings rush through her body. She wanted to block the voice tapping at her conscience, reminding her of a promise. She'd been sixteen when she made that promise. Sweet and innocent sixteen. She pushed those thoughts aside and let her heart dine on the sweet nectar of passion his kiss induced.

Lifting her into his arms, he carried her through to the kitchen, propped her on a stool, and kissed her again. "Pancakes?" he whispered against her lips.

Although her stomach groaned, she felt full, content. "Maple syrup and a dollop of cream on top," she murmured.

He laughed, pulled her into his arms, kissed her again, only this time deeper, more passionately than before. She felt his hands pressing to explore and pulled away before she was powerless to resist, using her hunger as an excuse, she ordered him to the other side of the bench.

Breakfast over, happy to watch him and his broad shoulders loading the dishwasher, she heard the sound of the garage door opening. Next thing, Sophie burst into the kitchen babbling about church and Jesus. Alicia held tight to her thoughts. Hadn't she heard those stories over and over as a child: stories of love and hope and joy. And Pastor Reed, vivid in her memory, presiding over the funeral, telling her how 'sometimes bad things happen to good people'. Bitterness swelled in her stomach. And she remembered her detest for him as he spoke those words.

"Something smells good." Hanging her keys on a row of hooks, Dee Dee sniffed the air, turned and smiled at Alicia.

"Pancakes … eh … a dollop of cream, and maple syrup. A favourite, so I'm led to believe," said Nick, pressing the button on the dishwasher.

"Talking of food, the markets are open today. I thought we

could take a look around and then maybe do lunch at one of the cafés," suggested Dee Dee.

The warm weather had drawn many folks from indoors to enjoy the thoroughfare along the coast and inhale the pungent smell of the ocean. The markets were full of multipurpose stalls, with a collection of people haggling for various trinkets, jewellery, or a range of handmade jams and sauces. Many pulled trollies piled with locally-grown produce.

Anyone watching would think they were a typical family, thought Alicia as she strolled along holding Nick's hand. Sophie, who hadn't stopped bouncing since they arrived, deserved all of this – a father, a grandmother, siblings – all of it. She even looked healthier, her cheeks as pink as rose petals.

"When did you arrive here?" She had forgotten to ask Nick earlier.

"Flew in yesterday and unfortunately, fly home tonight." Putting his arm around her shoulder he gave her a quick squeeze. "Not disappointed I came, are you?"

"No, not disappointed." She could no longer deny the relief she'd felt when she'd seen him but the feelings of betrayal lingered. She needed to know why he had told Matthew about them.

"Mummy! Mummy!" screamed Sophie, tugging on Dee Dee's hand. "Look!"

The words balanced on Alicia's lips were sucked away on a gasp as her gaze followed Sophie's outstretched arm. One of the two things Sophie wanted most in her life was, to Alicia's horror, staring her in the face.

"Please! Please, can you buy it for me?"

A dreadful feeling this wasn't about to end well, she dropped to her knees in front of Sophie and cupped her face. "Darling, please don't make a fuss. You know I can't take a bike on the plane and I definitely can't keep it at the hotel."

Sophie wrenched her face from Alicia's hands, anger etched in her expression. Hands on hips, she stamped her foot. "All the other kids have a daddy and a bike. Why won't you buy me one! You're mean and I hate you so much."

Alicia tried to grab Sophie's top before she dashed off through the crowds but missed and landed on her hands.

Nick, quick to react, seized Sophie by the waist and hoisted her into his arms.

"I hate her," she said.

When Alicia glanced over at Dee Dee, the worried expression made her recoil. She wanted to scream to the world, it wasn't my fault Sophie grew up without a father, or a bike, or any of the other things most children took for granted.

Sophie calmed under Nick's firm control. Whatever he said had obviously worked its magic. Sophie inched towards Alicia to offer an apology. She cupped the child's head against her hips, bent to drop a kiss on the curly mop.

Alicia could feel Dee Dee's penetrating stare boring into the side of her face and couldn't bring herself to meet the older woman's gaze. Afraid of the 'what' questions those eyes might be asking, she turned to gaze across the water. As she watched the white spray lift off the rolling waves, she had an overwhelming urge to throw herself at the mercy of the sea.

Unfair! Oh, she could tell Nick all about unfair. The question she asked herself was: would he still want the burden of her and Sophie if she did.

The touch of warm, soft flesh moving across her shoulders broke through her thoughts. "Alicia dear, I've been thinking. Would you mind dreadfully if I bought the pink bike for Sophie? It would give me such pleasure."

"That's very kind of you but what would I do with it, I can't take it home."

"You won't have to. There's plenty of room for a bike in my garage."

"It could be a long time, maybe a year, before the Company returns to Queensland then you would be stuck with a bike in your garage."

"Truth is, I've been planning a trip to Melbourne for a few months. I don't know if Nick mentioned that I have a holiday home in Brighton. I could fly the bike as extra luggage and maybe the two of you – or just Sophie, if it coincides with the school holidays – could come for a visit."

"Oh, my stars, that seems like an awful lot of trouble. I don't know what to say?"

"Just say yes."

"Please, Mummy, please say yes."

After Dee Dee paid for the bike, Sophie wobbled off down the path with Alicia running after her, desperate to save innocent pedestrians enjoying the sunshine from imminent collisions. They parked the bike outside an open-air restaurant and chose a table in front of the prized possession.

"All she needs now is a daddy," said Nick, guiding Alicia to a seat.

Fully aware of her face changing colour, Alicia pretended she hadn't heard his comment, and concentrated on hooking the strap of her bag over the back of the chair. When she finally looked up, her jaw dropped open. "Michael!" she called across the table.

It must have been over a year since she'd last seen Michael Gillespie. He looked different: had changed his hair into a more sophisticated style, and gained a bit of muscle. He smiled at her in the same gentle way she remembered and loved. He was always a handsome man but somehow, he seemed more mature, more manly. Maybe the break-up with Brandon had caused him to grow up, take stock and re-invent himself. Perhaps he had met someone else.

Crushed in his firm embrace, she let the familiar smell of David Beckham aftershave tickle her nostrils. "Still a fan?" she said, rubbing her nose.

Nodding he huffed out a laugh. "What are you doing on the Gold Coast?"

"Holidaying on my two-day break. The Company is performing *Manon* in Brisbane."

He hesitated; glanced around. Alicia guessed he was looking for Brandon and was pleased to know he was safely back in Brisbane. "And Sophie? Where's my little girl?" Sophie, whose eyes were glued to the pink bike, turned when she heard her name.

"Sophie, come and say hello." Michael knelt down; held open his arms.

Alicia liked Michael. He'd always been kind to her and Sophie. But the memory of her darling Brandon and his broken heart lingered. Watching him cuddle and tease Sophie, reminded her of how much he wanted a child of his own. Sophie kept turning to check on her bike, more interested in the pink contraption not going walkabout than in Michael.

"I've missed my little girl and our ice cream treats together."

"Mummy still buys me an ice cream, don't you, Mummy? And Dee Dee – that's Dee Dee over there – well, she bought me a pink bike, didn't you, Dee Dee?"

The mention of Dee Dee's name reminded Alicia of her manners. "Oh, forgive me, everyone. Michael Gillespie, this is Nick Coleman and his mother, Dee Dee Johnson."

Nick, a curious expression on his face, rose to his feet and shook hands. Dee Dee nodded.

"Michael is a freelance photographer and journalist. You may have read some of his articles in The Age or Sydney Morning Herald."

"Which reminds me," he chipped in. "We never did do that photoshoot you promised me."

"Drop in to the studio when next you're in Melbourne and we'll organise a time."

"Done. I really must go. I have friends waiting outside. But tell me, how long are you on the Gold Coast?"

"We'll be back in the city Tuesday. The show must go on."

He quietened; stepped a little closer. "Meet me for lunch, say twelve o'clock tomorrow?" He spoke in a low, toneless voice. "There are so many things left unsaid."

Alicia's stomach tightened: she had nothing to say to Michael. Alicia had never asked Brandon what went wrong with their relationship, and Brandon had never offered any information. Somehow going to lunch with him felt close to betrayal. But the sad, pathetic look on his face pushed her sympathy button and she didn't have the heart to refuse. "Dee Dee, would you mind very much if I joined Michael for lunch tomorrow."

"Of course not. It will give me an opportunity to take my favourite girl for a ride on her new bike and maybe a swim, if she behaves."

Michael hesitated, his hands shoved in his pockets. Lifting his head, he whispered, "How is he?"

Words failed her. There didn't seem a point to respond. What could she say, he's great, doing well with Kieran?

Seeming to understand her silence, he gave a quick nod, saluted Nick and Dee Dee and scooted off to join his friends.

Alicia eased down beside Nick at the table; sensed the distance occupying the space between them. She knew he was upset about her meeting with Michael but she wasn't quite sure why. Did he expect her to not have friends?

"Old boyfriend?"

She laughed at that, positive he was joking. Surely Nick, being a man of the world, would know Michael was gay. "He's a photographer Louis uses to take photos of us dancers for promotional purposes. Only now he is permanently contracted by the Herald Sun as a journalist and a lot more in demand. And a lot more expensive." It was on the tip of her tongue to tell Nick about

Michael's relationship with Brandon but, respecting Brandon's privacy, she decided against it. He laid his hand on her leg, gave it a squeeze and she returned his smile, glad to see him relaxed.

They held hands, like a normal couple in the throes of finding love, when they left the restaurant to join the crowds meandering along the foreshore. She glanced down at the fingers entwined with hers. Rare feelings of true happiness surfaced. He was breaking down her defences, drawing her into a world, she had once feared.

They arrived home in the afternoon. In the brief time before Nick's flight to Melbourne, alone together in the sunroom of his mother's villa, Alicia firmly tucked between his arms, he lifted her chin. "You seemed very friendly with that photographer fellow?"

"Michael? Yes, I suppose I am." Although what she was going to talk to him about tomorrow played heavily on her conscience.

"He's obviously fond of Sophie."

"Yes, he adores her. Always buys her an ice cream when he comes to the Arts Centre." It's a pity, she thought, that Sophie didn't return his affections, apart from loving his ice creams.

"Where are your parents?"

She glanced up at him, taken aback by his question. His face was set, his eyes steady, unchanging. It was a simple enough question. So why the sharp note, the false smile, or the challenge she detected in the stubborn tilt of his chin. And why now? For some reason she felt it had something to do with her meeting up with Michael. The longer she stayed silent, the faster his smile faded.

"Another secret. Another reason you're glad I know so little about you. Is that how it goes?"

Her mouth opened to give him some kind of an explanation when the sound of a horn broke through the tension. Without another word he lifted her from his lap and strode from the room. No reaction, no anger, just a blank departure. She could hear him saying farewell to his mother and Sophie, and wondered what to do. Before she had a chance to decide, he pushed through the door and, taking her by the hand, pulled her gently outside to the waiting taxi.

He threw his bags in the trunk and the driver slammed it shut. Turning, he pulled her up against him. With his fingers entwined through her hair, he eased back her head until her lips parted.

"I want you to know I never told Matthew about us. But I have told you most things about myself. I wish you would afford me the same consideration. Trust is a major part of a relationship and without it we have nothing." Nick paused for breath. "Tell me you believe me about Matthew. If not, I give you back your own words —"

Silencing him with her mouth, she kissed him long enough to ease his concerns and increase the taxi driver's impatience.

Chapter Eleven

Alicia stared at the tail lights of the taxi disappearing into the darkness. She fingered her lips still pulsing from the pressure of his kiss. Perched on the garden wall, enjoying the calm night air, she toyed with the speck of happiness peeping over her horizon. Her need of Nick was growing the more they were together but so too were the warning bells pealing in her head. She was losing control, something she had promised herself never to let happen. But hadn't he flown all the way from Melbourne to see her? So, what did that mean? Could she allow herself to believe that he was beginning to love her?

When she entered the house, Dee Dee was sitting on the settee with a sleepy-eyed Sophie huddled at her side, reading Beatrix Potter. She stared at the two of them. Her mother used to read Peter Rabbit to her when she was about Sophie's age and her favourite character was Mr Jeremy Fisher.

"It's seven o'clock, darling. Time for bed."

Sophie, rubbing her eyes, gave in easily to her mother's request. Alicia tucked her in, promising to check the bike was safely stowed in the garage before she too went to bed.

Having showered and changed, Alicia wandered up the passage in her shorty pyjamas, attempting to drag a brush through her tangled, wet hair.

"Alicia! Come and sit down. Can I get you a cup of tea or coffee?"

"I might pass." She patted her stomach, rolled her eyes at Dee Dee. "I'm full to the brim. Dinner was delicious - salmon and salad are a favourite. But thanks for asking." Alicia dropped cross-legged on the carpet in front of the TV and continued brushing her hair.

"Would you like me to do that for you? I have it on good authority I don't pull at the knots."

Alicia cast a glance towards the outstretched hand. Visions of herself sitting at her mother's feet having her hair braided, unfurled. Everything inside her wanted to refuse the offer but knowing how rude that would appear she edged closer and handed Dee Dee the brush.

Soft fingers, fluttering against her skin, gathered her hair into their hands. Dee Dee started to hum a familiar song, and recognising the tune from her years in church, Alicia bit hard on her bottom lip. She shut her eyes, tried counting to ten to block the sound but, instead, her mother's soft chuckles rang in her ears.

"Your hair is very beautiful, my dear. Did you know that a sinner woman washed Jesus' feet with her tears and dried them with her hair?" said Dee Dee. "I have a strong notion her hair would have been very similar to yours, rich and silky."

Alicia's tightly boxed grief slowly unravelled and she gripped her hands together, fighting for control. With each of Dee Dee's strokes, her mother's ghostly presence dominated: her laugh, her voice, her firm, gentle touch on her neck.

"Does your mother have hair like yours, Alicia?"

Her mother was only forty when she was killed and her hair was still long and vibrant and full of colour. Alicia's eyes brimmed with tears but she was too scared to wipe them away for fear Dee Dee might notice. The brushing stopped.

Dee Dee hunkered beside her on the floor, lifted Alicia's hand in hers. "I didn't mean to upset or hurt you, dear."

Shaking her head, Alicia struggled to speak past the lump in her throat. "You didn't."

"Maybe not this time but someone has. I see it in your eyes."

Embarrassed, Alicia tried to stem the flow but the stress of the past few weeks had opened the flood gates.

"Would you like to talk about it?"

She wiped over her face, shook her head and hugged her knees to her chest.

"Would it help if I told you, God and I are very good listeners?"

The mention of God brought her tears to an abrupt end, substituting them with anger. "Don't talk to me about God. God destroyed my life."

"Why would you say that? He loves you."

"Loves me! How strange, and yet he took everything I loved from me."

"Are you sure it was God who took it from you?"

"I'm sure. And do you know what He left me with …?"

Alicia, her hand fisted, punched lightly at her chest.

"No, dear. Tell me."

"An empty promise."

"What do you mean?"

What did she mean? She meant life, and life more abundant. Isn't that what He promised. Even her parents believed that lie and guess what, they're dead. And her life was far from abundant. Her life was lonely. Heated words bubbled to the surface. "You see this life in front of you?" Lip quivering, Alicia yanked at her top, twisted it into a knot. "Do you want me to tell you what it's full of?"

Dee Dee placed her hand on Alicia's arm, stroked the soft flesh.

Alicia's chest, full of everything she spent every day fighting to suppress, rose. Words pushed to vent spleen. She wanted to stop but couldn't. "Pain and grief and loneliness! All of it is eating away at me." And guilt, but that was her secret and hers alone.

"It doesn't have to be that way. Let me help you. Tell me what to do."

Alicia scrambled to her feet; backed away. How could this woman help her? Not even John Spencer with all his training had the power or knowledge to heal her broken heart. Books, exercises, strategies, were just the bandages, never the cure. Three years she had listened to him spruik his rubbish and for what? To watch him fall victim to a blonde with a shapely figure, denying his own declared values? "Nothing! There's nothing you or anyone can do."

Dee Dee rose and stepped closer. "All I ask is a chance to try."

Alicia shook her head. She didn't take chances with her emotions. She had just enough fight left in her to see Sophie safely into adulthood, then she could let go. No complications, no pity, no trying to put together the shattered pieces. Only survival until the end, then peace.

"May I tell you something?"

Those pleading eyes held a tale Alicia guessed she would rather not hear. She wanted to beg her not to say something that meant nothing but a bunch of kind words. Words that would ease Dee Dee's heart but leave Alicia's with destructive hope. But lacking the courage to deny the woman, she nodded.

"For as long as I can remember, I have always … wanted a daugh …"

Alicia put her hands over her ears. Pain clawed. She didn't want to hear what Dee Dee had to say. *Daughter … you want a daughter. I want my parents, my family and the life I thought I was promised.*

Dee Dee reached out; tried to touch her. Alicia stiffened. "Please, please don't … I'm sorry … I don't mean to offend you but I need to be … alone." She stepped away, confused, embarrassed and very sorry. Tears ran thick and full, blurring her vision as she groped her way down the passage to her room, shutting the door quietly behind her. She slumped onto the bed. Misery flooded through her as if she was poisoned, along with a deep, deep yearning to be cherished like a daughter. "Oh! God, why? What have I done to you? You know how much I miss my mother, so why do you keep tormenting me with snippets of hope? Why won't you leave me alone?"

⁎

The next day, Alicia spotted Michael waving to her from the restaurant. He had chosen a table under the shade of a white umbrella. She was glad she'd accepted his invitation. It gave her a chance to escape the uncomfortable atmosphere after her emotional scene the night before. Although Dee Dee acted as though nothing unusual had happened, humming happily as she cooked porridge for breakfast, Alicia sensed her unease. She attempted to apologise for her behaviour but Dee Dee, shaking her head, put her hand on Alicia's arm and said she had nothing to apologise for. But somehow that made it worse, more embarrassing, if that was possible.

Michael rose and greeted her with a quick hug. "Thanks for coming. I know how strapped for time you are on these tours."

She had always enjoyed Michael's company and listening to him talk about photography and the places he had travelled. But it was his dry sense of humour mixed with an acutely perceptive nature she found most appealing. She hoped this meeting didn't change her opinion. After they finished eating, his conversation turned to Brandon, prodding for information she couldn't reveal.

"We keep to ourselves when it comes to relationships, Michael. He never told me anything about the breakup or why it happened. But I can tell you, he was upset for months afterward."

"He got it all wrong. He thought I cheated on him but I didn't. I've tried so many times to ring and explain, but he won't answer my calls."

"I'm so sorry, Michael, I really am." Conscious not to betray Brandon's trust, she twice tried to change the subject, only to be cut short, confronted with another question.

"Is he with someone else?"

"Michael, please don't ask me. It really is a violation of Brandon's privacy." He looked so sad, she wished with all her heart

220

she could help him.

"It's just, I miss him."

With little else left to talk about, they arranged to meet the next time they were both in Melbourne. Relieved to be finally released from the inquisition, she happily kissed him goodbye.

In no hurry to return home, she ambled along the winding trail. She looked up to see an ice cream outlet and went over to check out the different flavours. Sitting on the limestone wall, licking homemade English Toffee in a waffle cone, she sat back to enjoy the beauty of the indigo sea tunnelling into foamy waves on the foreshore, and pondered her evening with Dee Dee. What was it about this woman that affected her so intensely? That she reminded Alicia of her mother, there was no doubt. The way she walked, talked, the clothes she wore, even the way she brushed Alicia's hair. But it was more than a mere resemblance that had her rattled. Finishing the last of her ice cream, she hopped off the wall.

Walking home, she wondered if it might be their spirituality which linked her mother and Dee Dee together, the way they naturally connected every part of their lives to God.

Before the accident, she too believed in His promises. Since she was a child her parents had taken her, her brother, Simon, and Sophie to church. She grew up believing the words the pastor preached. As hard as she tried, she could never completely let go of her faith.

She wanted to hate God so she could blame Him for their death, instead of herself. The accident had occurred on Flinders Street near the ballet shop. If only she hadn't asked her mother to pick up her ballet shoes, they might still be alive. Why hadn't He protected them? They were devoted, loving Christians who served him faithfully year after blessed year, and for what? To have their lives zapped away like mere bugs, leaving her with this crippling guilt.

Later that evening, with Sophie in bed, Dee Dee invited Alicia to join her in the sunroom. "Phillip and I built this room onto the house, so we could enjoy the view of the ocean in the cooler months. I often sit out here on my own and reminisce about the past. My darling Phillip, I miss him every day." Letting out a wistful sigh as she made herself comfortable on the settee. "I've been thinking … would you mind if Sophie stayed here with me for the week? She could ride her bike down to the beach for a swim and I'd love the company."

Alicia didn't know how to answer. She had only ever left Sophie once – for a few days back in Perth with Aunt Beryl when she and Brandon had flown to Melbourne to watch the Australian Ballet Company perform Swan Lake.

"Perhaps I shouldn't have asked: I can see you are reluctant."

Yes, she was reluctant, and if she was perfectly honest, selfish. She hated the thought of being alone. She knew Dee Dee was right: Sophie would love to go swimming and ride her new bike. "You're right. It will do Sophie good. She deserves a little holiday away from the theatre." *And from me,* she thought sadly.

Early the next morning, Dee Dee dropped Alicia off at the hotel. Standing on the sidewalk, waving goodbye, feelings of loss hit hard. She looked up at the gold-trimmed doors and shivered. The thought of entering without Sophie by her side made her feel hollow and incomplete, as if a part of herself was missing. Sophie was more than Sophie; she was … *them* … all wrapped up in one little girl.

She rang each day to see how Sophie was going. It hurt to hear her so happy: full of stories about Dee Dee and the fun they were having together. 'Much better than being with Linda,' she told Alicia.

Aware of her mood, Brandon invited her for a drink with him and some of the other dancers from the Company, after the show. She hated the thought of being alone in an empty hotel room, but she didn't feel like sitting in a bar trying to talked to people who had nothing more on their minds but fun. She would ruin their night and she knew Brandon would worry about her.

Curled up under the covers, the pillow spooned to her body to soften the loneliness. She wondered if she had made the right decision not to go with Brandon and his friends. Any company had to be better than none. Sleep refused to come and when it did it was broken by nightmares of the past. Standing in her pyjamas watching the city lights from her hotel window she thought about Nick. She hadn't spoken to him since she had left his mother's condo. She tried convincing herself it didn't matter. But she knew that wasn't true. She missed him more than she cared to admit. Picking up the phone, heedless of time, she rang his number and waited. As the seconds ticked away so did her courage and she hung up. What was she going to tell him, that she was lonely? It sounded ridiculous, when she had a Company of dancers in the same hotel, including Brandon. Tears poured down her cheeks and she threw the phone on the floor. *Unfair! What a joke! My whole life is unfair. I can't even spend a few nights alone without falling to pieces.*

She stared at the phone vibrating on the floor and brushed away her tears. It had to be him. "Hello."

"Baby, what's wrong? Are you alright?"

The anxiety in his voice made her cringe. "Ye … yes, I'm fine."

"So why did you ring? I know something is wrong. Talk to me, Alicia … tell me what's the matter."

She could feel the tears returning and swallowed hard. "I'm sorry."

"You're sorry! Sorry about what? For God's sake, tell me why you rang or I'm done trying to figure this puzzle out."

Alicia panicked, sobbed into the phone. "I … can't sleep. Your … mother … Sophie … I … please don't hang up!"

The silence seemed to last a lifetime. His exasperated sigh whistled down the line.

"Darling, listen to me. Get into bed and keep the phone close to your ear."

"You won't hang up?"

"No, my Sweet, I won't hang up."

She listened to him tell her stories about his childhood, how his father left him and his mother for a young actress suffering with delusions of grandeur spinning through her blonde head. The last thing she remembered him saying was something about a doctor – Brow or Brand – before she fell asleep. It was nine o'clock when she woke with the phone tangled in her hair. But her heart was still.

He rang the next night and the next, talking to her, telling her about his school days, college, his marriage, and his work until she drifted off to sleep.

***

Alicia was waiting at the front of the hotel when Dee Dee picked her up Sunday morning. "Hello, Dee Dee. Hello, Darling," she said as she followed her overnight bag onto the backseat. "You look very pleased with yourself this morning, Madam. Did you miss me, even a little bit?" Alicia lifted her hand, fingers parted to define a little bit.

Sophie laughed, stretched her arms wide. "From the ground to the sky."

"Fibber," Alicia said, strapping herself in. "I bet you hardly gave me a second thought. Too busy riding that pink bike."

"That would be the truth," said Dee Dee. "Have you had breakfast, Alicia?"

"Actually, no. I slept in."

"Good, nor have we."

With less traffic on the roads, being a Sunday, the drive home was relatively quick. Breakfast was toast with jam and a quick cup of coffee, no time for porridge or pancakes this morning. Alicia thought Dee Dee seemed in a hurry to be somewhere, which she soon realised to be true.

"Alicia dear, Sophie and I are going to church this morning and hoped you would join us. We don't have much time so if you'd like to come, we have to leave in ten minutes."

Sophie, swallowing the last mouthful of toast, bounced off the chair. "Please come, Mummy. I know you'll love it. You can meet Jesus."

Did she want to meet Jesus? "Uhm … I … I don't know. I have nothing to wear." The perfect excuse, so she thought.

"You look fine as you are," said Dee Dee.

Thirty minutes later they were standing on the steps of the Eternity Community Church, Alicia's nails digging into her palms. What was she doing? She had promised herself she would never step foot inside a church again. The thought of listening to another preacher spew forth lies about love, faith, and hope made her feel sick. She had buried those beliefs along with her dead family. The only truth she understood about God was to run as fast and far from his message as she could. "Dee Dee, I …"

Dee Dee slipped her arm through hers, squeezed her hand. "Alicia, this is Mrs Bradley, Laura if you prefer. She's a very dear friend of mine."

She'd hardly finished saying hello before Dee Dee had her through the door and up the aisle. Each step was like trudging through quicksand. The further in she went the deeper she sank. With her heart pounding she lifted her eyes to a field of smiling faces. Alicia thought she remembered everything about church but she'd forgotten the sickly veil of pretence.

Dee Dee sat in between Alicia and Sophie, talked briefly to friends in the front row. A young man walked on to the platform, picked up his guitar and struck a chord. Moments later an entire band joined him, prompting people to find their seats. The crowd started clapping, taking their cue from the beat of the drums.

Teenagers surged to the front, bopped in time to the music. A familiar song tapped at her memory and she silently sang along as her gaze traversed the congregation. There, in the midst of the players, she saw her parents, sitting in their favourite seats, a baby bouncing on her mother's lap, two young teenagers, one so fair the other brunette, alongside. They looked happy, like a family. God, the Joker, had tricked her yet again. Why hadn't she said no, no, no and no again to Dee Dee, and stayed home!

Everybody stood as the pastor claimed his place at the pulpit. He joined in, clapping and singing. Finally, the band stopped and he motioned for everyone to be seated, including the musicians. Smiling down on his flock, he welcomed all visitors. His gaze rested on her. She knew that look. She could almost feel him rubbing his hands together. A newcomer. She knew exactly what came next. *A lecture on your sins and God's mercy to forgive. But God hadn't been merciful, to her had he!*

The pastor titled his sermon *The Lost Sheep*. She girded her mind, barricading it with a shield of resistance. But she heard well enough.

"Jesus gives life to the broken, heals the bitter soul," said the pastor.

She almost laughed. Oh, yes, she was alive and bitter. He got that bit right. But it was grief, not Jesus, that kept her bitter soul fed.

His little speech on comfort cut deep and she clamped her lips together to stop from calling out loud enough for the whole congregation to hear so they would know the truth: *Where was God's comfort when I mourned.*

"He gave us beauty for ashes, so put on the garment of praise for the spirit of heaviness."

Alicia shook her head. Beauty for ashes. She failed to see how anything beautiful came from her family's ashes. How could she praise God for the heaviness that hung around her neck like a giant pendant everywhere she went. Before she realised what was happening, Dee Dee had slipped her arm around her shoulder. She didn't want to be touched or comforted: it was too late for that. But she couldn't deny his words felt like shards of truths - truths she wanted to ignore - slicing through the walls of her heart. The longer he preached the harder it became to deny the volcanic emotions erupting within.

"Just like the shepherd who loses a sheep, God never gives up on the lost."

Is that what she was, a lost sheep? There were certainly times in the past when she had felt so lost she had wanted to die. Was this God's way of shepherding her back into his flock? Could she do this again? Was He the comforter she yearned for? She had never questioned her decision to accuse God for her family's death. Doubt niggled. Was it really God's fault another vehicle had run a red light and rammed into the side of her father's car, killing her family? Could grief have clouded her judgment?

"Remember, Beloved, on His shoulders, His stripes bore our pain."

Did He bear her pain? Emotions, embedded deep in her psyche – pain, grief, loneliness, fear to love, bitterness and secrecy – spewed from her mouth in spluttered sobs.

She felt Dee Dee's arm tighten. "God and I love you, darling."

Alicia shook her head. It was too dangerous to believe Dee Dee loved her. But the need was great: a deep and desperate need to be loved and cherished. "Don't say those things to me unless you mean them."

"As God, be my judge, I speak the truth."

Fighting the tears, Alicia closed her eyes and bowed her head as the pastor led the congregation in a closing prayer. He prayed to create clean hearts and renew righteous spirit in all God's creatures. Everyone said Amen, and the band, gathered on the stage, started playing Amazing Grace. The congregation began to sing and for the first time in years she let the meaning of those words sink deep into her soul. *He saved a wretch like me.*

***

At the end of that long and emotional day, the two women sat in companionable silence on the front patio and watched the stars twinkle into existence. Alicia felt as though someone had oiled the strings of tension in her chest, allowing a blessed peace to swing free. She smiled at Dee Dee.

"You look better."

"I feel better."

"You didn't eat much for dinner. Are you sure you're not hungry?"

"Positive, thanks."

"Can I ask you something, Alicia?"

From the look on Dee Dee's face she had a strong suspicion her question would be threatening. Could she take a chance? Only one way to find out. She nodded.

"The night I brushed your hair I felt your pain. Something dreadful has happened to you in the past, something to do with your mother. Am I correct?"

It seemed ages before Alicia could bring herself to speak. *Yes, you are correct.* Could she trust Dee Dee enough to share her story? Maybe this was the start of learning to let go, to let the healing process begin. "Apart from two counsellors I've seen, Brandon is the only person in my life I truly trust. Of course, there are many others back home in Perth who know what happened but I have never shared my heart with any of them."

Her gaze strong, her voice gentle, Dee Dee asked, "Why?"

The answer was simple. "It hurts too much."

"Is it truly that bad?"

Bad was a strange word to use. If only it were as easy as the word 'bad'. She wished it were bad. Bad seemed good, even amusing. But there was nothing amusing about their death and she wondered if a word existed that described her tragedy. She stole a glance at Nick's mother. What would she think if she told the truth about Sophie? Being a Christian, she might consider her lies despicable. She might even tell Nick. "Yes," she said. "It is, it's that bad."

"I see."

"No, you don't, you can't." Alicia looked out across the ocean. "It's tragic and painful and twisted. I have lived a lie for a long time."

Dee Dee hesitated, shrugged her shoulders. "Well, I won't judge you, Alicia, if that's what's worrying you."

"You may change your mind once you hear the truth."

"I doubt it. I have seen many things in my life. Nothing so great I can't forgive."

"If I decide to tell you, first, you have to promise me something."

"Of course, anything."

Alicia looked straight at Dee Dee as she spoke. "And if you break your promise to me, neither you nor Nick will ever see me or Sophie again." She noted the subtle lift of the eyebrows but continued to hold her gaze as Dee Dee mulled over the challenge.

"Then I promise."

"You must promise me not to repeat a word of what I tell you to Nick. I will never forgive you if you do." Alicia regretted her need to be firm, but if her relationship with Nick failed, she needed to survive. Sophie needed her to survive. The less Nick knew, the less vulnerable she would feel and the greater her chance of continuing her life, as she knew it, would be.

"I give you my word as a Christian and a woman of integrity. I will never repeat what you tell me. Not to Nick. Not to anyone."

Alicia opened her mouth to speak but nothing came out. "I don't know how to start. The feelings are buried so deep."

"I have all night."

All night is probably how long her story would take to unravel, she thought, as she let her mind roll back to the fateful day, six years ago. "I arrived home early from the ballet Academy in Perth to an empty house. Two police officers turned up on my doorstep minutes later. They told me there had been an accident involving my parents. They never mentioned my brother."

She could still feel the chill creeping over her flesh from the cold whitewashed walls of the waiting room in the hospital. She remembered watching the lips of a man – obviously the doctor with splashes of blood on his white coat – speaking cruel words about her family until she wanted to strike him.

"I went with the police in their car to the hospital. The doctor told me my mother and father had died in the ambulance, my brother on the operating table."

Alicia stopped, still haunted by the memory of her terrified scream when she had eventually processed what the doctor was telling her. "A four-wheel drive …" She pushed her fingers against her mouth, waited for the moment to pass. "I don't think I'll ever be able to talk about it easily."

"I'm not surprised," said Dee Dee, dabbing at her eyes with a tissue.

"I'd never spent a single day without my mum and here I was at seventeen facing a life without my family. I was beyond terrified. I think I collapsed. They must have given me something to help me sleep because I woke the next morning in a hospital bed with my best friend, Brandon, holding my hand. We've been together ever since, Brandy and I. He's still holding my hand in a way. I told him I couldn't go on without them and that I wanted to die. He reminded me why dying wasn't an option. Do you want to know why dying wasn't an option?"

Dee Dee blew her nose, nodded tearfully.

"Because God in His glory cheated me out of my only refuge."

"Cheated you?" repeated Dee Dee, frowning.

"Yes! He cheated me. And do you want to know how He did that?"

With her fingers guarding her mouth, Dee Dee nodded.

"Because my … p … parents…" Dee Dee shifted forward, but Alicia lifted her hand to stop her coming closer, shook her head. If she intended to tell Dee Dee the whole story, she need to stay strong. "They left me something… that made death … impossible."

Spreading out her hands Dee Dee mouthed the word, 'What?'

Alicia dropped her head, acutely aware of her listener's watchful eyes. If it wasn't for Sophie and Brandon, she reminded herself, she probably would have ended her life. "They left me something I couldn't ignore or throw away," she said, inhaling the night air for courage. "Every day I woke, not because I wanted to, but because I had to."

"I don't understand."

"I hope you will when I finish telling you the truth."

"Debt … was it money troubles or something?"

"No! A bit more complicated than that." The words came out on a whispered rush. "They left me a baby," she said, twisting her fingers.

"What do you mean … a baby?

"A girl. They left me a beautiful … Baby… girl, who survived the crash."

Dee Dee's shocked expression soon morphed into realisation and her jaw dropped. "Sophie!" she gasped. "She's your mother's child!" She dragged her chair closer and reached for Alicia's hand. "Oh, darling, I'm so deeply, deeply sorry. I've been struggling to wrap my head around your tragedy and then add a baby to the mix, seems almost … unbelievable. And so young and alone. Oh dear. I beg pardon …" said Dee Dee, sobbing into her tissue.

The memory of Brandon, back in Perth, trying to manoeuvre

Sophie's cot to fit inside the boot of their clapped-out car and banging his head, brought a smile. "I wasn't completely alone. I did have Brandon. I don't know what I would have done without him. We lived together in my parents' house. Shared everything, from Sophie to the washing. I love him with all my heart, he's my best friend and my family. Sophie adores him. To her, he is her uncle."

"He sounds like a remarkable young man. I'd love to meet him." Dee Dee paused, shuffled in her seat. "But why the secrecy?"

Alicia eased back in her seat, pondering Dee Dee's question. "Oh, I don't know, it somehow just happened. It started with Sophie calling me mummy. Although I was shocked at first, I realised it had advantages. People who didn't know the truth simply assumed I'd landed myself in trouble. But a sister: well, I didn't want to have to explain. I hated the sympathetic looks, the million questions — how come you have the care of your sister, what happened to your parents and so on. After their death, I went into a very dark place. I became withdrawn … reclusive. My secrecy became my invisible shield, protecting me from the curious. Coming to Melbourne was like escaping, leaving everything behind and starting again. It made sense to continue as we were. Not even Louis, the Company's director, knows the truth."

"Phew!" said Dee Dee, flopping back on the chair.

"Please don't think I don't love Sophie. She means the world to me. Without her and Brandon … who knows?"

"Oh, my dear! Such a thought never entered my head. Quite the contrary. But there is something I find …" Dee Dee paused, pursed her lips, "… bewildering. Apart from Brandon, you don't seem to have had anyone you could turn to. An aunt or uncle, grandparents perhaps?"

Alicia stifled a laugh. She could still see the relief on her Aunt Pat's face when she'd told her extended family of her plans. "My mother's sister, Aunt Beryl, and her husband, Stan, lived next door, and her brother, Uncle Robert, and his wife, Aunt Pat, lived in the country. They held a family conference shortly after the funeral, without me I might add, and decided that Sophie should stay in the city with Aunt Beryl, and I was to go to the country and live with Uncle Robert and Aunt Pat. The most sensible solution, they said. I was too numb to think for myself."

"It was Brandon's idea, really, that changed everything. His life was almost as miserable as mine. I have only met Brandon's father once but it was enough. His father hated everything about him and – in his words – 'his pansy lifestyle'. Brandon is gay you see.

"I did guess," said Dee Dee.

It was only a matter of time before his father kicked him out of the house. He begged me not to go with Uncle Robert. He figured with Aunt Beryl next door to help out with Sophie, we could live together in my family's home and continue dancing. The scheme was perfect, except for my lack of courage. That changed the day I walked in on them all gathered in my aunt's kitchen discussing my future. Not knowing how they would react, I told them about Brandon's idea. The relief on their faces was so pronounced, I realised how difficult my life and Sophie's would have been, living unwanted in someone else's home. The rest is history."

After several sighs, Dee Dee found her voice. "Your story is overwhelming sad and yet inspiring, in a way. Suffice to say, I think you are a rather remarkable young woman, Alicia."

"Oh, how I wish that was true. I battle the grief of their loss daily. I miss them so much, especially my mother. I feel empty inside, as though my life has no purpose without them."

"I understand you feeling that way, but what about Sophie and Brandon. Where would they be without you?"

"Sophie will grow up, find her way in life and Brandon will one day move on, then what?"

"Well … you might fall in love …" She hesitated, glanced through the glass windows at the photo of Nick hanging on the sunroom wall.

Nick! Nick and his beautiful face had begun to fill Alicia with frightening hope. He was fast becoming the air she breathed. She stood up, swung around to face his mother. "Nick has changed everything."

"For better or worse?"

"I'm not sure, but I have this terrible fear he'll break my pathetic heart."

"Don't be frightened, Alicia. Nick is a good man. I ought to know, I'm his mother."

Alicia smiled. "My parents were Christians. They raised me in a church very similar to the one we went to today. Not long before my mother was due to give birth to Sophie, we spent the afternoon cleaning out the linen cupboard. She wanted to make room for Sophie's baby clothes." Alicia stopped, fixed in thought. "I found my mother's wedding dress. It was so beautiful, that rich satin material with embroidery across the bodice and puffy sleeves… well anyway, I held it up against me and my mother asked me if I'd like to wear it on my wedding day." Mimicking her mother, Alicia continued. "'Only virgins can wear this dress,' she said, one hand on her hip and the other pointing at my face. Her mother and grandmother and Aunt Beryl all wore it on their wedding day. It's something of a family tradition and I promised her … I promised her I would wear it on my wedding day. That promise will never be broken, it's all I have left to give a much loved and missed mother."

"And neither it should."

Alicia shook her head. "You don't understand."

"No, I certainly don't. It's God desire that his daughters should come to the marriage bed untouched."

"Maybe God does, but what about Nick?" asked Alicia. "Oh! I've been so careless. Look at him. He's sophisticated, handsome, clever, not to mention, experienced. How long do you think I can deny him what other girls would give willingly? I have nothing to offer him but a broken heart and a child who isn't even my own."

"You underestimate him. He's drunk from many cups and still thirsts for something more. He loves you, I'm sure of it."

Alicia wondered if she should continue. The truth might upset Dee Dee but she decided, one way or another, she had to say it. "No, he doesn't."

"What do you mean? Hasn't he told you he loves you?" Dee Dee looked puzzled.

"No, he hasn't. Not a word. I'm not very worldly when it comes to men, and I have no idea what Nick thinks, but he's not stupid. He knows there is something wrong, something awful I'm not telling him. I need to protect myself. I'm not going to bare my heart to a man who doesn't love me. For all I know he could be amusing himself at my expense. And I definitely don't want his pity. If he doesn't love me … well then, I need to survive with my heart and my secrets my own … for Sophie." Alicia worried over the puzzled look on Dee Dee's face.

"I don't understand why Nick hasn't declared himself to you but I do understand why you feel the way you do. Believe me when I say, no matter what happens between the two of you, I will never let you down or forsake you."

Alicia believed Dee Dee meant every word but deep down she knew if she and Nick parted, she would never see Dee Dee again.

Chapter Twelve

At the close of the Brisbane season, Dee Dee had invited Alicia to stay at her villa before flying to Sydney to join Mason, for the week's orientation. When Sophie found out she had to go away again to Sydney, she begged her mother to let her go home with Brandon. Unable to face another stint on her own, Alicia insisted Sophie come with her. She used Dee Dee's invitation to the Gold Coast, riding her precious bike, to help ward off the expected tantrum.

Alicia stood in front of the hotel, holding one of Sophie's hands while Dee Dee held the other. They waited for the Company to board the coach before heading to the coast.

"Now don't forget … if Sergio falls and breaks his leg tell Mason to give me a call. Happy to take his place," said Brandon hoisting his bag over his shoulder.

"I'm sure to. I can see it now, Sergio sprawled out on the floor holding his broken leg and writhing in pain, and compassionate me advising Mason to call you immediately while ignoring the groans coming from below."

"Worth a try."

"Goose." Alicia kissed him goodbye. Right before he was about to board the bus, he picked up his favourite Button, hugged her in a warm embrace, and jumped aboard.

"Tally Ho," he called from his window as the bus pulled away from the kerb, making Sophie giggle.

Later that evening over dinner, she thought about her day and how strange it felt saying goodbye to Brandon. She would miss his steady influence. Remembering his parting comment, brought a lazy smile.

"Something I missed?" said Dee Dee, scooping the last of her supper onto a fork.

"I was thinking about Brandon and his funny comment about Sergio, should he break his leg. Unfortunately, that is where my amusement ends. There is nothing funny about being a principal in another company; in fact, I'm scared to death. I've never danced without Brandon before."

"I know exactly how you feel. When Philip died, I thought I would never be able to step foot out of this place again. But of course, I did." Dee Dee gathered up the empty plates, put them on the sink. "Do you remember me mentioning I have a holiday house on the Victorian coast." Alicia nodded.

"I also have an older sister living there who I haven't seen for such a long time. I've been thinking of paying her a visit. The change would do me good. If you have no objections, I thought I might come with you to Sydney and fly to Melbourne when you're done. I could look after Sophie during the day, take her to the zoo, or a theme park, maybe do some shopping. The wardrobe is looking a little tired. What do you think?"

Alicia stared at her in disbelief.

"Can I take my bike?" Sophie pretend-rode her bike around the kitchen.

Dee Dee laughed. "I think Sydney might be a bit crowded for biking but I promise to fly it over to Nick and he can look after it until we get to Melbourne."

"Do you mean it? Would you really come with us to Sydney? It would only be a week." Alicia placed her cup on the saucer, edged forward.

"Yes! Up until now, I haven't had a good reason to go back. There's so much to see and do. Sophie and I could sightsee during the day while you're at rehearsals, and at night, we could all go for dinner in the city."

The faraway look in Dee Dee's eyes was enough to convince
Alicia, Dee Dee meant what she said. They spent the following day
preparing the house to be locked up for a few months and helping
Dee Dee pack.

⁂

Dodging the early-morning traffic, Alicia ran up Macquarie
Street, along Circular Quay 3 to the open walkway of the Sydney
Opera House and up the steps to the main plaza. The Aussie Ballet
Company often performed at the Opera House but it never ceased
to amaze her, the enormity, the opulence and the spectacular
architecture of the building. She loved the way it sat on the water
like a large proud whale, displaying its dorsal fins, the Sydney
Harbour Bridge as its spine. Nothing she'd yet seen compared to
the theatre's size, and she experienced a sense of true insignificance
in the wider world as she entered the building.

Dancers were gathered in small groups, some on the stage
warming up, others lurking in the iron-constructed web backstage.
Disorientated, she approached a girl walking towards her. "Could
you please tell me where I might find Mr Mason?" She cleared her
throat, conscious of sounding as nervous as jelly wobbling on a
plate. The girl pointed to the end of the room and she looked up
to see Mason coming towards her, a welcoming smile on his face.

"Alicia, you've arrived," he said, taking both her hands. "How
is the hotel?" He didn't wait for an answer as he led her through
the studio doors. The few dancers at the *barre*, or on the floor tying
ribbons, stopped talking. She lifted her chin and remembered the
advice of Madam Dobrovka - her old ballet teacher from the
Academy in Perth: Ignore emotion and focus on what you're doing.
Mixing it with Dee Dee's advice, she prayed for the good Lord to
ease her pulsating nerves.

Mason placed his arm around her shoulders and hailed a male dancer whom she recognised immediately as the famous Russian-born American, Sergio Vassilkovski, who Mason had discovered on one of his trips to the United States, and offered him a contract with Sydney Dance Company. One look at his stony face confirmed what she had already suspected. Sergio deemed it an insult to be partnering a young unknown. He stared at her through narrow eyes, barely tipping his head, when introduced.

Mason directed her to the change rooms. Heads turned sharply in her direction when she walked in. She offered a weak smile but received little response. Even before she'd pulled her gear from her bag, the room had emptied. She quickly changed. Rushing back into the studio, she headed for the one space left at the end of the *barre*.

To Alicia, dance was like a drug, detaching her from the real world. The harder she worked, the faster her tension dissipated. She thought about her time as a student back in Perth, how she would block the world around her by pretending to soar through the clouds, landing at heaven's door. How long ago that seemed. One day at a time, sweet Jesus, the pastor at Dee Dee's Church had said. In this case, one ballet step at a time.

Mason never took his eyes off her during class. The intensity of his scrutiny bordered on embarrassing and she was glad when class ended. Most of the dancers left the room; some stayed on the sidelines to watch rehearsal, Jacinta Westwood, the Company's most respected prima ballerina, one of them.

"Alicia, Sergio. Come here," called Mason.

After wiping the sweat from her face, she hurried to centre floor and waited for Sergio who seemed to be more interested in talking with another dancer.

"Thanks for joining us, Sergio." Aware of the chip in Mason's voice, Alicia kept her eyes lowered.

"I know it's early days but I would like to start rehearsal

immediately. The quicker you two connect emotionally and physically the better."

"I watched her do class," said Sergio, flicking his glance to heaven, his implication clear.

That was a slap to her ego. Determined not to get flustered, she exhaled slowly.

"I've named this ballet *Reticence*, after my mother. *Reticence* means caginess, silence, reserved, which exactly describes her personality. I need you to listen to me, hear the heartbeat in the music, feel my mother's character and grab hold of the emotion I am trying to convey to the audience with your body."

"I'll try my best, Mr Mason."

"Please, call me Lauren."

"And what am I, her silent lackey?"

"No! What you are is a temperamental bore. I'm sure Damson would be happy to partner Alicia, if you would prefer." Sergio shot her a contemptuous look.

"Right. Let's start." Mason inclined his head towards Sergio waiting for what appeared, a positive response. He simply shrugged his shoulders. Mason proceeded to explain the more difficult moves in his choreography.

Her nerves peaking, Alicia faltered often. She even tripped over Sergio's foot, like a bumbling fool.

He stepped back, hands on hips, shaking his head. "Lauren, please! Give me a break!"

Lauren placed his hand on her shoulder, gave it a reassuring squeeze.

"I'm so sorry. I'm a bit nervous," she said to Sergio who was looking as if she were a child from the Academy. Determined to make him eat that look, she clamped tight on her jaw and remembered how she had managed to get this far.

Sergio took every opportunity to denigrate her. The more he sighed, groaned or mumbled, the harder she worked to change his attitude. And as she danced, she prayed, re-affirming her confidence. She even considered asking God, on more than one occasion, to give her enough strength to resist the temptation to knock Sergio flat.

"Something funny?" he asked, annoyed.

Her smile died. "Yes, but I doubt you would appreciate the joke." At the sardonic curl of his upper lip, she immediately regretted her outburst. If she ended upside down on her head during the next lift, she would have only herself to blame.

It was midday when Mason finally stopped for a break. Although it had been a gruelling few hours, the lion, she thought, had calmed, and hopefully, it had something to do with his appreciation of her skill. By the end of the day, she could almost believe the upward curve of his mouth might actually be the hint of a smile.

During the course of the day, many of the dancers from the Company had popped their heads through the doors to catch a glimpse of rehearsal. Some lingered, and she sensed approval. But back in the change room, she realised approval was a long way from acceptance. Some battles, she mused, were better fought with quiet dignity.

Over the week, Mason proved to be a demanding taskmaster, with few breaks between hours of repetitive hard work. But she felt compensated by her increasing success in drawing out Sergio's better side.

"Alicia, come. I want to try that lift again." Sergio moved *centre floor*. Taking hold of her waist he wedged his hands under her ribs for support and lifted her onto his shoulder. "You do realise I am falling a little more in love with you each day?" he said, dropping her into *a fish*. From there he hoisted her into *arabesque,* held her balanced as she *developed devant* and letting go of his hand, fell back into his arms in *lunge position*, their lips inches apart. "I think it's because of your eyes. They are so brilliant. When I look into them, they make me want to sweep you off your feet." He lifted her into his arms, held her so tight she couldn't escape. "Are you just a little in love with me?"

"I thought you didn't like me."

"Blah! I was a fool."

The tabloids often described him as a flamboyant Casanova and she was beginning to understand why. "You have too many lovers, Sergio, to fit me into your busy schedule. Hush now, Lauren will get angry." Sergio hoisted her up backward into the air, balancing her on the palm of his hand, strategically placed between her shoulder blades. Hanging over his hand it occurred to her that their relationship had moved to a more professional level.

"Concentrate, you two. Stop talking and focus. You're holding her all wrong, Sergio. No, no, no. Put her down." Hands on hips, Lauren waited. "By the way. I've arranged a photo shoot later this afternoon. The Sydney Herald is sending a freelance photographer ... I forget his name, Gilbert or something. Anyway, I want all of New South Wales and Victoria to see my masterpiece, and fill this theatre. So look sharp!"

When Michael Gillespie walked into the studio later that afternoon, a camera slung over his shoulder, Alicia couldn't contain her surprise. "Michael! You didn't tell me you were freelancing for this production."

"Thought I'd surprise you. Besides, it's only for a short time. Just filling in for James Emmerson, who's been sent to cover a story in the Middle East."

She kissed him on the cheek. "It's good to see you again."

"And you. You look like you caught a touch of the sun in Queensland. Love the Gold Coast ... how about you?"

"Yes, very much." The memory of waking up to find Nick in his mother's kitchen flashed across her mind.

Sergio cleared his throat.

"Oh! I do beg your pardon. Michael, I'd like you to meet, Sergio

Vassilkovski. Sergio, Michael Gillespie, and of course,
Lauren Mason, the director."

"Right! Now that we are all formally introduced, back to business. Sergio, could you try that backward lift again, only this time place your hand lower down her back so she hangs directly along your arm. And Alicia … bend a little more in your upper body … like this." He placed his hand between her shoulder blades thrusting out her chest and, with the other hand on her forehead, pushed her head back. "Better, yes that's good." He heeled his hand over his forehead, took a few steps backward, signalled them all into motion.

"Better! Much better. Yes, that's it … good … good … exactly. Try releasing her foot … lovely."

"You're like poetry in motion, Alicia," said Michael as he clicked away. "I love taking photos of you. You make the impossible seem easy."

"Oh, blah blah blah," said Sergio, lowering Alicia to the ground, obviously a little miffed by the lack of praise coming his way.

By the end of her orientation week in Sydney, her relationship with Sergio had improved to the point where she felt confident about the coming season. She knew Mason was satisfied with her work and the relationship that had developed between his two leading dancers. It had been a good idea to come early to Sydney, and she walked away from the theatre a lot more relaxed than when she'd first entered. Even the cold stares of the other dancers were less oppressive, giving her fresh hope for her return. She caught a glimpse of her reflection in the glass windows and to her surprise she looked happy.

Skipping down the steps amidst the masse, she thought about Brandon and how little she had missed him. Dee Dee had filled the gap, and Nick – lovely, lovely Nick – had called every night, filling her dreams.

Their final night in the hotel she spent packing for Melbourne.

She had put Sophie to bed and folding her last pair of tights into a bag when her mobile rang. She loved hearing Nick's voice: it soothed every nerve in her body. She walked into the bathroom so as not to wake Sophie, rested against the glass divider and shut her eyes, but they sprang open when he mentioned the hospital ball.

"I haven't been since my marriage break-up, couldn't bear the thought of it," he admitted. "I'll be working at the hospital in a few months, so I thought it appropriate I go. I would very much like you to come with me. Do you think Louis would give you the night off?"

"Yes, of course. I'm sure we have nothing between now and when I return to Sydney for Mason's season."

"Then I'll take that as a yes."

Curled on the couch in front of the TV, she tried to concentrate on the movie Dee Dee was watching, but her mind kept wandering to thoughts about the ball. Memories of the last dinner date with Nick and his friends made her cringe.

"Something wrong, my love? You look worried," said Dee Dee.

"Nick has asked me to go to the hospital ball with him."

"Wow! How exciting. So why the worried look?"

"The last time we went out with his friends, it didn't go so well. Besides, I don't have a dress, and even if I did …" She stopped.

"What?"

"Those women, they're so … Oh, you know …"

Dee Dee shook her head. "No! I'm afraid I don't."

"They're … they're very sexy, voluptuous. You know the type." She looked down at her chest, then at Dee Dee. "Skinny – yes, Sexy – no."

Dee Dee laughed. "Darling, there's more to a beautiful woman than 'voluptuous and sexy.' Besides I have no doubt Nick thinks you're sexy. Beat them at a different game. Wear something unbelievably stunning. Knock their eyes out."

"I wish." Mentally checking her wardrobe, she knew something unbelievably stunning didn't exist.

"Sydney is the fashion capital of Australia," said Dee Dee. "Why don't we do a little shopping in the morning. We have plenty of time. The plane isn't due to leave until late afternoon and we've already packed."

They left their bags with the concierge the next day and headed off early, up Pitt Street. After scanning several of the more well-known outlets, they finally discovered a boutique tucked away down a narrow arcade, dealing exclusively in evening wear. Alicia perused the dresses displayed on the mannequins. She didn't think she'd be able to pay for a sleeve let alone a whole dress.

"Let's have a look," said Dee Dee. "Just for fun."

Alicia lifted the plastic covering and gaped at the pale grey creation underneath. It reminded her of something a movie star would wear at the Oscars. She lifted the dress from the rack and held it against herself. She'd never seen anything so exquisite. "Don't touch it Sophie, good girl"

"Now that is gorgeous. Why don't you try it on?" said Dee Dee, pulling Sophie to stand with her.

"All Jonathon Denney dresses are exclusive," replied the assistant.

"I don't think I should. I might not want to take it off."

The assistant laughed. "A common problem in this store," she said. "Here let me hang it in the changeroom for you." Dee Dee indicated with her head for Alicia to follow.

The assistant lifted it from the hanger; undid the zip. "Let me help you. It's best if you step into it and pull it up." She flung back the curtains and Alicia walked out to get a better look in front of the full-length mirror.

The delicate fabric felt like the tingling breath of heaven's sigh on her bare flesh. The bodice fell in even folds from the jewelled straps to cling at her waist above the long flowing skirt. And the patterned array of diamantes sewn into the material falling from the waist to her hips sparkled as she moved. She stared at her reflection in the mirror and wondered if this was how Cinderella felt on the night of the ball. She turned a semi-circle, looked back over her shoulder at the sweeping cut of the dress circling her back. It was then she noticed the price tag dangling from the zip. "Could you tell me how much it costs, please?"

The assistant reached for the tag; turned it in her hand. "You must consider, dresses of this quality are all exclusive. You won't see another one like it."

Alicia sucked in her breath when she heard the price. "Dee Dee, it's too expensive. I could never afford this." She wanted to impress Nick and his friends but not at this exorbitant price. She would search through the shops in Melbourne when she returned.

Dee Dee sighed. "You do look stunning in it."

"I would have to agree," said the assistant. "Not often do we have clients with such a slim figure."

"Thank you both, but as much as I love the dress, I really can't afford it."

"I have some pocket money saved," said Sophie.

"Oh, darling, that's very sweet of you but Mummy isn't going to buy the dress."

"Please, Alicia, let me buy it for you. Nothing would give me more pleasure."

Alicia gasped, horrified by the suggestion. "Oh, Dee Dee, I appreciate the offer, I really do, but I couldn't possibly accept such an expensive gift."

Alicia thanked the disappointed assistant and, taking Sophie's hand, went straight to the change room. "You can help me take it off, then I promise we can go and get you some lunch."

It had been the longest week of Nick's life, waiting for Alicia to return. When the day finally arrived, he admonished himself for fussing around like a schoolboy in the throes of his first love.

He spent a ridiculous amount of time choosing what to wear to the airport to pick them up and in the end, settled for jeans and a simple polo shirt.

The arrival lounge was packed, and trying to be as inconspicuous as possible with a pink bike at his side proved difficult. He had rung earlier in the week, when the bike arrived from Brisbane, to have it stored at the airport until his mother, Alicia, and Sophie arrived home. After being hit in the shins by several clumsy souls tripping over the bike, anxious to find their bags, he regretted his decision.

Sophie saw him first. Letting go of Dee Dee's hand, she ran over and, side-stepping Nick's feet, grabbed the bike.

He tried to remain calm but, when he saw Alicia, he couldn't help himself – he scooped her up and kissed her full on the mouth. The feel of her small frame imprisoned in his arms, the smell of her hair, the touch of her warm lips filled him with desire. "Promise me you won't go away again," he whispered. She opened her mouth to speak, but he silenced her with another long kiss, knowing he'd asked the impossible.

"I think we should collect our luggage or they'll put it back on the plane," said Dee Dee, grinning.

They arrived back at Alicia's apartment in the dark. Nick lifted the bags from the car, careful not to scratch them on the bike pedal. The arrangement for the bike was that his mother would take it with her to Brighten, but that didn't stop Sophie whining, all the way home.

"It sounds like we have company," said Alicia, inserting the key to her apartment.

Inside, Brandon sat at the dinner table, drinking coffee. Opposite him sat a very tanned, blue-eyed, blond-streaked, straggly-haired male, popping the lid of a Heineken to have with his dinner. Nick, studying the face, thought something about him looked vaguely familiar.

"Alicia!" squealed Brandon as he leapt from his chair and swept her into a bear hug. "It's so good to see you. I've missed you … both." He put her down, whipped Sophie into his arms. "My beautiful girl. Uncle Brandon has missed his Button."

"My bike is in the car," she said, rubbing her eyes.

"That's it? The bike is in the car. Not … I miss my wonderful Uncle? I think, maybe Miss Grumpy Bum might be a bit tired." He looked across at Alicia, and pulled a wry face. "Sydney, plane, bike – slightly confused! Apartment – no room for a bike – forgot that bit, did we?"

Alicia rolled her eyes; put her finger to her lips to shush him.

"I'm not tired … I just want my bike."

"Of course, you're not," said Brandon putting her down and shaking hands with Nick. "And who, may I ask is this lovely lady … or can I guess?"

"Mum, I'd like you to meet Brandon Hastie, Alicia's dance partner, and flatmate. Brandon, my mother, Mrs Dee Dee Johnson."

"Ah, the penny drops. Nice to meet you, Mrs Johnson."

"Please call me Dee Dee. It's nice to meet you too, Brandon. I've heard so much about you I feel I know you already."

"All good, I hope,"

"Of course."

"And this … eh … is my brother, Jason."

Jason stood, beer in hand, and moved out from his chair, his broad smile revealing a set of sparkling white teeth. "G'day, everyone."

Puzzle solved, thought Nick, shaking hands with the bronze surfer. Although how these two men could be brothers was beyond him.

"Jason!" said Alicia, wide-eyed.

"Same mould, different batch," said Jason.

"I don't think you and Jason ever met," said Brandon, frowning.

How strange that Alicia has never met Brandon's brother, thought Nick.

"He was too busy playing league football. Crazy, eh! Ballet dancer, league footballer. Doesn't quite fit but there you have it, eh Jase? The horror of our parents' storybook.'

"Right on, matey!"

Sophie yawned.

"Excuse me, everyone, but I'd better put Sophie to bed."

"Hope you don't mind, Ally, but I've put Jason in Sophie's room. Could she sleep with you until we work something out?"

"Yes, of course."

"I want Nick to put me to bed."

"Your loyalty, Button, kills me." Brandon pulled a funny face, making her laugh.

"Are you really Uncle Brandon's brother?" asked Sophie.

"You bet-cha your bottom dollar."

"Then that makes you my Uncle too!" said Sophie, taking his hand and smiling up at him.

Brandon let out a whopping laugh. "That wiped the smile off your face, eh Uncle Jason?"

Nick found it interesting that Brandon had a brother. He switched his gaze from one to the other. He would never have picked them as brothers. One so tanned and muscular, the other lithe, wiry and delicate. He was also a little annoyed to discover Jason would be staying at the apartment and for an indefinite time.

On the drive to his aunt's where Dee Dee had arranged to stay for a few nights before heading off to her own house, she chided him for being ridiculous. 'A more sincere girl I have yet to meet,' she had said. But perhaps his mother had missed the appreciative look on the surfer's face when Alicia walked through the door.

It was late when he arrived back home. Not wanting to appear rude, he'd stayed for the customary cuppa at his aunts but left immediately after. Inside his house, he ripped off his shirt on the way to his room, threw it on the chair perched in the corner along with his jeans and fell into bed with a head full of thoughts about Alicia, Brandon, Sophie, and now the bronzed surfer.

***

A few days later a large package arrived at his door. His mother had rung earlier to tell him to expect a dress she had secretly purchased in Sydney for Alicia to wear to the hospital ball and had it sent to his address. Apparently, Alicia had strongly objected to Dee Dee buying the dress, so his mother paid for it by credit card while Alicia was in the change room. He stared at the long rectangular box balanced on the coffee table, the silver bow smiling at him. He fingered the ribbon; played with its tassels. His mother had described the dress as 'divine'. *It wasn't the dress that was divine,* thought Nick. He would deliver it tonight but first, he had to focus on work.

Nick left the station early that afternoon, depleted of enthusiasm and full of impatience. Working at Channel Seven held little interest for him since he'd received his letter of acceptance from the medical board. He felt as though his life was in limbo, waiting for the whistle to blow so he could launch into the real reason he existed. He wanted … needed to get his teeth back into medicine and he wanted Alicia by his side when he did.

He was relieved to find her alone when he entered her apartment, the box tucked safely under his arm. Sophie was already in bed, and Brandon had taken his brother out for dinner at a popular pub in town.

"That's a mighty big box."

The animated look on her face made him wish it was him who had bought the dress instead of his mother. He followed her into the lounge, put the box on the coffee table and pulled Alicia into his arms.

"I'm desperate to see what's in the box."

"It's a gift from my mother."

"Oh, my stars! I hope it's not what I think it is," she said, pulling out of his embrace and plonking herself on the sofa in front of the box.

Alicia reminded him of a little girl opening a present on her birthday. Lifting the lid then the tissue paper, she stared at the folds of jewelled-fabric glittering in the light, then at him.

"Nick, I can't accept this. It cost an absolute fortune." She settled the tissue paper over the dress and put the lid back on.

"I think you would offend mother if you gave it back," he said, joining her on the sofa. He turned to face her, grasped both hands. "I know her and she's not the type of person to buy on impulse. She wanted you to have it." He pulled her closer. "Why didn't you tell me you needed a dress. I would have bought you one."

She leant in, lips pouted, a mock scowl on her face.

Nick ran his fingers down her cheek, rested his forehead against hers. He was sick of taking this relationship slowly. Awash with adrenalin rushing under heated skin, he pressed his lips onto hers, teased, explored, demanded. Her long hair felt like silk in his fingers, and smoothing it against the skin on his cheek, he inhaled the sweet smell of honey. Gently, he eased her back on the couch and settled himself in the comfort of her arms. Loving the feel of her beneath him, his lips sought hers. He feathered kisses along her neck, feasting on the sting of perfume. With their legs entwined, he smoothed his hand down the outside of her thigh, up again, and a little purr sent his heart racing. Thrilled by the knowledge he was awakening her desire, he lifted his head, watched those green cat-like eyes darken, and kissed her with a passion he had long been denied. When she arched, he whispered her name, glided his hand beneath her blouse and fondled the warm, peaked flesh, firm in his hand. She gasped. And like a cold slap to his hot face, she pushed at his chest, writhing to be free. Stunned, he whipped his hand out from under her blouse, stroked back her hair from her face as he tried to calm her down. "Sh, sh! Baby, it's okay. It's okay, I won't hurt you."

"No, it is not that. But it's not okay." Pushing at his chest, she slid out from under him and scrambled, pink-faced, to her feet. "You don't understand."

With his pride bruised, he took a deep breath, climbed off the sofa, and straightened his shirt. "You're right. I don't understand." He kept his voice low; watched her fidget. "Talk to me! Tell me what's wrong. Help me to understand."

She stared at the floor, said nothing. He waited. The longer she stayed silent, the greater his frustration grew. She lifted the box from the table, shot him a thin smile. "I'd better put this away."

"That's it? You'd better put the dress away?"

She looked at him, her face an emotional battlefield. He stepped closer, gently touched her arm. "Did someone hurt you, is that it?" He watched and waited and hoped. "Say something. Anything! Just don't shut me out."

Wide frightened eyes held his. "I … I made a …"

"You made a what? What are you trying to tell me?"

She whispered something under her breath, turned and left the room with the box tucked under her arm.

"Alicia, don't … do … this …" The words died in his throat. He couldn't believe it. Everything in him wanted to smash through the door, beg her to talk to him, tell him what the problem was. Maybe he'd done something to upset her, or was it someone else who had left their mark? Only the sight of raw pain in her eyes stopped him.

But that didn't stop him from lashing out. "Did Michael Gillespie have this much trouble making it to first base?"

He swore under his breath, suddenly ashamed of his outburst. He knew his behaviour derived from a bruised ego, hers from something much deeper. Torn, he hovered a moment, stepped forward, then back. Fist to palm pumping air, he left the apartment before he did something else he might regret. But that didn't stop him from wanting to slam the door on his way out.

He drove home in a weighty mood. Experience told him she had never known true love. She may have had a child, but Sophie was not born out of love. What was it Gillespie had said in the restaurant? "Where's my little girl?" He repeated those words over and over.

Although his accent was slightly coloured by a stint in the States, Gillespie was obviously Australian. *Did he and Alicia know each other back in Perth? Is he Sophie's father?* Not that Sophie in any way resembled him and his dark complexion: she was all her mother. Alicia obviously cared for the man, so force was out of the question. *Unless it was a one-night stand.* Now, that did make sense, no emotion, just experimenting, like kids do, oblivious to the consequences. And what then? He left Perth under a cloud of shame only to meet up with her again years later in Melbourne? *By choice …?* Did she imagine she owed Gillespie her loyalty, Sophie being his daughter, and this was the reason she resisted Nick so fiercely? Perhaps she was waiting for Gillespie to accept responsibility for his actions and marry her, even though he was gay.

Then why did she pursue me? That thought hit him like a bomb — she hadn't pursued him at all — he had been doing all the chasing. Jenny had said go slow but this was ridiculous. He had known her for over six months. Surely, he thought, *it was long enough to have earned her affection.* She must know he was in love with her, why else would a man bother? He gave himself a few days to calm down and then called.

"I bought two tickets over a month ago, to La Traviata. It's tomorrow night, would you like to go?"

"I love Traviata. It's my moth … it's one of my favourite operas."

"Mother … is it? You have a mother. Another secret I shouldn't know about?”

"Nick, I …”

"Forget it. I'll pick you up tomorrow night at seven.” He kicked the bar stool knocking it to the ground, and hobbled off to the bathroom.

Chapter Thirteen

Alicia lay in bed, her hands tucked behind her head, trying to recall when she last saw her best friend so happy. Since his brother had arrived, the change in Brandon was remarkable. It seemed a switch had been flicked, releasing the pressure in his overheated pipes.

Jason told Brandon he'd decided to travel, see the world, find himself, and maybe see his brother along the way. Unfortunately for Alicia, where Brandon's happiness began, hers ended. Jason needed a place to live and had moved his gear into Sophie's room. Alicia didn't mind sharing with Sophie: it was a bit uncomfortable but space was the least of her concerns. She sensed Nick's disapproval of Jason and the casual way he had moved into the apartment as if it were his own.

She had worked with temperamental characters long enough to recognise signs of jealousy: the tilt of his upper lip when they shook hands, the way his gaze traversed Jason's body, his glib, impassive replies. She also recognised his growing frustration at her guarded behaviour. He wanted answers and he wanted her. The walls were closing in around her and she felt anxious about going to the opera.

At least a dozen pieces of clothing lay sprawled across the bed, each discarded in favour of another. In the end, she chose a pair of black polyester evening pants and matched them with a gold knitted long-sleeved top and black belt.

The theatre was full of chiffon-clad women, supported on the arms of bow tied men. Nick held her hand as they climbed the steps to the dress circle, but the silence between them was acute.

She skimmed her gaze across the auditorium, picturing her

mother amongst the glitter. She always wore the same black evening gown, long dangling earrings and a sequined shawl draped across her shoulders. Her thick brown hair would be pinned into a French Roll, the same elegant style Meryl Streep had once worn at the Oscars. She glanced at the fingers entwined with hers and wondered what her mother would think of Nick.

By the end of the first act she'd relaxed into the magic of Verdi's music, her thoughts disturbed when Nick asked, "Would you like something to drink?"

There was no expression attached to the question. She nodded: anything would be preferable to sitting in awkward silence. She followed Nick into the lounge where she waited for him to return with a lemon, lime, and bitters. He smiled when he handed her the glass.

"Nick … Darling!"

The low sensual voice almost caused him to choke on his drink. A purring blonde wrapped her free arm around Nick's neck and, pushing herself against him, pressed her scarlet lips onto his. Long, red fingernails poking around the stem of the wine glass reminded Alicia of talons on a crow's foot. Nick broke free of *Marylin Monroe's* clingy embrace to shake hands with the man in a white jacket hovering behind her.

"Leon, Stacy, I'd like you to meet Alicia Sommers. Alicia, Leon Prudenville and his partner, Stacy Logan." Nick's cool voice, his rigid stance, spoke volumes. She might be naïve but not so green that she didn't recognise signs of a past affair.

A quick scroll of those snake-sharp eyes was all the acknowledgment Alicia received.

"Darling! I was certain I knew most things about you, but opera … …! Had I known, we could have made it a foursome."

Bite your tongue, said the voice inside Alicia's head. Going anywhere with *that* woman would take some persuading. Nick half agreed but, by the embarrassed look on his face, she guessed his thoughts coincided with her own.

"Is it true, Nicky? At long last, you've accepted an invitation to the hospital ball."

Nick cleared his throat; glanced at Alicia. "Yes. Actually, we're both going."

Stacy scanned Alicia from head to toe as if she was choosing a side of lamb hanging in a butcher's shop. She turned slightly, lowered her voice, but not quite low enough. "Try not to get leg shackled again by a pretty face with no brains, Nicky. And save me a dance, will you, darling. Like old times."

The bell rang to announce the second act. Stacy leant forward so the halter neck of her dress fell far enough away to reveal all but her nipples as she whispered something in Nick's ear.

Alicia wondered how the thin shoe-string-straps didn't break under the weight of those hefty bosoms. Aghast at the woman's bad manners, she glanced at the man by the blonde's side. He looked very uncomfortable, a silly smile plastered on his face. She would have returned his smile if Nick hadn't whisked her away.

The minute the lights came up to end the show, Nick was on his feet, ushering her from the theatre faster than a bullet on its way to war. Alicia assumed his haste had something to do with dodging the over-enthusiastic Stacy Logan. The drive home proved even less enjoyable. The tension between them charged the atmosphere and crossing her legs, Alicia stared out the window at the street signs flashing by.

Nick kept a tight grip on the steering when he pulled up outside her apartment. "You have never been to my apartment," he said, staring at the windscreen. He sounded as if he was accusing her of something vile. "I've invited a few friends from the studio for drinks Sunday night as a sort of farewell party and I would like it if you came."

It wasn't an invitation but a command. All she wanted to do was escape, and so, dutifully, nodded her acceptance.

***

Sleek, clean and sophisticated, perfectly described Nick's home, Alicia thought as she inhaled the rustic smell of dark leather. She liked what she saw, a mahogany dining suite, matching chairs upholstered in brown leather; Chinese urns in opposite corners of the room, each filled with sprays of silk anthuriums set amongst an array of maidenhair ferns; books on oak shelves lining the far wall. The effect made her think of a lion, proud and stalwart.

Nick played the perfect host, introducing her to personalities from the station. As she rarely had time to watch television, she mostly smiled, sometimes nodding, careful not to say anything that would reveal her ignorance. She chatted to Clarissa, Nick's PA, whom she'd met at the station, and her boyfriend, Harry, who went off to get drinks for the three of them.

Clarissa kept peeking over Alicia's shoulder, and she wondered if she was boring the girl. When she slipped away to see what was keeping Harry, Alicia felt like a palm tree in a desert, standing alone. Her feet ached; she was tired, and the hours dragged slower than a snail climbing a mountain. It was close to midnight when Nick said goodnight to the last of his guests. She flopped onto the leather lounge and slipped off her shoes. The blisters on her feet which had formed during rehearsals in Sydney, still hadn't completely healed. With class at nine o'clock in the morning, she really needed to go home. Nick leant against the bench, watching her.

"Sore feet?"

Apart from introducing her to all his friends as one of the principal ballerinas of the Aussie Ballet Company, like a prize he'd won in a competition, they were the only friendly words he'd spoken to her all evening. Barefoot, she collected the last of the empty glasses from the coffee table, hoping he'd read the signs it was time for her to go, and moved past him to place them on the sink. Busy rinsing the last drops of wine from a glass, she didn't hear him approach. He curled his arm around her waist, kissed her neck. She rested against him, held her breath hoping he would say he loved her. She promised herself if he did, she would tell him everything.

Instead, the words she heard, stung like a bee. "Stay, darling," he said, his lips teasing her ear, his hand crawling upwards.

She bit back the disappointment, pushed out of his embrace.

"It's late Nick. I have to go."

He scowled. "You don't have to go Alicia."

She moved further away, straightened her top. "I have class in the morning."

"How convenient. Another excuse to run away?"

She kept walking and he rounded in front of her, blocking her path.

"Tell me the real reason you can't stay. What is it you're running away from? Is it me? Do I repulse you?"

"No! Nick, you… Leave it alone."

"I what? Leave what alone? Is it intimacy, Alicia? Is that it? Did something happen?" he asked, stepping towards her.

She saw no trace of affection in those eyes, only curiosity … accusation. Of course, he would think that. Why else would a woman reject him? Certainly not a skinny one like her and certainly not Stacy Logan. She should be flattered by his attention. Not every day did the wonderful Nick Coleman bestow his favours on Miss Nobody. *No! That isn't it*, she wanted to say to him. *And yes, something happened, only I'm in no state to discuss my broken heart with you in this mood.* "I really have to go, Nick."

He stared at her. "This wall you've put between us is unnatural. I'm a man and you, my love, are a woman. Didn't your mother teach you about the birds and the bees? You do have a mother? Forgive my ignorance but for some God-forsaken reason I'm not privy to the confidence circle. Brandon, Jason – does Jason know Alicia? And let's not forget the daddy of the group, the worthy Mr

John Spencer. You're right, you'd better go. I'll pick you up for the ball, seven o'clock next Saturday night. Parking will be tight, so we'd best not be late."

Unnatural. Is he saying I'm unnatural because I don't want to go to bed on demand? And yes, I had a mother, a much loved and treasured mother. Had he taken the time to ask her nicely she might have told him her mother was dead, along with her father and brother. His arrogance, however, negated any responsibility she might have felt to answer some of his questions. She had wanted to tell him the truth, make a clean breast of everything, but not now, not with his off-hand attitude. She pushed past him to collect her bag and shoes.

He held the front door open, followed her to the car and waited until she was safely locked inside before disappearing into the lift. *How dare he treat me with so little respect*, she thought pulling out of the carpark. *All because he didn't get his own way.*

She wondered how Nick knew she had confided in John Spencer. Unless, of course, Jenny mentioned to him she'd been seeing John professionally. There was no doubt in her mind John would never have been so unethical as to betray her confidence, so why would Jenny? She vowed to tell him everything after the ball.

***

Alicia lifted the dress from the cupboard, removed the plastic cover. She held the soft fabric against her body and, humming the Viennese Waltz, rocked back and forth. She glided the dress over her head, stared at her reflection in the full-length mirror. Apprehension lurked. An awful feeling of distress — perhaps a premonition — hovered like a grey cloud ready to burst and wash away any joy she had recently discovered.

The lining, smooth and silky against her skin, clung to her small frame, and the diamond earrings Nick had given her picked up the dove-grey colour of the dress. She pushed her feet into a pair of silver beaded stilettos which raised the dress enough to swish seductively around her legs. After one last twirl in front of the mirror she left her bedroom, and her confidence, behind.

"Oh my!" said Dee Dee, smoothing her hand over the skirt. "You look stunning, and your hair … I love the way it falls in soft flowing waves around your shoulders and back."

"Thank you for all of this, Dee Dee," she said twirling a circle for inspection. "Do you really think I look stunning?"

"Well, if my vote counts for anything, I think you look absolutely stunning." Brandon stepped forward, clasped both her hands. "But then I always have."

Alicia wrapped her arms around his neck, whispered, "I love you."

"That only leaves me," said Jason, "and well, what can I say? If Nick should drop dead between now and … no such luck … that would be the doorbell." He rose; strode off clicking his fingers on the way. "G'day mate. Phew! Look-king goood! Your date scrubs up okay, too, if you don't mind me saying."

"Jason, I'm glad you think so."

A wariness touched Nick's eyes making her feel edgy but when his gaze travelled from her head to her feet, lingering at her waistline and back to her eyes, his face softened and his tender smile washed away her fears.

"Mother," he said walking over to kiss her cheek, "why am I not surprised to see you here."

"I wouldn't have missed it for the world. Not often do I get to see my son in a tuxedo and his date looking like Hollywood."

"Brandon. Good to see you again."

Brandon nodded.

"Do you think my mummy looks 'absolutely stunning', like what Uncle Brandon says?" asked Sophie.

Nick crossed the room, lifted Alicia's hand to his lips, stared into her eyes. "Yes … I'd say she looked breathtakingly beautiful."

She lowered her gaze and peeked at him from under her lashes. She wanted to ask him if he felt the same way about the person inside the dress but decided to save that question for later.

She bent and kissed Sophie then Dee Dee, and blew a kiss to each of the brothers. Reaching to take Nick's out-stretched hand, she walked with him to his car. Nick turned her to face him, rested her back against his Range Rover. Gentle fingers traced the outline of her face, moving softly around her chin. From his pocket, he pulled out a small box; flipped the lid. She looked down at a diamond pendant twinkling under the street light.

"To match your earrings," he said, fastening it around her neck.

She bit down on her bottom lip, forced her throat to relax. Her thumb rubbed over the diamond, and she pressed it against her chest. "Thank you, it's beautiful."

A small crease appeared on his brow and the muscle under his eye twitched. The dark clouds above sent shivers along her spine and the unexplained heaviness she'd felt earlier returned. Nick was going to break her heart, maybe even as soon as tonight. She wanted to run back to the security of yesterday and never look forward again. "I'm sorry I've disappointed you, Nick." She placed a finger over his lips before he had a chance to respond. "I have this strange feeling – I can't explain it but promise you won't hate me."

He held her hand to his lips; shook his head. "Alicia, I could never hate you."

She wished he would say he loved her, give her something to hope for, but he didn't. "I want you to know something."

She hesitated, feeling the need to give a small piece of herself for him to believe in and searched for the right words. "Nobody has ever made me feel so alive as you have." He started to speak, but she took his face between her hands, kissed him long and hard; finished that sentence with the words, *'since their death'*, in her head.

Out front of the Langham Hotel, the valet opened the door for her as she alighted from Nick's Range Rover. The fresh evening air danced over her skin. Hand-in-hand they walked up the rich alabaster steps into the hotel foyer, under an array of golden globes hanging from the high ceiling. Not until she reached the top did she notice the man holding the camera. She felt the clasp on her hand, tighten.

"Michael!"

"Surprise, again!" said Michael.

The grip began to hurt. "Again?" came the curt remark from beside her. A quick glance at Nick's face and she felt the first drop of trouble.

"Stand still while I take your photo. Perfect. Now one on your own, if you wouldn't mind. Thanks," said Michael, as Nick stepped away. "You look positively gorgeous in that dress. As beautiful as you do in a tutu." He clicked away like a cricket, ignoring other guests who were making their way up the steps. He bent down on one knee. "Turn around and look back over your shoulder. That's a girl. The photos of you and the great Sergio were fabulous. Front page if it were up to me. Okay, all done. Thanks again." He saluted Nick.

Nick took her hand and they walked along the plush blue carpet. "Michael Gillespie in Sydney? What are the odds?"

"Yes, he was contracted by the Sydney Herald. Michael is the best photographer in Australia – why wouldn't Lauren Mason want him to take our photo's?"

Nick nodded but none too convincingly. He strode through the foyer, following the signs to the Grand Ballroom. Inside he read the list of names on the display board and, finding his, without a word weaved through the crowd to their table.

It hadn't occurred to Alicia that John and Jenny would be at the ball. John lifted his glass and nodded a salute. Alicia thought he looked a little perplexed to see them together. Jenny mouthed a quick hello.

Jenny tried talking across the table but the mix of music, conversations and the clatter of cutlery made it difficult, and she eventually gave up. Although Alicia didn't feel all that hungry dinner was a welcomed distraction. Several people, recognising Nick, stopped to congratulate him on his decision to return to the hospital. He stood to greet them, politely introduced her, and continued talking about his future plans at The Royal. As the night drifted on, she needed to go to the bathroom. Excusing herself, she picked up her bag and headed towards the double doors, past the dance floor and waved to John and Jenny doing the Jive. She wondered why Nick hadn't asked her to dance.

Deep in thought on the way back, she collided with a man who had stepped back from his chair and into the aisle.

"I do beg your pardon. I wasn't looking where I was going," she said.

"The fault is all mine," replied the man, latching onto her wrist to steady himself. With her arm still in his grip, he straightened. His unblinking gaze scanned her body, settled on her mouth. Repulsed, she tried to pull away but his grip tightened. "A fault, I must admit, I don't mind being responsible for." He moved closer, looked down his nose into her eyes. "Would you care to dance?"

"I'm very sorry, but I'm expected back at my table." Alicia craned her neck in search of Nick, hoping he would come to her rescue, but he stood in a group, facing her with his mouth slightly open. Then he turned away.

The man just smiled; pulled her on to the dance floor.

"Please let me go. You're hurting my arm."

His sinister laugh sent chills up her spine. He gathered her in a firm embrace, giving her little choice but to follow his lead as they circled the outer edge of the dance floor in a slow waltz. John and

Jenny swung past. She pulled an anxious face hoping to convey a message of distress and received a funny frown from Jenny. When the song finally stopped, she wrenched free and fled back to her seat ... and an empty table.

Half afraid the man would follow her, she searched the room for Nick; sighted him standing against the outer wall talking to Stacy Logan in her plunging V-neck dress. Stacy's hollow laugh rippled across the room at something amusing Nick must have said. Alicia was sure Stacy had seen her watching them, for she turned into Nick and pressed a long kiss on what appeared to be his willing lips.

The final straw snapped. The humiliation unbearable. Unable to believe Nick would do this to her, she fought back tears. The music stopped and people slowly returned to their seats. She had to get out before Nick came back. She tried to find him in the crowd, but too many people filled the spaces. A sickly smell of sweet perfume wafted to her nostrils; a pair of spongey breasts pushed into her back, and red claws curled over her upper arms.

"Nick and I have been lovers for years," hissed the snarling voice. Alicia, stiff with anger, searched for the nearest exit. "He prefers his women warm and sensual – bones aren't really his thing. He'll soon be working at the hospital and you, little girl, will be history."

The high-pitched laugh faded into the distance as Alicia fled the room. Pushing through the swinging door, she hurried across the foyer and down the steps into the drizzling rain, welcoming the burst of cool air on her hot face.

"Running away again, my love?"

Flinching, she tried to pull free of Nick's grip. "Leave me alone."

"Not this time," he said, ushering her across the street to the car park. "I think you owe me an explanation."

"I owe you nothing, least of all an explanation. Now let me go or I'll scream."

"Scream all you want, but you're getting in that car. I brought you to this ball and I'll make sure you get home safely."

"A taxi will do fine. Now let me go, your hurting my arm."

"I'm sorry, I didn't mean to hurt you," he said, releasing her. "But I'm taking you home and that's final."

Seething, she relented, knowing he wouldn't give up until she agreed.

Neither spoke on the drive home. She tried to understand how he could justify his anger towards her, considering his own behaviour with that woman. What had she done to warrant such appalling treatment? Surely it wasn't because Michael was at the ball. Not even Nick could be that ridiculous. The minute the car pulled up she would make a dash for the apartment.

But when he stopped the car, instead of running like she planned, she sat like a block of ice, waiting for him to explain. His hands remained on the steering wheel, his knuckles white like the pale stain of anger on his face. She wanted to scream so loud his ears would ache, but years of schooling herself to keep her emotions hidden behind the brick wall she'd built to protect herself from the world kicked in, and she said nothing. Disappointment permeated inside her.

Unable to stand another second, she opened the door and fled. But he caught her by the hand and pulled her under the palm tree out of the rain, the distress on his face frightening.

"Why! Just tell me why you danced with him? What were you thinking? You had an entire ballroom to choose from, and you picked him! Why? Help me to understand your logic." He surrendered both his arms to the air.

"I didn't pick him, Nick, as you rudely suggest. He …"

"Oh God, spare me another lie. Don't tell me you had no idea who he was?" He looked as though he wanted to wrap his hands around her neck.

"No … I didn't …"

"I'm sick to my guts with your lies and secrets. You had to know who he was. I described him down to the last detail. And in front of the entire hospital staff, you dance with him."

"I told you, I didn't dance with him. And I still don't know who *him* is!" She tried desperately to recall Nick telling her about this man and who he was but nothing sprang to mind.

"God, you're good. You're really good." He started pacing. "Years of burying the disgrace Rebecca brought upon me, and you … you … why? For God's-sake, why? What have I done to you that you would go to such outlandish lengths to humiliate me? Or is it John Spencer? Are you trying to make him jealous?"

He held his hands out, shook his head. "Jenny? Is it Jenny you have some kind of weird grudge against?"

"Nick! What are you saying?"

"Was this all part of some vindictive plan or something?"

"What? No … no!" He was making no sense and Alicia realised then that no matter how hard she tried to convince him of the truth he was never going to believe her. He was determined to believe the worst, but why … what was going on in his head?

"Great, I feel much better now." He wiped a hand over his face, flicked raindrops from his fingers. "One more thing. Let me guess. Another photoshoot that Gillespie happened to be at?"

Alicia stood speechless. He actually believed she knew Michael would be at the ball. If he had slapped her across the face, she wouldn't have been more shocked. As if scales had dropped from her eyes, she saw her mistake. Her continual silence about her past, her cagey and elusive attitude, had led him to create a fantastic scenario in his head. The black dog of despair was yelping, calling and she tightened her stomach muscles to steady the violent trembling, snaking up her spine.

"Speak to me."

"I don't know what you want me to say. Did I know Michael was going to be at the ball? The answer is, no, I didn't. Satisfied?"

"I don't believe you."

She spoke quietly. "Why would I lie, Nick?"

"Because it's what you do best." He dropped his arms as though he was defeated. "I don't know why I bother but I need to know. A simple yes or no. Is Michael Gillespie Sophie's father?"

Alicia almost laughed. But knowing how deeply he had let this fantasy twist his thinking, she bit her lip. How did a man as worldly as Nick not see that Michael was gay? It stood out like a mole on Michael's face. If she said no to his question, she doubted he would believe her. Then Stacy Logan's words echoed in her head. "He likes his women warm and sensual." Hadn't she known from the beginning this day would come. What a fool she'd been. Now the price of her stupidity must be paid.

The rain seeping through the branches was flattening her hair and running down her neck. If she didn't seek cover soon the dress would be soaked through, along with her heart. She wondered which storm was more disturbing.

"Why don't you answer me?"

"What do you think, Nick." No sooner had the words left her lips than she regretted them. The reaction on his face was wrenching. He believed Sophie was Michael's child. She felt her legs go weak. What had she done?

Nick groaned, slammed his fist into the tree trunk. "Are you sleeping with him?"

Am I sleeping with Michael Gillespie? That his opinion of her had sunk so low was so much more than depressing. Dear God, what was wrong with the man, she wondered. "Is this … what you …?" She couldn't finish, because she already knew the answer.

"Tell me!"

Not even Stacy Logan could force her to say yes to this vile accusation. Although it was dark, she could feel the fury burning in his eyes.

"Like a fool, I thought you were pure and sweet. I got that

wrong. Rebecca was child's play compared to you." He stepped so close she could taste his contempt. "You were right," he said spitting his anger at her. "You have disappointed me. If you were a man …"

"You would what, hit me?" She couldn't quite hear through the rain but she was sure he whispered the word *Never*. At least she hoped he did.

Defeated, he turned, and strode away to the car. Screeching the wheels from the kerb, he drove away, leaving her standing under the tree.

She stayed there until she could no longer hear the purr of the engine. Blinded by tears and rain, she gathered up the skirt of her dress and stumbled up the pathway to her apartment. Her shoe caught in the hem and she tripped up the stairs, bashing her chin on the concrete step above. She bit back a cry, wiped the splatter of blood from her chin. Keys! Where were her keys? She tried to steady her hand as she fumbled inside her purse.

Oh God, he thinks I'm sleeping with Michael Gillespie. A sob escaped. *Oh, Nicky, how could you get it so wrong?* Another sob and then another. She needed to get off the cold concrete slab and go inside.

Water pooled onto the tiled floor in the kitchen. Brandon was only a door away and she needed him – needed him to help her out of her dress – needed him to hold her until the pain subsided. Clasping her stomach, she called him again and again, until she heard his voice.

"Alicia? Alicia is that you?" He switched on the light, pinched at his eyes. "Oh, my God. Ally! What's happened? Where's Nick and how the hell did you get so wet?"

Undoing the zip, he slid the dress from her shoulders and steadied her while she stepped out of it. Standing in her underwear, soaked to the bone and shivering, she let go. The tears ran like a river down her face as she sobbed out her broken heart against his chest.

"The last time I saw that look in your eyes … If Nick did this to you, I'll kill him." He pressed his face against hers. "Oh Ally, tell me he didn't …"

"No, no … oh no," she said, shaking her head. "Brandy, don't…"

"Ssh, ssh, it's okay. I've been picking you up all my life, remember." She rested her head against his shoulder as he carried her into the bathroom.

***

Dee Dee was relieved when Alicia called her from the hotel in Sydney. She had said little about the ball before she left, which left her wondering. "Darling, how are you? I'm so glad you called. Flight okay?"

"Yes. Thank you."

"And Sophie, how is she?"

"She's fine. She's asleep."

There it was again, the lack of bounce in Alicia's voice, the short-pointed replies, saying little but revealing more than Dee Dee cared to hear. "So, tell me, how was the ball?"

"Big and brilliant."

"You're not saying much, darling. Is everything alright? Did Nick behave himself?"

Dee Dee's grip on the phone tightened as she waited for the reply. Instinct warned her something was very wrong.

"Yes, yes, of course. I'm a little tired that's all."

"Well, I'll call in a few days. Take care and God Bless. Bye for now."

Dee Dee stood staring at the phone. Worrying her bottom lip, she rehashed the conversation. She gave it two days then rang again but hung up feeling even more concerned. She hadn't seen or heard from Nick since the ball and wondered if she should pay her son a visit, when as providence would have it, Brandon called. "I'm glad you called. How did you get my number?"

"Sophie, actually. She rang me from Sydney."

Sensing trouble, Dee Dee sat down. "Something's wrong, isn't it?"

"Yes."

She placed her hand over her chest, rubbed at the first flutter of anxiety. "Go on."

"I don't know exactly what, but I think Alicia's in trouble."

"Oh no! Brandon, why? What do you mean?"

"The night of the ball … she came home dripping wet from head to toe and shivering. She refused to tell me what happened but it obviously broke her heart. I thought at first … but never mind that. I've only seen that look in her eyes once before, and I don't mind admitting, it frightened me. It cut me something cruel when she and Sophie left for Sydney. I always call her after a performance to see how she's going. She says she's okay, but I know she's not. I wouldn't have rung but for Sophie. She called me from the hotel, frightened and upset. She thinks her Mummy is dying and she will be left in Sydney all alone. I can't leave Singapore, I'm about to start a two-week season of *Manon*. I didn't know what else to do. Alicia would kill me if I rang Nick – not sure he would go to her, anyway."

"You did the right thing, Brandon. I had a feeling something was amiss. Leave it with me and don't worry. I'll book a flight to Sydney as soon as I can. Where is she staying?"

After scribbling down the name of the hotel Alicia and Sophie were staying in, she said goodbye to Brandon and considered her options. Not knowing her son's movements on a Sunday evening, she wondered if he would be home. Could she take a gamble and just show up at his home, or perhaps it would be best to call first. She went to the fridge, pulled out a carton of milk, almost added a drop to her coffee when she realised, she hadn't boiled the water and flicked on the kettle. She stared into the garden from the kitchen window, watched the roses sway in the breeze. When she finished the remainder of her sandwich, she decided to trust her instincts and drive over to his home later in the evening.

***

A dull light shone through the glass window of Nick's home.

"Mum!"

Dee Dee barely recognised the man standing in front of her. His clothes looked as though they hadn't been changed in days. He stank of whiskey and his chin sported a two-day growth. But it was the pain in his blood-shot eyes that worried her the most.

"I've seen you looking better, son."

He wiped his hand over his face, held the door open for her to enter. Once inside she suffered another shock. Left-over takeaway cartons cluttered the dining table, opened jars of condiments lined the benchtop and several days of dirty dishes filled the sink. She seated herself on the lounge, an empty bottle of Jameson perched on the coffee table, and scattered pages of the Sydney Herald spread across the floor. A photo of Alicia and Sergio, lip to lip in a tight embrace, stared up at her.

Nick sat opposite, his hands clasped between his legs. "Excuse the mess but I've been a little out of sorts lately." He looked up at Dee Dee, pulled a wry face. "I suppose she told you what happened?"

His bitterness was so flagrant Dee Dee wondered if he had a lemon in his mouth. "If by *she* you mean Alicia, then no, she didn't."

He let out a huff; pushed back his unwashed hair. "No, I suppose not. Telling the truth never was one of her strong points."

"Why are you so upset with her, Nick?"

"Upset! I suppose that's one way to describe how I feel. Another would be foolish – pathetically foolish." He dropped his head into his hands.

"I wish you would explain yourself. Perhaps I might agree." When he looked up, frowning, she cocked her head at him, hoping to convey she wasn't entirely sympathetic.

"I never seem to get it right."

"I can't imagine there being too much wrong with Alicia, my love."

"Fooled you too, did she?"

Dee Dee sighed through pouted lips. "Would you care to explain that remark."

"Which lie would you like to hear first?"

"Really! You honestly think Alicia has lied to you."

Nick inched back into the settee and stared into the distance.

"Let's see. Everything about her is either a secret or a lie. Perhaps when I've told you my side of the story you'll agree."

She doubted it but was interested to see what cock-and-bull story her son had concocted in his befuddled brain. "By all means go ahead and try me."

"Let's see ... a coincidental encounter with Jenny Spencer, I think, started this nightmare. We had coffee. An innocent cup of coffee with an old friend." He closed his eyes, rested his head back against the padding. "She looked upset and I asked her what the frown was all about. She said she was worried about John. I had this feeling there was more to her story than she was letting on. She mentioned a ballerina they had become acquainted with. I was suspicious, so I suggested I'd call in to see them, suss out the problem. Jenny mentioned she was coming for dinner that night, and would I like to join them afterwards for coffee." He shook his head in obvious disbelief. "Walked straight into Jezebel's trap."

"Jezebel's trap?" repeated Dee Dee, somewhat shocked.

"Yes. I'm sure you'll agree when I'm through."

"I doubt it but go on."

"She's been so secretive about her past: shut me down on every level. Gillespie … you remember the photographer fellow we met at lunch on the Gold Coast … well he seemed to be everywhere Alicia went. First in Queensland, as I mentioned, then Sydney, taking her photo and doing a write up on Mason's new ballet, and finally at the ball here in Melbourne. It just seemed too much of a coincidence. I put two and two together and came up with the correct answer. She practically admitted he was Sophie's father. I'm almost positive she's having an affair with him. But the final straw was her behaviour with Alex Braun. She danced with him, you know … at the ball. For that, I'll never forgive her."

Dee Dee sat watching him, not saying a word, as he related the scene between Alicia and Braun at the ball.

"I confronted her with it after I took her home. Hence the parting of ways."

After listening to the long sorry story, Dee Dee could barely contain her anger. "And you said all that to her?"

"Well … yes!"

She rose, needing to add force to her argument and stared down at him. "You're not going to like what I'm about to say to you, my boy, but it's high time someone did. Has it not occurred to you that your bitterness, which I may add you have kept well-nourished since Rebecca left you, has somewhat marred your judgment?"

He lifted his chin. Dee Dee noticed the tightening of his jaw.

"How so?"

She walked to the end of the sofa, spun around to face her son. "Let me get this straight. You actually believe this shy and rather nervous girl made it her business to dance with Alex Braun just to embarrass you. Why would she do that, Nick? What possible motive could she have for dancing with that awful man?"

Dee Dee moved closer, scanned his face, intent on his reaction. "I also know how anxious she was to make a good impression. She knew this ball meant a lot to you in view of your recent appointment and your history with the hospital. And from what I recall, Alex Braun has hated you since the day you met and would stop at nothing to see you humiliated." Not since his school days had Dee Dee addressed her son with such force. "Shall I continue?"

"By all means!" Nick shifted, strummed his fingers on his thigh.

She thought she detected the first signs of apprehension. "Let's start with Michael Gillespie. He turns up in Queensland which, in my view, judging by the surprised reaction from both parties, was purely coincidental. Wouldn't you agree?"

He shifted again; shrugged his shoulders.

"The second meeting you mentioned happened in Sydney. Now, correct me if I'm wrong, but isn't this fellow a photographer slash journalist freelancing for various newspapers. Seems the obvious choice to me, for such an assignment. Now we come to the third, apparently clandestine meeting – in front of a whole bunch of people, I might add – in Melbourne!" She stopped pacing and stared at him, her head on one side. "Really, Nick!"

Dee Dee walked to the window; listened to the stillness of the night as she waited for her heartbeat to slow before confronting Nick again. "So, let's put this together. Sophie is what, seven. So when Alicia is … uhm sixteen? … she falls pregnant to Michael Gillespie back in Perth. Three or four years later – Alicia, Brandon, and Sophie move to Victoria, where she and Brandon join the Ballet Company. Michael Gillespie, who just happens to be in … of all places … Melbourne - or was it planned - meets up with Alicia again and they decided to make a go of it. Does that sound about right?"

Without giving him a chance to reply she continued. "Unfortunately, the relationship breaks down but of course they are still the best of friends. In fact, such good friends that when they meet up in Queensland, which we both agree was accidental, she decides to sleep with him again … at lunch … for old time's sake. Do you think that's the kind of person she is, Nick? Sly and, let's not forget, slutty. Then, they secretly arrange to meet in Sydney and they resume their sordid ..." Dee Dee used her fingers to indicate quotation marks, "... *relationship*, uhm ... after rehearsing all day! But not, of course, at the hotel, because Sophie and I were a bit of a hiccup. Perhaps they went back to his hotel. Only ..."

She stood in front of him with her hands on her hips. "... I don't recall a time when she wasn't with us, except when she was rehearsing. I remember her pleasure when she told me what a surprise it was to see Michael and how he was filling in for some chap who was on an assignment in the Middle East."

"Making sense so far, son?" She raised her eyebrows, inclined her head as if she was waiting for a response. "So, on top of all that, are you telling me, as a man of the world, you didn't recognise Michael's interest would more likely incline towards you than Alicia?"

Scowling, Nick sat forward. "Of course, I did but I thought he might have come out of the closet recently."

"If that were true, why would he want to rekindle a dead flame with a woman?"

"Sophie."

"Oh yes, silly me, because he had spent so much time with his daughter thus far. Have you ever known him to pick her up from school, take her to the movies or keep her for the weekend? And why wouldn't she stay with her father when the Company goes on tours? Have you ever heard Sophie refer to him as daddy? Given that some thought, have we? No, I didn't think so."

"Maybe she doesn't know Gillespie is her father."

"For goodness sake, Nick, surely that would defeat the purpose of him coming to Melbourne?"

"Okay, so maybe you're right, but what about Braun. I told Alicia all about him: the arrogant way he held his head, his sloppy clothes, those beady eyes atop a hooked nose. Only a moron wouldn't have guessed who he was."

"Does that mean you think Alicia is a moron? That is beneath you, Nick, and very arrogant. How could she possibly have known him from a skewed up description out of the mouth of his arch-enemy."

"But …"

For the first time she saw doubt on his face.

"… I saw her on the dance floor with him."

"And was she smiling? Having a good time? Showing off?"

He rose from the couch, paced back and forth. When he turned back to face her, she saw panic in his eyes. "Then why the secrecy? And why … why would she encourage me to believe Gillespie was Sophie's father?"

"Only two reasons I can think of, the first being your stubbornness to believe the truth, and the second – well, I can only assume you must have done something provocatively moronic – let's use your words, Nick – that left her little choice."

One glance at his blood-drained face and she knew she'd struck a nerve.

"She said that she would disappoint me and I would hate her. I thought she meant …"

"… … she was having an affair with Michael Gillespie." Dee Dee finished it for him. "Honestly, Nick!"

"She never trusted me, Mum. I know nothing about her life. Nothing."

"Ask yourself why that is, son. What possible reason could there be why a woman wouldn't trust a man?"

"I love her with all my heart. I have since the first time I saw her at the Spencers'. She must have known."

"Why, Nick? Why must she? I'm sure she's well aware of your reputation. Did you tell her you loved her?"

"I … No. I wanted her to trust me first … confide in me what deep dark secret it is that haunts her."

"And how did that work for you, son?" Dee Dee pursed her lips.

He looked at her like a beaten man. Her heart ached for him but not enough to hold back the words beating to be released. "You need to get your heart right, my boy, before your bitterness destroys what little respect I, or anyone else, has for you." She walked to the door and, with her hand on the knob, turned to him. "I'm sorry to have to say this to you, Nick … Alicia may have disappointed you but not half as much as you will have disappointed her and, for the record, me too." And she left, shutting the door firmly behind her.

Chapter Fourteen

Alicia walked into her room at the Marriot Hotel with a resentful Sophie by her side. Scarcely a month ago, in this same hotel, Alicia had been happier than she'd been in years. Now she felt the worst. She tried not to think of the six weeks ahead: rehearsals then performances with no Brandon to lean on. How was she going to survive? *Dear God, help me,* she silently prayed.

"Hey, darling, why don't you unpack your case."

"I don't want to unpack my case. I want to go home! I don't like Sydney and I don't like this room!"

"We've been over this, Sophie. How many times do I have to tell you … Uncle Brandon had to go to Singapore with the Company?"

"Why couldn't I stay with Nick or Dee Dee?"

"You know why."

"It's your fault they don't want to see us anymore."

"Dee Dee does. She loves you, darling, you know that, but she can't take you to school each day from Brighton. It's too far."

Looking at a sulky-faced Sophie, who sat staring at the door, her arms tightly folded, Alicia felt the full force of the situation. She stopped unpacking and joined the little girl on the bed; slipped her arm around the small, trembling shoulders.

"I'm so sorry, darling, I really am, but there is nothing I can do about it now."

"I don't want to stay with some strange lady." Sniffing loudly, Sophie wiped her tears with her sleeve.

"Mr Mason said Mrs Hetherington is a very nice lady." Even

to herself, she didn't sound convincing. Not since her family's death had Alicia felt so bereft. Once again, the battle of grief needed to be fought. And the negative voice from the bottomless pit convinced her that her life was destined for misery. Happiness was for the chosen and she certainly didn't feel like she had a lucky charm around her neck.

Her eyes misted at the thought of never seeing Nick again, never feeling his strong and protective arms holding her, or his sweet and tender lips bringing her to life. *Loneliness*, thought Alicia, *eats away at your spirit like a slow cancer*. She rested her chin on Sophie's head and stared at the blank wall.

Later that night, Alicia lay with the Bible open on her chest. Knowing how hard tomorrow's rehearsal would be, she begged God for a good night's sleep. She asked Him to let the power of His spirit filter through the pages of His Book and heal her broken heart. She felt a warm sensation surge along her veins, easing the cold chill that had settled.

She woke to the morning light peaking around the edges of the curtain, the Bible still resting on her chest and she smiled at the round eyes staring at her.

"Sleep okay?"

Sophie nodded. *She looks better*, thought Alicia. "Time to get dressed and pack a few things for the day. We can grab breakfast from the café downstairs."

They arrived early at the Opera House so Alicia could spend time introducing Sophie to Sally Hetherington before class started.

"What will happen to me?"

"I'm sure Mrs Hetherington has something very special organised for you to do. Don't cry, darling," said Alicia, giving her a cuddle. "I'll be right here if you need me."

A knock on the dressing room door drew her attention. "This is probably her." Alicia hoped some of her attempt at enthusiasm might rub off on Sophie. She was greatly relieved to find Sally was in her mid-fifties, comfortably rotund, with a motherly twinkle in her eyes. "Sally, is it?"

Smiling, Sally nodded.

"Please come in." Alicia held the door open. "Sophie, this is Mrs Hetherington."

"Well hello, Sophie." Sally leant forward, hands clasped at her large bosom. "Please, call me Aunt Sally, everyone does. My, what pretty hair you have. All those curls, I bet they get knotty?"

Sophie nodded. Alicia noticed the crease between Sophie's eyebrows ease.

"I've packed a light snack and a bottle of water in case you need it." Alicia handed Sally a small bag.

"That's very thoughtful of you." Sally rubbed her hands together. "Right then, if it's okay with Mummy, I thought we might walk to the park for a picnic lunch and maybe buy an ice cream. Chocolate chip cookie is my favourite." Sally lifted her shoulders and, hunching them together, licked her lips.

A hint of a smile crossed Sophie's unhappy face.

"I'm sure Sophie would love that. She gets very restless cooped up at the theatre all day."

"I don't blame her. So would I. Well, better say goodbye to Mummy."

Sophie kissed Alicia goodbye and took Sally's outstretched hand. Before she shut the door, Sally gave Alicia a reassuring smile.

***

The days that followed were arduous, often extending late into the evening. Once Sally's shift ended, Sophie had to wait at the theatre until Alicia finished rehearsing.

"How much longer?" asked Sophie when Alicia came over to retrieve her towel from the *barre*. "I'm so hungry."

"Soon, darling," said Alicia wiping sweat from her neck.

"Alicia," called Mason. "Do that again, only this time try doing the *pirouettes* with your left leg in *attitude*."

Alicia hooked the towel over the *barre* and walked into the middle of the room. Her legs ached and she bent over, touching her palms to the ground to stretch her muscles. Mason waited, tapping his foot. As she struggled to maintain the level of excellence he demanded, the pain in her legs increased. She would be close to collapsing if he didn't stop rehearsals soon.

Sergio's energy was boundless. In between rehearsals he tickled and teased her as if she were his personal toy. Although she valued his knowledge and skill, doing everything and more he required, nothing replaced the unique relationship she and Brandon shared on and off stage, and she wished with all her heart he was with her. He had rung every night for the past month and she looked forward to hearing his voice with an aching heart.

Opening night was fast approaching and the tension strings strained to breaking point. The first full dress rehearsal presented several problems, which threw Mason into a state of perpetual anxiety. By the final dress rehearsal, all but a few minor problems with lighting had been ironed out.

The atmosphere around the dressing rooms on opening night, was quietly chaotic. Many dancers from the Company wished Alicia good luck – or *'Merde'* as they say in the dance world – for her premier performance. To help with the strain on her muscles, the physio had rubbed her legs with liniment after class. Each toe and both heels were tightly bound with plaster. Ballet shoes were placed in a row under the bench; costumes hung in order of appearance on the clothes rack against the back wall; and all manner of cosmetics, placed on a towel, covered the bench.

The final call came for dancers in the first act to make their way to the stage. Alicia joined Sergio in the wings. Like a true entertainer, he was pumped, thriving on the excitement.

"Reporters and several arts critics from the papers are here," he said, lunging forward to stretch his achilles tendon. Pushing resin into the tip of her toe-shoe, Alicia listened as the audience applauded the entrance of the conductor. The introduction completed, the curtains drew apart. Sergio dropped a kiss on her shoulder, wished her good luck as he ran onto the stage and into a shower of cheers.

The final *pas de deux* – slow, tender and technically challenging – drew the audience to their feet. Cheers of *Bravo* came from all directions. When the curtains closed for the last time the press scrambled backstage, eager to photograph Sydney's Valentino of dance and his new partner.

"Sergio, are you in love with the delightful Miss Sommers?" a journalist from the Herald Sun asked.

Sergio pulled Alicia into his arms and smacked a theatrical kiss on her lips. "Does that answer your question?" He laughed loudly; bowed low.

The photo of Sergio kissing Alicia made page two of the Sydney Telegraph, the Herald Sun and the Melbourne Sun. The reviews were everything, and more, that Mason had anticipated, ensuring a sell-out season.

Alicia was pleased Mason's ballet was a great success but as the season drew to an end the cramping in her legs became so severe it kept her awake at night. Not only did her legs ache but her head had started to throb, causing her appetite to wane and her weight to plummet. It was a wonder, she thought, that Sergio couldn't hear the pain-killers rattling in her stomach. The driving obsession to achieve slowly diminished, and in its place gnawed the dark dog of depression. She prayed for God to give her enough strength to fight the disease threatening to overtake her body.

With only two more performance to go, she lay in bed with a damp towel over her face, shivering from pain, exhaustion, and a fever. Sophie sat by her side holding her hand.

"Are you dying, Mummy?"

"No, darling, of course not. I'm just tired from last night's performance."

The knock on the door startled them both. Sophie jumped off the bed, but Alicia grabbed her top; held her back. "Wait." Nobody knocked on her door.

Crawling out from under the covers, she slipped into a cotton gown. "Who is it?" she called in a weakened voice.

"It's Dee Dee."

Sophie shrieked, ran to the door and flung it open; hurled herself into Dee Dee's outstretched arms. Alicia dropped onto the bed, fed on the cool rush of relief as she crawled back under the covers.

Dee Dee pushed through the door, one arm around the little girl clinging to her legs and her case in the other hand. "Let me in, darling. There's a good girl."

"I prayed to Jesus you would come," said Sophie.

"And here I am." Dee Dee dropped a kiss on Sophie's head, and ruffled the blonde curls.

"Promise you won't go away."

"Promise and honest. Now let me have a look at your mother." She put her case and scarf on the chair. Sophie latched hold of her hand and pulled her towards Alicia.

"Hmm. Cup of tea, a tepid bath, and food. Then, my girl, a doctor if you don't improve." Sitting on the edge of the bed, Dee Dee stroked Alicia's head, wiped the tears from her ashen face. "Why didn't you ring me, you silly girl? I would have come earlier," she said, clasping Alicia's hand, pulling the covers up under her chin. She went to check the contents of the kitchenette. 'Right! Kettle, there you are. Sophie, go run the bath for your mother. Cold tap first then the hot. I'll order room service: eggs on toast, I think. Then you and I will go out for breakfast while your mother sleeps.

It was early afternoon when Dee Dee and Sophie returned to find Alicia awake and packing for the theatre.

"Alicia, you can't dance like this, and you've lost so much weight," said Dee Dee, her hand on Alicia's brow. "You're still hot. Far too hot to dance."

"I feel much better. I really do. I only have to get through two more performances and I've finished. I'll be alright." Zipping up her bag she slipped on a pair of sandals. "I'll have to tell Sally, Sophie's sitter we won't need her anymore now that you're here. I usually meet her at the theatre. She brings Sophie back to the hotel after dinner and waits with her until I get home. This is so much better. I'm so glad you came." She hugged Dee Dee before heading for the door.

Dee Dee rose. "Alicia, don't do this. Cancel tonight. You're not well enough to dance. Let me call the theatre and explain."

"No, no. I'll be okay. I promise." Alicia blew them both a kiss and slipped away before Dee Dee had time to protest further.

She arrived at the theatre early and went straight to her dressing room where she found Sally waiting.

"I hope you don't mind, Sally, but Dee Dee is a dear friend and Sophie loves her to bits."

"Not at all. I'll explain to Lauren on my way out that you won't be needing my services any longer. I'd just like to say how much I have enjoyed looking after Sophie. She is a credit to you."

"Thank you, Sally. I know Sophie has enjoyed your company too." Alicia gratefully returned her hug. With time pressing she quickly changed into her tights and leotard. She soaked a small towel in cold water and went upstairs to join the Company.

When class finished, she rested against the theatre wall, the towel slung around her neck, gulping air.

"Darling, you don't look well." Sergio placed his hands on the wall, either side of her head.

"A bit hot, that's all."

He felt her forehead, frowned. "I do hope you aren't catching a cold, little one."

"Me too! Forgive me if I need an extra push sometimes. My legs feel like lead."

"Forgiven. Marry me and I'll push you in any position you like."

She let out a huff then smiled. "You'd be sorry if I said yes."

"We could leave out the marriage bit," he said kissing the tip of her nose.

She pulled the towel from her neck, slapped him gently on the shoulder. "Scoundrel!" she said, slipping underneath his arm.

She took a cool shower, hoping to reduce her temperature before putting on her make-up. When she bent to pick up her shoes, the blood rushed to her head and she gripped the bench for support as she waited for the dizziness to subside. One last look in the mirror, she quickly rushed out to join Sergio in the front wing, dabbing the sweat from her forehead with a tissue.

During interval she lay on the dressing room floor with her legs lifted up along the wall, desperate to ease the throbbing, until it was time to change. Half-way through the last act the shooting pains up her thighs became so intense it sent her breath into heavy labour. The more tender the choreography, the more strength she needed to control the *adagio*. Not a whisper sounded through the theatre as they performed the final *pas de deux*.

Alicia gathered the last ounce of her will, stepped *on pointe* to execute a *double*, then *triple pirouette*, ending with her arms outstretched and her right leg in *retiree devant*. In one final fluid movement, with Sergio's right hand between her shoulder blades and his left hand around her raised ankle, Sergio lifted her above his head. And propelling her upper body backwards she hung over his hand in the *crucifix* position with her supporting leg balanced along the length of his arm. Once he had her steady, he released her ankle and she hung from her cross in *Surrendered Reticence*. Applause exploded across the auditorium, bringing the ballet to an end and the curtains to a close.

"Alicia! Alicia, what's wrong?" called Sergio, her body dangling from his hand like a rag doll. He slowly lowered her unresponsive and limp frame, until it was safe enough to drop her into his arms. He checked her breathing. He was still staring at her chest when the curtains opened. The clapping died. Exercising his artistic wit, Sergio rose *to demi pointe,* pushed his hips forward, threw his head back, and ran off the stage with Alicia bouncing in his arms. The audience broke into a loud cheer.

Behind the wings Sergio sank onto one knee, laid Alicia on the floor. Other members of the Company gathered around. When the curtain went up, dancers ran out from all directions to take their final bow. The clapping continued, demanding Sergio and Alicia's return. Finally, Sergio ran onto the stage, alone. He waited for the clapping to cease. It was announced that due to unforeseen circumstances Miss Sommers would not be returning to the stage. Sergio bowed, blew kisses in appreciation, then left the stage and the murmurings behind.

***

Dee Dee woke to the piercing ring of the hotel phone. Stumbling from her bed, she answered to the eloquent voice of Lauren Mason.

"I beg your pardon but I don't know your name, mine is Lauren Mason. I'm terribly sorry to have woken you at this ungodly hour. Mrs Hetherington, Sophie's previous baby sitter, happened to mention a friend of Alicia had arrived and was staying at the hotel. I thought I'd better let you know that Alicia, poor love, collapsed at the end of tonight's performance. She has been taken by ambulance to the Alfred Hospital."

"Oh dear! I half expected … … never mind. Thank you so much for letting me know, Mr Mason. I appreciate the call." Half an hour later, she and a bleary-eyed Sophie were being taxied to the hospital. They waited in the visitors' area until they were admitted into emergency where Alicia, still unconscious, was being examined.

"Hello. I'm guessing you're her mother, Mrs Sommers," said the doctor picking up Alicia's chart. "My name is Dr Allan Davies I've just given her something to help her sleep."

"What's wrong with her?"

"A rare infection of the muscles called Idiopathic Inflammatory Myositis. Her muscles are severely inflamed. Thankfully, it was caught before any major damage. It's quite a painful condition. She'll need plenty of rest in the next few weeks, especially if she wants to continue dancing at a professional level. I've started her on a course of cortisone treatment, which I think should be sufficient at this stage. If not, take her to your local doctor for a referral."

"I see."

"She's very thin, even for a ballerina. My guess is she's been over-doing it: working too hard and not eating properly. She's malnourished and her immune system isn't working properly." He looked sharply at Dee Dee and replaced Alicia's chart.

Feeling like a bad mother, Dee Dee nodded. She was still staring at the curtain where the doctor had exited when one of the night nurses entered.

"I put her costume and ballet shoes in a plastic bag in this cupboard by the bed," she said. "Oh! And all her clips, hair net and diamanté hair comb – yes I think that's all – are in there too." She hunched her shoulders; dropped them just as quickly. "We've never had a ballerina in here before. Everyone was dying to know who she was. The paramedics said she's famous."

"Thank you," said Dee Dee. "Yes, she's the prima ballerina in Lauren Mason's new ballet, *Reticence,* with the Sydney Ballet Company."

"Really! How exciting," said the nurse, pulling open the curtains for the orderly to move Alicia from emergency to a ward.

Dee Dee winced when she walked into the room and saw the nurse adjusting the threadbare recliner, for her to rest on. She rubbed her back and prayed it stood the challenge. For two days Alicia remained in a semi-comatose state. The nurses checked her vitals regularly and the doctor checked her progress each day. Reluctant to leave Alicia for too long in case she woke up alone, Dee Dee busied herself reading magazines, children's story books to Sophie, and dressing Barbie dolls.

About to turn the last page of the latest gardening journal, Dee Dee heard a faint whisper of her name.

"Oh, darling, thank God." Closing the magazine, she pulled herself to her feet and clasped the frail outstretched hand. "You've been asleep for days."

"Sophie?" The voice sounded as thin and pale as Alicia looked.

"She's fine – helping the trolley lady distribute treats around the ward at the moment. You know how it goes – one for the patient – two for Sophie. Apart from a few bored moments, she's been spoiled rotten by the nurses."

"Thank you," Alicia said, struggling to keep her eyes open.

Dee Dee, anxious to leave the hospital and Sydney, was relieved when the doctor gave Alicia the all clear the following morning. As soon as she was able, she ducked back to the hotel, with Sophie, to pack and book the first available flight to Melbourne. She organised wheelchairs for Alicia to get her on and off the plane, at Sydney and Melbourne. Next, she rang Brandon to let him know her plans. He arranged to meet them at the airport.

Hours later, with Dee Dee pushing Alicia along and Sophie by her side, they came through the airport doors. Brandon crouched in front of her, took hold of both her hands. "Stupid goose. Sergio's supposed to fall and break his neck, not you."

She managed a weak smile. "Brandy, I'm okay," she said.

He nodded, laughing through his tears. Sophie put her arm around his shoulders and the three of them hugged.

"She's alright, Uncle Brandon. Dee Dee fixed her up."

"I know, Button. Brandon is a silly cry baby." Pulling himself together, he took Sophie and went to collect the cases. Once Alicia was secured inside the cab he said, "I've missed you, Ally. Performing *Manon* just wasn't the same without you."

"I missed you too, Brandy."

Once she'd fastened Sophie into her seat belt, Dee Dee placed her hand on Brandon's shoulder. "I'm glad you came to the airport, she needed that. Mr. Mason and Sergio rang several times to see how she was going. Unfortunately, she was still unconscious when they rang but I did leave a message at the theatre, to let them both know I had booked a flight for Melbourne. You must visit us whenever you're free. Bring your brother if you wish and, of course, your bathers. Brighton is a beautiful beach if you fancy a dip."

Brandon hugged his two-favourite girls, gave Dee Dee a quick squeeze and promised a visit as soon as he was free.

***

Nick had hit a brick wall. He'd rung Alicia's phone at least fifty times but she refused to answer and the same with Brandon. He stood at the window of his home, coffee in hand, staring into space. The receptionist at the Melbourne Art Centre had insisted Alicia was still in Sydney. When he rang the Marriott Hotel, they informed him she had checked out several days ago. Next, he tried calling her apartment but no one answered. In desperation, he'd driven back to the Arts Centre. The less-than-welcoming receptionist, maintained Alicia was still in Sydney and staying at the Marriot. He tried to argue the point but eventually gave up and left. Nothing made sense, he thought as he sipped his coffee. The receptionist *had* to be mistaken. Alicia had been gone for almost seven weeks and, according to his calculations, the Sydney season had finished a week ago. *So, where is she? She isn't in Sydney or Melbourne. Where else can she be?*

He thought about ringing his mother but after doing the sums he was sure she was still in Brighton, enjoying the change. At least she was, when he spoke to her last week.

The night of the hospital ball played over in his mind. His first big mistake was Gillespie. He'd always suspected the man was gay but the affection he'd displayed for Alicia and Sophie at the restaurant had blurred his judgment. The second, he mused as he took his cup to the sink and rinsed it clean, was Braun. Nobody knew better than Nick how much Braun detested him, and yet he'd failed to recognise the look on her face when she danced with Braun – it was one of fear and not, as he had supposed, spite. Braun would have done anything to humiliate him. If he hadn't been so consumed with himself, he might have read the signs. The thought of her imprisoned in that animal's arms made his blood boil.

Nobody has ever made me feel so alive as you have. Those simple words hounded him and he fought with his guilt. But it was his own vile behaviour with Stacy Logan that revolted him the most.

He could still hear his mother's voice telling him how much he'd disappointed her. Once he had accepted the truth of his mother's words, the shame of what he'd done saw him wandering the streets of Toorak, stopping outside the one place he knew would accept him, stupidity and all.

The church doors were open, the building empty, except for a few people chatting up front. He slipped in unnoticed – or so he thought – onto the back row, and respectfully lowered his head. It was time to make peace with his Maker. Perhaps it would allow him to let go of past hurts and move forward. Silence filled his mind. Deeply rooted seeds of unforgiveness he had nurtured for too long needed to be addressed. He remembered hearing someone once say that if you grabbed the anger burrowed in your chest and screwed it round and round until you could physically feel it leave your body, then throw it away and let honour fill its place, you would find your peace. He placed his hand on his chest, ready to give it a go when he glimpsed a trouser leg by his side. He looked up to see a well-groomed, pleasant-looking man, with a strong jaw and an easy-going smile.

"Do you mind if I sit here awhile?" Nick asked.

"These doors are always open," came the soft-spoken reply.

The minutes ticked by. The need to talk was great but Nick, not accustomed to expressing his feelings, considered how to start. "My life is a mess." He swallowed. "And it's my own stupid fault … again."

The man nodded, stretched his legs out in front.

An obvious sign he was ready to listen, thought Nick. "It's late."

"Is it? I hadn't noticed. Let me introduce myself." He held out his hand. "My name is Jeff. Pastor Jeff Johns."

"Nick … Coleman."

"I'm a good listener, Nick. Goes with the job."

"I've been such a fool – a blind, thoughtless, arrogant fool and I don't know what to do to fix it.

"Talking often helps."

Hesitant at first, the words splattered from Nick's mouth like a baby duck's first connection with water. He spoke about the rejection of his faith after his adulterous father had walked out on him and his mother. "I was eighteen and gutted. I thought my world had collapsed. How wrong I was: nothing but a mere crumble. The real crash came when my dear wife cheated on me with a senior colleague. I found them together in our bed." Nick slumped into the seat. "I resigned from the hospital, throwing away a promising career in medicine."

"That certainly is a lot to process."

Nick sighed. "The best is yet to come. Recently my mother accused me of nurturing my bitterness for years. She was right, of course. So much so that it has robbed me of the most precious thing I have ever known."

"And does this precious thing have a name?"

Nick felt the heat moving up his neck. "What makes you think it has a name?"

"When they're that precious, they usually do."

He said the name in his head, gulped on the vision of her sweet face. "Alicia Sommers."

"Nice."

"Nice doesn't quite do her justice. She's exquisitely beautiful, sweet, gentle and adorably innocent. God! I've been a complete fool!"

Pastor Jeff shifted, crossed his legs.

Nick raked his fingers through his unruly hair as he thought back to the day he'd bumped into Jenny Spencer on the street. It seemed so long ago. He leant back and dragged in his tired breath. Embarrassed at the tears forming in his eyes, he covered his face. He felt a strong hand grip his knee as he fought to regain his self-control.

"Sometimes, Nick, we have to hit rock bottom before God can take a burdened soul and turn it into something good." Nick shook his weary head.

Pastor Jeff hunched forward, clasped his hands together in reverence to God. Nick listened as the Pastor spoke about the resurrection. The words, full and vibrant, touched his soul. He thought about the death of Christ and how such a sacrifice was supposed to pave the way to hope, glory and ultimate freedom. Years of accrued dirt could be washed away, not by a simple pleading to be forgiven but a genuine desire for redemption. He felt the sadness of his misplaced bitterness swell inside him. He needed to let go and discover who he really was.

Nick envied the cool assurance of the man at his side. His faith was alive, filling him with a security of who he was and where he fitted in this world of mayhem.

"From all you told me, Nick, I do see a positive in the midst of this calamity."

Nick looked at him, a question in his eyes and a glimmer of hope in his heart.

"It seems to me God is working His purpose out very nicely. He's just waiting for the players to find their way." Nodding, Pastor Jeff, continued. "Although it may sound presumptuous of me, I have the distinct feeling that God is waiting for you to be the man He made you to be. Step up to the mark and take the bull by the horns, so to speak." He dropped his fist on Nick's knee. "Faith," he said, standing. "Have faith Nick, and trust your instincts."

Nick followed his lead. "My mother always said … one day God would bring me a woman who would challenge me to behave like a good man."

"Your mother is a wise woman."

The two men shook hands.

"Promise me something," said Pastor Jeff.

"Anything," Nick replied sincerely.

Pastor Jeff shot him a cheeky smile. "Come back … together."

Nick left the church with renewed confidence of finding Alicia and winning her back. But, having searched every place he thought she might be, his efforts proved fruitless. She seemed to have disappeared off the face of the earth. His contract with the TV station was about to expire and, with only a six-week interlude before he started his residency, he needed to get his life in order. He made a promise to God that he would do everything He asked of him if He would give her back to him.

The first step was to talk to Brandon, and so he found himself the next morning knocking on his door. When no one answered, he used his fist.

"Eh! Nick, isn't it?" Jason, still in his boxers, rubbed at his eyes.

"Jason!" Nick tried not to look surprised at finding him still asleep at nine o'clock in the morning.

"Big night," said Jason, a trifle embarrassed. "If you're after Brandon I think he's at the Arts Centre. Said something about an early start."

"Alicia?"

"Not too sure, but I think she's still in Sydney."

"Thanks."

Nick sat in his car, racking his brains. The only place left for him to go was back to the Arts Centre. He pulled up in the car park, perused the red brick building. It occurred to him Brandon might not be all that pleased to see him. He hadn't answered any of Nick's phone calls, and taking on an entire Company took a bit of gumption. Squaring his shoulders, he locked the car.

"Can I help you?" asked the receptionist in a decidedly bored voice.

Nick read the 'not-you-again' look. Determined not to be put off again he dropped the tone of his voice a few decimals. "I'd like to speak to Brandon Hastie."

"I'm sorry sir, but the Company is in class at the moment."

"Exactly where do they do class?" Nick looked down the passage ready to make a dash for the studio.

"Along the passage and around the corner until you come to the stairs but you can't disturb … Sir … Sir?"

"Thank you," he called over his shoulder. Ignoring her echoing protests, he strode past several stunned-looking dancers hoping none of them would call Security. What he thought looked like dressing rooms were on his right, studios to his left. He decided to follow the music coming from the top of the stairs. Pushing open the wooden doors, he stepped into a room full of dancers. Everybody, including the pianist, stopped and stared at him. He felt like an overgrown alien who had landed on earth. He scanned the crowd, stopping at the four men standing in the far corner. There was no mistaking the nasty curl of Brandon's upper lip.

Gliding along the floor, Brandon suddenly leapt into the air his legs split apart, front leg stretched forward, back leg propelling backwards whilst airborne then landing elegantly two feet in front of Nick. He took a breath, stepped closer, "I promised myself if and when I saw you again, Nick, I would smash my fist into your slimy face."

Observing the balled fists, Nick braced himself. The last thing he wanted was a punch up with her best friend in front of an audience of Brandon supporters. "I love her, Brandon, with all my heart."

"Really! I find that hard to believe."

Nick held his stare. "Please tell me where she is before I go crazy."

"Why? So, you can rip her apart again?"

"So I can beg her forgiveness."

Brandon took a moment before answering. "Hang you, Nick!"

"Hit me if you want. I know I deserve it." Several gasps echoed around the room.

"Not on my watch," yelled Helen Barsby, the ballet mistress. "Go outside if you're going to brawl."

"Don't do it, Brandy – he's bigger than you," yelled another male dancer, sending the Company into hysterics.

"Very funny, Andy. And thanks for the vote of confidence."

Brandon flexed his muscles, shadow-boxed the air. The Company cheered.

Nick, not without a sense of humour, joined in.

"Brandon!" cried Helen, stamping her foot.

"Okay, okay. Keep your shirt on. Come on, Nick. Let's go get a coffee. Won't be long," announced Brandon to an exasperated ballet mistress. Displaying his flexed muscles to his adoring fans, he pushed Nick through the door, told him to wait in the corridor while he changed. He suggested a café up the road, which would be less crowded.

"Who's Michael Gillespie?" Nick demanded as soon as they had ordered.

Brandon stared at him. "Michael Gillespie! Who told you about him?"

"Nobody. We bumped into him when I took Alicia to lunch on the Gold Coast."

"He's a photographer who worked for the Company for a while. Wonder what he was doing on the Gold Coast," he said half to himself. "Why?"

"She met him again in Sydney when she went there for that week of orientation and then again at the hospital ball."

"He's a freelance photographer-cum-journalist, mainly based in Melbourne but often sub-contracts for Sydney Herald. Takes work when and where he can. He's made quite a name for himself, actually. Anyway, what's that got to do with Alicia?"

"It just seemed too much of a coincidence." Nick glanced sheepishly at Brandon.

"A coincidence …?

"Always being in the same place as Alicia."

"Dah … he's a photographer. Hang on. Don't tell me … Oh, you great galah. You thought he and Alicia were …" Brandon hooked his fingers together, indicating a relationship, and Nick nodded.

"Michael's gay." Brandon paused, gave a wry look. Has Alicia told you anything at all about me?"

"No."

"That's my darling: loyal to the backbone." Brandon, elbow on the table, flicked flat his hand. "Michael Gillespie was my lover, Nick, not Alicia's. How could you not see that?"

Nick hunched his shoulders. "I had a suspicion, but they seemed so close. The night of the ball, I accused her of sleeping with him."

"No!" Brandon looked shocked, then let out a whopping laugh. "What did she say?"

"Nothing. But you haven't heard the worst of it. I asked her if

Gillespie was Sophie's father."

"Are you insane? Either that or a few pickets short of the fence." Brandon screwed up his face. "Had a suspicion. Nick … honestly! He's as camp as a row of tents. No wonder she came home a mess that night."

"Don't. I can't bear to think of that night and the dreadful things I said to her. Who is Sophie's father?'

"What! You still don't know?"

"No. I've done everything I could to make her talk to me but she's told me nothing. I'm so in the dark."

"I don't understand why she hasn't confided in you. I'm positive she loves you, in spite of the fact you're a drongo."

"I seriously doubt it, but thanks, I think, for the … eh … so called compliment." Nick stared at Brandon then shook his head. "I wasn't particularly nice to her at the ball. Just the thought of her and Gillespie … God, I wanted to beat the truth out of her."

He dropped his head into his hands; pulled on his hair.

"Sophie's father's dead," said Brandon in a sharp voice.

That brought Nick's head to attention. "Dead! What? Hang on. How?"

"Do you remember the night you brought her home from the hospital after she fell off the jetty, and you asked me about why she seemed so terrified?"

"I do."

"And I said I couldn't tell you. Well, nothing has changed. If I tell you the whole truth, she will never forgive me. But I can tell you this … the reason she guards her secrets so fanatically is intrinsically linked with the trauma she suffered. Alicia has this insane idea that if nobody ever knows anything about her, it will somehow protect her from ever being hurt again. You have to understand something, Nick: although she raised a child at a young age and it forced her to grow up fast, emotionally she lives in a … how can I describe it … a kind of vacuum? I'm no shrink but I know her well enough to understand that, apart from myself, nobody has ever been allowed to get close enough to know the real person behind the lovely face … except you."

"I see. And the Spencers?"

"Jenny knows nothing about Alicia's past and Alicia tells John exactly what she wants him to hear but you …" said Brandon waving his finger accusingly in Nick's face, "… are the first person she has allowed past the front door who doesn't have a distinct purpose in her life, and I'm sure she loves you … more than she cares to admit. I'll tell you something else. If I didn't think you loved her, I would never give her up without a fight."

Nick wiped his hand over his face. "I love her, Brandon, more than I've ever loved anyone, so don't get your boxing gloves out just yet. But I need to clear my head. I never dreamed … there is so much more to this story than I realised. I only wish I knew it."

"It's a tragic story, but it's also a complicated one. Ask her, make her tell you, and don't give up until you have the whole truth."

"And therein lies the problem."

"Why?"

"I've no idea where she is, which is why I'm here talking to you."

"Then I take it you don't know what happened to her in Sydney?"

"No. What? Tell me … is she alright?"

Brandon fell silent, fiddled with the spoon in his cup. "She collapsed on stage at the end of her second last performance; spent the next three days in the hospital unconscious. Doctor said she was suffering from exhaustion. He also said she'd contracted some kind of weird muscle infection – myo-something. Won't be able to walk for a while."

"Myositis … Oh, dear God, my poor girl!" He rested his mouth against his fist, guilt consuming his thoughts.

"Relax, she's okay. She's in very capable hands."

He glared at Brandon; gripped the edge of the table. "If you know where she is tell me before I go mad.”

“She’s with your mother.”

“My mother! But how …? My mother? I don’t understand.”

“Simple really if you think about it. Sophie rang me from Sydney. She thought Alicia was dying. I was in Singapore at the time. I couldn’t leave Louis in the lurch, not with Alicia away as well. So I rang the only person I could think of. Your mother flew to Sydney the next day. Lucky, because Alicia collapsed that night on stage. They’ve been with your mother ever since.”

Nick scraped back his chair and stood up. Brandon, swallowing the last of his coffee, rose too. “Brandon, thank you – I mean it, thank you … for everything. And … forgive me … I’ve been such a fool. What can I do to make it up to you?”

“Let go of my hand for starters. Blimey Charlie, that’s some grip,” said Brandon, splaying his fingers. His smile faded. “There’s something I need to get off my chest. Something important.” He flicked back his hair then cleared his throat. “I’ve loved her since I was a young boy. She’s not just a friend, she’s my family, all wrapped up in one. If you promise me, you’ll treat her well, love her and don’t hurt a hair on her head, then you have my blessing. And if you don’t … well, I’ll take up boxing and beat the crap out of you.”

Nick pulled him into a firm embrace; gave his promise.

Chapter Fifteen

The cramps in her legs plagued Alicia during the night and she hung them over the side of the bed in the spare room at Dee Dee's Brighton home hoping for some relief. Massaging her thighs, she knew the pain would eventually subside, but grief, her arch-enemy, was not so easy to reconcile. Too frightened to look down the tunnel of her empty life, she squeezed closed her eyes. Mother, father, brother and now Nick – would the list go on?

The vision of him with the voluptuous Stacy Logan flashed to her mind. How could she have been so naïve – to think a worldly man like Nick would prefer her to a sensual woman like Stacy? But she had hoped, and this was the result. Sobbing, she shoved the pillow over her face, slid off the bed onto the carpet, landing on her knees.

Curled in foetal position she asked God, why? What had she done to deserve to have been dealt this card, in life? A shiver ran along her spine, and the gentle voice from Heaven whispered through the ashes of her defeat. "Wait, Beloved, on Him who loves you."

Alicia rolled onto her back, glanced around the room, as hope formed in her breast. *Oh, dear God*, she prayed. *Please be real and not in my imagination.*

Closing her eyes, she let her mind drift back over the years. She was a little girl again, standing on a sandhill listening to the thunderous roar of the waves as they crashed into the generous land, she once called home. She could still feel the mist on her face from the spray when she raced to the water's edge. Two little children frolicked in the water under the watchful eyes of loving parents busy building sandcastles for their baby girl. A familiar street, a quiet suburb, a special house whose windows framed the picture of her youth, and rising up through each scene emerged her mother's face. The images were strong – if she just let go she could almost believe she was there, with them. And in that moment, it came to her what she had to do.

"Alicia!"

The sound of Dee Dee's voice startled Alicia from a deep sleep and she gasped into awareness. "Oh darling, I beg your pardon. I thought … never mind what I thought. Did you have a bad night?"

"I'm sorry, Dee Dee," she said, her heart beating wildly. "I didn't mean to frighten you. I must have fallen asleep."

Dee Dee helped her off the floor and onto the bed. "Are you alright?"

She thought for a moment. *Am I alright?* The memories, God's voice, her mother's face, all of it seemed like a re-run of yesterday – something she couldn't touch or feel but it was there, close. "I don't know," she said truthfully. "But there is something I do know, it's time to go home."

"Of course. Say when, and I'll drive you."

"No, Dee Dee, not to my apartment. I mean home, to Perth."

"Oh! I see."

Alicia wasn't sure Dee Dee did see why she needed to go home, but it was true. Louis had told her to take as much time as she needed to recover. Going home to Perth, walking along the beach at Scarborough and feeling the sand beneath her feet would help her decide what she wanted to do with the rest of her life. "I've lost my way, my purpose," she said. "And I don't know what I want anymore. I know this sounds crazy, but I need to go home, to feel my mother's presence again, hear her voice." She wiped her eyes.

A pause followed. "I understand."

Alicia hoped that were true.

After returning from Dee Dee's, Alicia glanced around her apartment, wondering if she would ever return. She loved living in Melbourne with its artistic vibe and easy lifestyle. She loved working with Louis and the challenges he presented to the Company. But the call to Perth was powerful, much stronger than she thought possible.

Sophie sat on the couch, swinging her legs. She looked unhappy and Alicia joined her. Drawing her into her arms, she kissed the blonde curls. "Would you like to go home, darling, to Perth? You were born there, you know."

Large, apprehensive eyes stared into Alicia's. "Will I like it, Mummy?"

"Yes, darling, I think you will. Do you remember your Auntie Beryl? We're going to stay with her."

"I used to help Uncle Stan in the garden."

"Yes, yes you did. Clever you to remember that. You know poor old Uncle Stan has gone to Heaven?"

Sophie nodded, a wistful look on her face.

Brandon flew through the door, Kieran hard on his heels. He stopped abruptly, threw open his arms, and Sophie sprang into them.

"Beautiful, beautiful girl, I've missed you to the moon and back." They squeezed each other tight; rubbed noses.

Sophie gripped his face between her hands. "I'm going home, Brandy, to Perth."

Alicia noted the narrowing of his eyes. He glanced at her for a brief second and then back to Sophie who was pulling his ears. "Lucky you," he said, shaking his head free from a giggling little girl's grip.

"Do you want to come?" asked Sophie as he lowered her to the ground. She looked up at him waiting for an answer and he ruffled her hair. "Maybe."

Hunkering onto his knees in front of Alicia, he lifted her legs by the ankles. "How are these going?"

She reached out and cupped his face. There was a story behind those eyes bursting to be told. "Better, much better. I can walk a bit now."

He nodded; settled his cheek into her palm. "Perth?"

She smiled into the lovely face; took his hand. Brandon was her life-line, the anchor that had secured her unbridled emotions for the last six years, supported her through the many despairing moments, and there were many. She owed him her life and her truth. "I need to go home, Brandy."

"Why?"

"Many reasons really, but mainly to work out what I want for my future. I'm not sure if Melbourne is where I want to stay for the rest of my life. Maybe it's time to go home, start again. I just don't know."

"Does this decision have anything to do with Nick?"

If she was on the path of honesty, then even to herself she had to acknowledge it had everything to do with Nick. He had shaken her determination, broken the spirit that had driven her for so long. Now she felt empty, weak and most of all lonely. "You know it does."

He sat on his heels, looked at Kieran then back at Alicia. The story she sensed he harboured was about to be revealed.

Brandon was never one to hold back.

"What?" she cried, glancing from one to the other.

"Well, you're not the only one who has decided to go away for the holidays. Kieran and I have, too."

"Where are you going?"

"To the States. There are a few companies advertising in the Dance Gazette for positions. Houston Ballet and Miami for starters. American Theatre and New York City, if I'm game."

"This is sudden."

"Not really. I've been thinking about it for a while. It's perfect timing. With Jason here to rent the apartment during the summer holidays – he's decided to stay for now – I can look around, see how I go. If nothing, I'll come back. Nothing ventured nothing gained."

***

The tiny package wrapped in sparkling gold paper twinkled on the front seat of Dee Dee's car as she drove home from the airport, having spent the night at her sister's. Each time it caught her eye, she felt the prick of tears. Alicia had given it to her before she and Sophie boarded the plane. Dee Dee guessed what was inside the box and pondered her son's reaction when she gave it to him. Which wouldn't be long away, she realised with a sinking heart as she pulled into her driveway alongside Nick's Range Rover.

Dee Dee sat in the car staring at the house wall, thinking about the last time she had visited her son at his house. It crossed her mind she might not be all that well received. She thrust the little package into her purse, lifted her overnight bag from the back seat and walked across the lawn to her house.

A strong male odour mixed with tension assaulted her nostrils when she stepped inside. Instead of going straight to her bedroom, she left her bag in the hallway and went into the living room.

Nick stood facing the window, legs apart, hands in his trouser pockets. Dee Dee felt a mild shock when he turned to face her. His loss of weight, messy hair and unshaved face, heightened the tension on his gaunt face. And there was a strain about his eyes she hadn't seen since he left Rebecca.

"Where is she, Mother?"

The sharp edge to his voice advised caution. "Nick, sit down and we'll talk."

"I don't want to sit down," he said, the muscles in his jaw twitching. "I want you to tell me where she is."

Feeling a little unsteady, she slipped into the recliner. "You're too late." The wild look in his eyes deepened and she clenched the arm of the chair.

"Too late for what?"

"She caught the plane for Perth this morning."

His rigid body swayed but his eyes never left her face, cutting into her heart like a razor. He took his hands from his pockets, stepped closer. "Why?" His voice was rough, choking.

"You didn't come."

As if he had been punched in the chest, Nick let out a sharp breath. Like a caged lion, he paced; punched his palm, stopped; threw back his head. A moan escaped as he slumped onto the couch and dropped his head into his hands. Dee Dee wept as she watched her son cry like a baby.

"Why didn't you tell me?"

"Oh, Nick!"

"I know! I know! Don't say it. I'm a fool. But God be my judge, I've tried to find her. Honestly, Mum, I have. But she won't answer her phone. Not that I blame her when I think of the things I said to her. After your visit I called her hotel in Sydney the next day and they swore she'd left. So I tried her apartment but each time, nothing. Finally, I went to the ballet studio and the receptionist insisted she was still in Sydney. I hit a dead end."

"So what brought you here?"

"Desperate, I went back to her apartment and knocked so hard I woke Jason from the dead. He said Brandon had gone to work early. I raced to the studio, walked in on the Company doing class. After Brandon decided not to punch me senseless, we went for coffee. He told me she was with you. Thank God there were no police around – I drove like the devil was after me. Must have missed you by minutes." He looked at his mother. "I have to find her."

"Darling ... Perth?"

He sat staring at the floor. At last, he lifted his head. "I have some unfinished business with Channel Seven. My contract runs out in a few days and then I'll fly over. I have five weeks before I start at the hospital. I'll knock on every door in Perth if I have to."

"You won't have to. She left me Aunt Beryl's address and phone number."

"Thank God!"

Dee Dee pursed her lips; inched forward. "Darling, could I ask a favour?"

"Of course, anything."

"Out of loyalty to my son I didn't offer to accompany Alicia and Sophie but I would love to go with you. Would you mind awfully? I've often wondered about Perth, what it's like. And ... well .... I've grown fond of them both."

His cheeky grin tugged at Dee Dee's heartstrings. "I'd like that as long as you promise to behave."

Dee Dee laughed. "Thank you, darling."

"If I ask you something, Mum, will you answer me truthfully?"

Dee Dee studied the troubled face staring at her. She would do anything to take away his pain but her promise to Alicia was something she didn't intend to break and she braced herself for the hard question. "I will."

"Are you in her confidence?"

"Yes, I am."

"Did you know the facts that night you dressed me down?"

"Yes."

"Then, for God's sake, why didn't you tell me?"

"The same reason I'll not tell you now. I gave her my word."

"But why?"

"Because, Nick, she thought – naively I admit – the less you knew, the less you could hurt her. She might have relented if you had told her you loved her but you didn't. She also told me she wouldn't survive a second time. She very nearly didn't in Sydney."

Nick stood up and walked back to the window, turned, words hovering on his lips. "I have a lot to thank you for."

Dee Dee stood; took her overgrown son in her arms, who gently rested his tired head on her bony shoulder. Fighting back tears, she affectionately patted his back and, breaking from his firm embrace, quickly returned to her comfortable chair before blubbering all over his crumpled shirt.

"A second time?" he said, his voice hoarse.

"That, you'll have to find out for yourself."

"Is it so bad?" he said returning to the couch.

"Worse than most people experience in a lifetime. I mean that Nick. She's been to hell and back. And then go on to achieve what she has at such a young age must have taken an enormous amount of courage. I still find it hard to believe she did what she did. Honestly, I do. It led me thinking. If I stood in her shoes would I have been able to do what she did? The answer is: I don't know but I'd like to think I would. Suffice to say, I hold her in very high esteem."

"How did I get it so wrong?"

"Everyone gets things wrong from time to time, my love. The important thing is to recognise your wrongs and make them right."

"This thing … this secret, trauma as you call it … that divides us … will I … will it …?"

"If you're asking me will it revolt you then the answer is, no. It is more likely to leave you … heartbroken. At least it did me. As I said, I still struggle to comprehend how she came through it all."

Nick stared down at his feet, shook his tired head. "My poor girl." He paused; took a deep breath. "There is something I need to tell you."

Dee Dee studied her son's face. "Will I be pleased, Nick?"

"I sincerely hope so." He paused. "After you left my house that night I went for a walk. As providence would have it, I ended up at City Church; spoke to Pastor Jeff. A good man and a good listener. It felt good to unload my trash after so many years. He asked me to come back, but not alone."

Dee Dee pulled a tissue from her sleeve and blew her nose. "I too have something I need to give you." She fetched her handbag from the hall, handed him the package. "She said to say thank you."

He clasped the small box in his hand, then slipped it into his pocket.

Chapter Sixteen

Three years had passed since Alicia had last seen her Aunt Beryl. The curly hair, now completely white, combed off her face, emphasised sad eyes bagged over wrinkled cheeks, and her thin lips barely parted when she smiled. Uncle Stan's death had aged her and at sixty-three, Aunt Beryl looked much older.

Any resentment Alicia may have harboured toward her aunt after her parents and Simon's death had simply vanished. In the few days she had been home, the relationship of old, she once shared with her aunt, had returned. She even told her aunt about Nick over a coffee in the warmth of her kitchen.

"Do you love him?" asked Beryl.

"With all my heart, Auntie. But it's no use. Strange how life works. To think a simple promise at sixteen would change my life forever."

"I still have the dress in the cupboard, you know."

"Really?" said Alicia, looking over at Sophie in the lounge room watching television. "You'd best leave it there. I have no use for it. Save it for Sophie."

"What do you intend to do now?" asked Beryl.

"I'm not sure. I was hoping that coming home might help me decide. Lauren Mason offered me a contract but there's a lot to consider. Sophie and her education for one, my commitment to Louis for another. Brandon's in the United States. He thought he might like a change. If he should secure a position with one of the bigger companies, I'm pretty sure he will accept it – mad if he didn't."

Aunt Beryl rose, collected the cups. "If you decide to stay in Perth, you have your parents' house, you know. Your uncle and I kept the place up to scratch and the finances in order."

Alicia nodded, wondering if she could bring herself to live there again. Although she loved Perth and the family home, there would always be memories lurking in every corner to remind her of her loss.

"I don't mean to sound pushy, but you've been here nearly a week, my girl. Time to bite the bullet. You can take my car, here's the keys."

She stared at the keys; her aunt had put on the table. Fisting her fingers around the bits of cold metal, she nodded at her aunt and quietly left the comfort of the warm house.

Still a little unsteady on her feet, she moved careful across the slushy grass. The old garage door creaked as she struggled to heave it open. She drove slowly up the driveway and onto the road, parked out the front of her parents' home, next door. Everything looked the same, and yet, strangely different. The pink and crimson roses, her mother's favourites, had been replaced with a small hedge lining the fence. A football rolled along the path ahead of the howling wind. Aunt Beryl said there was a young family living there now. Her parents would like that, it was built for a family. The front door swung open and a young boy bolted out, picked up his football and raced back inside. She caught a quick glimpse of his mother waiting in the hallway. New people and new memories were being formed. But the old ones would always remain in the secret crevices of yesterday. No, she thought, she didn't think she could live there again, even if she did return.

***

Nick soaked in the sights of Perth, awed by the clean, crisp landscape as he and his mother taxied from the airport to Mt.

Hawthorn where Alicia's aunt lived. Envy surged as the driver, meandering along with his arm resting along the rim of the door, drove them through the wide uncluttered streets. Perth wasn't a particularly lush green city but the salty smell of the sea hit him the further west they travelled. They finally pulled up out the front of the address Dee Dee had given the driver. The house looked tired, in need of a paint. And the old fashion veranda with its white painted railing and red-coated concrete reminded Nick of his grandparents' bungalow style home back in the States. He escorted his mother down the slabbed pathway, dodging branches protruding from the Illawarra Flame tree. Nick knocked hard on the side panels, rattling the glass panes. The wooden door creaked open. A petite grey-haired lady, maybe a few years older than his mother, peered through the flywire screen door.

"Can I help you?" she asked, poking at her short curls.

"I hope so. My name is Nick Coleman and …"

"Nick, Nick!" yelled Sophie, running into the hall and banging on the screen.

"Seems I best let you in."

Alicia's aunt unlocked the flywire door, held it open while they wiped their shoes on the outside mat, before entering. On closer observation, Nick noted the similarity between aunt and niece. The same small oval-shaped face, inquiring eyes set atop high cheekbones, and when she smiled, a hint of a dimple appeared in her right cheek.

Sophie tapped on Nick's thigh demanding attention, and he scooped her up, laughing. She wrapped her legs and arms around him, squeezed him with all her might.

"Wow, Precious. That's a mighty big hug for a small girl."

"You came! And Dee Dee, too! Mummy didn't tell me you were coming." Sophie pushed out of Nick's hold and threw herself at Dee Dee.

"Here, give me your coats. Perth's winter weather can be every bit as depressing as Melbourne's," said Beryl, holding out her hand. "I'm Beryl Maxwell, by the way, Alicia's aunt."

The mention of Alicia set Nick wondered where she was and how long her aunt intended keeping him in suspense. "Nick Coleman. Nice to meet you, Beryl. This is my mother, Dee Dee Johnson." Nick helped his mother with her coat, handed it to Beryl along with his own, who hung it on the hall stand in the corner.

"How do you do, Beryl. You don't mind me calling you Beryl?" Dee Dee, still holding Sophie's hand, smiled.

Beryl shook her head. "Not at all. Please come into the kitchen. It's much warmer in there and I'll make you a cup of tea."

Beryl ushered them into the kitchen, seated them at the table in the family room. Unlike her niece's apartment, photos filled the room, some displayed on furniture, others hanging in groups on the walls, some large, some small. He tried to find Alicia amongst them but it was too hard to determine, from where he sat.

Nick thought the house seemed too big for one woman to maintain and could only assume memories of a lifetime kept her rooted.

"And please call me Dee Dee.

"Mummy's not here," said Sophie, slipping onto the seat alongside Dee Dee.

"The story of my life," replied Nick.

Beryl checked the clock above the stove. "She left to go to the cemetery about an hour ago. Tea anyone, or would you prefer coffee?"

"A hot cup of tea sounds lovely, thanks Beryl. Milk, no sugar." Dee Dee removed her gloves, loosened the scarf around her neck. "I wasn't quite prepared for Perth's cold weather. But it's lovely and warm in your kitchen. A few more minutes and I'll be completely thawed out."

"Might pass on the tea, if you don't mind," said Nick, his mind on Alicia and the cemetery she was visiting.

Beryl nodded, waited for the kettle to boil, placed a cup of hot tea on the table in front of Dee Dee. "How was your flight over?"

Dee Dee took a quick sip. "Long and tiring. These old bones ain't what they used to be."

"How old are your bones, Dee Dee?" asked Sophie looking down at Nick's mother's legs. "Are they as old as Auntie Beryl's."

Dee Dee flashed a cheeky glance at Beryl. "Never you mind, young lady. Let's just say they are old enough to know better than to choose stockings over woollen pants."

Pleased to see his mother and Beryl getting along, Nick considered this an opportune moment to make his move.

"Cemetery! Is it far away?"

"Not really, dear."

Nick eyed his mother.

"Go, son. Beryl and I will spend the afternoon getting acquainted."

"I hope you don't think me rude leaving," said Nick, flicking through his mobile for the Uber app. The app informed him the car was only minutes away.

"Gracious no! Unfortunately, I can't offer you a lift as Alicia has taken the car."

"No problem. It's all good." He lifted his head to smile at Beryl but her glance was momentarily fixed on Sophie and his mother. Was that regret he saw in her sad eyes? It started him thinking when a horn sounded. He rose from the table, hoped the smile he gave Beryl conveyed a message of tenderness.

She blinked several times. "Yes dear, that'll be the taxi. Tell the driver to take you to Karrakatta. The family is buried in the Salvation Army Section. Would you like me to write that down or will you remember?"

He assured her he would remember and grabbing his coat on the way out, left the house.

The Uber pulled up at the main entrance to the cemetery. He lifted the collar of his coat, pushed his chilled hands in the pockets and wondered why nobody warned him about Perth's howling, winter winds. Fondling the little box in his pocket, he hurried to reception. Beryl had said 'the family' and he wondered who exactly 'the family' was.

A middle-aged woman with a broad Australian accent came outside and pointed him in the right direction.

Nick perused the grounds. As with most cemeteries, the neatly positioned burial plots with well-kept gardens and lawns separated the many sections. Cemeteries always gave him an eerie feeling and he rubbed at the imaginary ghost crawling through his hair. He paused at the cross-road; looked out across the site to see a lone figure kneeling over a stone slab in the upper ground. With her shoulders hunched and her long hair whipping circles in the wind, she looked a picture of misery against a grey, clouded backdrop.

He quickened his pace, matching the beat of his heart. The bitumen path gave way to a muddied, yellow sandy track, staining his polished leather shoes. Suddenly, she sat up and he hunched as low as he could inside his coat, careful she didn't recognise him and bolt before he had a chance to plead his case. Certain he was safe, he weaved through the marbled plots onto a path that led to the Salvation Army Section and ended at the foot of the grave where she knelt.

Slowly she turned her head towards him. Cold mist steamed from her parted lips as she mouthed his name. He wasn't sure if it was the icy wind or the shock of seeing him making her tremble. Unsteady on her feet, she gripped hold of the headstone to pull herself up. It occurred to him, she hadn't fully recovered from her illness. He started towards her, anxious to close the gap between them. Tightening the sides of her coat against the cold, she started walking away when she slipped on the wet grass and fell to her knees beside the adjacent grave. He snatched his hands from his pockets, hurdled a small shrub and grabbed hold of her arm to give her support.

"Don't you touch me," she said, wrenching her arm free from his grasp. He tried to help her to her feet but she slapped his hand away. Using the deceased Mr Brown's headstone for support, she brushed the mud from her pants and hands.

She was angrier than he'd thought she might be. Her deadpan expression looked colder than the grave she was leaning on. "Alicia, please give me a chance. Just listen to me, let me explain."

"I've done enough listening to you, thanks," she said, gathering her hair and tucking it into the collar of her coat. She'd barely taken ten steps when she slipped again, this time on the muddied gravel road. He caught her before she hit the ground. "Don't! I don't want you to touch me. Let me go! Let me go!" she said, trying to wriggle free of his grip. When a clap of thunder broke from a dark bulging cloud, she jumped and instinctively he pulled her closer.

She thumped her fist into his chest. "I asked you to let me go and I mean it!"

Nick glanced up at the dark sky wondering how long he had before the clouds burst apart. Something swiped past his face and he realised it was her hand. Shocked, he jerked away, loosening his hold. She twisted her arm free and started to walk up the path, carefully dodging the many rain-filled potholes, until she hit the bitumen road, and quickened her pace. Nick, ignoring the gale-force wind as it slapped his face, followed. She looked back over her shoulder, and before he had chance to prevent her, she stepped into a large puddle, where the rain had weathered away the bitumen. He heard the moan then the half-hearted sob. Splaying his legs either side of the puddle he lifted her free, and received an elbow to his ribs for his trouble.

Keeping her eyes lowered, she turned. "I'm sorry, I shouldn't have done that."

He stepped away from the puddle, took both her hands and

pulled her into his arms. She tried to wrestle free but he held her tight, determined not to let her go again. He stood his ground until the fight left her body. She was panting heavily. With one arm around her waist, he cupped her head with the other, resting his lips on her forehead. "Forgive me," he whispered against her cold skin.

"No! I won't!"

She summoned a fresh burst of energy, pushed against his chest, but he held fast. "I've missed you." He heard the hiss of her breath and flinched, knowing the battle was far from over.

"Missed me! Missed me! Oh, that's rich!" She flicked him a look; pushed at his chest. "What do you want, Nick? What are you doing here? No, don't answer, just let me go. Please!"

"No, not until you hear me out." He pulled her closer, smoothed his hand over her hair. It was time to man up. "I'm so sorry, Baby."

"Sorry? You're sorry? That's it, you're sorry?" She stopped struggling; looked him straight in the eye. "Well, don't let it worry you, Nick. Michael Gillespie and I have decided to get ..."

His arms tightened and she dropped her head onto his chest. Gripping the back of his coat, she started to cry. He stroked and kissed her head until he felt her sag against him.

She lifted her tear-stained face; stared into his eyes. She reminded him of the words he spat at her the night of the ball, outside her apartment, under the tree. "'Your silence says it all.' Remember saying that to me, the last time we spoke. Shall I go on .... 'Like a fool I thought you ... ...'"

"... ... were pure and sweet," he said, finishing the sentence for her.

"No Nick, you didn't think I was pure or sweet, did you? You thought I was having an affair with a man who happened to be ... ..."

"Oh, God, Alicia, don't. I'm so ashamed. You must believe me."

"Well, I don't believe you. How…?" She tried to wriggle away. "Forget it, I don't want to talk to you. Just let me go."

"No, I won't. How… what? Tell me what you were going to say."

"How could you think all those terrible things about me?"

"God, I don't know. You kept me so in the dark about everything, my imagination went crazy. Somewhere along the way, I lost my brains. I couldn't think straight. The past, my insecurities … everything … fear, you name it." He rested his lips on her temple, fed on that wonderful smell of Coco Chanel. "Forgive me Alicia, please forgive me."

She said nothing.

He touched his forehead against hers. "I love you."

He felt her tears, wet against his skin. She gripped his coat collar, buried her head in the fold. "No, you don't."

Her soft voice brought a smile. "Yes, I do, Alicia Sommers. I love every inch of you and more. You are the most perfect woman in the whole world, and I can't live without you."

"Then why didn't …?"

"… I tell you. Because I wasn't sure how you felt about me. I wanted you to trust me, talk to me, share your troubles so I could help you shoulder whatever it is breaking your beautiful heart." He looked back at the graves, then at the curly mop on his chest. "I screwed up. I love you, Baby, with all my heart." He lifted her chin. "Nobody has ever made me feel so alive as you do."

"Oh, Nick!"

She sobbed against his chest. Careful not to let her escape, he opened his coat and drew her inside. He trembled as the warmth of her body pressed against his. Lowering his lips onto hers, he kissed her with the intensity that weeks of uncertainty and emotion had provoked.

"I didn't come all this way to let you escape … again. I can't live without you."

"Eight weeks, Nick."

"I tried, Alicia. Honestly I did, but I kept coming to a dead end." He recounted every step from the hotel in Sydney to dragging a reluctant Brandon from the studio. He stared into her bright green eyes, cupped her head with both hands. "I've been out of my mind since the night of the ball. No excuses, but my stupid pride. Please say you forgive me."

When she said nothing, his tears fell. "The first time I ever saw you at the Spencers', I lost my heart. I have never loved anyone like I love you. I can't go on without you. Please, please forgive me."

"Oh Nick," she said, returning his kiss. He lifted her into his arms, their lips still attached, he carried her back to the gravesite where he first saw her and sat on the cold slab with her firmly planted on his lap. It was kiss-and-tell time and he needed answers. Tracing her face with his fingers, he asked, "Whose grave are we sitting on, Sweetheart?"

She shivered, pulled his coat around her legs and looked over at the granite headstone.

His gaze followed hers. A carving of an open book with inscriptions on both pages stared back at him. The engraved letters were stained from brown leaves of the peppermint tree above, making it hard to read but he could make out the name Sommers, and held his breath. "If I could take this pain away from you, darling, I would."

She turned into him, wrapped both arms around his neck, rested her chin on his shoulder. "My parents' and my brother's."

The family, her family. Three of them, in one grave, parents and a brother – that, he hadn't expected. He pulled her closer, smoothed his hand across her back. "All three?"

He felt her nod and his heart sank. He wanted to prompt her, but waited for her to tell him in her own time.

She raked her fingers through his hair, whispered into his neck. "It's a long story."

Every story, even his own, was long and painful, but death? His heart bled for her loss. "I'm not going anywhere."

"I could get heavy."

Nick laughed; patted her backside. Her soft sigh danced across his cheek and he kissed her again, thrilled to be comfortable in her affection.

"Strange," she said. "It happened exactly six years ago, today."

Nick's mind raced through the sums. Six years ago, … she was seventeen. About a year after Sophie was born. "*It* being?"

"The accident … that killed them. I came home from dancing to an empty house. I thought that was strange. Then I remembered mum saying they might take Sophie for a drive. She had a few chores to run, so I asked if she would mind picking up the pair of ballet shoes, I had ordered from the ballet shop on Flinders Street. That's where the crash happened, Nick … on Flinders Street, near the ballet shop."

She stopped twirling his hair. He felt her knuckles pressing into his back and rocked her back and forth.

"I was at the Academy. I … killed them … if I hadn't asked … maybe … maybe …"

Nick hugged a distraught and sobbing Alicia against his chest, whispered words of compassion that he hoped brought her some comfort. Conscious of his own grief fighting to escape, he lifted his face to heaven, let the cold air chill away the tears. "You just told me it was an accident. You can't blame yourself. No one can predict these things." He knew that to be true. Rebecca had been sleeping with Braun for months before he accidentally discovered the truth.

"I felt so guilty," she cried, searching his face. "It's haunted me for years. I've never told anyone … until now. Not even Brandon knows how one stupid pair of ballet shoes caused their death and left me fighting for life."

"Darling … how could you be responsible for something you

had no control over. People ask favours of their loved ones all the time. If we worried each time we did, no one would ever do anything for anyone. What kind of world would that be?"

"I know that now but when you are seventeen, alone and frightened, you don't."

"My darling, I'm so terribly sorry. Honestly, I am. I wish with all my heart I could have been there for you." He took her face in his hands, studied her beautiful features. "And I love you, Alicia, so very much."

She nestled into him, cradled his hand against her chest. "Soon after I arrived home from the Academy, there was a knock on the front door. Two policemen were standing there. I knew by the serious looks on their faces it wasn't good. A four-wheel drive had run a red light, slamming into Dad's side of the car. Mum was in the front next to Dad ..." Her voice caught on a sob. "... and Simon, my brother, was behind Dad in the back with So ... the shopping.

He watched the branches of a nearby willow whip the air and wondered what in Heaven's name he could say to ease her pain.

"When I arrived at the hospital, the doctor said the paramedics had done everything they could to save my parents but they'd both died in the ambulance on the way to hospital. Simon was still fighting for his life. 'Severe trauma to his head,' he said."

Nick continued to rock her back and forth, trying not to imagine what came next. "Easy, darling," he said, hitching her closer.

"Simon ..." she gasped.

Nick held her face against his, kissed every tear that fell. He wondered how she managed to survive, to live a normal life and at the same time, raise Sophie. Sophie! He wondered where she was at the time of the accident. "My poor, poor girl, why didn't you tell me?"

"I wanted to," she said, pulling a tissue from her sleeve and blowing her nose. "I came close so many times but something always went wrong."

"It would have helped me understand your fears, like that trip to the hospital."

"They never came home from the hospital. I had to leave them behind in that cold smelly place. I felt like I'd betrayed them. I was so sure I could hear them calling me, begging me not to leave them. My aunt had to prise my fingers off the door. Everything I loved and cherished had suddenly gone, just like that," she said, snapping her fingers. "You don't know how much I wanted to die, to end my miserable life and join them. I might have done if it wasn't for … …"

She swallowed her next word, peeked at him from under her lashes. He tugged on a ringlet of her hair, prompting her to continue. He noticed the crease in her brow deepen; wordless thoughts escaped on a rattled sigh.

She placed her forehead against his, took his face between her hands. "… for the next chapter in this story."

How much more can there be, thought Nick as he stroked her cheek with his thumb.

"There was someone who did survived the accident."

He knew Sophie had survived and wondered who else was in the car. "Who?"

"My sister."

"Your sister! Darling, that's wonderful." He inched back, and smiled. "But where is she? When can I meet her?"

"She's with Aunt Beryl." Alicia studied his shirt button, twisted it in her fingers.

"What? Does she live there?"

Alicia shook her head.

"I don't understand."

"I only hope you will when I've finished," she said, half to herself. "Dad's family all lived in Adelaide, so they didn't really count in the big picture of things. It was my Mum's family, Aunt

Beryl and her brother, my Uncle Robert, who took care of everything. Uncle Robert, being older, was named executor of my parents' will. Between them, they decided who would take care of us girls. My sister was to stay with Aunt Beryl and her husband, Uncle Stan, and I was to go and live with my Uncle Robert and his family down south in Busselton."

She shifted on his lap, pushed the hair from her face. "They never asked me what I wanted, if I minded going to the country to live, or considered how I felt leaving the family home, being separated from my sister. It was the best solution, they said. I didn't want to give up ballet and be someone's solution, but I had lost my will. At least that's what I thought, at first." She paused, hesitant. "I had my reasons for doing what I did."

"Sweetheart, I've no doubt you did." His mother did say he would be shocked and he braced himself, wondering if maybe Alicia's sister was incapacitated in some way, and kept in the back room. He chided himself, his over-active imagination was at work again.

"Brandon begged me not to leave him. He suggested we live together in my parents' home and continue our training at the Academy. I wasn't sure until I overheard my Aunt Pat call me 'an added burden' and that I would have to get a job to pay my way. That's when I started to wonder if Brandon could be right. I had to make a hasty decision before my uncle whipped me off to the country. Brandon and I have been together ever since, looking after … my sister … the way I knew my mother would want me to."

He'd been listening intently to her story. But when she stopped, he felt confused as if she had left out the important part. "But where is she … I still don't understand."

"I told you, she's at home with Aunt Beryl."

His confusion increased. What was it about this story he was missing? "Why didn't we meet her?"

Alicia took a deep breath. "You did."

He stared at her, his mind reverting back to Aunt Beryl's house. The only people he remembered in the house were his mother, Alicia's aunt and …

"Sophie! Sophie … is your sister!"

She nodded. "Yes, she is. And here," she patted the gravestone, "lies our beloved father."

"Sophie is your sister?" How had he not seen the obvious. Of course! Now he understood. All the pieces fell into place, her innocence, the hidden tragedy, and the secrets Jenny talked of, her fear of the hospital. Oh, no he wasn't upset, far from it. Sophie as a sister explained more than Alicia realised. "Of course, you have the same father. Does she know you're not her mother?"

"No."

"But why the secrecy?"

She took a deep breath, seeming to roll her mind back in time. "They were the most desperate days of my life. I was in such a dark place after they died – kind of like a breakdown. I didn't want to talk about it to anyone except Brandon. I sort of shut down, became almost reclusive. Then one day when Sophie was about eighteen months old, she called me Mummy. Although I was shocked at first, I realised lots of girls have babies out of wedlock. People asked fewer questions with Sophie as a daughter. It made sense and my life easier."

"Alicia." He lifted her hand to his lips, kissed her fingers. "You're a remarkable woman. And Brandon is a good man."

"Oh, Brandy! If it wasn't for him, I don't know how I would have survived. He saved my life! He's all I really had besides Sophie, and I love him with all my heart. We have been together every day since I lost them."

"You have me now." He silenced her reply with his lips. "Why Melbourne?"

"Louis offered us both a position with the Company after we graduated from the Academy. We grabbed it with both hands. It meant a new beginning." She poked him in the chest with her index finger. "So, you see, Michael Gillespie isn't Sophie's father."

For the first time since he could remember, Nick felt the blood rush to his face. "I'm very embarrassed about that. But why the hell didn't you tell me the truth?"

"Stacy Logan."

The flush deepened. "Oh God! I'm so ashamed."

"So you should be. You humiliated me in front of John and Jenny. Not to mention the fact you left me in the arms of that awful man."

"My only excuse is … when my wife cheated on me with Braun, it left me gutted. I don't think I ever really dealt with the humiliation. I let you down, Baby, and for that I will always be ashamed but I also let myself down. I thought I was better than that. It's quite humbling to realise you aren't as big a man as you thought you were."

"It takes a big man to admit that," she said, pulling his ear. "I can't believe you wouldn't know Michael was gay."

Nick shrugged; pulled a wry face. "I did. Deep inside, of course I knew, but you seemed so close and when he called Sophie 'our baby', I thought he must be 'bi' or something."

She rolled her eyes. "Are you serious?"

"Yes, unfortunately. A fool, I know. Don't punish me anymore, I feel bad enough."

"Oooh! I've only just started. Tell me about Alex Braun."

He flung back his head and groaned. "Alex and I go back a long way. His jealousy of me started in Uni when I beat him at the end of first-year finals. On for young and old after that. Paid me back by sleeping with my ex-wife. I should have known he was up to his old tricks; fell head-first into his trap."

"I think he deliberately bumped into me at the ball. He wouldn't let go of my wrist."

"I'm sure. Sounds just like him."

"There's one more thing and then I'm done," she said, giving him a quick nudge.

Nick pulled her closer; stretched his legs. "Thank God for that."

"When my mother was about to give birth to Sophie …" She stopped, and he could see she was wrestling with something.

"How many women have you been with, Nick?"

He didn't see that coming and sure as heck wasn't about to do the sums. "What's that got to do with anything?"

"Because I … you … well, you and me …"

"Hang on. Let's go back to the bit where your mother was about to give birth."

"I wish it was that simple. Since my parents' death, I have worked hard to give Sophie a good life. It hasn't been easy." The crease appeared on her brow, a look he was beginning to appreciate. "I'm not like other girls. I've listened to them in the change rooms and their lives are so different to mine. How old are you?"

He wound a curl behind her ear, ran his fingers down her cheek, wondering if his age would scare her off. "Thirty-four. Does that bother you?"

"No, it doesn't, but Sophie was one year old when they died, and I'd just turned seventeen. Seventeen, with a baby to care for. It shut my world inside a box. My life was nappies, bottles, and ballet. When other people went out, I went home. Do you understand what that was like? How it affected me? Don't look at me with that blank stare, like I'm making no sense."

"I'm sorry but I honestly have no idea what you're trying to tell me."

"I didn't want to … it never mattered … and I wasn't ready anyway … but then I met … Oh God, Nick, this is so difficult." She looked away and back again. "I feel so inadequate."

"Darling, are you joking? Most young women would have left the child and gone to live with their uncle in the country. But not my strong and beautiful girl."

"*My* strong and beautiful girl?" She raised her eyebrows.

He kissed her long and hard. "And don't you forget it. Please go on."

"Yes, sir." Dimples peeking, she saluted. But the smile quickly faded and the tension returned. "Do you know how old I was when I had my first date, first held a man's hand? How many times do you think I've been …" She paused. "… kissed?"

"Well I know you've been kissed by me. Not too many others, I hope."

Alicia turned bright red. "No, not too many others." She traced her fingers along his jawline, smoothed over his lips, sending his heart into a frenzy. "A few months before Sophie came along, I found my mother's wedding dress in the linen closet. My mother asked me if I would like to wear it on my wedding day and I said yes, I'd love to. It's a tradition, she said. All the women in our family have worn it. But it comes with a … condition. I made her a promise that I intend to keep. It's the only thing I have left to give a much loved and missed mother."

He felt his frenzied heart slow, fearful he might not meet the condition. "And …?"

Alicia turned, looked him in the eyes. "And …" She took a deep breath. "… I walk down the aisle … a virgin."

Nick released the breath he was holding. "Better get married tomorrow." He laughed at her startled expression, then frowned. "Hang on a minute. Am I correct in thinking that you thought because – how shall I put it – I'm experienced, I would expect you to be the same?"

Her bottom lip caught between her teeth, she nodded.

He tilted up her chin so she would look at him. Studying the beautiful face, he wondered how he came to deserve such a treasure. He also wondered if she had any idea how much he looked forward to loving her. "I would never ask you to give up something so dear to you. Besides, do you think me any less a man than your father? If he could wait, so can I."

Several moments passed before she spoke. "Nick?"

"Alicia."

"Can I ask you something … personal?"

"Yes, Baby, anything." He couldn't even begin to guess what was coming.

"I've heard stuff … girl stuff in the change rooms. Men, experienced men, well … maybe you will get … bored?"

"Maybe," he said, tickling her till she squirmed. "Nothing about you so far has been boring. I have great hopes for the future."

"Your mother …"

He cut her off. "What's my mother got to do with it?"

"Nothing, silly. I'm trying to tell you something."

"That's a relief. Mum and my wedding night? No, thanks."

"Don't joke, this is serious."

He held her tight, wondering what more she had to reveal.

"Your mother took me with her to church on the Gold Coast. I didn't want to go but afterward I felt different, changed. Not so broken, if that makes sense. I used to go regularly when my parents were alive, but when they died, I was angry, very angry, with God, and I stopped going. I get that bad things happen to good people and I don't blame God or myself anymore. If I go back to Melbourne …"

"If! I didn't come all this way to leave you behind."

Everything and more, he had ever hoped for in a woman was sitting on his lap and he didn't intend to let her get away. He wanted it all: Alicia, marriage, kids, and the white picket fence.

"I'd like to go back to church."

"You will, with me. I know just the place. Marry me and we'll go together." As he had promised Pastor Jeff.

"Sophie?"

Sophie, a sister. He couldn't believe how good knowing that

made him feel. "Will naturally live with us. Answer me before I go nuts."

"You have to promise me something first."

"Anything!"

She wrapped her arms around his neck, rested her lips on his ear. "Promise, you'll never leave me. I couldn't bear to lose anyone else."

"Oh, darling, never. I will never let you get away from me again. Never. You're my world, my reason, and I love you more than my own life. Now, tell me what I so desperately need to hear!"

"I love you, Nick Coleman."

He gently eased her back onto the grey slab. "Do you think your parents would mind me kissing you on their rather cold grave?"

Latching hold of his coat collar, she drew him to her. He took that as a 'no, they wouldn't'. If it weren't for the cold wind blowing down the neck of his coat, he would have kissed her longer. He sat up, and lifted her onto his lap, wondering how he had got it so wrong and yet it had all ended up so right. He thought about Pastor Jeff's words of wisdom. The past was the past, and he made a promise to God he would take better care of his future.

He took the small gold package from his pocket and handed it to Alicia. "How dare you give these backs," he teased. "I gave them to you as a gift."

She closed both her hands over his and drew them to her chilled lips. Their eyes locked. "You don't know how hard that was. I loved them so much, nearly as much as I love you."

He smiled, dropped a kiss on her lips. The day had darkened and the cold from the slab had begun to penetrate through to his bones. "It was nice to meet you, folks. And I promise to take great care of your precious girl." He affectionately patted the slab before he stood with Alicia cradled in his arms, and lowering her legs, he stretched his own. "Now," he said, wrapping her cold hand in his own. "It's time to go home."

She turned towards her family's grave. Blew three kisses. "Goodbye, my darlings. Until we're together again."